The Girl with No Shadow

The Girl
with No
Shadow

Joanne Harris

WILLIAM MORROW

An Imprint of HarperCollins*Publishers*

Designed by Betty Lew

ISBN-13: 978-1-60751-206-6

To A. F. H.

Contents

✳

ACKNOWLEDGMENTS

✳

Once again, heartfelt thanks to everyone who helped guide this book from baby steps to walking in heels. To Serafina Clarke, Jennifer Luithlen, Brie Burkeman, and Peter Robinson and Michael Carlisle; to my fabulous editor, Jennifer Brehl, and her assistant, Katherine Nintzel; to Ervin Serrano for his wonderful cover design, and to Betty Lew for her elegant page design; to my terrific publicists, Sharyn Rosenblum and Jamie Brickhouse, and to all my friends at William Morrow/HarperCollins, New York. Many thanks also to Laura Grandi in Milan and to Francesca Liversidge and everyone at Transworld, London. Thanks, too, to my P.A., Anne Riley; to Mark Richards for running the website; to Kevin for running everything; to Anouchka for enchiladas and *Kill Bill*; to Joolz, Anouchka's evil aunt, and to Christopher, Our Man in London. Special thanks go to Martin Myers, super-rep, who saved my sanity this Christmas, as well as to all the loyal reps, booksellers, librarians, and readers who ensure that my books are still kept on the shelves.

PART ONE

Death

Wednesday, 31 October
DÍA DE LOS MUERTOS

IT IS A RELATIVELY LITTLE-KNOWN FACT THAT, OVER THE COURSE OF A
single year, about twenty million letters are delivered to the dead. People
forget to stop the mail—those grieving widows and prospective heirs—and
so magazine subscriptions remain uncanceled; distant friends unnotified;
library fines unpaid. That's twenty million circulars, bank statements,
credit cards, love letters, junk mail, greetings, gossip and bills dropping
daily onto doormats or parquet floors, thrust casually through railings,
wedged into letter boxes, accumulating in stairwells, left unwanted on
porches and steps, never to reach their addressee. The dead don't care.
More importantly, neither do the living. The living just follow their petty
concerns, quite unaware that very close by, a miracle is taking place. The
dead are coming back to life.

It doesn't take much to raise the dead. A couple of bills; a name; a post-
code; nothing that can't be found in any old domestic garbage bag, torn apart
(perhaps by foxes) and left on the doorstep like a gift. You can learn a lot
from abandoned mail: names, bank details, passwords, e-mail addresses,
security codes. With the right combination of personal details you can
open up a bank account; hire a car; even apply for a new passport. The
dead don't need such things anymore. A gift, as I said, just waiting for collection.

Sometimes Fate even delivers in person, and it always pays to be alert.
Carpe diem, and devil the hindmost. Which is why I always read the obitu-

aries, sometimes managing to acquire the identity even before the funeral has taken place. And which is why, when I saw the sign, and beneath it the postbox with its packet of letters, I accepted the gift with a gracious smile.

Of course, it wasn't my postbox. The postal service here is better than most, and letters are rarely misdelivered. It's one more reason I prefer Paris; that and the food, the wine, the theaters, the shops, and the virtually unlimited opportunities. But Paris costs—the overheads are extraordinary—and besides, I'd been itching for some time to reinvent myself again. I'd been playing it safe for nearly two months, teaching in a lycée in the eleventh arrondissement, but in the wake of the recent troubles there I'd decided at last to make a clean break (taking with me twenty-five thousand euros' worth of departmental funds, to be delivered into an account opened in the name of an ex-colleague and to be removed discreetly, over a couple of weeks), and had a look at apartments to rent.

First, I tried the Left Bank. The properties there were out of my league; but the girl from the agency didn't know that. So, with an English accent and going by the name of Emma Windsor, with my Mulberry handbag tucked negligently into the crook of my arm and the delicious whisper of Prada around my silk-stockinged calves, I was able to spend a pleasant morning window-shopping.

I'd asked to view only empty properties. There were several along the Left Bank: deep-roomed apartments overlooking the river; mansion flats with roof gardens; penthouses with parquet floors.

With some regret, I rejected them all, though I couldn't resist picking up a couple of useful items on the way. A magazine, still in its wrapper, containing the customer number of its intended recipient; several circulars; and at one place, gold: a banker's card in the name of Amélie Deauxville, which needs nothing but a phone call for me to activate.

I left the girl my mobile number. The phone account belongs to Noëlle Marcelin, whose identity I acquired some months ago. Her payments are quite up-to-date—the poor woman died last year, aged ninety-four—but it means that anyone tracing my calls will have some difficulty finding me. My Internet account, too, is in her name and remains fully paid up. Noëlle is too precious for me to lose. But she will never be my main identity. For a start, I don't want to be ninety-four. And I'm tired of getting all those advertisements for stairlifts.

My last public persona was Françoise Lavery, a teacher of English at the Lycée Rousseau in the eleventh. Age thirty-two; born in Nantes; married and widowed in the same year to Raoul Lavery, killed in a car crash on the eve of their anniversary—a rather romantic touch, I thought, that explained her faint air of melancholy. A strict vegetarian, rather shy, diligent, but not talented enough to be a threat. All in all, a nice girl—which just goes to show you should never judge by appearances.

Today, however, I'm someone else. Twenty-five thousand euros is no small sum, and there's always the chance that someone will begin to suspect the truth. Most people don't—most people wouldn't notice a crime if it was going on right in front of them—but I haven't got this far by taking risks, and I've found that it's safer to stay on the move.

So I travel light—a battered leather case and a Sony laptop containing the makings of over a hundred possible identities—and I can be packed, cleaned out, all traces gone in rather less than an afternoon.

That's how Françoise disappeared. I burned her papers, correspondence, bank details, notes. I closed all accounts in her name. Books, clothes, furniture, and the rest I gave to the Croix Rouge. It never pays to gather moss.

After that I needed to find myself anew. I booked into a cheap hotel, paid on Amélie's credit card, changed out of Emma's clothes, and went shopping.

Françoise was a dowdy type, sensible heels and neat chignons. My new persona, however, has a different style. Zozie de l'Alba is her name—she is vaguely foreign, though you might be hard-pressed to tell her country of origin. She's as flamboyant as Françoise was not—wears costume jewelry in her hair; loves bright colors and frivolous shapes; favors bazaars and vintage shops, and would never be seen dead in sensible shoes.

The change was neatly executed. I entered a shop as Françoise Lavery, in a gray twinset and a string of fake pearls. Ten minutes later, I left as someone else.

The problem remains: where to go? The Left Bank, though tempting, is out of the question, though I believe Amélie Deauxville may be good for a few thousand more before I have to ditch her. I have other sources too, of course, not including my most recent—Madame Beauchamp, the secretary in charge of departmental finances at my erstwhile place of work.

It's so easy to open a credit account. A couple of spent utility bills; even an old driving license can be enough. And with the rise of online purchasing, the possibilities are expanding daily.

But my needs extend to far, far more than a source of income. Boredom appalls me. I need more. Scope for my abilities, adventure, a challenge, a change.

A life.

And that's what Fate delivered to me, as if by accident this windy late-October morning in Montmartre as I glanced into a shop window and saw the neat little sign taped to the door.

FERMÉ POUR CAUSE DE DÉCÈS

It's been some time since I last came here. I'd forgotten how much I enjoyed it. Montmartre is the last village in Paris, they say, and this part of the Butte is almost a parody of rural France, with its cafés and little *crêperies*; its houses painted pink or pistachio, fake shutters at the windows, and geraniums on every window ledge; all very consciously picturesque, a movie-set miniature of counterfeit charm that barely hides its heart of stone.

Perhaps that's why I like it so much. It's a perfect setting for Zozie de l'Alba. And I found myself there almost by chance; stopped in a square behind the Sacré-Coeur; bought a *café-croissant* at a bar called Le P'tit Pinson and sat down at a table on the street.

A blue tin plate high up on the corner gave the name of the square as Place des Faux-Monnayeurs. A tight little square like a neatly made bed. A café, a *crêperie*, a couple of shops. Nothing more. Not even a tree to soften those edges. But then for some reason, a shop caught my eye—some kind of a chichi *confiserie*, I thought, though the sign above the door was blank. The blind was half drawn, but from where I was sitting I could just see the display in the window, and the bright-blue door like a panel of sky. A small, repetitive sound crossed the square; a bundle of wind chimes hanging above the door, sending out little random notes like signals in the air.

Why did it draw me? I couldn't say. There are so many of these little shops along the warren of streets leading up the Butte de Montmartre, slouching on the cobbled corners like weary penitents. Narrow fronted and crookbacked, they are often damp at street level, cost a fortune to rent, and rely mainly on the stupidity of tourists for their continued existence.

The rooms above them are rarely any better. Small, sparse, and inconvenient; noisy at night, when the city below comes to life; cold in winter, and most likely unbearable in summer, when the sun presses down on the heavy stone slates and the only window, a skylight not eight inches wide, lets in nothing but the stifling heat.

And yet—*something* there had caught my interest. Perhaps the letters, poking out from the metal jaws of the postbox like a sly tongue. Perhaps the fugitive scent of nutmeg and vanilla (or was that just the damp?) that filtered from beneath the sky blue door. Perhaps the wind, flirting with the hem of my skirt, teasing the chimes above the door. Or perhaps the notice—neat, hand lettered—with its unspoken, tantalizing potential.

CLOSED DUE TO BEREAVEMENT

I'd finished my coffee and croissant by then. I paid, stood up, and went in for a closer look. The shop was a *chocolaterie*; the tiny display window crammed with boxes and tins, and behind them in the semidarkness I could see trays and pyramids of chocolates, each one under a round glass cloche like wedding bouquets from a century ago.

Behind me, at the bar of Le P'tit Pinson, two old men were eating boiled eggs and long slices of buttered bread while the aproned *patron* held forth at some volume about someone called Paupaul, who owed him money.

Beyond that the square was still almost deserted, but for a woman sweeping the pavement and a couple of artists with easels under their arms, on their way to the Place du Tertre.

One of them, a young man, caught my eye. "Hey! It's *you!*"

The hunting call of the portrait artist. I know it well—I've been there myself—and I know that look of pleased recognition, implying that he has found his muse; that his search has taken many years; and that however much he charges me for the extortionate result, the price can in no way do justice to the perfection of his oeuvre.

"No, it's not," I told him drily. "Find someone else to immortalize."

He gave me a shrug, pulled a face, then slouched off to rejoin his friend. The *chocolaterie* was all mine.

I glanced at the letters, still poking impudently from the letter box. There was no real reason to take the risk. But the simple fact was, the little shop drew me, like a shining something glimpsed between the cobbles, that might turn out to be a coin, a ring, or just a piece of tinfoil as it catches the light. And there was a whisper of promise in the air, and besides, it was Hallowe'en, the Día de los Muertos, always a lucky day for me, a day of endings and beginnings, of ill winds and sly favors and fires that burn at night. A time of secrets, of wonders—and, of course, the dead.

I took a last quick glance around. No one was watching. I was sure no one saw as, with a swift movement, I pocketed the letters.

The autumn wind was gusting hard, dancing the dust around the square. It smelled of smoke—not Paris smoke, but the smoke of my childhood, not often remembered—a scent of incense and frangipani and fallen leaves. There are no trees on the Butte de Montmartre. It's just a rock, its wedding cake icing barely concealing its essential lack of flavor. But the sky was a brittle, eggshell color, marked with a complex pattern of vapor trails, like mystic symbols on the blue.

Among them I saw the Ear of Maize, the sign of the Flayed One—an offering, a gift.

I smiled. Could it be a coincidence?

Death, and a gift—all in one day?

Once, when I was very young, my mother took me to Mexico City, to see the Aztec ruins and to celebrate the Day of the Dead. I loved the drama of it all: the flowers and the *pan de muerto* and the singing and the sugar skulls. But my favorite was the piñata, a painted papier-mâché animal figure, hung all over with firecrackers and filled with sweets, coins, and small, wrapped presents.

The object of the game was to hang up the piñata over a doorway and to throw sticks and stones at it until it split open, releasing the presents inside.

Death, and a gift—all in one.

It couldn't be a coincidence. This day, this shop, this sign in the sky—it was as if Mictecacihuatl herself had put them in my path. My very own piñata—

I turned away, smiling, and noticed someone watching me. There was a child standing very still about a dozen feet away: a girl aged eleven or twelve, in a bright red coat, with slightly scuffed brown school shoes and flossy black hair like that of a Byzantine icon. She looked at me without expression, head cocked slightly to one side.

For a moment I wondered if she'd seen me take the letters. Impossible to know for sure how long she'd been standing there; so I just gave her my most appealing smile and pushed the bundle of letters deeper into my coat pocket.

"Hello," I said. "What's your name?"

"Annie," said the girl, without smiling back. Her eyes were a curious blue-green-gray, her mouth so red it looked painted. Striking in the cool morning light; and as I watched, her eyes seemed to brighten still further, to take on the shades of the autumn sky.

"You're not from here, are you, Annie?"

She blinked at that; puzzled, perhaps, at how I knew. Paris children never talk to strangers; suspicion is hardwired into their circuitry. This girl was different—wary, perhaps, but not unwilling—and far from impervious to charm.

"How do you know?" she said at last.

Strike one. I grinned. "I can tell from your voice. What is it? The Midi?"

"Not quite," she said. But now she was smiling.

You can learn a lot from talking to children. Names, professions, the small details that give an impersonation that invaluable authentic touch.

Most Internet passwords consist of some child's name, a spouse's, even a pet's.

"Annie, shouldn't you be at school?"

"Not today. It's a holiday. Besides . . ." She looked at the door with its hand-lettered notice.

"Closed due to bereavement," I said.

She nodded.

"Who died?" That bright red coat seemed less than funereal, and there was nothing in her face that suggested grief.

Annie said nothing for a moment, but I caught the gleam in her blue-gray eyes, their expression slightly haughty now, as if debating whether my question might be impertinent or genuinely sympathetic.

I let her stare. I'm used to being stared at. It happens, sometimes, even in Paris, where beautiful women are more than plentiful. I say beautiful—but that's an illusion, the very simplest of glamours, barely magic at all. A tilt of the head, a certain walk, clothes befitting the moment, and anyone can do the same.

Well, *almost* anyone.

I fixed the girl with my brightest smile, sweet and cocky and slightly rueful, becoming for a second the tousled elder sister she has never had, the glamorous rebel, Gauloise in hand, who wears tight skirts and neon colors and in whose impractical shoes I know she secretly longs to be.

"Don't you want to tell me?" I said.

She looked at me for a second more. An elder child, if I ever saw one; tired, so tired of having to be good, and perilously close to the age of revolt. Her colors were unusually clear; in them I read some willfulness, some sadness, a touch of anger, and a bright thread of something that I could not quite identify.

"Come on, Annie. Tell me. Who died?"

"My mother," she said. "Vianne Rocher."

Wednesday, 31 October

VIANNE ROCHER. IT'S BEEN A LONG TIME SINCE I WORE THAT NAME. LIKE a coat, well loved but long since put away, I'd almost forgotten how good it felt, how very warm and comfortable. I've changed my name so many times—*both* our names, changing from village to village as we followed the wind—that I should have outgrown this wish by now. Vianne Rocher is long dead. And yet—

And yet I *enjoyed* being Vianne Rocher. I liked the shape of the word in their mouths. *Vianne*, like a smile. Like a word of welcome.

I have a new name now, of course, not so different from the old. I have a life; a better life, some might say. But it's not the same. Because of Rosette; because of Anouk; because of everything we left behind in Lansquenet-sous-Tannes, that Easter when the wind changed.

That wind. I see it's blowing now. Furtive but commanding, it has dictated every move we've ever made. My mother felt it, and so do I—even here, even now—as it sweeps us like leaves into this backstreet corner, dancing us to shreds against the stones.

V'là l'bon vent, v'là l' joli vent

I thought we'd silenced it for good. But the smallest thing can wake the wind: a word, a sign, even a death. There's no such thing as a trivial thing. Everything costs; it all adds up until finally the balance shifts and we're gone again, back on the road, telling ourselves—*well, maybe next time*—

Well, this time, there will be no next time. This time, I'm not running away. I don't want to have to start anew, as we have done so many times, before and since Lansquenet. This time, we stay. Whatever it takes. Whatever it costs us, we stay.

We stopped in the first village that didn't have a church. We stayed six weeks, and then moved on. Three months, then a week, a month, another week, changing our names as we went until the baby began to show.

Anouk was nearly seven by then. Excited at the thought of a baby sister; but I was so tired, so tired of those interminable villages with the river and the little houses and the geraniums in the window boxes and the way people looked at us—at her especially—and asked their questions, always the same.

Have you come far? Will you be staying with relatives here? Will Monsieur Rocher be joining you?

And when we answered, there'd be that look, that measuring look, taking in our worn clothes and our single case and that fugitive air that speaks of too many railway stations and passing places and hotel rooms left neat and bare.

And oh—how I longed to be free at last. Free as we had never been; free to stay in a single spot; to feel the wind and ignore its call.

But however hard we tried, rumor followed us. Some kind of scandal, the whispers said. Some priest was involved, so someone had heard. And the woman? A gypsy; in with the river people; claimed to be a healer; dabbled in herbs. And someone had died, the rumors said—poisoned, perhaps, or simply unlucky.

In any case, it didn't matter. The rumors spread like dogwort in summer, tumbling us, harrying us, snapping at our heels; and slowly, I began to understand.

Something had happened along our road. Something that had altered us. Perhaps we'd stayed a day—a week—too long in one of those villages. Something was different. The shadows had lengthened. We were running.

Running from what? I didn't know then, but I could already see it in my reflection; in hotel room mirrors and shiny shop fronts. I'd always worn red shoes; Indian skirts with bells on the hems; secondhand coats with daisies on the pockets, jeans embroidered with flowers and leaves. Now I tried to blend in with the crowd. Black coats, black shoes, black beret on my black hair.

Anouk didn't understand. "Why couldn't we have stayed this time?"

The perpetual refrain of those early days. I began to dread even the name of that place, the memories that clung like burs to our traveling clothes. Day by day we moved with the wind. And at night we'd lie side by side in some room above a café, or make hot chocolate over a camping stove, or light candles and make shadow bunnies on the wall and tell fabulous stories of magic and witches and gingerbread houses, and dark men who turned into wolves who, sometimes, never turned back again.

But by then, stories were all they were. The *real* magic—the magic we'd lived with all our lives, my mother's magic of charms and cantrips, of salt by the door and a red silk sachet to placate the little gods—had turned sour on us that summer, somehow, like a spider that turns from good luck to bad at the stroke of midnight, spinning its web to catch our dreams. And for every little spell or charm, for every card dealt and every rune cast and every sign scratched against a doorway to divert the path of malchance, the wind just blew a little harder, tugging at our clothes, sniffing at us like a hungry dog, moving us here and moving us there.

Still we ran ahead of it: picking cherries in season and apples in season and working for the rest of the time in cafés and restaurants, saving our money, changing our names in every town. We grew careful. We had to. We hid ourselves, like grouse in a field. We did not fly; we did not sing.

And little by little the Tarot cards were put aside, and the herbs went unused, and the special days went unmarked, and the waxing moons came and went, and the signs inked into our palms for luck faded and were washed away.

That was a time of relative peace. We stayed in the city; I found us a place to stay; I checked out schools and hospitals. I bought a cheap wedding ring from the *marché aux puces* and gave my name as Madame Rocher.

And then, in December, Rosette was born, in hospital on the outskirts of Rennes. We had found a place to stay for a while—Les Laveuses, a village on the Loire. We rented a flat above a *crêperie*. We liked it there. We could have stayed—

But the December wind had other ideas.

> *V'là l'bon vent, v'là l'joli vent*
> *V'là l'bon vent, ma mie m'appelle—*

My mother taught me that lullaby. It's an old song, a love song, a charm, and I sang it then to calm the wind; to make it leave us behind this time; to lull the mewing thing that I had brought back from the hospital. The tiny thing that neither fed nor slept but cried like a cat night after night, while around us the wind shrieked and tossed like an angry woman, and every night I sang it to sleep, calling it *good wind, pretty wind*, in the words of my song, as simple folk once named the Furies, addressing them as *Good Ladies* and *Kindly Ones*, in the hope of escaping their revenge.

Do the Kindly Ones pursue the dead?

They found us again by the side of the Loire, and once again, we had to flee. To Paris, this time—Paris, my mother's city and the place of my birth, the one place where I'd sworn we'd never go back to. But a city confers a kind of invisibility on those who seek it. No longer parakeets among the sparrows, we now wear the colors of the native birds—too ordinary, too drab for a second glance or even a first. My mother had fled to New York to die; I fled to Paris to be reborn. Sick or well? Happy or sad? Rich or poor? The city doesn't care. The city has other business to attend to. Unquestioning, it passes by; it goes its way without a shrug.

All the same, that year was hard. It was cold; the baby cried; we stayed in a little upstairs room off the Boulevard de la Chapelle, and at night the neon signs flashed red and green till it was enough to drive you mad. I could have fixed it—I know a cantrip that would have done it just as easily as switching off a light—but I had promised us *no more magic*, and so we slept in little slices between the red and green, and Rosette went on crying until Epiphany (or so it seemed), and for the first time our *galette des Rois* was not homemade, but from a shop, and no one felt much like celebrating anyway.

I hated Paris so much that year. I hated the cold and the grime and the smells; the rudeness of the Parisians; the noise from the railway; the violence; the hostility. I soon learned that Paris is not a city. It's just a mass of Russian dolls boxed one inside the other, each with its customs and prejudices, each with its church, mosque, synagogue; all of them rife with bigots, gossips, insiders, scapegoats, losers, lovers, leaders, and objects of derision.

Some people were kind: like the Indian family who looked after Rosette while Anouk and I went to the market, or the grocer who gave us the damaged fruit and vegetables from his stall. Others were not. The bearded men who averted their gaze when I walked with Anouk past the mosque in Rue Myrrha; the women outside the Eglise St. Bernard who looked at me as if I were dirt.

Things have changed a lot since then. We have found our place at last. Not half an hour's walk from Boulevard de la Chapelle, Place des Faux-Monnayeurs is another world.

Montmartre is a village, so my mother used to say, an island rising out of the Paris fog. It's not like Lansquenet, of course, but even so, it's a good place, with a little flat above the shop and a kitchen at back, and a room for Rosette and one for Anouk, under the eaves with the birds' nests.

Our *chocolaterie* was once a tiny café, run by a lady called Marie-Louise Poussin, who lived up on the first floor. Madame had lived here for twenty years; had seen the death of her husband and son; and now in her sixties and in failing health, still stubbornly refused to retire. She needed help; I needed a job. I agreed to run her business for a small salary and the use of the rooms on the second floor, and as Madame grew less able to cope, we changed the shop to a *chocolaterie*.

I ordered stock, managed accounts, organized deliveries, handled sales. I dealt with repairs and building work. Our arrangement has lasted for over three years, and we have become accustomed to it. We don't have a garden, or very much space, but we can see the Sacré-Coeur from our window, rising above the streets like an airship. Anouk has started secondary school—

the Lycée Jules Renard, just off the Boulevard des Batignolles—and she's bright, and works hard; I'm proud of her.

Rosette is almost four years old, although, of course, she does not go to school. Instead she stays in the shop with me, making patterns on the floor with buttons and sweets, arranging them in rows according to color and shape, or filling page after page in her drawing books with little pictures of animals. She is learning sign language and is fast acquiring vocabulary, including the signs for *good, more, come here, see, boat, yum, picture, again, monkey, ducks* and most recently—and to Anouk's delight—*bullshit.*

And when we close the shop for lunch, we go to the Parc de la Turlure, where Rosette likes to feed the birds, or a little farther to Montmartre cemetery, which Anouk loves for its gloomy magnificence and its many cats. Or I talk to the other shop owners in the quartier: to Laurent Pinson, who runs the grubby little café-bar across the square; to his customers, regulars for the most part, who come for breakfast and stay till noon; to Madame Pinot, who sells postcards and religious bric-a-brac on the corner; to the artists who camp out on the Place du Tertre hoping to attract the tourists there.

There is a clear distinction here between the inhabitants of the Butte and the rest of Montmartre. The Butte is superior in every respect—at least, to my neighbors of the Place des Faux-Monnayeurs—a last outpost of Parisian authenticity in a city now overrun with foreigners.

These people never buy chocolates. The rules are strict, though unwritten. Some places are for outsiders only; like the *boulangerie-pâtisserie* on the Place de la Galette, with its art deco mirrors and colored glass and baroque piles of macaroons. Locals go to Rue des Trois Frères, to the cheaper, plainer *boulangerie*, where the bread is better and the croissants are baked fresh every day. In the same way, locals eat at Le P'tit Pinson, all vinyl-topped tables and plat du jour, whereas outsiders like ourselves secretly prefer La Bohème, or even worse, La Maison Rose, which no true son or daughter of the Butte would ever frequent, any more than they would pose for an artist at the terrace of a café on the Place du Tertre, or go to mass at the Sacré-Coeur.

No, our customers are mostly from elsewhere. We do have our regulars; Madame Luzeron, who drops by every Thursday on her way to the cemetery and always buys the same thing—three rum truffles, no more, no less, in a gift box with a ribbon around it. The tiny blond girl with the bitten fingernails, who comes in to test her self-control. And Nico from the Italian restaurant on the Rue Caulaincourt, who visits almost every day, and whose exuberant passion for chocolates—and for everything—reminds me of someone I once knew.

And then there are the occasionals. Those people who just drop by for a look, or for a present, or an everyday indulgence: a twist of barley; a box of violets; a block of marzipan or a *pain d'épices*; rose creams or a candied pineapple, steeped in rum and studded with cloves.

I know all their favorites. I know what they want, although I'd never tell. That would be too dangerous. Anouk is eleven now, and on some days I can almost feel it, that terrible knowledge, trembling inside her like an animal in a cage. Anouk, my summer child, who in the old days could no more have lied to me than she could have forgotten how to smile. Anouk, who used to lick my face and bugle—*I love you!*—in public places. Anouk, my little stranger, now grown stranger still, with her moods and her strange silences and her extravagant tales, and the way she sometimes looks at me, eyes narrowed, as if trying to see something half-forgotten in the air behind my head.

I've had to change her name, of course. Nowadays I am Yanne Charbonneau, and she is Annie—though she'll always be Anouk to me. It's not the actual names that trouble me. We've changed them so many times before. But something else has slipped away. I don't know what, but I know I miss it.

She's growing up, I tell myself. Receding, dwindling like a child glimpsed in a hall of mirrors—Anouk at nine, still more sunshine than shadow, Anouk at seven, Anouk at six, waddling duck-footed in her yellow Wellingtons, Anouk with Pantoufle bounding blurrily behind her, Anouk with a plume of cotton candy in one small pink fist—all gone now, of course, slipping away and into line behind the ranks of future Anouks. Anouk at thirteen, discovering boys, Anouk at fourteen, Anouk, impossibly, at twenty, marching faster and faster toward a new horizon—

I wonder how much she still remembers. Four years is a long time to a child of her age, and she no longer mentions Lansquenet, or magic, or worse still, Les Laveuses, although occasionally she lets something slip—a name, a memory—that tells me more than she suspects.

But seven and eleven are continents apart. I have done my work well enough, I hope. Enough, I hope, to keep the animal in its cage, and the wind becalmed, and that village on the Loire nothing more than a faded postcard from an island of dreams.

And so I keep my guard on the truth, and the world goes on as always, with its good and bad, and we keep our glamours to ourselves, and never interfere, not even for a friend, not even so much as a rune sign sketched across the lid of a box for luck.

It's a small enough price to pay, I know, for nearly four years of being left alone. But I sometimes wonder quite how much we have already paid for that, and how much more there is to come.

There's an old story my mother used to tell, about a boy who sold his shadow to a peddler on the road in exchange for the gift of eternal life. He got his wish and went off pleased at the bargain he had struck—for what use is a shadow, thought the boy, and why should he not be rid of it?

But as months passed, then years, the boy began to understand. Walking abroad, he cast no shadow; no mirror showed him back his face; no pool, however still, gave him the slightest reflection. He began to wonder if he was invisible; stayed in on sunny days; avoided moonlit nights; had every mirror in his house smashed and every window fitted with shutters on the inside—and yet he was not satisfied. His sweetheart left him, his friends grew old and died. And still he lived on in perpetual dusk until the day when, in despair, he went to the priest and confessed what he had done.

And the priest, who had been young when the boy made his deal, but who now was yellow and brittle as old bones, shook his head and said to the boy: "That was no peddler you met on the road. That was the devil you bargained with, son, and a deal with the devil usually ends in someone or other losing their soul."

"But it was only a *shadow*," protested the boy.

Once more, the old priest shook his head. "A man who casts no shadow isn't really a man at all," he said, and turned his back and would say no more.

And so at last the boy went home. And they found him the next day, hanging from a tree, with the morning sun on his face and his long, thin shadow in the grass at his feet.

It's only a story. I know that. But it keeps coming back to me, late at night when I can't sleep and the wind chimes jangle their alarm and I sit up in bed and lift up my arms to check my shadow against the wall.

More often now, I find myself checking Anouk's as well.

Wednesday, 31 October

OH, BOY. VIANNE ROCHER. OF ALL THE STUPID THINGS TO SAY. WHY DO I say these stupid things? Sometimes I really just don't know. Because she was listening, I suppose, and because I was angry. These days I feel angry a lot of the time.

And maybe too it was because of the shoes. Those fabulous, luminous high-heeled shoes in lipstick, candy cane, lollipop red, gleaming like treasure on the bare cobbled street. You just don't see shoes like that in Paris. Not on regular people, anyway. And we *are* regular people—at least Maman says so—though you wouldn't know it, sometimes, the way she goes on.

Those *shoes*—

Tak-tak-tak went the lollipop shoes and stopped right in front of the *chocolaterie* while their owner looked inside.

From the back, at first I thought I knew her. The bright red coat that matched her shoes. Coffee-cream hair tied back with a scarf. And were there bells on her print dress, and a jingling charm bracelet around her wrist? And what was that—that faintest gleam in the wake of her, like something in a heat haze?

The shop was shut for the funeral. In a moment, she would be gone. But I really wanted her to stay, and so I did something I shouldn't, something Maman thinks I've forgotten about, something I haven't done for a very long time. I forked my fingers behind her back and made a little sign in the air.

A breeze, vanilla-scented, nutmeg milk, dark roast of cocoa beans over a slow fire.

It isn't magic. Really it isn't. It's just a trick, a game I play. There's no such thing as real magic—and yet it works. Sometimes, it works.

Can you hear me? I said. Not in my voice, but a shadow-voice, very light, like dappled leaves.

She felt it then. I know she did. Turning, she stiffened; I made the door shine a little, ever so slightly, the color of the sky. Played with it, pretty, like a mirror in the sun, shining it on and off her face.

Scent of woodsmoke in a cup; a dash of cream, sprinkle of sugar. Bitter orange, your favorite, 70 percent darkest chocolate over thick-cut oranges from Seville. Try me. Taste me. Test me.

She turned around. I knew she would. Seemed surprised to see me but smiled all the same. I saw her face—blue eyes, big smile, little bridge of freckles across the nose—and I liked her so much right away, the way I liked Roux when we first met—

And then she asked me who had died.

I couldn't help it. Maybe it was because of the shoes; maybe because I knew Maman was standing behind the door. Either way it just came out, like the light on the door and the scent of smoke.

I said, "Vianne Rocher," a little too loudly, and just as I'd said it, Maman came out. Maman in her black coat with Rosette in her arms and that look on her face, that look she gets when I misbehave, or when Rosette has one of her Accidents.

"Annie!"

The lady with the red shoes looked from her to me, and back to my mother again.

"Madame—Rocher?"

She recovered fast. "That was my—maiden name," she said. "Now it's Madame Charbonneau. Yanne Charbonneau." She gave me that look again. "I'm afraid my daughter's a bit of a joker," she told the lady. "I hope she hasn't been annoying you?"

The lady laughed right down to the soles of her red shoes. "Not at all," she said. "I was just admiring your beautiful shop."

"Not mine," said Maman. "I just work here."

The lady laughed again. "I wish I did! I'm supposed to be looking for a job, and here I am, ogling chocolates."

Maman relaxed a little at that and put Rosette down to lock the door. Rosette looked solemnly at the red-shoe lady. The lady smiled, but Rosette didn't smile back. She rarely does for strangers. In a way, I was pleased. I found her, I thought. I kept her here. For a while, at least, she belongs to me.

"A job?" said Maman.

The lady nodded. "My flatmate moved out last month, and there's no way I can pay for the whole flat on nothing but a waitress's salary. My name's Zozie—Zozie de l'Alba—and by the way, I *love* chocolate."

You couldn't help liking her, I thought. Her eyes were so blue, her smile like a slice of summer watermelon. It dropped a little as she looked at the door.

"I'm sorry," she said. "It's a bad time. I hope it wasn't a relative?"

Maman picked up Rosette again. "Madame Poussin. She lived here. I suppose she would have said she ran the place, although to be honest, she didn't do much."

I thought of Madame Poussin, with her marshmallow face and her blue-checked pinafores. Rose creams were her favorites, and she ate far more of them than she ought to have done, though Maman never said anything.

It was a stroke, Maman said, which sounds quite nice, like a stroke of luck, or someone smoothing down the bedclothes over a sleeping child. But it came to me then that we would never see Madame Poussin *ever again*, and I felt a kind of dizziness, like looking down and seeing a big sudden hole right at your feet.

I said, "Yes, she did," and began to cry. And before I knew it her arms were around me, and she smelt of lavender and delicious silk, and her voice in my ear was whispering something—a cantrip, I thought, with a twist of surprise, a cantrip, just like the days in Lansquenet—and then I looked up and it wasn't Maman there at all. It was Zozie, her long hair touching my face and her red coat shining in the sun.

Behind her, Maman, in her funeral coat and her eyes dark as midnight, so dark that no one can ever, ever tell what she's thinking. She took a step—

still carrying Rosette—and I knew that if I stayed she would put her arms around us both, and I wouldn't be able to stop crying, though I couldn't possibly tell her why, not now, not ever, and especially not in front of the lady with the lollipop shoes.

So instead I turned and ran down the bare white alleyway so that for a moment I was one of them, free as the sky. It's good to run: you take giant strides; you can be a kite with your arms outstretched; you can taste the wind; you can feel the sun racing ahead; and sometimes you can almost outrun them, the wind and the sun and your shadow at your heels.

My shadow has a name, you know. His name is Pantoufle. I used to have a rabbit called Pantoufle, so Maman says, although I can't quite remember now whether he was real or simply a toy. *Your imaginary friend,* she sometimes calls him, but I'm almost sure he was really there, a soft gray shadow at my heels, or curled up in my bed at night. I like to think of him sometimes still, keeping watch over me as I sleep, or running with me to beat the wind. Sometimes I feel him. Sometimes I see him even now, though Maman says that's just my imagination and doesn't like me talking about it, even as a joke.

Nowadays Maman hardly ever jokes, or laughs the way she used to do. Perhaps she's still worried about Rosette. I know she worries about me. I don't take life seriously enough, she says. I don't have the right kind of attitude.

Does Zozie take life seriously? Oh, boy. I'll bet she doesn't. No one could, wearing those shoes. I'm sure that's why I liked her at once. Those red shoes, and the way she stopped at the window to look, and the way I was sure she could see Pantoufle—not just a shadow—at my heels.

Wednesday, 31 October

WELL, I LIKE TO THINK I HAVE A WAY WITH CHILDREN. PARENTS TOO; IT'S
part of my charm. You can't be in business without a certain charm, you
know, and in my particular line of business, when the prize is something
far more personal than mere possessions, it's essential to *touch* the life you
take.

Not that I was particularly interested in this woman's life. Not then, at
least—although I will admit I was already intrigued. Not so much by the
deceased. Nor even by the shop itself—pretty enough, but far too small,
and limiting, to someone of my ambitions. But the woman intrigued me,
and the girl—

Do you believe in love at first sight?

I thought not. Neither do I. And yet—

That flare of colors through the half-open door. That tantalizing hint
of things half-seen and half-experienced. The sound of the wind chimes
over the threshold. These things had awakened first my curiosity, and second my spirit of acquisition.

I'm not a thief, you understand. First and foremost I'm a *collector*. I have
been since I was eight years old, collecting charms for my bracelet, but now
I collect individuals—their names, their secrets, their stories, their lives.
Oh, some of it's for profit, of course. But most of all I enjoy the chase; the
thrill of pursuit; the seduction; the fray. And the moment at which the
piñata splits—

That's what I love best of all.

"Kids." I smiled.

Yanne sighed. "They grow so fast. A blink, and they're gone." Way down the alley, the girl was still running. "Don't go far!" Yanne called.

"She won't."

Yanne looks like a tamer version of her daughter. Black bobbed hair, brows straight, eyes like bitter chocolate. The same crimson, stubborn, generous mouth, lifting a little at the corners. The same obscurely foreign, exotic look, though beyond that first glimpse of colors through the half-open door, I could see nothing to justify the impression. She has no accent; wears well-worn clothes from La Redoute; plain brown beret at a slight angle, sensible shoes.

You can tell a lot from a person by looking at their shoes. These were carefully without extravagance: black and round-toed and relentlessly uniform, like the ones her daughter wears for school. The ensemble slightly down-at-heel, a shade too drab; no jewelry but for a plain gold ring; just enough makeup to avoid making a statement.

The child in her arms may be three at most. The same watchful eyes as her mother, though her hair is the color of fresh pumpkin and her tiny face, no bigger than a goose egg, is a blur of apricot freckles. An unremarkable little family, at least on the surface; and yet I couldn't rid myself of the idea that there was something more that I couldn't quite see, some subtle illumination not unlike my own—

Now *that*, I thought, would be worth collecting.

She looked at her watch. "Annie!" she called.

At the end of the street Annie waved her arms in what might have been exuberance or revolt. In her wake, a gleam of butterfly blue confirms my impression of something to hide. The little one, too, has more than a hint of illumination, and as for the mother—

"You're married?" I said.

"I'm a widow," she said. "Three years ago. Before I moved here."

"Really," I said.

I don't think so. It takes more than a black coat and a wedding ring to make a widow, and Yanne Charbonneau (if that's her name) doesn't look like a widow to me. To others, perhaps, but I can see more.

So why the lie? This is Paris, for pity's sake—here, no one is judged on the absence of a wedding band. So what little secret is she hiding? And is it worth my finding out?

"It must be hard, running a shop. Here, of all places." Montmartre, that strange little stone island with its tourists and artists and open drains, and beggars and strip clubs under the linden trees, and nightly stabbings down among the pretty streets.

She gave a smile. "It's not so bad."

"Really?" I said. "But now that Madame Poussin's gone—"

She looked away. "The landlord's a friend. He won't throw us out." I thought I saw her flush a little.

"Good business here?"

"It could be worse."

Tourists, ever on the lookout for overpriced tat.

"Oh, it's never going to make us a fortune—"

As I thought. Barely worthwhile. She's putting a brave face on it, but I can see the cheap skirt; the frayed hem on the child's good coat; the faded, illegible wooden sign above the *chocolaterie* door.

And yet there is something oddly attractive about the crowded shop window with its piles of boxes and tins, and its Hallowe'en witches in darkest chocolate and colored straw, and plump marzipan pumpkins and maple-candy skulls just glimpsed beneath the half-closed shutter.

There was a scent too—a smoky scent of apples and burnt sugar, vanilla and rum and cardamom and chocolate. I don't even really *like* chocolate; and yet I could feel my mouth watering.

Try me. Taste me.

With my fingers I made the sign of the Smoking Mirror—known as the Eye of Black Tezcatlipoca—and the window seemed to glow briefly.

Uneasy, the woman seemed to sense the flare, and the child in her arms gave a silent mew of laughter and held out her hand—

Curious, I thought.

"Do you make all the chocolates yourself?"

"I used to, once. But not anymore."

"It can't be easy."

"I manage," she said.

Hm. Interesting.

But *does* she manage? Will she continue to manage now that the old woman's dead? Somehow I doubt it. Oh, she looks capable enough, with her stubborn mouth and her steady gaze. But there's a weakness inside her, in spite of all that. A weakness—or perhaps a strength.

You have to be strong to live as she does; to bring up two children alone in Paris; to work all hours in a business that brings in, if she's lucky, just enough to cover the rent. But the weakness—that's another matter. That child, for a start. She fears for her. Fears for them both, clings to them as if the wind might blow them away.

I know what you're thinking. Why should I care?

Well, call me curious if you like. I trade in secrets, after all. Secrets, small treacheries, acquisition, inquisition, thefts both petty and grandiose, lies, damn lies, prevarications, hidden depths, still waters, cloaks and daggers, secret doors, clandestine meetings, holes and corners, covert operations and misappropriation of property, information and more.

Is that so wrong?

I suppose it is.

But Yanne Charbonneau (or Vianne Rocher) is hiding something from the world. I can smell the scent of secrets on her, like firecrackers on a piñata. A well-placed stone will set them free, and then we'll see if they are secrets that someone such as I can use.

I'm curious to know, that's all—a common enough characteristic of those fortunate enough to be born under the sign of One Jaguar.

Besides, she's lying, isn't she? And if there's anything we Jaguars hate more than weakness, it's a liar.

Thursday, 1 November

ALL SAINTS

ANOUK WAS RESTLESS AGAIN TODAY. PERHAPS THE AFTERMATH OF YESterday's funeral—or perhaps just the wind. It takes her like that sometimes, cantering her about like a wild pony, making her willful and thoughtless and tearful and strange. My little stranger.

I used to call her that, you know, when she was small and there were just the two of us. Little stranger, as if she were on loan from somewhere or other, and one day they'd be coming to take her back. She always had that about her, that look of *otherness*, of eyes that see things much too far, and of thoughts that wander off the edge of the world.

A *gifted* child, her new teacher says. *Such extraordinary powers of imagination, such vocabulary for her age*—but already, there's a look in her eye, a measuring look, as if such imagination is in itself suspect, a sign, perhaps, of a more sinister truth.

It's my fault. I know that now. To bring her up in my mother's beliefs seemed so natural at the time. It gave us a plan; a tradition of our own; a magic circle into which the world could not enter. But where the world cannot enter, we cannot leave. Trapped inside a cocoon of our own making, we live apart, eternal strangers from the rest.

Or we did, until four years ago.

Since then, we have lived a comforting lie.

Don't look so surprised, please. Show me a mother, and I'll show you a liar. We tell them how the world *should* be: that there are no such things as monsters or ghosts; that if you do good, then people will do good to you; that Mother will always be there to protect you. Of course we never call them lies—we mean so well, it's all for the best—but that's what they are, nevertheless.

After Les Laveuses, I had no choice. Any mother would have done the same.

"What was it?" she said again and again. "Did we make it happen, Maman?"

"No, it was an accident."

"But the wind—you said—"

"Just go to sleep."

"Couldn't we magic it better, somehow?"

"No, we can't. It's just a game. There's no such thing as magic, Nanou."

She stared at me with solemn eyes. "There is," she said. "Pantoufle says so."

"Sweetheart, Pantoufle isn't real either."

It's not easy being the daughter of a witch. Harder still being the mother of one. And after what happened at Les Laveuses I was faced with a choice. To tell the truth and condemn my children to the kind of life I'd always had: moving constantly from place to place; never stable; never secure; living out of suitcases; always running to beat the wind—

Or to lie, and to be like everyone else.

And so I lied. I lied to Anouk. I told her none of it was real. There was no magic, except in stories; no powers to be tapped and tested; no household gods, no witches, no runes, no chants, no totems, no circles in the sand. Anything unexplained became an Accident—with a capital letter—sudden strokes of luck, close calls, gifts from the gods. And Pantoufle—demoted to the rank of "imaginary friend" and now ignored, even though I can still sometimes see him, if only from the corner of my eye.

Nowadays, I turn away. I close my eyes till the colors have gone.

After Les Laveuses, I put all of those things away, knowing that she might resent me—hate me, a little, perhaps—for a while—hoping one day she would understand.

"You have to grow up someday, Anouk. You have to learn to tell the difference between what's real and what isn't."

"Why?"

"It's better this way," I told her. "Those things, Anouk—they set us apart. They make us different. Do you *like* being different? Wouldn't you like to be included, just for once? To have friends, to—"

"I *did* have friends. Paul and Framboise—"

"We couldn't stay there. Not after that."

"And Zézette and Blanche—"

"Travelers, Nanou. River people. You can't live on a boat forever, not if you want to go to school—"

"And Pantoufle—"

"Imaginary friends don't count, Nanou."

"And Roux, Maman. Roux was our friend."

Silence.

"Why couldn't we stay with Roux, Maman? Why didn't you tell him where we were?"

I sighed. "It's complicated."

"I miss him."

"I know."

With Roux, of course, everything's simple. Do what you want. Take what you want. Travel wherever the wind takes you. It works for Roux. It makes him happy. But I know you can't have everything. I've been down that road. I know where it leads. And it gets so hard, Nanou. So very hard.

Roux would have said: *you care too much.* Roux with his defiant red hair and reluctant smile and his beloved boat under the drifting stars. *You care too much.* It may be true; in spite of everything I care too much. I care that Anouk has no friends in her new school. I care that Rosette is nearly four years old, so alert, and yet without speech, like the victim of some evil spell, some princess stricken dumb for fear of what she might reveal.

How to explain this to Roux, who fears nothing and cares for no one? To be a mother is to live in fear. Fear of death, of sickness, of loss, of accidents, of strangers, of the Black Man, or simply those small everyday things that somehow manage to hurt us most: the look of impatience, the angry word, the missed bedtime story, the forgotten kiss, the terrible moment when a mother ceases to be the center of her daughter's world and becomes just another satellite orbiting some less significant sun.

It has not happened—at least, not yet. But I see it in the other children; in the teenage girls with their sullen mouths and their mobile phones and their look of contempt at the world in general. I have disappointed her, I know that. I am not the mother she wants me to be. And at eleven, though bright, she is still too young to understand what I have sacrificed, and why.

You care too much.

If only things could be that simple.

They are, replies his voice in my heart.

Once, maybe, Roux. Not anymore.

I wonder if he has changed at all. As for myself—I doubt he'd know me. He writes to me from time to time—he got my address from Blanche and Zézette—briefly, at Christmas, and on Anouk's birthday. I write to him at the post office in Lansquenet, knowing that he sometimes passes by. I have not mentioned Rosette in any of my letters. Nor have I mentioned Thierry at all; my landlord Thierry, who has been so kind and so very generous, and whose patience I admire more than words can say.

Thierry Le Tresset, fifty-one; divorced, one son, a churchgoer, a man of rock.

Don't laugh. I like him very much.

I wonder what he sees in me.

I look in the mirror nowadays and there's no reflection looking back; just a flat portrait of a woman in her thirties. No one special; just a woman of no exceptional beauty or character. A woman like all the rest, which is precisely what I mean to be, and yet today the thought depresses me. Perhaps because of the funeral: the sad, underlit chapel of rest with the flowers left over from the previous client; the empty room; the absurdly enormous wreath from Thierry; the indifferent clergyman with the runny nose; the piped music (Elgar's "Nimrod") from the crackling speakers.

Death is banal, as my mother used to say, weeks before her own death on a crowded street in Midtown New York. Life is extraordinary. *We* are extraordinary. To embrace the extraordinary is to celebrate life.

Well, Mother. How things change. In the old days (not *so* old, I remind myself) there would have been a celebration last night. All Hallows' Eve: a magical time; a time of secrets and of mysteries; of sachets to be sewn in red silk and hung around the house to ward off evil; of scattered salt and spiced wine and honey cakes left on the sill; of pumpkin, apples, firecrackers, and the scent of pine and woodsmoke as autumn turns and old winter takes the stage. There would have been songs and dancing round the bonfire; Anouk in greasepaint and black feathers, flitting from door to door with Pantoufle at her heels, and Rosette with her lantern and her own totem—with orange fur to match her hair—prancing and preening in her wake.

No more—it hurts to think of those days. But it isn't safe. My mother knew—she fled the Black Man for twenty years, and though for a while I thought I'd beaten him, fought for my place and won the fight, I soon realized that my victory was just an illusion. The Black Man has many faces, many followers, and he does not always wear a clerical collar.

I used to think I feared their God. Years later, I know it's their *kindness* I fear. Their well-meaning concern. Their pity. I have felt them on our trail these past four years, sniffing and sneaking in our wake. And since Les Laveuses they have come so much closer. They mean so well, the Kindly Ones; they want nothing but the best for my beautiful children. And they will not relent till they have torn us apart; until they have torn us all to pieces.

Perhaps that's why I have never confided in Thierry. Kind, dependable, solid Thierry, my good friend, with his slow smile and his cheery voice and his touching belief in the cure-all properties of money. He wants to help— has already helped us so much this year. A word from me, and he would again. All our troubles could be over. I wonder why I hesitate. I wonder why I find it so hard to trust someone, to finally admit that I need help.

Now, close to midnight, I find my thoughts straying, as they often do at such times, to my mother, the cards, and the Kindly Ones. Anouk and Rosette are already asleep. The wind has dropped abruptly. Below us, Paris simmers like a fog. But above the streets the Butte de Montmartre seems to float like some magical city of smoke and starlight. Anouk thinks I have burned the cards; I have not read them for over three years. But I have them still, my mother's cards, scented with chocolate and shuffled to a gloss.

The box is hidden beneath my bed. It smells of lost time and the season of mists. I open it, and there are the cards, the ancient images, woodcut as they were centuries ago in Marseille: Death; the Lovers; the Tower; the Fool; the Magus; the Hanged Man; Change.

It is not a true reading, I tell myself. I pick the cards at random, without any idea of the consequences. And yet I cannot rid myself of the thought that something is trying to reveal itself, that some message lies within the cards.

I put them away. It was a mistake. In the old days I would have banished my night demons with a cantrip—*tsk-tsk, begone!*—and a healing brew, some incense and a scatter of salt on the threshold. Today I am civilized; I brew nothing stronger than camomile tea. It helps me sleep—eventually.

But during the night, and for the first time in months I dream of the Kindly Ones, snuffling and slinking and sneaking through the backstreets of old Montmartre, and in my dream I wish I had left just a pinch of salt on the step—or a medicine bag above the door—for without them the night can enter unchecked, drawn in by the scent of chocolate.

PART TWO

One Jaguar

Monday, 5 November

I CAUGHT THE BUS TO SCHOOL, AS USUAL. YOU WOULDN'T THINK THERE was a school here but for the plaque that marks the entrance. The rest is hidden behind high walls that might belong to offices or a private park or something different altogether. The Lycée Jules Renard; not so large by Paris standards, but to me it's practically a city.

My school in Lansquenet had forty pupils. This has eight hundred boys and girls; plus satchels, iPods, mobile phones, tubes of underarm deodorant, schoolbooks, lip salves, computer games, secrets, gossip and lies. I have just one friend there—well, *almost* a friend—Suzanne Prudhomme, who lives on the cemetery side of Rue Ganneron and who sometimes calls in at the *chocolaterie*.

Suzanne—who likes to be called Suze, like the drink—has red hair, which she hates, and a round, pink face, and she is always about to begin a diet. I actually rather like her hair, which reminds me of my friend Roux, and I don't think she's fat at all, but she complains about these things all the time. She and I used to be really good friends, but she can be moody nowadays and sometimes says quite nasty things for no reason, or says she won't talk to me anymore if I don't do exactly what she wants me to.

Today, she wasn't talking to me again. That's because I wouldn't come to the pictures last night. But the cinema's expensive enough already, and then there's popcorn and Coke to buy—and if I don't buy any, Suzanne notices and makes jokes at school about my never having any money—and besides, I knew that Chantal would be there too, and Suzanne's different when Chantal's around.

Chantal is Suzanne's new best friend. She always has money to go to the cinema, and her hair is always perfectly neat. She wears a Tiffany diamond cross, and once, at school, when the teacher told her to take it off, Chantal's father wrote a letter to the newspapers saying that it was a disgrace that his daughter should be victimized for wearing the symbol of her Catholic faith when Muslim girls were allowed to get away with those head scarves. It caused quite a fuss, actually; and afterward both crosses and head scarves were banned from school. Chantal still wears hers, though. I know because I've seen her with it on in gym. The teacher pretends not to notice. Chantal's father has that effect on people.

Just ignore them, Maman says. *You can make other friends.*

Don't think I haven't tried; but it seems that whenever I do find someone new, Suze finds a way to get to them. It's happened before. It's nothing you could put your finger on, but it's there all the same, like a perfume in the air. And suddenly the people you thought were your friends start avoiding you and being with her; and before you know it, they're *her* friends, not yours, and you're alone.

So all today Suze wouldn't talk, and sat with Chantal in all her lessons, and put her bag on the seat next to her so that I couldn't sit there, and every time I looked at them they seemed to be laughing at me.

I don't care. Who wants to be like those two?

But then I see them with their heads together, and I can tell from the way they're not looking at me that they're laughing at me again. Why? What *is* it about me? In the old days at least I *knew* what made me different. But now—

Is it my hair? Is it my clothes? Is it because we've never bought anything at the Galeries Lafayette? Is it because we never go skiing to Val d'Isère, or to Cannes for the summer? Is it some kind of a label on me, like on a cheap pair of trainers, that warns them that I'm second-rate?

Mamam has tried so hard to help. There's nothing unusual about me; nothing to suggest we haven't got money. I wear the same clothes as everyone else. My schoolbag is the same as theirs. I see the right films, read the right books, listen to the right music. I ought to fit in. But somehow I still don't.

The problem is me. I just don't match. I'm the wrong shape, somehow, the wrong color. I like the wrong books. I watch the wrong films in secret. I'm different, whether they like it or not, and I don't see why I should pretend otherwise.

But it's hard when everyone else has friends. And it's hard when people only ever really like you when you're being someone else.

When I came in this morning the others were playing with a tennis ball in the classroom. Suze was bouncing it to Chantal, who was bouncing it to Lucie, then across to Sandrine, and around the class to Sophie. No one said anything as I came in. They all just kept playing with the ball, but I noticed that no one ever passed it to me, and when I called out—*over here!*—no one seemed to understand. It was as if the game had changed; without anyone actually saying so, now it was about keeping the ball away from me, yelling *Annie's It*, making me jump, spinning it wide.

I know it's stupid. It's only a game. But it's like that every day at school. In a class of twenty-three, I'm the odd number; the one who has to sit on her own; the one who has to share the computers with two other pupils (usually Chantal and Suze) instead of one; who spends break alone, in the library or just sitting on a bench while the others go around in groups, laughing and talking and playing games. I wouldn't mind if someone else was It sometimes. But they never are. It's always me.

It's not that I'm shy. I *like* people. I get on with them. I like to talk, or play tag in the playground; I'm not like Claude, who's too shy to say a word to anyone and who stutters whenever a teacher asks him a question. I'm not touchy like Suze, or snobby like Chantal. I'm always here to listen if someone's upset—if Suze gets into a quarrel with Lucie or Danielle, then it's me, not Chantal, she comes to first—but just when I think we're getting somewhere, she goes and starts some new thing, like taking pictures of me in the changing room with her mobile phone and showing them to everyone. And when I say, *Suze, don't do that*, she just gives me that look and says *it's only a joke*, and so I have to laugh, even when I don't want to, because I don't want to be the one with no sense of humor. But it really doesn't feel funny to me. Like the tennis ball game, it's only funny when you're not It.

Anyway, that's what I was thinking as I came back on the bus, with Suze and Chantal giggling on the backseat behind me. I didn't look round but pretended to read my book, although the bus was bumpy and the page blurred into nothing in front of my eyes. Actually my eyes were watering a bit—and so I just looked out the window, though it was raining and nearly dark, and everything very Paris-gray as we approached my stop just after the Métro station by Rue Caulaincourt.

Maybe I'll take the Métro from now on. It's not so close to the school itself, but I like it better: the biscuity smell of the escalators; the rush of air when the trains come in; the people; the crowds. You see all kinds of strange people in the Métro. People of all races: tourists; Muslim women with the veil; African traders with their pockets filled with fake watches and ebony carvings and shell bracelets and beads. There are men dressed as women, and women dressed as film stars, and people eating strange food out of brown paper bags, and people with punk hair, and tattoos, and rings in their eyebrows, and beggars and musicians and pickpockets and drunks.

Maman prefers me to take the bus.

Of course. She would.

Suzanne giggled, and I knew she'd been talking about me again. I stood up, ignoring her, and moved toward the front of the bus.

It was then that I saw Zozie, standing in the aisle. No lollipop shoes for her today, but a pair of purple platform boots with buckles all the way up to the knee. Today she was wearing a short black dress over a lime green roll-neck pullover; her hair had a bright pink streak in it, and she looked fabulous.

I couldn't help it. I said so.

I was sure she would have forgotten me by now, but she hadn't. "Annie! It's you!" She gave me a kiss. "This is my stop. Are you getting off?"

I looked back and caught Suzanne and Chantal staring, forgetting even to giggle in their surprise. Not that anyone would have giggled at Zozie. Or that she would have cared if they had. I could see Suzanne with her mouth hanging open (not a good look for Suzanne); next to her, Chantal was nearly the same shade as Zozie's pullover.

"Friends of yours?" said Zozie as we got off the bus.

"As if," I said and rolled my eyes.

Zozie laughed. She laughs a lot, quite loudly, actually, and never seems to mind if people stare. She was very tall in those platform boots. I wished I had some.

"Well, why don't you get some?" said Zozie.

I shrugged.

"I have to say that's a very—*conventional* look you've got." I love the way she says *conventional*, with a gleam in her eye that's quite different from just making fun. "Now I had you down as more of an original, if you get my drift."

"Maman doesn't like us to be different."

She raised her eyebrows. "Really?"

Again, I shrugged.

"Oh, well. Each to his own. Listen, there's a spectacular little place just down the road that does the most wonderful *saint-honorés* this side of paradise—so why don't we just stop by there to celebrate?"

"Celebrate what?" I said.

"I'm going to be a neighbor of yours!"

Well, of course I know I'm not supposed to go off with strangers. Maman tells me often enough, and you can't live in Paris without picking up a few cautious habits. But this was different—this was Zozie—and besides, I was meeting her in a public place, an English tea shop I hadn't seen before which did have, as she'd promised, the most fabulous cakes.

I wouldn't have gone there on my own. Places like that make me nervous—all glass tables and ladies in furs drinking fancy teas in bone china cups, and waitresses in little black dresses who looked at me in my school clothes with my hair all over the place, and looked at Zozie in her purple platform boots as if they couldn't believe either of us.

"I love this place," said Zozie in a low voice. "It's hilarious. And it takes itself so seriously—"

It took its prices seriously too. Way out of my league—ten euros just for a pot of tea, twelve for a cup of hot chocolate.

"It's all right. My treat," said Zozie, and we sat down at a corner table while a sulky-looking waitress who looked like Jeanne Moreau handed us the menu as if it gave her a pain.

"You know Jeanne Moreau?" said Zozie, surprised.

I nodded, still feeling nervous. "She was fabulous in *Jules et Jim*."

"Not with that poker up her arse," said Zozie, indicating our waitress, now all smiles around two expensive-looking ladies with identical blond hair.

I gave a snort of laughter. The ladies looked at me, then down at Zozie's purple boots. Their heads went together, and I suddenly thought of Suze and Chantal and felt my mouth go dry.

Zozie must have noticed something, because she stopped laughing and looked concerned. "What's wrong?" she said.

"I don't know. I just thought those people were laughing at us." It's the kind of place Chantal's mother takes her to, I tried to explain. Where very thin ladies in pastel cashmere drink lemon tea and ignore the cakes.

Zozie crossed her long legs. "That's because you're not a clone. Clones fit in. Freaks stand out. Ask me which one I prefer."

I shrugged. "I guess."

"You're not convinced." She gave me her mischievous grin. "Watch this." And she flicked her fingers at the waitress who looked like Jeanne Moreau, and just as she did, at exactly the same time, the waitress stumbled in her high heels and dropped a whole pot of lemon tea onto the table in front of her, soaking the tablecloth and dripping hot tea into the ladies' handbags and onto their expensive shoes.

I looked at Zozie.

Zozie grinned back. "Neat trick, hey?"

And then I laughed, because *of course* it was an accident, and no one could have foreseen what was going to happen, but to me it looked exactly as if Zozie had *made* the teapot fall, with the waitress fussing over the mess, and the pastel ladies with their wet shoes, and no one watching us at all, or laughing at Zozie's ridiculous boots.

So we ordered cakes from the menu then, and coffee from the special bar. Zozie had a *saint-honoré*—no dieting for *her*—and I had a frangipane and we both had vanilla latte, and we talked for longer than I thought, about Suze, and school, and books, and Maman, and Thierry, and the *chocolaterie*.

"It must be great, living in a chocolate shop," said Zozie, starting her *saint-honoré*.

"It's not as nice as Lansquenet."

Zozie looked interested. "What's Lansquenet?"

"A place we used to live before. Down south somewhere. It was cool."

"Cooler than Paris?" She looked surprised.

So I told her about Lansquenet, and Les Marauds where we used to play, Jeannot and I, by the banks of the river; and then I told her about Armande, and the river people, and Roux's boat with its glass roof and the little galley with its chipped enamel pans, and the way we used to make the chocolates, Maman and I, late at night and early in the morning, so that everything used to smell of chocolate, even the dust.

Afterward I was surprised at how much I'd talked. I'm not supposed to talk about that, or any of the places we were before. But with Zozie it's different. With her, it feels safe.

"So with Madame Poussin gone, who's going to help your mother now?" said Zozie, scooping froth from her glass with a little spoon.

"We'll manage," I said.

"Does Rosette go to school?"

"Not yet." For some reason I didn't want to tell her about Rosette. "She's very bright, though. She can draw really well. She signs, and she even follows the words in her storybooks with her finger."

"She doesn't look much like you."

I shrugged.

Zozie looked at me with that gleam in her eye, as if she was going to say something else, but didn't. She finished her latte and said: "It must be tough, not having a father."

I shrugged. Of course I have a father—we just don't know who he is—but I wasn't going to say *that* to Zozie.

"Your mother and you must be very close."

"Nn-hm." I nodded.

"You look alike—" She stopped and smile-frowned a little, as if trying to figure out something that puzzled her. "And there's something about you, isn't there, Annie, something I can't quite put my finger on—"

I didn't say anything to that, of course. Silence is safer, Maman says, so that what you say can't be used against you.

"Well, you're not a clone, that's for sure. I bet you know a few tricks—"

"Tricks?" I thought of the waitress and the spilled lemon tea. I looked away, feeling suddenly awkward again, wishing someone would come with the bill so that I could say good-bye and run back home.

But our waitress was avoiding us, chatting with the man behind the coffee bar, laughing now and flicking her hair, the way Suze does sometimes when Jean-Loup Rimbault (that's a boy she likes) is standing nearby. Besides, I've noticed that about waiters and waitresses: even when they serve you on time, they never want to bring you the bill.

But then Zozie made a little forked sign with her fingers, so very small I might have missed it. A little forked sign, like flicking a switch, and the waitress who looked like Jeanne Moreau turned round, as if someone had prodded her, and brought us the bill at once on a tray.

Zozie smiled and took out her purse. Jeanne Moreau waited, looking bored and sulky, and I half-expected Zozie to say something—after all, someone who can say *arse* in an English tea shop surely isn't shy about speaking their mind.

But she didn't. "Here's fifty. You can keep the change." And she handed the waitress a five-euro note.

Well, even I could see it was a five. I saw it quite clearly as Zozie put it on the tray and smiled. But somehow the waitress didn't see.

Instead she said: "*Merci, bonne journée,*" and Zozie made that sign with her hand and put away her purse as if nothing had happened—

And then she turned and winked at me.

For a second I wasn't sure I'd seen it right. It might just have been a normal kind of accident—after all, the place was crowded, the waitress was busy, and people sometimes make mistakes.

But after what had happened with the tea—

She smiled at me, just like a cat that could scratch you even as it sits purring on your knee.

Tricks, she'd said.

Accident, I thought.

I suddenly wished I hadn't come, wished I hadn't called to her that day in front of the *chocolaterie*. It's only a game—it's not even real—and yet it feels so dangerous, like a sleeping thing that you can only poke so many times before it opens its eyes for good.

I looked at my watch. "I have to go."

"Annie. Relax. It's half past four—"

"Maman worries if I'm late."

"Five minutes won't hurt—"

"I have to go."

I think I expected her to stop me, somehow; to make me turn back, as the waitress had. But Zozie just smiled, and I felt stupid at having panicked like that. Some people are just suggestible. The waitress was probably one of them. Or maybe they both made a mistake—or maybe I did.

But I knew I hadn't. And she knew I'd seen. It was in her colors. And in the way she looked at me—half-smiling, as if we'd shared something more than just cake—

I know it's not safe. But I like her. I really do. I wanted to say something to make her understand—

On impulse I turned and found her still smiling.

"Hey, Zozie," I said. "Is that your real name?"

"Hey, Annie," she mocked. "Is that yours?"

"Well, I—" I was so stunned that for a second I nearly told her. "My *real* friends call me Nanou."

"And do you have many?" she said, smiling.

I laughed and held up a single finger.

Tuesday, 6 November

WHAT AN INTERESTING CHILD. YOUNGER THAN HER CONTEMPORARIES IN some ways, but so much older in others, she has no difficulty in speaking with adults, but with other children she seems awkward, as if trying to assess their level of competence. With me she was expansive, funny, talkative, wistful, willful but with an instinctive caution as soon as I touched—ever so lightly—on the subject of her strangeness.

Of course, no child wants to be seen as different. But Annie's reserve goes further than this. It's as if she's hiding something from the world, some alien quality that might be dangerous if it were discovered.

Other people may not see it. But I'm not other people, and I find myself drawn to her in a way I find impossible to resist. I wonder if she knows *what* she is, if she understands—if she has any inkling of the potential in that sullen little head.

I met her again today, on her way home from school. She was—not cool, precisely, but certainly less confiding than yesterday, as if aware of a mark overstepped. As I said, an interesting child, and all the more so for the challenge she presents. I sense that she is not impervious to seduction; but she is careful, very careful, and I will have to work slowly if I am not to frighten her away.

And so we simply talked for a while—I made no mention of her otherness, or the place she calls Lansquenet, or the chocolate shop—and then we went our separate ways, but not before I had told her where I lived, and where I'm working nowadays.

Working? Everyone needs a job. It gives me an excuse to play, to be with people, to observe them and to learn their little secrets. I'm not in need of the money, of course, which is why I can afford to take the first convenient job on offer. The one job any girl can find without difficulty in a place like Montmartre.

No, not *that*. Waitressing, of course.

It's been a long, long time since I worked in a café. These days I don't have to—the pay's lousy and the hours are worse—but I feel that being a waitress somehow suits Zozie de l'Alba, and besides, it gives me a good vantage point from which to observe comings and goings in the neighborhood.

Le P'tit Pinson, tucked into the corner of the Rue des Faux-Monnayeurs, is an old-style café from the dingy days of Montmartre, dark and smoky and paneled in layers of grease and nicotine. Its owner is Laurent Pinson, a sixty-five-year-old native Parisian with an aggressive mustache and poor personal hygiene. Like Laurent himself, the café's appeal is generally limited to the older generation—who appreciate its modest pricing and its plat du jour—and the whimsical like myself, who enjoy its owner's spectacular rudeness and the extreme politics of its elderly patrons.

Tourists choose the Place du Tertre, with its pretty little cafés and gingham-topped tables along the cobbled lanes. Or the art deco *pâtisserie* on the lower Butte, with its jeweled array of tarts and confits. Or the English tea shop on Rue Ramey. But I'm not interested in tourists. I'm interested in that *chocolaterie*, which I can see quite clearly from across the square. From here I can see who comes and goes, I can count the customers, monitor deliveries, and generally acquaint myself with the rhythms of its little life.

The letters I stole on that first day have proved less than useful in practical terms. A stamped invoice dated 20 October, marked PAID IN CASH, from Sogar Fils, a confectionery supplier. But who pays in cash nowadays? An impractical, senseless means of payment—doesn't this woman have an account?—which leaves me as ignorant as I was before.

The second envelope was a sympathy card for Madame Poussin, signed Thierry, with a kiss. Postmarked London, with a *see you soon, and please don't worry* casually appended.

File that away for later use.

The third, on a faded postcard of the Rhône, was even less informative.

Heading north. I'll drop by if I can.

Signed *R*, the card was addressed only to "Y and A," though the writing was so careless that the *Y* looked more like a *V*.

The fourth, junk mail peddling financial services.

Still, I tell myself. There's time.

"Hey! It's you!" The artist again. I know him now; his name is Jean-Louis, and his friend with the beret is Paupaul. I see them often at Le P'tit Pinson, drinking beer and chatting up the ladies. Fifty euros pays for a pencil sketch—call it ten for the sketch, and forty for the flattery—and they have their spiel down to a fine art. Jean-Louis is a charmer—plain women are particularly susceptible—and it is his persistence, rather than his talent, that holds the secret of his success.

"I won't buy it, so don't waste your time," I told him as he opened his pad.

"Then I'll sell it to Laurent," he said, with a wink. "Or maybe I'll just keep it myself."

Paupaul pretends indifference. He's older than his friend, and his style is less exuberant. In fact he rarely speaks at all but stands at his easel in the corner of the square, scowling furiously at the paper and occasionally scratching at it with frightening intensity. He has an intimidating mustache and makes his patrons sit at length, while he scowls and scratches and mutters violently to himself before producing a work of such bizarre proportions that his customers are awed into paying up.

Jean-Louis was still sketching me as I made my way among the tables. "I'm warning you. I charge," I said.

"Consider the lilies," said Jean-Louis airily. "They do not toil, neither do they demand a sitter's fee."

"Lilies don't have bills to pay."

This morning I called in at the bank. I've been doing it every day this week. To withdraw twenty-five thousand euros in cash would certainly bring me the wrong kind of attention, but several withdrawals of modest size—a thousand here, two hundred there—are barely remembered from one day to the next.

Still, it never pays to be complacent.

And so I went in, not as Zozie, but as the colleague in whose name I opened the account—Barbara Beauchamp, a secretary with a hitherto unblemished record of trust. I made myself drab for the occasion; although true invisibility is impossible (besides being far too conspicuous), drabness is open to anyone, and a nondescript woman in a woolly hat and gloves can pass almost unseen anywhere.

Which is why I sensed it immediately. An odd sensation of scrutiny as I stood at the counter; an unprecedented alertness in their colors; a request to wait as they processed my cash; the scent and sound of something not quite right.

I did not wait for confirmation. I left the bank as soon as the cashier was out of sight, then slipped the checkbook and card into an envelope and posted it in the nearest letter box. The address was fictitious; the incriminating items will spend three months passing from one post office to the next until they end up in the dead-letter depot, never to be found. If I ever need to dispose of a body, I'll do the same, sending parceled hands and feet and bits of torso to blurry addresses across Europe and back, while police search in vain for the shallow grave.

Not that murder was ever my taste. Still, you should never completely dismiss any possibility. I found a convenient clothes store in which to change back from Madame Beauchamp to Zozie de l'Alba and, with an eye for anything out of the ordinary, returned by a roundabout route to my bed-and-breakfast in lower Montmartre and contemplated the future.

Damn.

Twenty-two thousand euros remained in Madame Beauchamp's fake account—money that had cost me six months' planning, research, performance, and honing of my new identity. No chance of retrieving it now; although it was unlikely that I would be recognized from the bank's blurry camera footage, it was more than likely that the account had been frozen, pending police investigation. Face it, the money was lost forever, leaving me with little more than an extra charm on my bracelet—a mouse, as it happens, quite appropriate for poor Françoise.

The sad truth is, I tell myself, there's no future in craftsmanship any more. Six wasted months, and I'm back where I started. No money, no life.

Well, *that* can change. All I need is a little inspiration. We'll start with the chocolate shop, shall we? With Vianne Rocher, from Lansquenet, who for reasons unknown has recast herself as Yanne Charbonneau, mother of two, respectable widow of the Butte.

Do I sense a kindred spirit? No. But I do recognize a challenge. Though there's little enough to be had from the *chocolaterie* at present, Yanne's life is not entirely without appeal. And, of course, she has that child. That very interesting child.

I'm staying in a place just off the Boulevard de Clichy, ten minutes' walk from Place des Faux-Monnayeurs. Two rooms the size of a postage stamp at the top of four flights of narrow stairs, but cheap enough to suit my needs and discreet enough to preserve my anonymity. From there I can observe the streets; plot comings and goings; become a part of the scenery.

It's not the Butte, which is out of my league. In fact, it's rather a big step down from Françoise's nice little place in the eleventh. But Zozie de l'Alba doesn't belong; and it suits her to live below the salt. All kinds of people live here: students, shopkeepers, immigrants, masseuses both registered and unregistered. There are half a dozen churches in this small area alone (debauch and religion, those Siamese twins); the street yields more litter than fallen leaves; there's a perpetual smell of drains and dog shit. On this side of the Butte the pretty little cafés have given way to cheap takeaways and general stores, around which the tramps congregate at night, drinking red wine from plastic-topped bottles before bedding down in the steel-shuttered doorways.

I'll probably tire of it soon enough; but I do need a place to lie low for a while, until the heat on Madame Beauchamp—and Françoise Lavery—dies down. It never hurts to be cautious, I know—and besides, as my mother used to say, you should always take time to pick the cherries.

Thursday, 8 November

WHILST WAITING FOR MY CHERRIES TO RIPEN, I HAVE MANAGED TO collect a certain amount of local knowledge on the inhabitants of Place des Faux-Monnayeurs. Madame Pinot, the little partridge of a woman who runs the newsagent-souvenir-bric-a-brac shop, has a busy mouth for gossip and has acquainted me with the neighborhood through her eyes.

Through her I know that Laurent Pinson frequents the singles bars, that the fat young man from the Italian restaurant weighs over three hundred pounds but still goes into the *chocolaterie* at least twice a week, and that the woman with the dog who passes every Thursday at ten o'clock is Madame Luzeron, whose husband had a stroke last year and whose son died when he was thirteen. Every Thursday she goes to the cemetery, says Madame Pinot, with that silly little dog in tow. Never misses. Poor old thing.

"What about the *chocolaterie?*" I asked, selecting *Paris-Match* (I hate *Paris-Match*) from a small shelf of magazines. Above and below the magazines there are colorful displays of religious tat: plaster Virgins, cheap ceramics; snow globes of the Sacré-Coeur; medallions; crucifixes; rosaries; incense for all occasions. I suspect Madame may be a prude; she looked at the cover of my magazine (which shows Princess Stephanie of Monaco, bikinied and cavorting blurrily on some beach somewhere), and pulled a face like the back end of a turkey.

"Not much to say, really," she said. "Husband died down south somewhere. But she's fallen on her feet all right." The busy mouth puckered again. "I reckon there'll be a wedding before long."

"Really?"

She nodded. "Thierry le Tresset. He owns the place. Let it out cheap to Madame Poussin because she was some kind of friend of the family. That's where he met Madame Charbonneau. And if ever I saw a man head over heels—" She rang up the magazine on the till. "Still, I wonder if he knows what he's taking on. She must be twenty years younger than he is—and he's always away on business, and her with two kids, one of them *special*—"

"Special?" I said.

"Oh, haven't you heard? Poor little thing. That's got to be a burden for anyone—and if *that* wasn't bad enough," she said, "you're not telling me the shop makes much of a profit, what with the overheads, and the heating, and the rent—"

I let her talk for a little while. Gossip is currency to people like Madame, and I sense that I have already given her much to think about. With my pink-streaked hair and scarlet shoes I too must be a promising source of tittle-tattle. I left the shop with a cheery good-bye and the sense that I'd made a good start, and returned to my place of employment.

It's the best vantage point I could have hoped for. From here I can see all Yanne's customers, monitor comings and goings, keep track of deliveries, and keep my eye on the children.

The little one is a handful; not noisy, but mischievous, and despite her small size, rather older than I originally guessed. Madame Pinot tells me she's nearly four years old and has yet to speak her first word, although she seems to know some sign language. A *special* child, Madame tells me, with that tiny sneer she reserves for blacks, Jews, travelers, and the politically correct.

A special child? Undoubtedly. Exactly *how* special remains to be seen.

And, of course, there's Annie too. I see her from Le P'tit Pinson—every morning just before eight and every afternoon after half past four—and she speaks to me cheerily enough: of her school, and her friends, her teachers, the people she sees on the bus. It's a start, at least; but I sense she's holding back. In a way, it pleases me. I could put that strength to use—with the right education I'm sure she'd go far—and besides, you know, the greater part of any seduction lies in the chase.

But I'm already tired of Le P'tit Pinson. My first week's wages will barely cover my expenses, and Laurent is far from easy to please. Worse, he has begun to notice me: I see it in his colors and in the way he slicks his hair, in the new, special care he gives to his appearance.

It's always a risk, of course, I know. He would not have noticed Françoise Lavery. But Zozie de l'Alba has a different charm. He doesn't understand it; he dislikes foreigners, and this woman has a certain look, a gypsy look that he mistrusts—

And yet, for the first time in years, he finds himself choosing what to wear: discarding this tie (too loud, too wide); balancing the merits of this suit and that; considering that old bottle of eau de toilette, last used at someone's wedding, vinegary with age now, leaving brown stains on the clean white shirt. . . .

Normally I might encourage this, play up to the old man's vanity in the hope of a few easy pickings: a credit card, some money, perhaps; maybe a cash box hidden somewhere, a theft that Laurent would never report.

At any normal time, I would. But men like Laurent are easy to find. Women like Yanne, however—

Some years ago, when I was somebody else, I went to the cinema to see a film about ancient Romans. A disappointing film in many ways: too slick with fake blood and Hollywood redemption. But it was the gladiator scenes that struck me as particularly unrealistic, those audiences of computer-generated people in the background, all shouting and laughing and waving their arms in neat patterns, like animated wallpaper. I'd wondered at the time if the makers of that film had ever *watched* a real crowd. I do—I generally find the crowd far more interesting than the spectacle itself—and though they were convincing enough as animation, they had no colors, and there was nothing real about their behavior.

Well, Yanne Charbonneau reminds me of those people. She is a figment in the background, realistic enough to the casual observer, but operating according to a sequence of predictable commands. She has no colors—or if she has, she has become adept at hiding them beneath this screen of inconsequence.

The children, however, are brightly illuminated. Most children have brighter colors than adults, but even so Annie stands out, her color-trail of butterfly blue flaring defiantly against the sky.

There's something else as well, I think—some kind of a shadow in her wake. I saw it again as she played with Rosette in the alley outside the *chocolaterie*, Annie with that cloud of Byzantine hair torched into gold by the afternoon sun, holding her little sister's hand as Rosette splashed and stamped at the speckled cobblestones in her primrose yellow Wellington boots.

Some kind of shadow. A dog, a cat?

Well, I'll find out. You know I will. Give me time, Nanou. Just give me time.

Thursday, 8 November

THIERRY WAS BACK FROM LONDON TODAY, WITH AN ARMFUL OF PRESENTS for Anouk and Rosette, and a dozen yellow roses for me.

It was twelve-fifteen, and I was ten minutes away from closing for lunch. I was just gift wrapping a box of macaroons for a customer, and looking forward to a quiet hour with the children (Thursday is Anouk's free afternoon). I looped pink ribbon around the box—a gesture I'd performed a thousand times—tied the bow, then pulled the ribbon taut against the blade of the scissors to curl it.

"Yanne!"

The scissors slipped, spoiling the curl. "Thierry! You're a day early!"

He's a big man, tall and heavy. In his cashmere coat he more than filled the little shop doorway. An open face; blue eyes; thick hair, still mostly brown. Moneyed hands still used to working; cracked palms and polished fingernails. A scent of plaster dust and leather and sweat and *jambon-frites* and the occasional guilty, fat cigar.

"I missed you," he said, and kissed my cheek. "I'm sorry I couldn't make it back in time for the funeral. Was it terrible?"

"No. Just sad. No one came."

"You're a star, Yanne. I don't know how you do it. How's business?"

"OK." In fact, it's not; the customer was only my second that day, not counting the ones who just come to look. But I was glad of her presence when he arrived—a Chinese girl in a yellow coat, who would no doubt enjoy her macaroons but who would have been far happier with a box of chocolate-coated strawberries. Not that it matters. It's not my concern. Not anymore, anyway.

"Where are the girls?"

"Upstairs," I said. "Watching TV. How was London?"

"Great. You should come."

As a matter of fact I know it well; my mother and I lived there for nearly a year. I'm not sure why I haven't told him this, or why I have allowed him to believe that I was born and raised in France. Perhaps a yearning for ordinariness: perhaps a fear that if I mention my mother he may look at me differently.

Thierry is a solid citizen. A builder's boy made good through property, he has had very little exposure to the unusual and the uncertain. His tastes are conventional. He likes a good steak; drinks red wine; loves children, bad puns, and silly rhymes; prefers women to wear skirts; goes to mass through force of habit; has no prejudice against foreigners but would prefer not to see quite so many of them about. I do like him—and yet the thought of confiding in him—in anyone—

Not that I need to. I've never needed a confidant. I have Anouk. I have Rosette. When did I ever need anyone else?

"You're looking sad." The Chinese girl had gone. "What about lunch?"

I smiled. Lunch cures sadness in Thierry's world. I wasn't hungry; but it was that or have him in the shop all afternoon. So I called Anouk, wheedled and struggled Rosette into her coat, and we went across the road to Le P'tit Pinson, which Thierry likes for its dilapidated charm and greasy food, and I dislike for the same reasons.

Anouk was restless, and it was time for Rosette's nap, but Thierry was full of his London trip: the crowds, the buildings, the theaters, the shops. His company is renovating some office buildings near Kings Cross, and he likes to oversee the work himself, going down by train on Monday and coming back for the weekend. His ex-wife Sarah still lives in London with their son, but Thierry is at pains to reassure me (as if I needed it) that he and Sarah have been estranged for years.

I don't doubt it; there's no subterfuge in Thierry, no side. His favorites are the simple wrapped milk chocolate squares you can buy from any supermarket in the country. Thirty percent cocoa solids; anything stronger, and he sticks out his tongue like a little boy. But I do love his enthusiasm—and I envy him his plainness and his lack of guile. Perhaps my envy exceeds my love—but does it matter so very much?

We met him last year when the roof sprang a leak. Most landlords would have sent a workman—if we were lucky—but Thierry has known Madame Poussin for years (an old friend of his mother's, he said), and he fixed the roof himself, staying for hot chocolate and playing with Rosette.

Twelve months into our friendship now, and we have already become an old couple, with our favorite haunts and our comfortable routines, although Thierry has yet to stay the night. He thinks I'm a widow, and touchingly wants to "give me time." But his desire is there, unvoiced and untested—and would it really be so bad?

He has broached the subject only once. A single oblique reference to his own mansion flat on Rue de la Croix, to which we have been invited many times and which longs, as he says, for a woman's touch.

A woman's touch. Such an old-fashioned phrase. But then, Thierry is the old-fashioned type. In spite of his love of gadgetry, his mobile phone, and his surround-sound stereo, he remains loyal to old ideals; to a simpler time.

Simple. That's it. Life with Thierry would be very simple. There would always be money for necessary things. The rent for the *chocolaterie* would always be paid. Anouk and Rosette would be cared for and safe. And if he loves them—and me—isn't that enough?

Is it, Vianne? That's my mother's voice—sounding very like Roux these days. *I remember a time when you wanted more.*

As you did, Mother? I told her silently. Dragging your child from place to place, always, forever on the run. Living—just—from hand to mouth, stealing, lying, conjuring; six weeks, three weeks, four days in a place and then move on; no home, no school, peddling dreams, shuffling cards to map our journeys, wearing seam-stretched hand-me-downs, like tailors too busy to mend our own clothes.

At least we knew what we were, Vianne.

It was a cheap comeback, and one I would have expected from her. Besides, I know what I am. Don't I?

We ordered noodles for Rosette and plat du jour for the rest of us. It was far from crowded, even for a weekday; but the air was stale with beer and Gitanes. Laurent Pinson is his own best customer; but for that, I really think he would have closed down years ago. Jowly, unshaven, and bad tempered, he views his customers as intruders on his free time and makes no secret of his contempt for everyone but a handful of regulars who are also his friends.

He tolerates Thierry, who plays the brash Parisian for the occasion, erupting into the café with a *"Hé, Laurent, ça va, mon pote!"* and the slap of a big banknote on the bar. Laurent knows him for a property man— has enquired about the price his own café might fetch, rebuilt and refurbished—and now calls him *M'sieur Thierry* and treats him with a deference that might be respect, or perhaps the hope of a deal to come.

I noticed he was looking more presentable today—shiny suited and smelling of cologne, shirt collar buttoned over a tie that had first seen the light of day some time in the late 1970s. Thierry's influence, I thought; though later I came to change my mind.

I left them to it and sat down, ordered coffee for myself and Coke for Anouk. Once we would have had hot chocolate, with cream and marshmallows and a tiny spoon with which to scoop it—but now it's always Coke for Anouk. She doesn't drink hot chocolate nowadays—some diet thing, I thought at first—and it feels so absurd to be hurt by that, like the first time she refused her bedtime story. Still such a sunny little girl; and yet increasingly I sense these shadows in her, these places to which I am not invited. I know them well—I was the same—and isn't a part of my fear just that: the knowledge that, at her age, I too wanted to run, to escape my mother in as many ways as I possibly could?

The waitress was new and looked vaguely familiar. Long legs, pencil skirt, hair tied up in a ponytail—I finally recognized her by her shoes.

"It's Zoë, isn't it?" I said.

"Zozie." She grinned. "Some place, eh?" She made a comic little gesture, as if ushering us in. "Still"—she lowered her voice to a whisper—"I think the landlord's sweet on me."

Thierry laughed out loud at that, and Anouk gave her a sideways smile.

"It's only a temporary job," Zozie said. "Until I come up with something better."

The plat du jour was choucroute garnie—a dish I associate somehow with our time in Berlin. Surprisingly good for Le P'tit Pinson, which fact I attributed to Zozie and not to some renewed culinary zeal in Laurent.

"With Christmas coming up, won't you need some help in the shop?" said Zozie, transferring sausages from the grill. "If so, then I'm a volunteer." She flung a glance over her shoulder at Laurent, feigning disinterest from his corner. "I mean, obviously I'd hate to leave all this—"

Laurent made a percussive sound, something between a sneeze and a call to attention—*mweh!*—and Zozie raised her eyebrows comically.

"Just think about it," she said, grinning, then turned, picked up four beers with a deftness born of years of bar work, and carried them, smiling, to the table.

She didn't say much to us after that—the bar filled up, and as usual, I was busy with Rosette. Not that she's such a difficult child—she eats much better now, although she dribbles more than a normal child, and still prefers to use her hands—but she can behave oddly at times, looking fixedly at things that aren't there, starting at imaginary sounds or laughing suddenly for no reason. I'm hoping she will grow out of it soon—it has been weeks since her last Accident—and although she still wakes up three or four times a night I can manage on only a few hours, and I'm hoping the sleeplessness will pass.

Thierry thinks I overindulge her; more recently he has begun to speak of taking her to a doctor.

"There's no need. She'll talk when she's ready," I said, watching Rosette eat her noodles. She holds the fork with the wrong hand, though there are no other signs that she is left-handed. In fact, she is rather clever with her hands and especially loves to draw. Little stickmen and women, monkeys—her favorite animal—houses, horses, butterflies, clumsy as yet, but recognizable, in every available color—

"Eat properly, Rosette," said Thierry. "Use your spoon."

Rosette went on eating as if she hadn't heard. There was a time I feared she was deaf; now I know she simply ignores what she feels to be unimportant. It's a pity she does not pay more attention to Thierry; rarely laughs or smiles in his company; rarely shows her sweet side, or signs any more than absolutely necessary.

At home, with Anouk, she laughs and plays; sits for hours with her book; listens to the radio; and dances like a dervish around the flat. At home, barring Accidents, she is well behaved; at naptime we lie in bed together, as I used to with Anouk. I sing to her and tell her stories, and her eyes are bright and alert, lighter than Anouk's, and green and clever as a cat's. She sings along—after a fashion—to my mother's lullaby. She can just hold a tune, but still relies on me for the words:

> V'là l'bon vent, v'là l'joli vent,
> V'là l'bon vent, ma mie m'appelle.
> V'là l'bon vent, v'là l'joli vent,
> V'là l'bon vent, ma mie m'attend.

Thierry speaks of her being "a little slow" or "a late developer," and suggests that I get her "checked out." He has not yet mentioned autism, but he will—like so many men of his age, he reads *Le Point* and believes that this makes him an expert on most things. I, on the other hand, am only a woman, besides being a mother, which has addled my sense of objective judgment.

"Say *spoon*, Rosette," Thierry says.

Rosette picks up the spoon and looks at it curiously.

"Come on, Rosette. Say *spoon*."

Rosette hoots like an owl and makes the spoon perform an impertinent little dance on the tablecloth. Anyone would think she is making fun of Thierry. Quickly I take the spoon from Rosette. Anouk pinches her lips to stop herself from laughing.

Rosette looks at her and grins.

Quit it, signs Anouk with her fingers.

Bullshit, signs Rosette with hers.

I smile at Thierry. "She's only three—"

"Nearly four. That's old enough." Thierry's face takes on the bland expression he adopts when he feels I am being uncooperative. It makes him look older, less familiar, and I feel a sudden sting of irritation—unfair, I know, but it can't be helped. I don't appreciate interference.

I am shocked at how close I come to actually saying it aloud; then I see the waitress—Zozie—watching me with a frown of amusement between her long blue eyes, and I bite my tongue and keep silent.

I tell myself that I have much to be grateful for in Thierry. It's not just the shop, or the help that he has given us over the past year; or even the presents for myself and the children. It's that Thierry is so much larger than life. His shadow covers the three of us; beneath it we are truly invisible.

But he seemed unusually restless today, fidgeting with something in his pocket. He looked at me quizzically over his *blonde*. "Something wrong?"

"I'm just tired."

"What you need is a holiday."

"A holiday?" I almost laughed. "Holidays are for selling chocolates."

"You're going to keep on with the business, then?"

"Of course I am. Why shouldn't I? It's less than two months to Christmas, and—"

"Yanne," he interrupted me. "If I can help in any way—financial or otherwise—" He reached out his hand to touch mine.

"I'll manage," I said.

"Of course. Of course." The hand returned to his coat pocket. He means well, I told myself; and yet something in me rebels at the thought of intrusion, however well meant. I have managed alone for so long that the need for help—*any* kind of help—seems like a dangerous weakness.

"You'll never run the shop alone. What about the kids?" he said.

"I'll manage," I repeated. "I'm—"

"You can't do everything on your own." He was looking slightly annoyed now; shoulders hunched, hands jammed into his coat pockets.

"I know that. I'll find someone."

Once more I glanced at Zozie, busy now with two platters of food in each hand, joking with the belote players at the back of the room. She looks so very much at ease, so independent, so very much *herself* as she hands out the plates, collects the glasses, fends off wandering hands with a laughing comment and a pretend slap.

Why, I was like that, I told myself. *That was me, ten years ago.*

Well, not even that, I thought, because surely Zozie could not be so much younger than me, but so much easier in her own skin, more thoroughly Zozie than I was ever Vianne.

Who *is* Zozie? I ask myself. Those eyes see much farther than dishes to be washed, or a banknote folded under the rim of a plate. Blue eyes are easier to read, and yet the trick of the trade that has served me so often—if not so well—along the years, for some reason fails to work at all with her. Some people are like that, I tell myself. But dark or light, soft-centered or brittle, bitterest orange or rose cream or *manon blanc* or vanilla truffle, I have no idea whether she even likes chocolate at all, still less her favorite.

So—why is it I think that she knows mine?

I looked back at Thierry, to find that he was watching her too.

"You can't afford to hire any help. You're barely making ends meet as it is."

Once more, I felt a flash of annoyance. Who does he think he is? I thought. As if I'd never managed alone, as if I were a child playing shop with my friends. Certainly, business in the *chocolaterie* has not been good over the past few months. But the rent is paid till the New Year, and surely we can turn it around. Christmas is coming, and with luck—

"Yanne, perhaps we need to talk." The smile had gone, and now I could see the businessman in his face; the man who had started out at fourteen with his father to renovate a single derelict flat near Gare du Nord and had become one of the most successful property dealers in Paris. "I know it's hard. But really, it doesn't have to be. There's a solution to everything. I know you were devoted to Madame Poussin—you helped her a lot, and I appreciate that—"

He thinks that's true. Perhaps it was; but I'm also aware that I used her too, as I used my imagined widowhood as an excuse to delay the inevitable; the terrible point of no return—

"But perhaps there's a way forward from here."

"Way forward?" I said.

He gave me a smile. "I see this as an opportunity for you. I mean, obviously we're all sorry about Madame Poussin, but in a way, this liberates you. You could do whatever you wanted, Yanne—although I think I've found a place you'll like—"

"You're saying I should give up the *chocolaterie?*" For a moment his words sounded like a foreign language.

"Come on, Yanne. I've seen your accounts. I know what's what. It's not your fault, you've worked so hard, but business is terrible everywhere and—"

"Thierry, please. I don't want this now."

"Then what *do* you want?" Thierry said with exasperation. "God knows, I've humored you long enough. Why can't you see I'm trying to help you? Why won't you let me do what I can?"

"I'm sorry, Thierry. I know you mean well. But—"

And then I saw something in my mind. It happens sometimes, at unguarded moments: a reflection in a coffee cup; a glimpse in a mirror; an image floating its clouds across the glossy surface of a batch of newly tempered chocolate.

A box. A little sky blue box—

What was in it? I couldn't say. But a kind of panic bloomed in me; my throat was dry, I could hear the wind in the alleyway, and I wanted nothing more at that moment than to take my children and run and run—

Pull yourself together, Vianne.

I made my voice as bland as I could. "Can't this wait till I've sorted things out?"

But Thierry is like a hunting dog, cheery, determined, and impervious to argument. His hand was still in his coat pocket, fiddling with something inside.

"I'm trying to *help* you sort it out. Don't you see that? I don't want you killing yourself with work. It isn't worth it, just for a few miserable boxes of chocolates. Maybe it suited Madame Poussin. But you're young, you're bright, your life isn't over—"

And now I knew what it was I'd seen. I could see it, quite clearly in my mind's eye. A little blue box from a Bond Street jeweler, a single gem, carefully chosen with the help of a female shop assistant, not too large but of perfect clarity, nestling against the velvet lining. . . .

Oh, please, Thierry. Not here. Not now.

"I don't need any help right now." I gave him my most brilliant smile. "Now eat your choucroute. It's delicious—"

"You've hardly touched it," he pointed out.

I scooped a mouthful. "See?" I said.

Thierry smiled. "Close your eyes."

"What, here?"

"Close your eyes and hold out your hand."

"Thierry, please—" I tried to laugh. But it sounded harsh in my throat, a pea in a gourd, rattling to escape.

"Close your eyes and count to ten. You'll like it. I promise. It's a surprise."

What could I do? I did as he said. Held out my hand like a little girl, felt something—small, the size of a wrapped praline—drop into my palm.

When I opened my eyes Thierry was gone. And the Bond Street box was there in my hand, just as I'd seen it a moment before, with the ring—an icy solitaire—gleaming out from its bed of midnight blue.

Friday, 9 November

THERE, I TELL YOU. JUST AS I THOUGHT. I WATCHED THEM THROUGHOUT that tense little meal: Annie with her gleam of butterfly blue; the other, red-gold, too young as yet for my purposes but no less intriguing; the man—loud, but of little account; and lastly the mother, still and watchful, her colors so muted that they hardly seem to be colors at all, but some reflection of the streets and the sky in water so troubled it defies reflection.

There's definitely a weakness there. Something that might give me the edge. It's the hunter's instinct I've developed over the years; the ability to sense the lame gazelle without even opening half an eye. She's suspicious, and yet some people *want* to believe so much—in magic, in love, in business proposals guaranteed to treble their investment—and it makes them vulnerable to one such as myself. These people fall for it every time, and how can I help it if they do?

I first began to see the colors when I was nine. Just a little gleam at first; a sparkle of gold from the corner of my eye, a silver lining where there was no cloud, a blur of something complex and colored in among a crowd. As my interest grew, so did my ability to see these colors. I learned that everyone has a signature, an expression of their inner being that is visible only to a certain few, and with the help of a fingering or two.

Mostly there isn't a lot to see; the majority of folk are as dull as their shoes. But occasionally you can glean something worthwhile. A flare of anger from an expressionless face. A rose banner flying over a pair of lovers. The green-gray veil of secrecy. It helps when dealing with people, of course. And it helps at cards, if money runs short.

There's an old finger sign known by some as the Eye of Black Tezcatlipoca, by others as the Smoking Mirror, that helps me to focus on the colors. I learned to use it in Mexico; and with practice and knowledge of the right fingerings I could tell who was lying; who was afraid; who was cheating on his wife; who was anxious about money.

And little by little I learned to manipulate the colors that I saw; to give myself that rosy glow, that gleam of something special. Or—when a certain discretion was required—the opposite: the comforting cloak of unimportance that allows me to pass unseen and unremembered.

It took me a little longer to recognize these things as magic. Like all children reared on stories, I'd expected fireworks: magic wands and broomstick rides. The real magic of my mother's books seemed so dull, so fustily *academic*, with its silly incantations and its pompous old men, that it hardly counted as magic at all.

But then, my mother *had* no magic. For all her study, for all her spells and candles and crystals and cards, I never saw her turn so much as a cantrip. Some people are like that; I saw it in her colors long before I told her so. Some people just don't have what it takes to make a witch.

But my mother had the knowledge, if not the skill. She ran an occult bookshop in the suburbs of London, and all kinds of people came and went. High magicians, Odinists, Wiccans by the score, and the occasional would-be Satanists (invariably acne ridden, as if adolescence had never quite passed them by).

From her—from them—I finally learned what I needed to know. My mother was certain that by allowing me access to all forms of occultism, I would eventually choose my own path. She herself was a follower of an obscure sect who believed dolphins to be the enlightened race, and who practiced a kind of "earth magic" that was as harmless as it was ineffective.

But everything has its uses, I found, and over the years, with excruciating slowness, I was able to pick out the crumbs of practical magic from the useless, ludicrous, and outright fake. I found that most magic—when it's there at all—is hidden beneath a suffocating drift of ritual, drama, fasting, and time-consuming disciplines devised to give a sense of mystery to what is basically just a matter of finding what works. My mother loved the ritual—I just wanted the recipe book.

So I dabbled in runes, in cards, in crystals and pendulums and herbology. I steeped myself in the *I Ching*; cherry-picked the Golden Dawn; rejected Crowley (but for his Tarot pack, which is rather beautiful), pored earnestly over my Inner Goddess and laughed myself into convulsions over *Liber Null* and the *Necronomicon*.

But most fervently I studied Mesoamerican beliefs: those of the Maya, the Inca, and above all, the Aztec. For some reason these had always held a special appeal, and from them I learned about sacrifice, and the duality of the gods, and the malice of the universe, and the language of colors, and the horror of death; and how the only way to survive in the world is to fight back as hard and as dirty as you can.

The result was my System, minutely gleaned over years of trial and error and consisting of: some solid herbal medicine (including some useful poisons and hallucinogens); some fingerings and magical names; some breathing and limbering exercises; some mood-enhancing potions and tinctures; some astral projection and self-hypnosis; a handful of cantrips (I'm not fond of spoken spells, but some of them work); and a greater understanding of the colors. Including the ability to manipulate them further: to become, if I chose, what others expected; to cast glamour over myself and others; to change the world according to my will.

Throughout it all, and to my mother's concern, I remained unaffiliated to any group. She protested; felt that it was somehow immoral for me to winnow what I liked from so many lesser, flawed beliefs, and would have liked me to join a nice, friendly, mixed-gender coven—where I would have a social life and meet unthreatening boys—or to embrace her own aquatic school of thought, and follow the dolphins.

"But what do you actually *believe*?" she would say, worrying at her strings of beads with a long, nervous finger. "I mean, where's the *soul* of it; where's the *avatar*?"

I shrugged. "Why does there have to be a soul? I care what *works*, not

how many angels can dance on the head of a pin, or what color candle to burn
for a love spell." (Actually, I'd already discovered that in the seduction de-
partment, colored candles are vastly overrated when compared to oral sex.)

My mother just sighed in her sweetest way and said something about
following my own path. So I did, and I have been following it ever since. It
has led me to many interesting places—here, for example—but never have
I encountered evidence to suggest that I am not unique.

Until now, perhaps.

Yanne Charbonneau. It rings too nicely to be entirely plausible. And
there's something in her colors, some suggestion of deceit, although I suspect that she has developed ways to hide herself, so that I can only glimpse
the truth when her defenses are lowered.

Maman doesn't like us to be different.

Interesting.

And what was the name of that village again? Lansquenet? I must look it
up, I told myself. There may be some clue to be found there, past scandal perhaps, some trace of a mother and child that may cast light on this shadowy pair.

Searching Internet sites from my laptop, I found only two references
to the place—both websites dedicated to folklore and festivities of the
southwest, in which the name of Lansquenet-sous-Tannes was linked to a
popular Easter festival, first held a little over four years ago.

A *chocolate* festival. No surprise.

So. Did she get bored with village life? Did she make enemies? Why
did she leave?

Her shop was completely deserted this morning. I watched it from Le
P'tit Pinson, and no one came in till half past twelve. A Friday, and no one
came; not the grossly fat man who never shuts up, not even a neighbor or a
tourist in passing.

What's wrong with the place? It should be buzzing with customers.
Instead, it's half-invisible, hiding in the corner of the whitewashed square.
Surely that's bad for business. It wouldn't take much to gild it a little, to
enhance the place, to make it shine, as it did the other day—and yet she
does nothing. Why, I wonder? My mother spent her life trying vainly to be
special—why does Yanne exert so much effort in pretending otherwise?

Friday, 9 November

THIERRY CALLED ROUND AT TWELVE O'CLOCK. I'D BEEN EXPECTING HIM, OF course, and I'd spent a sleepless night worrying about how I was going to handle our next meeting. How I wish I'd never drawn those cards—Death, the Lovers, the Tower, Change—because now it almost feels like Fate, as if this were inevitable, and all the days and months of my life set out like a row of dominoes ready to fall. . . .

Of course it's absurd. I don't believe in Fate. I believe we have a choice; the wind can be stilled, and the Black Man fooled, and even the Kindly Ones appeased.

But at what cost? I ask myself. And that's what keeps me awake at night, and that's what made me tense up inside as the wind chimes rang out their warning note and Thierry came in with that look on his face—that stubborn look he gets sometimes that speaks of unfinished business.

I tried to stall. I offered him hot chocolate, which he accepted without much enthusiasm (he prefers coffee), but which gave me a reason to keep my hands busy. Rosette was playing with her toys on the floor, and Thierry watched her as she played: lining up rows of loose buttons from the button box to make concentric patterns on the terra-cotta tiles.

On a normal day he would have commented; made some observation about hygiene, perhaps, or worried that Rosette might choke on the buttons. Today he said nothing, a warning sign that I tried to ignore as I set about making the chocolate.

Milk in the pan, *couverture*, sugar, nutmeg, chilli. A coconut macaroon on the side. Comforting, like all rituals; gestures handed down from my mother to me, to Anouk, and maybe to her daughter too, someday in a future too distant to imagine.

"Great chocolate," he said, eager to please, cupping the little demitasse in hands best suited to building walls.

I sipped mine; it tasted of autumn and sweet smoke, of bonfires and temples and mourning and grief. I should have put some vanilla in, I told myself. Vanilla, like ice cream—like childhood.

"Just a little bitter," he said, helping himself to a sugar lump. "So—how about a break this afternoon? A stroll along the Champs-Elysées—coffee, lunch, shopping. . . ."

"Thierry," I said. "That's very sweet, but I can't just close shop for the afternoon."

"Really? It looks completely dead."

Just in time, I stopped the sharp retort. "You haven't finished your chocolate," I said.

"And you haven't answered my question, Yanne." His eyes flicked to my bare hand. "I notice you're not wearing the ring. Does that mean the answer's no?"

I laughed without meaning to. His directness often makes me laugh, although Thierry himself has no idea why. "You surprised me, that's all."

He looked at me over his chocolate. His eyes were tired, as if he hadn't slept, and there were lines bracketing his mouth that I hadn't noticed before. It was a hint of vulnerability that troubled and surprised me; I'd spent so long telling myself I didn't need him that it had never occurred to me that *he* might need *me*.

"So," he said. "Can you spare me an hour?"

"Give me a minute to change," I said.

Thierry's eyes lit up at once. "That's my girl! I knew you would."

He was back on form again, the small moment of uncertainty gone. He stood up, cramming his macaroon into his mouth (I noticed he'd left the chocolate). He grinned at Rosette, still playing on the floor.

"Well, *jeune fille*, what do you think? We could go to the Luxembourg, play with the toy boats on the lake—"

Rosette looked up, her eyes bright. She loves those boats, and the man who rents them; would stay there all summer if she could. . . .

See boat, she signed, emphatically.

"What did she say?" said Thierry, frowning.

I smiled at him. "She says that sounds like a pretty good plan."

I was struck by a sudden affection for Thierry, for his enthusiasm, his goodwill. I know he finds Rosette difficult to cope with—her eerie silence, her refusal to smile—and I appreciated the effort he was making.

Upstairs, I discarded my chocolate-smeared apron and put on my red flannel dress. It's a color I haven't worn in years; but I needed something to combat that cold November wind, and besides, I thought, I'd be wearing a coat. I wrestled Rosette into anorak and gloves (a garment which, for some reason, she despises), and then we all took the Métro to the Luxembourg.

So curious to be a tourist still, here in the city of my birth. But Thierry thinks I'm a stranger here, and he takes such joy in showing me his world that I cannot disappoint him. The gardens are crisp and bright today, pebbled with sunlight beneath a kaleidoscope of autumn leaves. Rosette loves the fallen leaves, kicking through them in great exuberant arcs of color. And she loves the little lake and watches the toy boats with solemn enjoyment.

"Say *boat,* Rosette."

"Bam," she says, fixing him with her catlike gaze.

"No, Rosette, it's *boat,*" he says. "Come on now, you can say *boat.*"

"Bam," says Rosette, and makes the sign for *monkey* with her hand.

"That's enough." I smile at her, but inside, my heart is beating too fast. She has been so good today, running about in her lime green anorak and red hat like some wildly animated Christmas ornament, occasionally calling— "*Bam-bam-bam!*"—as if shooting down invisible enemies, still not laughing (she rarely does) but concentrating with fierce intent, her lip pushed out, her brows drawn together, as if even running could be a challenge not to be taken frivolously.

But now there's danger in the air. The wind has changed; there's a gleam of gold from the corner of my eye, and I'm beginning to think it's time—

"Just one ice cream," Thierry says.

The boat does a clever little flip in the water, turning ninety degrees to starboard and heading out for the middle of the lake. Rosette looks at me mischievously.

"Rosette, no."

The boat flips again, now pointing at the ice cream stand.

"All right, just one."

We kissed as Rosette ate her ice cream by the side of the lake, and he was warm and vaguely tobacco scented, like somebody's father, his cashmere-coated arms folded bearlike over my too-thin red dress and my autumn coat.

It was a good kiss, beginning with my cold fingers and finding its clever, earnest way toward my throat and finally my mouth, unfreezing what the wind had frozen, little by little, like a warm fire, repeating *I love you, I love you* (he says that a lot), but under his breath, like Hail Marys delivered in haste by an eager child too keen for redemption.

He must have seen something in my face. "What's wrong?" he said, serious again.

How to tell him? How to explain? He watched me with sudden earnestness, his blue eyes watery with the cold. He looked so guileless, so *ordinary*— unable, for all his business acumen, to understand our kind of deceit.

What does he see in Yanne Charbonneau? I've tried so hard to understand. And what might he see in Vianne Rocher? Would he mistrust her unconventional ways? Would he sneer at her beliefs? Judge her choices? Feel horror, perhaps, at the way she lied?

Slowly, he kissed my fingertips, putting them one by one in his mouth. He grinned. "You taste of chocolate."

But the wind was still blowing in my ears, and the sound of the trees all around us made it immense, like an ocean, like a monsoon, sweeping the sky with dead-leaf confetti and the scent of that river, that winter, that wind.

An odd little thought came to me then—

What if I told Thierry the truth? What if I told him everything?

To be known; to be loved; to be understood. My breath caught—

Oh, if only I dared—

The wind does curious things to people: it turns them around, it makes them dance. In that moment it made Thierry a boy again, tousle-haired, bright-eyed and hopeful. The wind can be seductive that way, bringing wild thoughts and wilder dreams. But all the time I could hear that warning—and even then I think I knew that for all his warmth and all his love, Thierry le Tresset would be no match for the wind.

"I don't want to lose the chocolate shop," I told him (or maybe the wind). "I need to keep it. I need it to be mine."

Thierry laughed. "Is that all?" he said. "Then marry me, Yanne." He grinned at me. "You can have all the chocolate shops you want, and all the chocolates. And you'll taste of chocolate all the time. And you'll even *smell* of it—and so will I—"

I couldn't help laughing at that. And then Thierry took my hands and spun me around on the dry gravel, making Rosette hiccup with laughter.

Perhaps that's why I said what I did; a moment of fearful impulsiveness, with the wind in my ears and my hair in my face and Thierry holding on for all he was worth, whispering *I love you, Yanne,* against my hair in a voice that sounded almost afraid.

He's afraid to lose me, I suddenly thought, and that was when I said it, knowing that there could be no turning back after this, and with tears in my eyes and my nose pink and running from the wintry cold.

"All right," I said. "But quietly . . ."

His eyes widened a little at the suddenness of it.

"You're sure?" he said, a little breathlessly. "I thought you'd want—you know." He grinned. "The dress. The church. The choir singing. Bridesmaids, bells—the whole shebang."

I shook my head. "No fuss," I said.

He kissed me again. "As long as it's yes."

And for a moment it was so good; the small, sweet dream right there in my hands. Thierry's a good man, I thought. A man with roots, with principles.

And money, Vianne, don't forget that, said the spiteful voice inside my head, but the voice was faint, and getting fainter as I gave myself to the small, sweet dream. Damn her, I thought, and damn the wind. This time it would not blow us away.

Friday, 9 November

TODAY I QUARRELED WITH SUZE AGAIN. I DON'T KNOW WHY IT HAPPENS SO much; I want to be friends, but the more I try, the harder it gets. This time it was about my hair. Oh, boy. Suze thinks I should get it straightened.

I asked why.

Suzanne shrugged. We were alone in the library during break—the others had gone to buy sweets at the shop, and I was trying to copy some geography notes, but Suze wanted to talk, and there's no stopping her when that happens.

"Looks weird," she said. "Like Afro hair."

I didn't care, and told her so.

Suze made the fish-mouth face she always makes when someone contradicts her. "So—your dad wasn't black, was he?" she said.

I shook my head, feeling like a liar. Suzanne thinks my father's dead. But he *might* have been black for all I know. For all I know he might have been a pirate, or a serial killer, or a king.

"Because, you know, people might think—"

"If by *people*, you mean Chantal—"

"No," said Suzanne crossly, but her pink face went a shade pinker, and she didn't quite meet my eyes as she said it. "Listen," she went on, putting her arm around my shoulders. "You're new to this school. You're new to *us*. The rest of us went to the primary school. We learnt to fit in."

Learn to fit in. I had a teacher called Madame Drou, back in the days at Lansquenet, who used to say the exact same thing.

"But you're different," said Suze. "I've been trying to help—"

"Help me how?" I snapped, thinking of my geography notes and how I never, *never* get to do what I want when she's around. It's always *her* games, *her* problems and her *Annie please stop following me around* when somebody better comes along. She knew I didn't mean to snap, but she looked hurt anyway, pushing back her (straightened) hair in what she thinks is a very adult fashion and saying, "Well, if you won't even *listen*. . . ."

"All right," I said. "What's wrong with me?"

She looked at me for a moment or two. Then the lesson bell rang, and she gave me a sudden, brilliant smile and handed me a folded piece of paper.

"I made a list."

I read the list in geography class. Monsieur Gestin was talking to us about Budapest, where we'd lived once, for a while, though I don't remember much about it now. Only the river, and the snow, and the old quarter, which looks so like Montmartre to me somehow, with its winding streets and its steep stairways and the old castle on the little hill. The list was written on half a sheet of exercise-book paper in Suze's neat, pudgy hand. There were tips on grooming (hair straight, nails filed, legs shaved, always carry deodorant); dress (no socks with skirts, wear pink, but not orange); culture (chick-lit good, boy-books bad); films and music (recent hits only); what to watch on television, websites (as if I had a computer anyway), how to spend my free time; and what type of mobile phone to carry.

I thought at first it was another joke; but after school, when I met her queuing for the bus, I realized she was serious. "You have to make an ef-fort," she said. "Otherwise people will say you're weird."

"I'm not weird," I said. "I'm just—"

"Different."

"What's so bad about being different?"

"Well, Annie, if you want to have friends . . ."

"Real friends shouldn't care about that kind of thing."

Suze went red. She often does when she's annoyed, and it makes her face clash with her hair. "Well, I *do*," she hissed, and her eyes went to the front of the queue.

There's a code in queuing for the bus, you know, just as there's a code when you're going into class, or picking teams in games. Suze and I stand about halfway. In front of us there's the A-list: the girls who play basketball for the school; the older ones who wear lipstick, who roll their skirts up at the waistband and smoke Gitanes outside the school gates. And then there are the boys: the best-looking ones; the team members; the ones who wear their collars turned up and their hair gelled.

And there's the new boy: Jean-Loup Rimbault. Suzanne has a crush on him. Chantal really likes him too—though he never seems to notice either of them much and never joins in any of their games. I began to see what was going on in Suze's mind.

Freaks and losers stand at the back. First, the black kids from the other side of the Butte, who keep to their group and don't talk to the rest of us. Then Claude Meunier, who stutters; Mathilde Chagrin, the fat girl; and the Muslim girls, a dozen or so of them, all in a bunch, who caused such a fuss about wearing their head scarves at the beginning of term. They were wearing them now, I noticed as my eyes went to the back of the queue; they put them on the minute they leave the school gates, even though they're not allowed them at school. Suze thinks they're stupid to wear head scarves, and that they should be like us if they're going to live in our country—but she's just repeating what Chantal says. I don't see why a head scarf should make a difference any more than a T-shirt, or a pair of jeans. Surely what they wear is their business.

Suze was still watching Jean-Loup. He's quite tall, good-looking, I suppose, with black hair and a fringe that covers most of his face. He's twelve, a year older than the rest of us. He should be in a higher form. Suze says he was kept back last year, but he's really bright, always top of the class. A lot of the girls like him; but today he was just trying to be cool, leaning against the bus stop, looking through the viewfinder of the little digital camera he never seems to be without.

"Oh, my *God*," whispered Suze.

"Well, why don't you talk to him for once?"

Suze shushed me furiously. Jean-Loup looked up briefly at the noise, then went back to his camera. Suze went even redder than before. "He *looked* at me!" she squeaked, then, hiding behind the hood of her anorak, turned to me and rolled her eyes. "I'm going to get highlights. There's a place that Chantal goes to for hers." She grasped my arm so hard it hurt. "I know," she said. "We could go together! I'll get highlights, and you can get yours straightened."

"Stop going on about my hair," I said.

"Come on, Annie! It'll be cool. And—"

"I said *stop it!*" Now I was beginning to feel really angry. "Why do you keep going on about it?"

"Oh, you're hopeless," said Suze, losing her temper. "You look like a freak, and you don't even care?"

That's another thing she does, you know. Makes a sentence sound like a question when it isn't.

"Why should I?" I said. By now the anger had become something like a sneeze, and I could feel it coming, building, ready to burst whether I liked it or not. And then I remembered what Zozie had said in the English tea shop and wished I could do something to take the smug look off Suzanne's face. Not something bad—I'd never do that—but something to teach her, all the same.

I forked my fingers behind my back and spoke to her in my shadow-voice—

See how you like it, for a change.

And for a second, I thought I saw something. A flash of something across her face; something that was gone before I'd really seen it.

"I'd rather be a freak than a clone," I said.

Then I turned and walked to the back of the queue, with everyone staring and Suze wide-eyed and ugly, quite ugly with her red hair and her red face and her mouth hanging open in disbelief as I stood there and waited for the bus to arrive.

I'm not sure if I expected her to follow me or not. I thought perhaps she would, but she didn't; and when the bus came at last she sat next to Sandrine and never even looked at me again.

——◦◦✦◦◦——

I tried to tell Maman about it when I got home, but by then she was trying to talk to Nico *and* wrap a box of rum truffles *and* fix Rosette's snack at the same time and I couldn't quite find the words to tell her how I felt.

"Just ignore them," she said at last, pouring milk into a copper pan. "Here, watch this for me, will you, Nanou? Just stir it gently while I wrap this box. . . ."

She keeps the ingredients for the hot chocolate in a cabinet at the back of the kitchen. At the front she has some copper pans, some shiny molds for making chocolate shapes, the granite slab for tempering. Not that she uses them anymore; most of her old things are downstairs in the cellar, and even before Madame Poussin died, there was scarcely any time for making our specials.

But there's always time for hot chocolate, made with milk and grated nutmeg, vanilla, chilli, brown sugar, cardamom, and 70 percent *couverture* chocolate—the only chocolate worth buying, she says—and it tastes rich and just slightly bitter on the back of the tongue, like caramel as it begins to turn. The chilli gives it a touch of heat—never too much, just a taste—and the spices give it that churchy smell that reminds me of Lansquenet somehow, and of nights above the chocolate shop, just Maman and me, with Pantoufle sitting to one side and candles burning on the orange-box table.

No orange-boxes here, of course. Last year Thierry got us a complete new kitchen. Well, he would, wouldn't he? He is the landlord, after all—he's got lots of money, and besides, he's supposed to fix the house. But Maman insisted on making a fuss and cooking him a special dinner in the new kitchen. Oh, boy. Like we'd never had a kitchen before. So even the mugs are new now, with *Chocolat* written on them in fancy lettering. Thierry bought them—one for each of us and one for Madame Poussin—though he doesn't actually *like* hot chocolate. (I can tell because he adds too much sugar.)

I used to have my own cup, a fat red one that Roux gave me, slightly chipped, with a painted letter *A* for *Anouk*. I don't have it now; I don't even remember what happened to it. Perhaps it got broken or left behind. It doesn't matter, anyway. I don't drink chocolate anymore.

"Suzanne says I'm weird," I said as Maman came back into the kitchen.

"Well, you're not," she said, scraping the inside out of a vanilla pod. The chocolate was nearly ready by now, simmering gently in the pan. "Want some? It's good."

"No thanks."

"OK."

She poured some for Rosette instead and added sprinkles and a dollop of cream. It looked good and smelled even better, but I didn't want to let it show. I looked in the cupboard and found half a croissant from breakfast and some jam.

"Pay no attention to Suzanne," said Maman, pouring out chocolate for herself into an espresso cup. I noticed neither she nor Rosette was using the *Chocolat* mugs. "I know her type. Try to make friends with somebody else."

Well, easier said than done, I thought. Besides, what's the point? It wouldn't be me they were friends with at all. Fake hair, fake clothes, fake *me*.

"Like who?" I said.

"*I* don't know." Her voice was impatient as she put the spices back into the cupboard. "There must be someone you get on with."

It isn't my fault, I wanted to say. Why does she think *I'm* the difficult one? The problem is that Maman never really went to school—learned everything the practical way, so she says—and all she knows about it now is what she's read in children's books, or seen through the wrong side of some school yard railings. From the other side, believe me, it's not all jolly hockey sticks.

"Well?" Still that impatience, that tone that says *you should be grateful, I worked hard to get you here, to send you to a proper school, to save you from the life I had*—

"Can I ask you something?" I said.

"Of course, Nanou. Is anything wrong?"

"Was my father a black man?"

She gave a start, so small that I wouldn't have seen it if it hadn't been in her colors.

"That's what Chantal says at school."

"Really?" said Maman, beginning to slice up some bread for Rosette. Bread, knife, chocolate spread. Rosette with her little monkey fingers turning the bread slice over and over. A look of intense concentration in Maman's face as she worked. I couldn't tell what she was thinking. Her eyes were as dark as Africa, impossible to read.

"Would it matter?" she said at last.

"Dunno." I shrugged.

She turned to me then, and for a second she looked almost like the old Maman, the one who never cared what anyone thought.

"You know, Anouk," she said slowly, "for a long time I didn't think you even needed a father. I thought it would always be just the two of us, the way it was with my mother and me. And then Rosette came along, and I thought, well maybe—" She broke off, and smiled, and changed the subject so fast that for a minute I didn't realize that she hadn't actually changed it at all, like one of those fairground acts with the three cups and a ball. "You do like Thierry, don't you?" she said.

I shrugged again. "He's OK."

"I thought you did. He likes *you*."

I bit the corner off my croissant. Sitting in her little chair, Rosette was making an airplane out of her slice of bread.

"I mean, if either of you didn't like him—"

Actually, I don't like him that much. He's too loud, and he smells of cigars. And he's always interrupting Maman when she's talking, and he calls me *jeune fille*, like it's a joke, and he doesn't get Rosette at all, or understand when she signs at him, and he's always pointing out long words and what they mean, as if I'd never heard them before.

"He's OK," I said again.

"Well—Thierry wants to marry me."

"Since when?" I said.

"He mentioned it first to me last year. I told him I didn't want to be involved with anybody just then—there was Rosette to think of, and Madame Poussin—and he said he was happy to wait. But now we're alone. . . ."

"You didn't say yes, did you?" I said, too loudly for Rosette, who put her hands over her ears.

"It's complicated." She sounded tired.

"You always say that."

"That's because it's always complicated."

Well, I don't see why. It seems simple to me. She's never been married before, has she? So why would she want to get married now?

"Things have changed, Nanou," she said.

"What things?" I wanted to know.

"Well, the *chocolaterie*, for a start. The rent's paid till the end of the year. But after that . . ." She gave a sigh. "It won't be easy making it work. And I can't just take money from Thierry. He keeps offering, but it wouldn't be fair. And I thought. . . ."

Well of course I'd known there was *something* wrong. But I'd thought she was sad about Madame. Now I could see it was Thierry instead, and her worry that I might not fit in with their plan.

Some plan. I can see us now. Maman, Papa, and the two little girls, like something out of a story by the Comtesse de Ségur. We'd go to church; eat *steak-frites* every day; wear dresses from Galeries Lafayette. Thierry would have a picture of us on his desk, a professional portrait, with Rosette and me in matching outfits.

Don't get me wrong; I *said* he's OK. But—

"Well?" she said. "Cat got your tongue?"

I bit a little piece from my croissant. "We don't need him," I said at last.

"Well, we need *someone*, that's for sure. I thought at least you'd understand that. You need to go to school, Anouk. You need a proper home—a father—"

Don't make me laugh. A father? As if. *You choose your family*, she always says, but what choice does she think she's giving me?

"Anouk," she said. "I'm doing it for you. . . ."

"Whatever." I shrugged and took my croissant out into the street.

Saturday, 10 November

I DROPPED IN AT THE CHOCOLATERIE THIS MORNING AND BOUGHT A BOX of liqueur cherries. Yanne was there, with the little one in tow. Though the shop was quiet, she looked harried, almost uncomfortable at seeing me, and the chocolates, when I tried them, were nothing special.

"I used to make these myself," she said, handing me the cherries in a paper twist. "But liqueurs are so fussy, and there's never the time. I hope you like them."

I popped one into my mouth with well-feigned greed. "Fabulous," I said, through a sour paste of pickled cherry. On the floor behind the counter, Rosette was singing softly to herself, sprawled among a scatter of crayons and colored paper.

"Doesn't she go to nursery school?"

Yanne shook her head. "I like to keep an eye on her."

Well, of course, I can see that. I see other things too, now that I happen to look for them. The sky blue door hides a number of things that regular customers overlook. First, the place is old and in some considerable disrepair. The window is attractive enough with its display of pretty little tins and boxes, and the walls are painted a cheerful yellow, but even so the damp awaits, lurking in corners and beneath the floor, speaking of too little money and not enough time. Some care has been taken to hide this: a scrawl of cobweb-gold across a nest of cracks, a welcoming shimmer in the doorway, a luscious quality to the air that promises more than those second-rate chocolates.

Try me. Test me.

Discreetly, with my left hand, I conjured the Eye of Black Tezcatlipoca. Around me, the colors flared, confirming my suspicions on that first day. Someone has been at work here, and I don't think it was Yanne Charbonneau. There is a youthful, naïve, exuberant aspect to this glamour that speaks of a mind as yet untrained.

Annie? Who else? And the mother? Well. There's something about her that needles me, something I've seen only once—on that first day as she opened the door at the sound of her name. She had brighter colors then, all right; and something tells me she has them still, even though she chooses to conceal them.

On the floor, Rosette was drawing, still singing her little wordless song. *"Bam-bam-bammm . . . Bam-badda-bammm . . ."*

"Come on, Rosette. Time for your nap."

Rosette did not look up from her drawing. The singing grew a little louder, now accompanied by the rhythmic thumping of a sandaled foot against the floor. *"Bam-bam-bamm . . ."*

"Now, Rosette," said Yanne gently. "Time to put the crayons away."

Still no reaction from Rosette.

"Bam-bam-bamm . . Bam-badda-bammm . . ." At the same time, her colors bloomed from chrysanthemum-gold to brilliant orange, and she laughed, reaching out, as if to grasp falling petals. *"Bam-bam-bamm . . . Bam-badda-bamm . . ."*

"Shh, Rosette!"

And now I could feel a tension in Yanne. It was not just the embarrassment of a mother whose child will not behave, but more like the sense of approaching danger. She picked up Rosette—still warbling unconcerned—flinging me a grimace of apology as she did so.

"I'm sorry," she said. "She's gets like this when she's overtired."

"It's OK. She's cute," I said.

A pot of pencils fell from the countertop. Pencils rolled across the floor.

"Bam," said Rosette, pointing at the fallen pencils.

"I need to put her to bed now," said Yanne. "She gets too excited if she doesn't have her nap."

I looked at Rosette again. She didn't look tired at all, I thought. It was the mother who looked exhausted: pale and washed out with her too-sharp haircut and her cheap black sweater, which made her face seem paler still.

"Are you all right?" I said.

She nodded.

Above her, the single lightbulb began to flicker. These old houses, I thought to myself. The wiring's always out-of-date.

"Are you sure? You're looking a little pale."

"Just a headache. I'll manage."

Familiar words. But I doubt she will; she clings to the child as if I might snatch her from her arms.

Might I, do you think? Twice married (though on neither occasion under my own name), and still I've never once thought of having a child. The complications are endless, so I've heard, and besides, in my line of work, the last thing I can afford is excess baggage.

And yet . . .

I drew the cactus sign of Xochipilli in the air, keeping my hand well out of view. Xochipilli the silver-tongued; the god of prophecy and dream. Not that I'm particularly interested in prophecies. But careless talk can bring rewards, so I have found, and information of any kind is currency for someone in my line of business.

The symbol gleamed and floated for a second or two, dispersing like a silvery smoke ring in the dark air.

For a moment, nothing happened.

Well, to be honest, I hadn't expected much of a result. But I was curious; and didn't she owe me a little satisfaction, after all the effort I've made on her behalf?

So I made the sign again. Xochipilli the whisperer, unlocker of secrets, bringer of confidences. And this time, the result was beyond all my expectations.

First, I saw her colors flare. Just a little, but very bright, like a flame in the hearth as it encounters a pocket of gas. Almost at the same time, Rosette's sunny mood altered abruptly. She arched back in her mother's arms, throwing herself backward with a whimper of protest. The flickering lightbulb popped with a sudden sharp report—and at the same time, a pyramid of biscuit tins fell over in the window display with a clatter fit to wake the dead.

Yanne Charbonneau was taken off balance, and she took a step sideways, striking her hip against the counter.

There was a little open-fronted cabinet on the counter, which housed a collection of pretty glass dishes filled with sugared almonds in pink, gold, silver, and white. It wobbled—instinctively Yanne reached out a hand to steady it—and one of the dishes fell to the floor.

"*Rosette!*" Yanne was almost in tears.

I heard the dish pulverize on impact, skittering bonbons across the terra-cotta tiles.

I heard it go but did not look down; instead I watched Rosette and Yanne—the child aflame in her colors now, the mother so still she might as well have been stone.

"Let me help." I bent down to scoop up the mess.

"No, please—"

"I've got it," I said.

I could feel the nervous tension in her, banked and ready to explode. It was surely not the loss of the dish—in my experience women like Yanne Charbonneau don't go to pieces over a bit of broken glass. But the oddest things can trigger the blast: a bad day, a headache, the kindness of strangers.

And then I saw it from the corner of my eye, hunched beneath the countertop.

It was a bright orange-gold, and clumsily drawn, but it was clear enough from the long curly tail and bright little eyes that it was supposed to be some kind of monkey. I turned abruptly to see it face-on, and it bared its pointed teeth at me before blinking back into empty air.

"*Bam,*" said Rosette.

There was a long, long silence.

I picked up the dish—it was blue Murano glass, delicately fluted at the edges. I'd heard it smash like the sound of firecrackers going off, scattering shrapnel across the tiles. And yet here it was, unbroken in my hand. No accident.

Bam, I thought.

Under my feet I could still feel the spilled bonbons grinding like teeth. And now Yanne Charbonneau was watching me in a fearful silence that spun and spun like a silk cocoon.

I could have said, *well, that was lucky*, or just put back the dish without a word, but it was now or never, I told myself. *Strike at once, while resistance is low. There may not be another chance.*

And so I stood up, looked Yanne straight in the eyes, and leveled at her all the charm that I could muster.

"It's all right," I said. "I know what you need."

For a moment she stiffened and held my gaze, her expression all defiance and haughty incomprehension.

Then I took her arm and smiled.

"Hot chocolate," I told her gently. "Hot chocolate, to my special recipe. Chilli and nutmeg, with Armagnac and a dash of black pepper. Come on. No arguments. Bring the brat."

Silently she followed me into the kitchen.

I was in.

PART THREE

Two Rabbit

Wednesday, 14 November

I NEVER WANTED TO BE A WITCH. NEVER EVEN DREAMED OF IT—THOUGH my mother swore she could hear me calling months before I appeared on the scene. I don't remember that, of course. My early childhood was a blur of places, scents, and people passing fast as trains; crossing borders without papers; traveling under different names; leaving cheap hotels at night; seeing the dawn in a new place every day, and running, always running, even then. As if the only way to survive was to run through every artery, vein, capillary on the map, leaving nothing—not even our shadows—behind.

You choose your family, Mother said. My father had apparently not been chosen.

"What would we need with him, Vianne? Fathers don't count. It's just you and me."

Tell the truth, I didn't miss him. How could I? I had nothing against which to measure his absence. I imagined him dark, and slightly sinister; a relative, perhaps, of the Black Man we fled. And I loved my mother. I loved the world we had made for ourselves, a world we carried with us wherever we went; a world just out of reach of ordinary folk.

Because we're special, she would say. We saw things; we had the knack. You choose your family—and so we did, wherever we went. A sister here, a grandmother there; familiar faces of a scattered tribe. But as far as I could tell, there were no men in my mother's life.

Except for the Black Man, of course.

Was my father the Black Man? It gave me a start to hear Anouk come so

close. I'd considered it myself, as we fled all shirttailed and carnival-colored
and ragged with the wind. The Black Man wasn't real, of course. I came to
think my father was the same.

Still, I was curious; and from time to time I would scan the crowds—
in New York or Berlin, in Venice or Prague—hoping perhaps to see him
there—a man, alone, with my dark eyes. . . .

Meanwhile, we ran, my mother and I. First it seemed for the sheer joy
of running; then, like everything else, it became a habit, then a chore. In the
end I began to think that running was the only thing that kept her alive as
the cancer ran through her, blood, brain, and bone.

It was then that she first mentioned the girl. Ramblings, I thought at
the time, born of the painkillers she was taking. And she *did* ramble as the
end approached: told stories that made no sense at all; spoke of the Black
Man; talked earnestly with people who weren't there.

That little girl, with the name that so resembled mine, could have been
another figment of those uncertain times—an archetype, an anima; a snip-
pet from a newspaper; some other little lost soul with dark hair and dark
eyes, stolen away from outside a cigarette kiosk one rainy day in Paris.

Sylviane Caillou. Vanished as so many do; stolen from her car seat aged
eighteen months, in front of a chemist's near La Villette. Stolen away with
her changing bag and toys, last seen wearing a cheap silver baby bangle with
a lucky charm—a little cat—dangling from the clasp.

That wasn't me. It couldn't have been. And even if it was, after all this
time . . .

You choose your family, Mother said. As I chose you and you chose me.
That girl—she wouldn't have cherished you. She wouldn't have known how
to care for you: how to slice the apple widthways to show the star inside,
how to tie a medicine bag, how to banish demons by banging on a tin pan,
how to sing the wind to sleep. She wouldn't have taught you any of that—

And didn't we do OK, Vianne? Didn't I promise we'd be OK?

I have it still, that little cat charm. I don't remember the baby bangle—
probably she sold it or gave it away—but I half-remember the toys, a red
plush elephant and a small brown bear, much loved and missing an eye.
And the charm is still there in my mother's box, a cheap thing, such as a

child might buy, tied with a piece of red ribbon. It's there with her cards, and a few other things: a photograph of us taken when I was six, a stash of sandalwood, some newspaper clippings, a ring. A drawing I did at my first school—my only school—in the days when we were still going to settle down someday.

Of course I never wear it. I don't even like to touch it now; there are too many secrets locked in there, like scent that needs only human warmth to release it. As a rule I don't touch anything in that box—and yet I don't quite dare to throw it away. Too much ballast slows you down—but too little and I could blow away like a dandelion seed, losing myself forever on the wind.

Zozie has been with me for four days now, and already her personality has begun to affect everything she touches. I don't know how it happened—a temporary moment of weakness, perhaps. I certainly hadn't intended to offer her a job. For a start, I can't afford to pay her much, though she's happy to wait until I can—and it seems so natural for her to be here, as if she has been with me all my life.

It began on the day of the Accident—the day she made the chocolate and drank it with me in the kitchen, hot and sweet with fresh chillies and chocolate curls. Rosette drank some in her little mug, then played on the floor as I sat in silence—Zozie watching me with that smile, and her eyes all narrowed like a cat's.

The circumstances were exceptional. On any other day, at any other time, I would have been better prepared. But on *that* day—with Thierry's ring still in my pocket, and Rosette at her worst, and Anouk so quiet since she heard, and the long empty day stretching ahead—

At any other time, I would have held fast. But on that day—

It's all right. I know what you need.

What, exactly? What does she know? That a dish that was broken came back whole? It's too absurd; no one would believe it, still less that a four-year-old child had performed the trick, a four-year-old child who can't even talk.

"You look tired, Yanne," Zozie said. "Must be hard, looking after all this."

Silently I nodded.

The memory of Rosette's Accident sat between us like the last piece of cake at a party.

Don't say it, I told her silently, just as I'd tried to tell Thierry. *Don't say it, please; don't put it in words.*

I thought I felt her brief response. A sigh; a smile; a glimpse of something half-seen in shadow. A soft shuffle of cards, scented with sandalwood.

A silence.

"I don't want to talk about it," I said.

Zozie shrugged. "So drink your chocolate."

"You saw it, though."

"I see all sorts of things."

"Such as?"

"I can see you're tired."

"I don't sleep well."

She looked at me in silence for a time. Her eyes were all summer, freckled with gold. *I ought to know your favorites,* I thought, almost dreamily. *Perhaps I've simply lost the knack....*

"Tell you what," she said at last. "Let me look after the shop for you. I was born in a shop—I know what to do. You take Rosette and have a lie-down. If I need you, I'll shout. Go on. I'll enjoy it."

That was just four days ago. Neither of us has referred to that day since then. Rosette, of course, does not yet understand that in the real world, a broken dish must stay broken, however much we may wish it otherwise. And Zozie has made no effort to broach the subject again, and for that I am grateful. She knows that *something* happened, of course, but seems content to let it go.

"What kind of a shop were you born in, Zozie?"

"A bookshop. You know, the New Age kind."

"Really?" I said.

"My mother was into that kind of thing. Shop-bought magic. Tarot cards. Selling incense and candles to blissed-out hippies with no money and bad hair."

I smiled, though it made me a little uneasy.

"But that was a long time ago," she said. "I don't remember much of it now."

"But do you still—believe?" I said.

She smiled. "I believe we can make a difference."

Silence.

"And you?"

"I used to," I said. "But not anymore."

"May I ask why?"

I shook my head. "Later, perhaps."

"OK," she said.

I know, I know. It's dangerous. Every action—even the smallest—has consequences. Magic comes at a high price. It took me a long time to understand that—after Lansquenet, after Les Laveuses—but now it seems so very clear, as the consequences of our journeying widen around us like ripples on a lake.

Take my mother, so generous with her gifts, handing out good luck and goodwill as, inside her, the cancer grew like the interest from a deposit account she never even knew she had. The universe balances its books. Even such a small thing as a charm, a cantrip, a circle drawn in sand—all must be paid for. In full. In blood.

There's a symmetry, you see. For every piece of luck, a blow; for everyone we helped, a hurt. A red silk sachet over our door—and somewhere else, a shadow falls. A candle burned to banish ill luck—and somebody's house across the road catches fire and burns to the ground. A chocolate festival; the death of a friend.

A piece of malchance.

An Accident.

That's why I can't confide in Zozie. I like her too much to lose her trust. The children seem to like her too. There's something youthful about her somehow, something more akin to Anouk's age than mine, that makes her more approachable.

Perhaps it's her hair—long, loose, and dyed pink at the front—or her exuberantly colored charity-shop clothes, flung together like the contents of a child's dressing-up box, but oddly right on her, somehow. Today she is wearing a nip-waisted 1950s dress in sky blue, with a pattern of sailboats, and yellow ballet shoes, quite wrong for November—not that she cares. Not that she would ever care.

I remember being like that once. I remember that defiance. But motherhood changes everything. Motherhood makes cowards of us all. Cowards, liars—and sometimes worse.

Les Laveuses. Anouk. And—oh! That wind.

Four days—and I am still surprised to find myself relying on Zozie, not just to keep an eye on Rosette, as Madame Poussin used to do, but also for all kinds of little things in the shop. Wrapping, packaging, cleaning, ordering. She says she likes it—tells me she always dreamed of working in a *chocolaterie*—and yet she never helps herself to the stock, as Madame Poussin often did, or exploits her position by asking for samples.

I haven't yet mentioned her to Thierry. I'm not sure why, except that I feel he will not approve. Perhaps because of the extra cost; perhaps because of Zozie herself, who is as far removed from the staid Madame Poussin as it is possible to be.

With customers she is cheerily—sometimes worryingly—informal. She talks constantly as she wraps boxes, weighs chocolates, points out novelties. And she has a knack for making people talk about themselves: enquires about Madame Pinot's backache; chats with the postman on his round. She knows Fat Nico's favorites, flirts outrageously with Jean-Louis and Paupaul, the would-be artists touting for customers around Le P'tit Pinson, and chats with Richard and Mathurin, the two old men she calls "The Patriots," who sometimes arrive at the café at eight in the morning and rarely leave until dinnertime.

She knows Anouk's school friends by name, asks after her teachers, discusses her clothes. And yet she never makes me feel uncomfortable; never asks the questions anyone else in her place would ask.

I felt the same with Armande Voizin—back in the days of Lansquenet. Unruly, mischievous, naughty Armande, whose scarlet petticoats I still sometimes see out of the corner of my eye, whose voice imagined in a crowd—so eerily like that of my mother—still sometimes makes me turn and stare.

Zozie is nothing like her, of course. Armande was eighty when I knew her: dried up, cantankerous, and old. And yet I can see her in Zozie—her exuberant style, her appetite for everything. And if Armande had a spark of what my mother called *magic* . . .

But we do not speak of these things now. Our pact is silent, but nonetheless strict. Any indiscretion—even as much as a spark lit—and once again, the little house of cards goes up in flames. It's happened before, in Lansquenet, in Les Laveuses, and in a hundred places before that. But not anymore. No. This time, we stay.

She came in early today, just as Anouk was leaving for school. I left her alone for less than an hour—just time enough to take Rosette for a walk—and when I got back the place looked brighter, somehow; less cluttered, more attractive. She'd changed the display in the shop window, spreading a swatch of dark blue velvet onto the pyramid of tins that filled it, and on top she had placed a pair of bright red, shiny, high-heeled shoes, brimming over with foil-wrapped chocolates in red and gold.

The effect is eccentric but arresting nevertheless. The shoes—the same red shoes she was wearing on that first day—seem to shine in the dark shop window, and the sweets like buried treasure spill across the velvet in cubes and fragments of colored light.

"I hope you don't mind," said Zozie as I came in. "I thought it could do with a bit of a lift."

"I like it," I said. "Shoes and chocolates . . ."

Zozie grinned. "Twin passions of mine."

"So—what's your favorite?" I asked. Not that I *really* wanted to know, but professional curiosity made me ask. Four days, and I am no closer to guessing her favorite than I was before.

She shrugged. "I like them all. But the bought ones aren't the same, are they? You used to make your own, you said?"

"I did. But then I had more time."

She looked at me. "You've got plenty of time. Let me look after the front of the shop, and you can work your magic in the back."

"Magic?"

But Zozie was already making plans—seemingly unaware of the impact of that casual word—plans for a line of handmade truffles, the simplest of all chocolates to make; and then, perhaps some *mendiants*—my own favorites—sprinkled with almonds, sour cherries, and fat yellow sultanas.

I could do it with my eyes closed. Even a child can make *mendiants*, and Anouk had often helped me in the days of Lansquenet, selecting the plumpest raisins, the sweetest cranberries (always keeping a generous portion aside for herself), and arranging them on the discs of melted chocolate, dark or light, in careful designs.

I haven't made *mendiants* since then. They remind me too much of those days, of the little bakery with the wheat sheaf over the door, of Armande, of Joséphine, of Roux—

"You can ask what you like for handmade chocolates," Zozie was saying, oblivious. "And if you put out a couple of chairs, made a bit of space *here*"—she showed me the spot—"then people could even sit down for a while, have a drink, perhaps, a slice of cake. It would be nice, wouldn't it? Friendly, I mean. A way of getting them inside."

"Hm."

I wasn't altogether sure. It sounded too much like Lansquenet. A *chocolaterie* should remain a place of business; its patrons should be customers and not friends. Otherwise one day the inevitable happens; and the box, once opened, cannot be shut. Besides, I knew what Thierry would say. . . .

"I don't think so," I said at last.

Zozie said nothing but gave me a look. I feel I have disappointed her, somehow. An absurd feeling—and yet—

When did I become so fearful? I ask. When did I begin to care so much? My voice sounds dry and fussy, like that of some prude. I wonder, does Anouk hear it too?

"OK. It was just an idea."

And where's the possible harm? I thought. It's only chocolate, after all; a dozen or so batches of truffles, just to keep myself in practice. Thierry will think I am wasting my time; but why should that stop me? What do I care?

"Well—I suppose I *could* make a few boxes for Christmas."

I still have my pans, the copper ones and the enamel, all carefully wrapped and boxed in the cellar. I have even kept the granite slab on which I temper the melted chocolate; the sugar thermometers; the plastic and the ceramic molds; the dippers and scrapers and slotted spoons. Everything is there, clean and stored and ready to go. Rosette might enjoy it, I thought—and Anouk.

"Great!" said Zozie. "You can teach me too."

Well, why not? What harm could there be?

"All right," I said. "I'll give it a try."

So that was that. Back in business at last, without any fuss. And if any qualms remain in my mind—

There can be no harm in a batch of truffles. Or a tray of *mendiants*, or a cake or two. The Kindly Ones do not concern themselves with such trivial things as chocolates.

Or so I hope—as with every day Vianne Rocher, Sylviane Caillou, and even Yanne Charbonneau recede more safely into the past, becoming smoke, becoming history, a footnote, names upon a faded list.

The ring upon my right hand feels strange against fingers long accustomed to being bare. That name—Le Tresset—feels even stranger. I try it on, as if for size, halfway between a smile and not.

Yanne Le Tresset.

It's just a name.

Bullshit, says Roux, that veteran name changer, shape-shifter, gypsy, and pinpointer of home truths. *It's not just a name. It's a sentence.*

Thursday, 15 November

SO THERE IT IS. SHE'S WEARING HIS RING. *THIERRY*, OF ALL PEOPLE—
Thierry, who doesn't like her hot chocolate, or know anything about her,
not even her real name. She says she hasn't made any plans. She says she's
still getting used to it. Wearing it like a pair of shoes that need breaking in
before they feel right.

A simple wedding, Maman says. A registry office, no priest, no church.
But we know better. He'll get his way. The whole hog, with Rosette and me
in matching frocks. It's going to be terrible.

I said so to Zozie, and she pulled a face and said *each to his own*, which
was a laugh, really, because no one in their right mind could imagine that
those two could ever be really in love.

Well, maybe *he* does. What does he know? He came round again last
night and took us out—not to P'tit Pinson this time, but to an expensive
place on the river, where we could see the boats go by. I wore a dress, and
he said I looked very nice, but I ought to have brushed my hair, and Zozie
looked after Rosette at the shop, because Thierry said it wasn't a suitable
place for a small child (though we all knew that wasn't the real reason).

Maman was wearing the ring he'd given her. A great, fat, hateful diamond, perched on her hand like a shiny bug. She doesn't wear it in the shop
(it gets in the way of everything), and last night she kept playing with it,
twisting it round and round on her finger, as if it felt uncomfortable.

Getting used to it yet? he says. As if we could ever get used to that, or
to him, or to the way he treats us, like spoiled children, to be bought and

bribed. And he gave Maman a mobile phone, *just to keep in touch*, he said—*I can't believe you've never had one before*—and afterward we had champagne (which I hate) and oysters (which I also hate), and a chocolate soufflé ice cream, which was quite nice, but not as nice as the ones Maman used to make, as well as being very, very small.

And Thierry laughed a lot (at least, at first), and called me *jeune fille*, and talked about the *chocolaterie*. Turns out he's going to London again, and this time he wanted Maman to go with him, but she was too busy, she said, and maybe after the Christmas rush.

"Really?" he said. "I thought you said business was slow."

"I'm trying something new," said Maman and told him about the new line of truffles she was planning, and how Zozie was helping out for a while, and how she was bringing her old things out of storage. She talked about it for a long time, and her face was pink, the way it gets when she's really into something, and the more she talked, the quieter Thierry got, and the less he laughed, so that finally she stopped talking and looked a bit embarrassed.

"Sorry," she said. "You don't want to hear all this."

"No, it's fine," said Thierry. "And this was Zozie's idea, was it?" He didn't sound too pleased about it.

Maman smiled. "We like her a lot. Don't we, Annie?"

I said we did.

"But do you think she's management material? I mean, she may be all right, but let's face it, in the long run you're going to need a bit more than some waitress you poached off Laurent Pinson."

"Management material?" said Maman.

"Well, I was thinking, when we're married, you might actually want someone to run the place."

When we're married. Oh, boy.

Maman looked up. She was frowning a little.

"Well, I know you want to run the shop, but surely you don't need to be there all the time? There'd be all kinds of things to do instead. We'd be free to travel, to see the world. . . ."

"I've seen it," she said, a little too fast, and Thierry gave her a funny look.

"Well, I hope you don't expect me to move in above the *chocolaterie*," he said, with a grin to show he was joking. He wasn't, though; I could tell from his voice.

Maman said nothing and looked away.

"Well, what about you, Annie?" he said. "I bet *you'd* like to travel the world. How about America? Wouldn't that be cool?"

I hate it when he says "cool." I mean, he's *old*—he's fifty at least—and I know he tries, but it's just so embarrassing, don't you think?

When Zozie says "cool," it's as if she means it. It's as if she actually invented the word. America *would* be cool with Zozie in it. Even the *chocolaterie* looks cooler now, with the gilt mirror in front of the old glass case, and her lollipop shoes in the window like magic slippers filled with treasure.

If Zozie was here, she'd sort him out, I thought, remembering the Jeanne Moreau waitress in the English tea shop. Then I felt bad—almost as if I'd done something wrong, as if just thinking about it might cause an Accident.

Zozie wouldn't care about that, said the shadow-voice inside my head. Zozie would just do as she pleased. And would that be so bad? I thought. Well, of course it would. But all the same . . .

This morning as I was getting ready for school I caught Suze looking into the new shop window, nose pigged up against the glass. She ran off as soon as she saw me—we're still not really talking right now—but for a minute I felt so bad that I had to sit down on one of the old armchairs Zozie had brought in from somewhere, and imagine Pantoufle sitting there listening, with his black eyes shining in his whiskery face.

You know, it isn't even that I *like* her that much. But she was so nice, when I was new; she used to come to the *chocolaterie* and we'd talk, or watch TV, or go to the Place du Tertre and watch the artists, and once she bought me a pink enameled pendant from one of the stalls there, a little cartoon dog with BEST FRIEND written on it.

It was only a cheap thing, and I've never liked pink, but I'd never had a Best Friend, either—not a real one anyway. It was nice; it made me feel good just having it, even though I haven't worn it for ages.

And then Chantal came along.

Perfect, popular Chantal with her perfect blond hair and her perfect clothes and that way she has of sneering at everything. Now Suze wants to be exactly like her, and I'm just the one who stands in when Chantal has something better to do, or, more often, I'm just a convenient stooge.

It isn't fair. Who decides these things? Who was it decided that Chantal deserved to be the popular one, even though she never raised a finger for anyone, or cared about anyone but her little self? What makes Jean-Loup Rimbault more popular than Claude Meunier? And what about the others? Mathilde Chagrin, or those girls in their black head scarves? What is it about them that makes them freaks? What is it about *me*?

I was talking in my shadow-voice, and I didn't notice Zozie come in. She can be very quiet sometimes, you know, quieter even than me, which was odd, because today she was wearing the kind of clacky wooden-soled clog-things that you can't help making a noise with. Except that these were fuchsia-pink, which made them kind of fabulous.

"Who was that you were talking to?"

I hadn't realized I'd said it aloud.

"No one. Just me."

"Well, there's no harm in that."

"I guess." I still felt awkward sitting there; very conscious of Pantoufle watching, quite real today actually with his stripy nose going up and down just like a proper rabbit's. I see him more clearly when I'm upset—that's why I shouldn't talk to myself. Besides, Maman always says that it's important to tell the difference between what's real and what isn't. It's when you can't tell the difference that Accidents happen.

Zozie smiled and made a little sign, a bit like an "OK" sign, with her thumb and index finger joined to make a circle. She looked at me through the circle, and then she dropped her hand again. "You know, I often talked to myself as a kid. Or rather, to my invisible friend. I used to talk to her all the time."

I don't know why I was so surprised. "You?"

"Her name was Mindy," Zozie said. "My mother said she was a spirit guide. Of course, my mother believed in all those things. In fact, she believed in pretty much *everything*—crystals, dolphin magic, alien abduction, the Yeti—you name it, my mother was a believer." She grinned. "Still, some of it works—doesn't it, Nanou?"

I didn't know what to say to that. *Some of it works*—what did that mean? It made me feel uncomfortable—but a little excited at the same time. Because this wasn't just a coincidence, or an Accident, like what had happened in the English tea shop. Zozie was talking about real magic, talking quite openly, as if it was really true and not some kids' game I'd had to grow out of.

Zozie believed.

"I have to go." I picked up my bag and made for the door.

"You say that so often. What is it? A cat?" She shut one eye and looked at me once more through the circle of her thumb and forefinger.

"I don't know what you mean," I said.

"Little guy, big ears."

I looked at her. She was still smiling.

I knew I shouldn't talk about it. Talking only makes things worse—but I didn't want to lie to Zozie. Zozie never lies to me.

I sighed. "He's a rabbit. He's called Pantoufle."

"Cool," said Zozie.

And that was that.

Friday, 16 November

STRIKE TWO. AND I'M IN AGAIN. ALL IT TAKES IS A WELL-PLACED BLOW, and the piñata begins to weaken and split. The mother is the weak link; and with Yanne on my side, Annie follows as sweetly as summer follows spring.

That lovely child. So young, so bright. I could do great things with such a child—if only her mother were out of the way. But one thing at a time, eh? The mistake now would be to push my advantage too far. The child is still cautious and may still withdraw if I press too hard. And so I'll wait, and work on Yanne, and to tell the truth I'm enjoying it. A single mother, with a business to run and a young child constantly underfoot—trust me to become indispensable, to become her confidante, her friend. She needs me; Rosette, with her endless curiosity and her knack for getting into all the wrong places, will give me all the excuse I need.

Rosette intrigues me more and more. So small for her age, with that pointed face and widely spaced eyes, she might almost be a kind of cat, scuttling about the floor on her hands and knees (a technique she prefers to walking upright), poking her fingers into holes in the wainscoting, repeatedly opening and closing the kitchen door, or making long and complicated arrangements of small objects on the floor. She must be watched at all times, for although she is usually quite good, she seems to have no sense of danger, and when she becomes upset or frustrated, she may sometimes indulge in violent (though often soundless) tantrums, swaying wildly from side to side, sometimes to the point of striking her head against the floor.

"What's wrong with her?" I asked Annie.

She looked at me warily, as if calculating whether it was safe to tell. "No one really knows," she said. "A doctor saw her once, you know, when she was just a little baby. He said it might be something called *cri-du-chat*, but he wasn't sure, and we never went back."

"*Cri-du-chat?*" It sounds like a medieval affliction, something brought on by the cry of a cat.

"She made this noise. Just like a cat. I used to call her the Cat Baby." She laughed and quickly looked away, almost guiltily, as if just talking about it might be somehow dangerous. "She's all right, really," said Annie. "She's just different, that's all."

Different. That word again. Like *Accident*, it seems to hold a special resonance for Annie, something more than its everyday meaning. Certainly, she is accident-prone. But I sense that this means something other than pouring paint water into her Wellingtons, or putting toast slices into the video player, or poking her fingers into the cheese to make holes for invisible mice.

Accidents happen when she's around. Like the Murano dish that I could swear was broken, though now I'm not sure at all. Or the lights, which sometimes switch on and off, even when there's no one there. Of course, that might simply be the eccentric wiring of a very old house. I may have imagined the rest of it. Then again, *may and might never made a wrong thing right*, as my mother used to say, and I'm not in the habit of imagining things.

The past few days have been busy for us. A bustle of cleaning, restructuring, and ordering of stock, with all Yanne's copper pans and molds and ceramics to bring out of storage—in spite of her careful packing, many of the pans were tarnished and spotted with verdigris, and as I looked after the front of the shop, Yanne spent hours in the kitchen, polishing and cleaning until at last every piece was done.

"It's only for fun," she keeps saying, as if slightly ashamed of her enjoyment, as of some childish habit she should have outgrown. "It's not really serious, you know."

Well, it looks serious enough from where I'm standing. No game could be so meticulously planned.

She buys only the best *couverture*, from a fair trade supplier down near Marseille, and pays for it all in cash. A dozen blocks of each kind, to begin with, she says; but I already know from her eager response that a dozen blocks will not be enough. She used to make all her own stock, so she tells me, and though I'll admit I didn't quite believe it at first, the way she has thrown herself back into the business tells me that she was not exaggerating.

The process is deft and peculiarly therapeutic to watch. First comes the melting and tempering of the raw *couverture*: the process that enables it to leave its crystalline state and take on the glossy, malleable form necessary to make the chocolate truffles. She does it all on a granite slab, spreading out the melted chocolate like silk and gathering it back toward her using a spatula. Then it goes back into the warm copper, the process to be repeated until she declares it done.

She rarely uses the sugar thermometer. She has been making chocolates for so long, she tells me, that she can simply sense when the correct temperature has been reached. I believe her; certainly over the past three days I have been watching her, she has never produced a less than flawless batch. During that time I have learned to observe with a critical eye: to check for streaks in the finished product; for the unappealing pale bloom that denotes incorrectly tempered chocolate; for the high gloss and sharp snap that are the indicators of good-quality work.

Truffles are the simplest to make, she tells me. Annie could make them when she was four, and now it is Rosette's turn to try, solemnly rolling out the truffle balls across the cocoa-dusted baking sheet, face smeared, a bright-eyed racoon in melted chocolate. . . .

For the first time, I hear Yanne laughing aloud.

Oh, Yanne. That weakness.

Meanwhile, I'm practicing some tricks of my own. It's in my interest for this place to do well, and I have worked hard to enhance its appeal. In view of Yanne's sensitivity, I have had to be discreet; but the symbols of Cinteotl, the Ear of Maize, and the Cacao Bean of Lady Blood Moon, scratched under the lintel of the doorway and embedded into the front step, should ensure that our little business thrives.

I know their favorites, Vianne. I can read it in their colors. And I know that the florist's girl is afraid; that the woman with the little dog blames herself; and that the fat young man who never shuts up will be dead before he is thirty-five if he does not make an effort to lose some weight.

It's a gift, you know. I can tell what they need. I can tell what they fear; I can make them dance.

Had my mother done the same, she would never have struggled as she did; but she mistrusted my practical magic as "interventionist" and hinted that such misuse of my skills was at best selfish and, at worst, doomed to bring terrible retribution on both of us.

"Remember the Dolphin Creed," she said. *"Meddle ye not, lest the Way be forgot."* Of course the Dolphin Creed was awash with this kind of sentiment—but by then my own System was well under construction, and I had long since decided that not only had I forsaken the Dolphin Way, but also that I was born to be a meddler.

The question is, where to begin? Will it be with Yanne or Annie? Laurent Pinson or Madame Pinot? There are so many lives here, intertwined; each one with its secrets, dreams, ambitions, hidden doubts, dark thoughts, forgotten passions, unspoken desires. So many lives just there for the taking; there for the tasting, for someone like me.

The girl from the florist's came in this morning. "I saw the window," she whispered. "It looks so nice—I couldn't help just looking in."

"It's Alice, isn't it?" I said.

She nodded, looking round with small-animal wariness at the new displays.

Alice, we know, is painfully shy. Her voice is a wisp; her hair, a shroud. Her kohl-rimmed eyes, which are rather beautiful, peep out from beneath a mass of white-bleached fringe, and her arms and legs poke out awkwardly from a blue dress that might once have belonged to a ten-year-old.

Her shoes are enormous platform boots that look far too heavy for her little stick legs. Her favorite is milk chocolate fudge, though she always buys the plain dark squares because they contain only half the calories. Her colors are gilded with anxiety.

"Something smells good," she said, sniffing the air.

"Yanne's making chocolates," I told her.

"*Making* them? She can do that?"

I sat her down in the old armchair I found in a Dumpster down Rue de Clichy. It's shabby, but quite comfortable; and like the shop, I intend to make something of it within the next few days.

"Try one," I said. "It's on the house."

Her eyes gleamed. "I shouldn't, you know."

"I'll cut it in half. We'll share it," I said, perching on the arm of the chair. So easy to scratch the seductive sign of the Cacao Bean with my fingernail; so easy to watch her through the Smoking Mirror as she pecked at her truffle like a baby bird.

I know her well. I've seen her before. An anxious child; always aware of not being good enough, of not being entirely like the others. Her parents are good people, but they are ambitious, they are demanding; they make it plain that failure is not an option, that nothing can ever be too good for them and for their little girl. One day, she misses dinner. It makes her feel good—emptied, somehow, of all the fears that weigh her down. She misses breakfast, dizzy with that new, exhilarating feeling of control. She tests herself and finds herself wanting. Rewards herself for being so good. And here she is now—*such a good girl, trying so hard*—twenty-three and still looks thirteen, and still not quite good enough, still not quite there—

She finished the truffle. "*Mmmm,*" she said.

I made sure she saw me eat one too.

"It must be so hard, working here."

"Hard?" I said.

"I mean, *dangerous.*" She flushed a little. "I know that sounds stupid, but that's how I'd feel. Having to look at chocolates all day—handling chocolates—and always with the smell of chocolate. . . ." She was losing some of her shyness now. "How do you do it? How come you're not just eating chocolates all day long?"

I grinned. "What makes you think I don't?"

"You're thin," said Alice. (In fact I could easily give her fifty pounds.)

I laughed. "Forbidden fruits," I said. "So much more tempting than the ordinary kind. Here, have another."

She shook her head.

"Chocolate," I said. "*Theobroma cacao*, the food of the gods. Make it with pure ground cocoa beans, chillies, cinnamon, and just enough sugar to take away the bitterness. That's how the Mayans used to make it, over two thousand years ago. They used it in ceremonies to give themselves courage. They gave it to their sacrificial victims just before they ripped out their hearts. And they used it in orgies that lasted for hours."

She stared at me with widened eyes.

"So you see—it *can* be dangerous." I smiled. "Better not to have too much."

I was still smiling when she left the shop with a box of twelve truffles in her hand.

Meanwhile, from another life—

Françoise Lavery made the papers. Seems I was wrong about the bank's camera footage: the police got a fairly good set of pictures of my last visit, and some colleague or other recognized Françoise. Of course, further investigation proved that there *was* no Françoise and that her story was fake from beginning to end. The results are somewhat predictable. A rather grainy staff photograph of the suspect appeared in the evening paper, followed by several editorials suggesting that she might have had more sinister motives for her imposture than money. It was even possible, gloated *Paris-Soir*, that she may have been a sexual predator, targeting young boys.

As if, as Annie would say. Still, it makes for a good headline, and I expect to see that photograph several times more before its newsworthiness fades. Not that it troubles me at all. No one would see Zozie de l'Alba in that mousy little piece of work. In fact most of my colleagues would have been hard put to see Françoise herself—glamours don't transfer well to celluloid, which is why I never tried for a career in the movies, and the photograph looks less like Françoise and more like a girl I used to know, the girl who was always It at St. Michael's-on-the-Green.

I don't often think about that girl now. Poor girl, with her bad skin and her freak mother with the feathers in her hair. What chance did she have?

Well, she had the same chance everyone has; the chance you're dealt the day you are born, the *only* chance. And some spend their lives making excuses, and blaming the cards, and wishing they'd had better ones, and some of us just play the hand, and up the stakes, and use every trick, and cheat where we can—

And win. And win. Which is all that matters. I like to win. I'm a very good player.

The question is, where to begin? Certainly, Annie could do with a little help—something to boost her confidence, to start her on the right path.

The names and symbols of One Jaguar and Rabbit Moon, written in marker on the bottom of her schoolbag, ought to take care of her social skills; but I think she needs a little more. And so I give her the Hurakan, or Hurricane, the Vengeful One, to make up for all those times of being It.

Not that Annie would think so, of course. There's a regrettable lack of malice in the child, and all she really wants is for everyone to be friends. I'm sure I can cure her of that, however. Revenge is an addictive drug, which, once tasted, is seldom forgotten. After all, I should know.

Now, I'm not in the business of granting wishes. In my game, it's every witch for herself. But Annie is a genuine rarity—a plant that, if nurtured, may produce spectacular blossom. In any case, there's precious little opportunity to be creative in my line of work. Most of my cases are easy to crack; there's no need for craftsmanship when a cantrip will do just as well.

Besides, for once, I can sympathize. I remember what it was like to be It every day. I remember the joy of settling scores.

This is going to be a pleasure.

Saturday, 17 November

THE FAT YOUNG MAN WHO NEVER SHUTS UP IS CALLED NICO. HE TOLD me so this afternoon, coming in to investigate. Yanne had just finished a batch of coconut truffles, and the whole place smelled of them; that mulled, earthy scent that catches at the throat. I think I said I don't like chocolate—and yet that scent, so like the incense in my mother's shop, sweet and rich and troubling, acts upon me like a drug, making me reckless, impulsive—making me want to interfere.

"Hey, lady! Like your shoes. Great shoes. Fabulous shoes." That's Fat Nico; a man in his twenties, I'd say at a guess, but weighing a good three hundred pounds, with curly hair to his shoulders and a puffy, screwed-up face like that of a giant baby perpetually on the brink of laughter or tears.

"Why, thank you," I said. Actually they're among my favorites: high-heeled pumps from the 1950s in faded green velvet, with ribbons and crystal buckles on the toes. . . .

You can often tell a person by their shoes. His were two-tone, black and white; good shoes but downtrodden like slippers at the heel, as if he couldn't be bothered to put them on properly. Still lives at home, so I would guess—a mummy's boy if ever I saw one—rebelling quietly through his shoes.

"What's that smell?" He'd caught it at last, his big face turning toward the source. In the kitchen behind me, Yanne was singing. A rhythmic sound, as of a wooden spoon against a pot, suggested that Rosette was joining in. "Smells like someone's doing some cooking. Point me to it, Shoe Lady! What's for lunch?"

"Coconut truffles," I said with a smile.

In less than a minute he'd bought the lot.

Oh, I don't flatter myself on this occasion that it was any of my doing. His type is absurdly easy to seduce. A child could have done it; and he paid by Carte Bleue, which made it the work of an instant to collect his number (after all, I must keep in practice), although I do not mean to use it as yet. Such a clear trail might lead to the *chocolaterie*; and I'm enjoying myself far too much to jeopardize my position at this stage. Later, perhaps. When I know why I'm here.

Nico is not the only one to have noticed a difference in the air. Just this morning I sold an astonishing eight boxes of Yanne's special truffles—some to regulars, some to strangers lured in from the streets by that earthy, seductive scent.

In the afternoon, it was Thierry le Tresset. Cashmere coat, dark suit, pink silk tie and handmade brogues. Mmmm. I love a handmade shoe; glossy as the flank of a well-groomed horse and whispering *money* from every perfect stitch. Perhaps I was wrong to overlook Thierry; he may be nothing special from an intellectual point of view, but a man with money is always worth a second glance.

He found Yanne in the kitchen, with Rosette, both of them laughing fit to split. Seemed slightly put out that she had to work—he came back from London today just to see her—though he agreed to call back after five.

"Well, why on earth didn't you check your phone?" I heard him say from the kitchen door.

"I'm sorry," said Yanne (half laughing, I thought). "I don't really know about things like that. I suppose I must have forgotten to turn it on. Besides, Thierry—"

"God help us," he said. "I'm marrying a cave woman."

She laughed. "Call me a technophobe."

"How can I call you anything if you won't answer the phone?"

He left Yanne with Rosette then, and came round to the front for a word with me. He mistrusts me, I know. I'm not his type. He may even consider me a bad influence. And, like most men, he sees only the obvious: the pink hair; the eccentric shoes; the vaguely bohemian look that I have worked so hard to cultivate.

"You're helping Yanne. That's nice," he said. He smiled—he's really very charming, you know—but I could sense the wariness in his colors. "What about the P'tit Pinson?"

"Oh, I still work there in the evenings," I said. "Laurent doesn't need me all day—and really, he isn't the easiest of bosses."

"And Yanne is?"

I smiled at him. "Let's say Yanne doesn't have such—roving hands."

He looked startled, as well he might. "I'm sorry. I thought—"

"I know what you thought. I know I don't quite look the part. But really, I'm just trying to help Yanne. She deserves a break—now don't you agree?"

He nodded.

"Come on, Thierry. I know what you need. A *café-crème* and a milk chocolate square."

He grinned. "You know my favorite."

"Of course," I said. "I've got the knack."

After that, it was Laurent Pinson—for the first time in three years, so Yanne says—all stiff and churchy and trying too hard in his cheap and shiny brown shoes. He hummed and hawed for a laughable time, occasionally casting a jealous glance at me over the glass countertop, then opted for the cheapest chocolates he could find and asked me to wrap them as a gift.

I took my time with scissors and string, smoothing down the pale blue tissue paper with the tips of my fingers, wrapping it all in a double bow of silver ribbon and paper rose.

"Someone's birthday?" I said.

Laurent gave his habitual grunt—*mweh!*—and fingered out the correct change. He has not yet spoken to me of my defection, though I know he resents it, thanking me with exaggerated politeness as I hand him the box.

I have no doubt as to the meaning of Laurent's sudden interest in gift-wrapped chocolates. He means it as a gesture of defiance, indicating that there is more to Laurent Pinson than meets the eye and warning me that if I am fool enough to ignore his attentions, then someone else will benefit in my place.

Let them benefit. I sent him away with a cheery smile and the spiral sign of the Hurakan scratched onto the lid of his chocolate box with the pointed tip of a fingernail. It's not that I bear any especial malice toward Laurent—although I'll admit I wouldn't grieve if the café were struck by lightning, or some client got food poisoning and sued the management. It's just that I have no time to deal with him sensitively at this time, and besides, the last thing I want is a love-struck sexagenarian following me around, getting in the way of business.

I turned as he left and saw Yanne watching.

"Laurent Pinson, buying chocolates?"

I grinned. "I told you he was sweet on me."

She laughed at that, then looked abashed. Rosette peeped out from behind her knee, a wooden spoon in one hand, a melted something in the other. She made a sign with her chocolatey fingers.

Yanne handed her a macaroon.

I said, "The homemade chocolates have all sold out."

"I know." She grinned. "Now I suppose I'll have to make some more."

"I'll help, if you like. Give you a break."

She paused at that. Seemed to consider it, as if it were something much more than simply making chocolate.

"I promise you, I'm a fast learner."

Of course I am. I've had to be. When you have had a mother like mine, either you learn fast or you don't survive. An inner-city London school, fresh from the ravages of the comprehensive system and packed with thugs, immigrants, and the damned. That was my training ground—and I learned fast.

My mother had tried to teach me at home. By the time I was ten, I could read, write, and do the double lotus. But then the Social Services got involved; pointed out Mother's lack of qualifications; and I was packed off to St. Michael's-on-the-Green, a pit of roughly two thousand souls, which swallowed me up in less than no time.

My System was still in its infancy then. I had no defenses; I wore green velvet dungarees with appliquéd dolphins on the pockets, and a turquoise headband to align my chakras. My mother picked me up at the school gates; on the first day, a small crowd gathered to watch. On the second, someone threw a stone.

Hard to imagine that kind of thing now. It happens, though—and for far less. It happened here, at Annie's school—and for nothing more than a head scarf or two. Wild birds will kill exotic ones: the budgies and the lovebirds and the yellow canaries—escaped from their cages, hoping to get a taste of the sky—usually end up back on the ground, plucked raw by their more conformist cousins.

It was inevitable. For the first six months I cried myself to sleep. I begged to be sent to some other school. I ran away; I was brought back; I prayed fervently to Jesus, Osiris, and Quetzalcoatl to save me from the demons of St. Michael's-on-the-Green.

Unsurprisingly, nothing worked. I tried to adapt: changed my dungarees for jeans and a T-shirt, took up smoking, hung out with the crowd, but it was already too late. The bar had been set. Every school needs its freak; and for the next five years or so, I was it.

It was then that I could have used someone like Zozie de l'Alba. What use was my mother, that second-rate, patchouli-scented wannabe witch, with all her crystals and dream catchers and glib talk of karma? I didn't care about karmic retribution. I wanted my retribution to be *real*: for my tormentors to be laid low, not later, not in some future lifetime, but paid back in full, in blood, and in the present.

And so I studied, and studied hard. I made up my own curriculum from the books and pamphlets in Mother's shop. The result was my System, every piece honed and refined and stored and practiced with only one objective in mind.

Revenge.

I don't suppose you'll remember the case. It made the news at the time, of course; but there are so many similar stories now. Tales of perennial losers armed with handguns and crossbows, blowing themselves into high school legend in a single bloody, glorious, suicidal spree.

That wasn't me at all, of course. Butch and Sundance were no heroes of mine. I was a survivor: a scarred veteran of five long years of bullying, name-calling, punching, thumping, taunting, pinching, vandalism, and petty theft, the subject of much spiteful locker room graffiti and a perpetual target for everyone.

In short, I was It.

But I bided my time. I studied and learned. My curriculum was unorthodox, some might say profane, but I was always top of the class. My mother knew little about my research. If she had, she would have been appalled. Interventionist magic, as she liked to call it, was the very antithesis of her belief, and she held a number of quaint theories promising cosmic retribution on those who dared to act for themselves.

Ah, well. I dared. And when at last I was ready, I went through St. Michael's-on-the-Green like a December wind. My mother never guessed the half of it—which was probably a good thing, as I'm sure she would have disapproved. But I'd made it. I was just sixteen, and I had passed the only exam that mattered.

Annie, of course, has a way to go. But with time, I hope to make something rather special of her.

And so, Annie. About that revenge.

Monday, 19 November

TODAY SUZE CAME TO SCHOOL WITH HER HEAD IN A SCARF. APPARENTLY the hairdresser, instead of giving her highlights, has made her hair fall out in clumps. Some reaction to the peroxide, the hairdresser says—Suze told her she'd had it before, but she lied, and now the hairdresser says it isn't *her* fault, that Suzanne's hair was already damaged by all the ironing and straightening she's done to it, and that if Suzanne had told her the truth in the first place, she would have used another solution and none of this would have happened.

Suzanne says her mother's going to sue the company for distress and emotional trauma.

I think it's hilarious.

I know I shouldn't—Suzanne's a friend. Although perhaps she isn't— not quite. A friend stands up for you when you're in trouble and never goes along when someone's being mean. *Friends put out*, is what Zozie says. With real friends, you're never It.

I've been talking to Zozie a lot lately. She knows what it's like to be my age, and to be different. Her mother had a shop, she says. Some people didn't like it much, and once, someone even tried to set it on fire.

"A bit like what happened to us," I said, and then I had to tell her the rest, about how we blew into the village of Lansquenet-sous-Tannes at the beginning of Lent and set up our chocolate shop right in front of the church, and about the curé who hated us, and all our friends, and the river people, and Roux, and Armande, who died just the way she had lived, with no regrets and no good-byes and with the taste of chocolate in her mouth.

I don't suppose I should have told her all that. But it's quite hard not to, with Zozie. And anyway, she works for us. She's on our side. She understands.

"I hated school," she told me yesterday. "I hated the kids and the teachers too. All those people who thought I was a freak, and who wouldn't sit with me because of the herbs and stuff Mum used to put into my pockets. Asafetida—*God*, that's rank—and patchouli, because it's supposed to be spiritual, and dragon's blood, that gets everywhere and leaves these red stains— And so the other kids used to laugh at me, and say I'd got nits, and say I smelled. And even the teachers got drawn in, and one woman—Mrs. Fuller, she was called—gave me a talk about personal hygiene. . . ."

"That's rotten!"

She grinned. "I paid them back."

"How?"

"Another time, perhaps. The point is, Nanou, that for a long time I thought it was my fault. That I really *was* a freak, and I'd never amount to anything."

"But you're so clever—and besides, you're gorgeous."

"I didn't feel clever or gorgeous then. I never felt good enough, or clean enough, or nice enough for them. I never bothered to do any work. I just assumed everyone was better than me. I talked to Mindy all the time—"

"Your invisible friend—"

"And, of course, people laughed. Though by then it hardly mattered what I did. They'd have laughed at me anyway."

She stopped talking, and I looked at her, trying to imagine her in those days. Trying to imagine her without her confidence, her beauty, her style . . .

"The thing about beauty," Zozie said, "is that actually it doesn't have much to do with looks at all. It's not about the color of your hair, or your size, or your shape. It's all in *here*." She tapped her head. "It's how you walk, and talk, and think—and whether you walk about like *this*—"

And then suddenly she did something that really startled me. *She changed her face.* Not like *pulling* a face, or anything; but her shoulders slumped, and she turned her eyes away, and her mouth drooped somehow, and she made her hair into a limp kind of curtain, and suddenly she was someone else, someone else in Zozie's clothes, not *ugly*, not quite, but someone you wouldn't turn round to see twice, someone you'd forget as soon as they'd gone.

"—or like *this*," she said, and she shook her hair and straightened up and just like that she was Zozie again, brilliant Zozie with her jingling bangles and her black-and-yellow peasant skirt and her pink-streaked hair and bright yellow patent platform shoes that would have just looked weird on anyone else, but on Zozie they looked terrific, because she was Zozie, and everything does.

"Wow," I said. "Could you teach me that?"

"I just did," she said, laughing.

"It looked like—magic," I said, and blushed.

"Well, most magic really *is* that simple," said Zozie matter-of-factly, and if anyone else had said it I might have thought they were making fun of me, but not Zozie. Not her.

"There's no such thing as magic," I said.

"Then call it something else." She shrugged. "Call it attitude, if you like. Call it charisma, or chutzpah, or glamour, or charm. Because basically it's just about standing straight, looking people in the eye, shooting them a killer smile, and saying, *fuck off, I'm fabulous.*"

I laughed at that, and not just because Zozie had said the f-word. "I wish I could do that," I said.

"Try it," said Zozie. "You might be surprised."

Of course I was lucky. Today was exceptional. Even Zozie couldn't have known. But I did feel different, somehow; more alive, as if the wind had changed.

First there was Zozie's whole attitude thing. I'd promised her I'd try it, and so I did, feeling just a bit self-conscious this morning with my hair just washed and a little of Zozie's rose perfume on as I looked at myself in the bathroom mirror and practiced my killer smile.

I have to say, it didn't look bad. Not perfect, of course, but really, it makes a world of difference if you stand up straight and say the words (even if it's only in your head).

I *looked* different too: more like Zozie, more like the type of person who might swear in an English tea shop and not give a damn.

It isn't magic, I told myself in my shadow-voice. From the corner of my eye I could see Pantoufle, looking slightly disapproving, I thought, his nose going up and down.

"It's all right, Pantoufle," I said softly. "It isn't magic. It's allowed."

Then there was Suze and the head scarf, of course. I hear she's going to have to wear the scarf until her hair grows out, and it's not a good look for Suzanne at all. She looks like an angry bowling ball. Plus people have started going *Allah Akhbar* when she walks past, and Chantal laughed, and Suze was upset, and now they've fallen out completely.

So then Chantal spent all lunchtime with her other friends, and Suze came to complain and to cry on my shoulder, but I suppose I wasn't feeling too sympathetic just then, and besides, I was with someone else.

Which brings me to the third thing.

It happened this morning, during break. The others were playing the tennis ball game, except for Jean-Loup Rimbault, who was reading as usual, and a few loners (the Muslim girls, mostly) who never play at anything.

Chantal was bouncing the ball to Lucie, and when I came in, she said, "*Annie's It!*"—and then everyone was laughing and throwing the ball across the room to one another and shouting, "*Jump! Jump!*"

Another day I might have joined in. It's a game, after all, and it's better to be It than to be left out altogether. But today I'd been practicing Zozie's attitude.

And I thought: *what would she do?* And I knew straight away that Zozie would rather die than be It.

Chantal was still shouting, "Jump, Annie, jump!" as if I were a dog, and for a second I just looked at her, as if I'd never seen her properly before.

I used to think she was pretty, you know. She ought to be; she spends enough time on her appearance. But today I could see her colors too, and Suzanne's; and it was so long since I'd seen them that I couldn't help staring now at how *ugly*—how really ugly—both of them were.

The others must have seen something too, because Suze dropped the ball and no one picked it up. Instead I sensed them forming a circle, as if there was a fight in the air, or something extra special to see.

Chantal didn't like me staring at all. "What's wrong with *you* today?" she said. "Don't you know it's rude to stare?"

I just smiled and kept on staring.

Behind her, I saw Jean-Loup Rimbault look up from the book he was reading. Mathilde was watching too, her mouth open just a little bit; and Faridah and Sabine had stopped talking in their corner, and Claude was smiling, just a bit, the way you do when it's raining and the sun comes out unexpectedly for just a second.

Chantal gave me one of her sneery looks. "*Some* of us can afford to get a *life*. I guess *you* just have to make your *own* entertainment."

Well, I knew what Zozie would have said to that. But I'm not Zozie; I hate scenes, and part of me just wanted to sit down at my desk and hide myself inside a book. But I'd promised I'd try; so I straightened up, looked her in the eye, and shot them all with my killer smile.

"Fuck off," I said. "I'm fabulous." And, picking up the tennis ball, which had come to rest just between my feet, I bounced it—*pok!*—off Chantal's head.

"You're It," I said.

And, making my way to the back of the room, I stopped in front of Jean-Loup's desk, where Jean-Loup wasn't even pretending to read anymore but was watching me with his mouth half-open in surprise.

"Want a game?" I said.

I led the way.

W̲e talked for quite a long time. It turns out that we like a lot of the same things: old films in black-and-white, photography, Jules Verne, Chagall, Jeanne Moreau, the cemetery. . . .

I'd always thought he looked a bit stuck-up—he never plays with the others, perhaps because he's a year older, and he's always taking pictures of weird things with that little camera of his—and I'd only spoken to him because I knew it would annoy Chantal and Suze.

But actually he's OK; laughed at my story of Suze and her list; and when I told him where I lived, said, "You live in a *chocolaterie?* How terrific is that?"

I shrugged. "OK, I guess."

"Do you get to eat the chocolates?"

"All the time."

He rolled his eyes, which made me laugh. Then—

"Hold it," he said and pulled out that little camera of his—silver-colored, and not much bigger than a box of kitchen matches—and cocked it at me. "Gotcha," he said.

"Hey, stop it," I told him, turning away. I don't like pictures of myself.

But Jean-Loup was looking into the camera's little screen. He grinned. "Look at this." He showed it to me.

I don't see many pictures of me. The few I have are formal ones, taken at some passport place, all white background and no smile. In this one, I was laughing, and he'd taken the picture at a mad kind of angle, with me just turning toward the camera, my hair a blur and my face lit up—

Jean-Loup grinned. "Go on, admit it—it's not so bad."

I shrugged. "It's OK. Been doing it long?"

"Since I first went into the hospital. I've got three cameras; my favorite's an old manual Yashica that I only use for black-and-white; but the digital one's pretty good, and I can carry it anywhere."

"What were you in the hospital for?"

"I've got this heart condition," he said. "That's why I was kept back a year. I had to have two operations and miss four months of school. It was totally lame." (*Lame* is Jean-Loup's favorite word.)

"Is it serious?" I asked.

Jean-Loup shrugged. "I actually died. On the operating table. I was officially dead for fifty-nine seconds."

"Wow," I said. "Have you got a scar?"

"Loads of them," said Jean-Loup. "I'm practically a freak."

And then, before I knew it, we were talking properly; and I'd told him about Maman and Thierry; and he'd told me how his parents had divorced when he was nine, and how his father had remarried last year, and how it didn't matter how nice she was, because—

"Because it's when they're nice that you hate them most," I finished with a grin, and he laughed, and just like that, we were suddenly friends. Quietly, without a fuss; and somehow it didn't matter anymore that Suze preferred Chantal to me, or that I was always It when we played the tennis ball game.

And waiting for the school bus, I stood with Jean-Loup at the front of the queue, and Chantal and Suze glared from their place in the middle but didn't say anything at all.

Monday, 19 November

ANOUK CAME HOME FROM SCHOOL TODAY WITH AN UNACCUSTOMED
bounce in her step. She changed into her play clothes, kissed me exuberantly for the first time in weeks, and announced that she was going out with
a friend from school.

I didn't press her for more details—Anouk has been so moody recently
that I didn't want to dampen her spirits—but I kept an eye out just the
same. She hasn't mentioned the subject of friends since her quarrel with
Suzanne Prudhomme, and although I know better than to interfere in
what may be nothing more than a children's squabble, it makes me so sad
to think of Anouk being left out.

I've tried so hard to make her fit in. I've invited Suzanne countless
times, made cakes, arranged visits to the cinema. But nothing seems to
make a difference; there's a line that separates Anouk from the rest, a line
that seems more pronounced as the days go by.

Today was different, somehow; and as she set off (at a run, as always) I
thought I could see the old Anouk, racing across the square in her red coat,
her hair flying like a pirate's flag and her shadow hopping at her heels.

I wonder who the friend was. Not Suzanne, in any case. But there's
something in the air today, some new optimism that makes light of my
concerns. Maybe it's the sun, back again after a week of cloudy skies. Maybe
it's the fact that, for the first time in three years, we have actually *sold out* of
gift boxes. Maybe it's just the scent of chocolate, and how good it is to be
back at work again, to handle the pans and the ceramics, to feel the granite

slab grow warm beneath my hands, to make those simple things that give people pleasure. . . .

Why did I hesitate so long? Could it be that it still reminds me too much of Lansquenet—of Lansquenet and Roux, and Armande and Joséphine, and even the curé Francis Reynaud—all those people whose lives took a different turn just because I happened to pass by?

Everything comes home, my mother used to say; every word spoken, every shadow cast, every footprint in the sand. It can't be helped; it's part of what makes us who we are. Why should I fear it now? Why should I fear anything here?

We have worked so hard over the past three years. We have persevered. We deserve success. Now, at last, I think I can feel a change in the wind. And it's all ours. No tricks, no glamours, just plain hard work.

Thierry's in London again this week, supervising his Kings Cross project. This morning, he sent flowers again, a double handful of mixed roses, tied with raffia, with a card that reads:

TO MY FAVORITE TECHNOPHOBE—LOVE, THIERRY

It's a sweet gesture—old-fashioned and just a little childish, like the milk chocolate squares he likes so much. It makes me feel slightly guilty to think that in all the rush of the past two days, I've barely thought about him at all, and his ring—so awkward to wear when making chocolate—has been lying in a drawer since Saturday night.

But he'll be so pleased when he sees the shop and all the progress we have made. He doesn't know much about chocolate—still thinks of it as just for women and children and has quite failed to notice the growing popularity of high-quality chocolate over the past few years—so that it's hard for him to envisage the *chocolaterie* as a serious concern.

Of course, it's early days yet. But Thierry, when you see us again, I think I can promise you'll be surprised.

Yesterday we began to redecorate the shop. Another of Zozie's ideas, not mine, and at first I'd dreaded the disruption, the mess. But with Zozie,

Anouk, and Rosette helping out, what might have been a chore somehow ended up being a mad kind of game, with Zozie on the ladder painting the walls, her hair tied up in a green scarf and yellow paint all over one side of her face, and Rosette with her toy brush, attacking the furniture, and Anouk stenciling blue flowers and spirals and animal shapes across the wall, and all the chairs out in the sunny street, covered in dust sheets and speckled with paint.

"It doesn't matter, we'll paint them too," said Zozie when we discovered Rosette's little handprints on an old white kitchen chair. And so Rosette and Anouk made a game of it, with trays of ready-mix poster paint, and when they had finished the chair looked so cheery, with multicolored hand-prints covering it all over, that we all did the same with the other chairs, and with the small secondhand table that Zozie had bought for the front of the shop.

"What's happening? You're not closing down?"

That was Alice, the blond girl who drops by almost every week but hardly ever buys anything. She hardly ever says anything either, but the stacked furniture, the dust sheets, and the multicolored chairs drying in the street were enough to startle her into speech.

When I laughed she looked almost alarmed but stopped to admire Rosette's handiwork (and to accept a homemade truffle on the house, as part of the celebration). She seems quite friendly with Zozie, who has spoken to her once or twice in the shop, and she especially likes Rosette and knelt beside her on the floor to measure her own small hands against Rosette's smaller, paint-smudged ones.

Then it was Jean-Louis and Paupaul, coming to see what all the fuss was about. Then Richard and Mathurin, the regulars from Le P'tit Pinson. Then Madame Pinot from around the corner, pretending to be on some kind of errand but darting an eager look over her shoulder at the chaos outside the *chocolaterie*.

Fat Nico dropped by and commented with his usual exuberance on the shop's new look. "Hey, yellow and blue! My favorite colors! Was that your idea, Shoe Lady?"

Zozie smiled. "We all contributed."

Actually she was barefoot today, her long, shapely feet gripping the rickety stepladder. Some of her hair had escaped the scarf; her bare arms were exotically gloved with paint.

"Looks fun," said Nico wistfully. "All the little baby hands." He flexed his own hands, which are large and pale and chubby, and his eyes shone. "Wish I could try, but I guess you're all done, hey?"

"Go ahead," I told him, indicating the trays of poster paint.

He extended a hand toward a tray. There was red paint inside, only slightly grubby now. He hesitated for a moment, then dabbed his fingertips with a quick movement into the paint.

He grinned. "Feels pretty good," he said. "Like mixing pasta sauce without a spoon." He stretched out his hand again, this time letting the paint cover the palm.

"Over here," said Anouk, indicating a place on one of the chairs. "Rosette missed a bit."

Well, as it turned out, Rosette had missed lots of bits, and after that Nico stayed awhile to help Anouk with the stenciling, and even Alice stayed to watch, and I made hot chocolate for everyone, and we drank it like gypsies, out on the step, and laughed and laughed when a group of Japanese tourists came past and photographed us all sitting there.

As Nico said, it felt pretty good.

"You know," said Zozie, when we were clearing away the painting things ready for the morning, "what this shop really needs is a name. There's a sign up there"—she pointed to the faded strip of wood hanging above the door—"but it doesn't look as if there's been any actual writing on it for years. How about it, Yanne?"

I gave a shrug. "You mean just in case people don't realize what it is?" As a matter of fact, I knew exactly what she meant. But a name is never just a name. To name a thing is to give it power, to invest it with an emotional significance that, until now, my quiet little shop has never had.

Zozie wasn't listening. "I think I could do a pretty good job. Why don't you let me try?" she said.

I shrugged again, feeling uneasy. But Zozie had been so very good, and her eyes were shining with such eagerness that I gave in. "All right," I said. "But nothing fancy. Just *chocolaterie*. Nothing too chichi."

What I meant, of course, was *nothing like Lansquenet*. No names, no slogans. It was already enough that somehow my discreet plans for redecorating had turned into a psychedelic paint war.

"Of course," said Zozie.

And so we took down the weathered sign. (Closer examination revealed the ghostly inscription PAYEN FRÈRES, which could have been the name of a café or something different altogether.) The wood was faded but intact, Zozie declared; with a little rubbing down and some fresh paint, she thought she might make something reasonably durable.

We went our separate ways then: Nico to his place on the Rue Caulaincourt, Zozie to her tiny bedsit on the other side of the Butte, where, she promised, she would work on the sign.

I could only hope it wouldn't be too garish. Zozie's color schemes tend toward extravagance, and I had visions of a sign in lime green and red and brilliant purple—perhaps with a picture of flowers or a unicorn—that I would have to display or hurt her feelings.

And so it was with a slight feeling of trepidation that this morning I followed her out of the shop—with my hands over my eyes, at her request—to see the result.

"Well?" she said. "What do you think?"

For a moment I couldn't speak. There it was: hanging above the door, as if it had always been there, a rectangular yellow sign with the name of the shop carefully lettered in blue.

"It's not too chichi, do you think?" There was a trace of anxiety in Zozie's voice. "I know you said write something plain, but this just came to me and—well—what do you think?"

Seconds passed. For a time I could not take my eyes away from that sign—the neat blue letters, that name. My name. Of course it was a coincidence: what else could it be? I gave her the brightest smile I could. "It's lovely," I said.

She sighed. "You know, I was starting to worry."

And she gave me a smile and tripped over the threshold—which, by some trick of the sun or the new color scheme, now seemed almost luminous—leaving me craning my neck at a sign that read, in Zozie's neat, cursive script:

Le Rocher de Montmartre
CHOCOLAT

PART FOUR

Change

Tuesday, 20 November

So now i'm officially best friends with Jean-Loup. Suzanne was away today, so I didn't get to see her face, but Chantal made up for both of them, looking really quite ugly all day long, and pretending not to look at me while all her friends just stared and whispered.

"So are you going out with him?" said Sandrine in chemistry. I used to like Sandrine—a bit—before she fell in with Chantal and the rest. Her eyes were round as marbles, and I could see the eagerness in her colors as she kept saying, "Have you kissed him yet?"

If I'd really wanted to be popular, then I suppose I'd have said yes. But I don't need to be popular. I'd rather be a freak than a clone. And Jean-Loup, for all his popularity with the girls, is nearly as much of a freak as I am, with his films and his books and his cameras.

"No, we're just friends," I told Sandrine.

She gave me a look. "Well, *don't* tell me, then." And stomped off in a sulk to rejoin Chantal, and whispered and giggled and watched us all day, while Jean-Loup and I talked about all sorts of things and took pictures of them staring at us.

I think the word is *puerile*, Sandrine. We're just friends, like I said, and Chantal and Sandrine and Suze and the others can just fuck off—we're fabulous.

Today after school we went to the cemetery together. It's one of my favorite places in Paris, and Jean-Loup says it's one of his too. Montmartre cemetery, with all its little houses and monuments and pointy-roofed chapels and skinny obelisks and streets and squares and alleys and flat-blocks for the dead.

There's a word for it—*necropolis*. City of the dead. And it *is* a city; those tombs could almost be houses, I think, lined up side by side with their little gates neatly closed, and their gravel neatly raked, and flower boxes in their mullioned windows. Neat little houses all the same, like a minisuburbia for the dead. The thought made me shiver and laugh at the same time, and Jean-Loup looked up from his camera and asked me why.

"You could almost live down here," I said. "A sleeping bag and a pillow—a fire—some food. You could hide away in one of these monuments. No one would know. The doors all shut. Warmer than sleeping under a bridge."

He grinned. "You ever slept under a bridge?"

Well, of course I had—once or twice—but I didn't want to tell him that. "No, but I've got a good imagination."

"You wouldn't be scared?"

"Why should I?" I said.

"The ghosts . . ."

I shrugged. "They're only ghosts."

A feral cat strolled out from one of the narrow stone lanes. Jean-Loup snapped it with his camera. The cat hissed and went skittering off among the tombs. Probably saw Pantoufle, I thought; cats and dogs are sometimes afraid of him, as if they know he shouldn't be there.

"One day I'm going to see a ghost. That's why I bring my camera here."

I looked at him. His eyes were bright. He really believes—and he cares too, which is what I like so much about him. I hate it when people don't care, when they move through life without caring or believing in anything.

"You're really not scared of ghosts?" he said.

Well, when you've seen them as often as I have, you tend not to worry about that kind of thing—but I wasn't going to tell Jean-Loup *that*, either. His mother's quite the Catholic. She believes in the *Holy* Ghost. And exorcisms. And communion wine turning into blood—I mean, how gross is that? And always having fish on Friday. Oh, boy. Sometimes I think I'm a ghost myself. A walking, talking, breathing ghost.

"The dead don't do anything. That's why they're here. That's why the little doors in these chapel-of-rest places don't have handles on the inside."

"And dying?" he said. "Are you scared of that?"

I shrugged. "I guess. Isn't everyone?"

He kicked a stone. "Not everyone knows what it's like," he said.

I was curious. "So what *is* it like?"

"Dying?" He shrugged. "Well, there's this corridor of light. And you see all your dead friends and relatives waiting for you. And they're all smiling. And at the end of the corridor there's a bright light, really bright and—*holy*, I guess, and it talks to you, and it says you have to go back to your life now, but not to worry, because you'll be back one day and go into the light with all your friends and . . ." He stopped. "Well, that's what my mum thinks, anyway. That's what I told her I saw."

I looked at him. "What *did* you see?"

"Nothing," he said. "Nothing at all."

There was a silence as Jean-Loup looked through his viewfinder at the avenues of the cemetery with all their dead. *Ping* went the camera as he pressed the switch.

"Wouldn't it be a joke," he said, "if all of this was for nothing?" *Ping.* "What if there's no heaven after all?" *Ping.* "What if all those people are just *rotting*?"

His voice had got quite loud by then, and some birds that had been perching on one of the tombs went off in a sudden clap of wings.

"They tell you they know it all," he said. "But they don't. They lie. They always lie."

"Not always," I said. "Maman doesn't lie."

He looked at me in a funny way, as if he were much, much older than me, with a wisdom born of years of pain and disappointment.

"She will," he said. "They always do."

Tuesday, 20 November

ANOUK BROUGHT IN HER NEW FRIEND TODAY. JEAN-LOUP RIMBAULT, a nice-looking boy a little older than she is, with an old-fashioned politeness that sets him apart. Today he came over directly from school—he lives on the other side of the Butte—and instead of going out straight away sat in the shop for half an hour, talking to Anouk over biscuits and mocha.

It's good to see Anouk with a friend, although the pang it causes me is no less strong for being irrational. Pages of a lost book. *Anouk at thirteen,* the silent voice whispers; *Anouk at sixteen, like a kite on the wind . . . Anouk at twenty, thirty, and more—*

"A chocolate, Jean-Loup? On the house."

Jean-Loup. Not quite a usual name. Not quite a usual boy, either, with that dark, measuring look he shows to the world. His parents are divorced, I hear; he lives with his mother and sees his father three times a year. His favorite chocolate is bitter almond crisp—rather an adult taste, I thought; but then he is a curiously adult and self-possessed young man. His habit of watching everything through the viewfinder of his camera is slightly disconcerting; it's as if he is trying to distance himself from the world outside, to find in the tiny digital screen a simpler, sweeter reality.

"What's that picture you've just taken?"

Obediently, he showed me. At first sight it looked like an abstract, a dazzle of colors and geometric shapes. Then I saw it: Zozie's shoes, shot at eye level, deliberately out of focus among a kaleidoscope of foil-wrapped chocolates.

"I like it," I said. "What's that in the corner?" It looked as if something outside the frame had cast a shadow into the picture.

He shrugged. "Maybe someone was standing too close." He leveled his camera at Zozie, standing behind the counter with a mass of colored ribbons in her hands. "That's nice," he said.

"I'd rather not." She didn't look up, but her voice was sharp.

Jean-Loup faltered. "I was just—"

"I know." She smiled at him, and he relaxed. "I just don't like being photographed. I find I rarely look like myself."

Now *that*, I thought, I could understand. But the sudden glimpse of insecurity—and in Zozie, of all people, whose cheery approach to everything makes any task look effortless—made me a little uneasy, and I began to wonder if I wasn't relying too heavily on my friend, who must have her own problems and concerns, like everyone else.

Well, if she does, she is hiding them well; learning fast, and with an ease that has surprised us both. She comes in at eight every day just as Anouk leaves for school, and spends the hour before opening time watching as I demonstrate the various chocolate-making techniques.

She knows how to temper *couverture*; how to gauge the different blends; how to measure the temperatures and to keep them constant; how to achieve the best kind of gloss; how to pipe decorations onto a molded figure or make chocolate curls with a potato peeler.

She has a knack, as my mother would have said. But her real skill is with our customers. I'd noticed it before, of course: her knack for dealing with different people; her memory for names; the infectious nature of her smile; and the way she manages to make everyone feel special—however crowded the shop may be.

I've tried to thank her, but she just laughs, as if working here were a kind of game, something she does for fun, not money. I've offered to pay her properly, but so far she has always refused, although now the closure of Le P'tit Pinson means that once more she's out of a job.

I mentioned it again today.

"You deserve a proper wage, Zozie," I said. "You're doing far more now than just helping out occasionally."

She shrugged. "Right now you can't afford to pay anyone a full wage."

"But seriously . . ."

"Seriously." She arched an eyebrow. "You, Madame Charbonneau, should stop worrying about other people and look after Number One for a change."

I laughed at that. "Zozie, you're an angel."

"Yeah, right." She grinned. "Now shall we get back to those chocolates?"

Wednesday, 21 November

IT'S FUNNY, THE DIFFERENCE A SIGN CAN MAKE. OF COURSE, MINE WAS more of a beacon, of sorts, shining out into the Paris streets.

Try me. Taste me. Test me.

It works; today we saw strangers and regulars alike, and no one left without something—a gift box, beribboned, or some little treat. A sugar mouse; a brandied plum; a handful of *mendiants* or a kilo of our bitterest truffles, packed loosely in their cocoa powder like chocolate bombs ready to explode.

Of course it's still too early to claim success. The locals, especially, will take longer to seduce. But already I sense a turn in the tide. By Christmas, we will own them all.

And to think I first assumed there was nothing for me here. This place is a gift. It draws them in. And think of what we could collect—not just the money, but the stories, the people, the *lives*—

We? Well, of course. I'm prepared to share. Three of us—four, if we count Rosette—each of us with our own special skills. We could be extraordinary. She's done it before, in Lansquenet. She covered her trail, but not well enough. That name—Vianne Rocher—and the small details I have gleaned from Annie were enough to plot her trajectory. The rest was easy: a few long-distance telephone calls, some back editions of a local newspaper, dated four years ago; one of them showing a grainy, yellowed photograph of Vianne, smiling brashly from the doorway of a chocolate shop, while a tousled someone—Annie, of course—looks out from beneath her outstretched arm.

La Céleste Praline. Intriguing name. Vianne Rocher enjoyed her share of whimsy, though you wouldn't think it to see her now. In those days she was unafraid; wore red shoes and jangling bracelets and long, wild hair like a comic-book gypsy. Not entirely a beauty, perhaps—her mouth is too large, her eyes not entirely wide enough—but any witch worth her spell-book could tell that she was alight with glamours. Glamours to change the course of lives; glamours to charm, to heal, to hide.

So—what happened?

Witches don't just quit, Vianne. Skills like ours beg to be used.

I watch her as she works in the back, making her truffles, her choco-late liqueurs. Her colors have brightened since we first met, and now that I know where to look, I see the magic in everything she does. And yet she seems unaware of this, as if she could blind herself to what she is by simply ignoring it long enough, the way she ignores her children's totems. Vianne is no fool—so why does she behave like one? And what will it take to open her eyes?

She spent this morning in the back room; a scent of baking drifted through. In front—a pot of chocolate. In less than a week, the place has altered almost beyond recognition. Our table and chairs, handprinted by the children, give the place a holiday look. There is something of the school yard in those primary colors, and however neatly they are aligned, there's always a vague impression of disorder. There are pictures on the walls now: framed, embroidered sari squares in hot pink and lemon yellow. There are two old armchairs rescued from a Dumpster; the springs are shot, and the legs are bowed. But I have made them comfortable, using nothing but a couple of meters of plush fabric, in a fuchsia leopard print, and some gold material from a charity shop.

Annie loves them, and so do I. But for our size, we might almost be a little café from one of the trendier quarters of Paris—and the timing couldn't be better for us.

Two days ago, Le P'tit Pinson was closed down (not *quite* unexpect-edly) following an unfortunate food-poisoning incident and a visit from the health inspector. I've heard say that Laurent has at least a month's worth of cleaning and refurbishment before he's allowed to reopen the café, which means that his Christmas clientele is likely to suffer.

So he ate the chocolates after all. Poor Laurent. The Hurakan works in mysterious ways. And some people bring these things down on themselves, as lightning rods draw the lightning.

Still, all the more for us, I say. We don't have a license for alcohol, but hot chocolate, cakes, biscuits, macaroons—and, of course, the siren call of bitter truffle, mocha liqueurs, dipped strawberries, walnut cluster, apricot cup—

Till now, our shopkeepers have stayed away, slightly wary of the changes here. They are so used to thinking of the *chocolaterie* as a tourist trap, a place where locals fear to tread, that it will take all my powers of persuasion to entice them to our door.

But it helps that Laurent has been seen inside. Laurent, who detests any kind of change, who lives in a Paris of his own imagination where only native Parisians are allowed. Like all alcoholics, he has a sweet tooth—besides, where will he go, now that his café has closed down? Where will he find an audience for his endless catalog of complaints?

He came in yesterday at lunchtime, sulky but palpably curious. It's the first time he's been here since we refurbished, and he took in the improvements with a sour look. As luck would have it, we had customers: Richard and Mathurin, who had dropped in on their way to their usual game of *pétanque* in the park. They looked slightly embarrassed to see Laurent—as well they might, being long-standing regulars of Le P'tit Pinson.

Laurent shot them a look of disdain. "Someone's doing well," he said. "What's this supposed to be—a bloody café, or something?"

I smiled. "Do you like it?"

Laurent made his favorite noise. "*Mweh!* Everyone thinks they're a bloody café. Everyone thinks they can do what I do."

"I wouldn't dream of it," I said. "It's not easy to create an authentic atmosphere nowadays."

Laurent snorted. "Don't start me on *that*. There's the Café des Artistes down the road—the owner's a Turk, wouldn't you guess—and the Italian coffee place next to it, and that English tea shop, and any number of Costas and Starbucks—bloody Yanks think they *invented* coffee—" He glared at me, as if I too might harbor American ancestry. "I mean, what about *loyalty?*" he bugled. "What about good, old-fashioned, French *patriotism?*"

Mathurin is quite deaf and genuinely may not have heard him, but I was pretty sure Richard was pretending.

"That was nice, Yanne. Better go."

They left the money on the table and fled without looking back as Laurent's face grew slightly redder, and his eyes bulged alarmingly.

"Those two old faggots," he began. "The number of times they've dropped in for a beer and a game of cards—and now, the minute things go wrong. . . ."

I gave him my most sympathetic smile. "I know, Laurent. But chocolate-houses are quite traditional, you know. In fact, I believe that historically they actually *precede* coffeehouses, which makes them totally authentic and Parisian." I guided him, still blustering, to the table the others had just vacated. "Why don't you sit down and try a cup? On the house, of course, Laurent."

Well, that was only the start of it. For the price of a drink and a chocolate praline, Laurent Pinson is on our side. It's not that we need his custom, of course—he's a parasite, filling his pockets with lump sugar from the bowl and sitting for hours over a single demitasse—but he's the weak link in this little community, and where Laurent goes, the others will follow.

Madame Pinot popped round this morning—she didn't actually buy anything, but she did have a good look round, and left with a chocolate on the house. Jean-Louis and Paupaul did the same; and I happen to know that the girl who bought truffles from me this morning works in the *boulangerie* on the Rue des Trois Frères and will spread the word to her customers.

It's not just the taste, she will try to explain. The rich dark truffle, flavored with rum; the hint of chilli in the blend; the yielding smoothness of the center and the bitterness of the cocoa-powder finish . . . none of these explain the strange allure of Yanne Charbonneau's chocolate truffles.

Perhaps it's the way they make you feel: stronger, perhaps; more powerful; more alert to the sounds and scents of the world; more aware of the colors and textures of things; more aware of yourself; of what's under the skin; of the mouth, of the throat, of the sensitive tongue.

"*Just one*," I say.

They try. They buy.

They buy so many that Vianne was busy all day today, leaving me to run the shop and serve hot chocolate to those who came in. We can seat six, with a little goodwill—and it is a strangely attractive place; quiet and restful, yet cheery as well, where folk can come to forget their troubles, and sit and drink their chocolate, and talk.

Talk? And how! The exception is Vianne. Still, there's time. Start small, I say. Or rather, *big*, in Fat Nico's case.

"Hey, Shoe Lady! What's for lunch?"

"What do you *want* it to be?" I said. "Rose creams, chilli squares, coconut macarooooons." I drew out the word suggestively, knowing his passion for coconut.

"Whoa! I shouldn't."

It's an act, of course. He likes to put up a token resistance; grins sheepishly, knowing that I am not fooled.

"Try one," I say.

"I'll just have half."

Broken sweets, of course, don't count. Nor does a small cup of chocolate, with four more macaroons on the side, or the coffee cake that Vianne brings in, or the frosting he cleans from the mixing bowl.

"My ma always used to make extra," he said. "So I'd have more to lick from the bowl at the end. Some days she'd make so much frosting that even I couldn't eat it all—" He stopped abruptly.

"Your ma?"

"She died." His baby face drooped.

"You miss her," I said.

He nodded. "I guess."

"When did she die?"

"Three years ago. She fell down the stairs. I guess she was a little overweight."

"That's hard," I say, trying not to smile. *A little overweight* to him must mean something in the region of three hundred pounds. His face takes on a blank expression—his colors shift into the spectrum of dull greens and silvery grays that I associate with the negative emotions.

He blames himself, of course. I know. The stair carpet was loose, perhaps; he was late from work; he stopped by the *boulangerie* for a fatal ten minutes too long or sat down on a bench to watch the girls go by—

"You're not the only one," I said. "Everyone feels the same, you know. I blamed myself when my mother died. . . ."

I took his hand. Beneath the flab his bones felt small, like a child's.

"It happened when I was sixteen. I've never stopped thinking it was somehow my fault." I gave him my most earnest look, forking my hand behind my back to stop myself from laughing. Of course I believed it—and with good reason.

But Nico's face lit up at once. "That true?" he said.

I nodded.

I heard him sigh like a hot-air balloon.

I turned away to hide a smile and busied myself with the chocolates that were cooling on the counter at my side. They smelt innocent, like vanilla and childhood. Nico's type rarely makes friends. Always the fat boy, living alone with his fatter ma; lining up his substitutes against the arm of the sofa while she watches him eat with anxious approval.

You're not fat, Nico. Just big-boned. There you are, Nico. Such a good boy.

"Perhaps I shouldn't," he said at last. "My doctor says I oughta cut down."

I raised an eyebrow. "What does he know?"

He shrugged. The ripples went all the way down his arms.

"You feel OK, don't you?" I said.

That sheepish smile. "I guess I do. The thing is . . ."

"What?"

"Well—girls." He flushed. "I mean, what do they see? This great big fat guy. I thought if I lost a little weight—toned up a bit—then maybe, you know . . ."

"You're not so fat, Nico. You don't need to change. You'll find someone. Just wait and see."

Once more he sighed.

"So. What's it to be?"

"I'll have a box of the macaroons."

I was tying the bow when Alice came in. I'm not sure why he *needs* a bow—we both know that box will be open long before he gets it home—but for some reason he likes it that way, tied with a length of yellow ribbon, incongruous between his big hands.

"Hi, Alice," I said. "Just take a seat. I'll be with you in a minute."

In fact, it was five. Alice needs time. She stares at Nico fearfully. He's a giant beside her—a *hungry* giant—but Nico has become unexpectedly mute. He bridles—all three hundred pounds of him—and a flush creeps over his broad face.

"Nico, meet Alice."

She whispers hello.

It's the easiest thing in the world to do. With the fingernail, to scratch a sign along the satin of the chocolate box. It might be anything—an accident—but then again it might be the beginning of something: a turn in the road; a path into another life—

All change.

Once more she whispers something. Looks down at her boots—and sees the box of macaroons.

"I love 'em," says Nico. "Try one with me?"

Alice begins to shake her head. But he looks nice, she tells herself. There's something about him, in spite of his bulk; something reassuringly childish, almost vulnerable. And there's something about his eyes, she thinks; something about him that makes her feel that maybe—just maybe—he understands.

"Just one," he says.

And the symbol scratched on the lid of the box begins to gleam with a pale light—it's Rabbit Moon, for love and fertility—and instead of her usual plain chocolate square, Alice shyly accepts a cup of frothy mocha, with a macaroon to accompany it, and they leave at the same time (if not quite together), she with her small box, he with his large one, into the November rain.

And as I watch, Nico opens a red umbrella of giant proportions bearing the legend MERDE, IL PLEUT! and holds it over little Alice. The sound of her laughter is distant and bright, like something remembered rather than heard. And I watch them down the cobbled road, she skipping in the puddles with her giant boots, he solemnly holding that absurd umbrella over them both, like a cartoon bear and an ugly duckling in some fractured fairy tale, on their way to a great adventure.

Thursday, 22 November

THREE MISSED CALLS FROM THIERRY'S PHONE, AND A PHOTOGRAPH OF the Natural History Museum with a text message reading: CAVE WOMAN! TURN ON UR FONE! It made me laugh but not quite easily; I don't share Thierry's passion for all things technical, and after trying unsuccessfully to text him back, I hid the phone in the kitchen drawer.

Later, he rang. It seems he's not going to be able to get back this weekend, although he promises he will next week. In a way, I'm a little relieved. It gives me time to get things in order; to prepare my stock; to become accustomed to this new shop of mine, its habits and its customers.

Nico and Alice were back today. Alice bought a small box of chocolate fudge squares—a very small box, but she ate them herself—and Nico, a kilo of macaroons.

"Can't get enough of these bad boys," he said. "Just keep 'em coming, Yanne—OK?"

I couldn't help smiling at his exuberance. They sat at a table in the front of the shop. She had mocha, and he had hot chocolate with cream and marshmallows while Zozie and I remained discreetly aloof in the back kitchen—unless a customer came in—and Rosette pulled out her drawing pad and began to draw pictures of monkeys, long-tailed and grinning, in every color in the box.

"Hey, that's good," said Nico as Rosette handed him a picture of a fat purple monkey eating a coconut. "I guess you must like monkeys, eh?"

He did a monkey face for Rosette, who gave a crow of laughter and signed—*Again!* She's laughing more often. I've noticed that. At Nico, at me, at Anouk, at Zozie—perhaps, next time Thierry calls, she will start to connect with him a little more.

Alice laughed too. Rosette likes her best, perhaps because she is so small, almost a child herself in her short print dress and pale blue coat. Perhaps because she so rarely speaks, even with Nico, who talks enough for the both of them.

"That monkey looks like Nico," she said. With adults her voice is wispy and reluctant. With Rosette, she has a different tone. Her voice is rich and comical, and Rosette responds with a brilliant smile.

So Rosette drew monkeys for all of us. Zozie's is wearing bright red mittens on all four hands. Alice's monkey is electric blue, with a tiny body and a ridiculously long and curly tail. Mine is embarrassed, hiding its furry face in its hands. She has a knack, no doubt about it: her drawings are crude but oddly alive; and she manages to convey facial expressions with only a couple of strokes of the pen.

We were still laughing when Madame Luzeron came in with her little fluffy peach-colored dog. Madame Luzeron dresses well, in gray twinsets that hide her expanding waist, and well-cut coats in shades of charcoal and black. She lives in one of the big stucco-fronted houses behind the park; goes to mass every day, to the hairdresser's every other day—except on Thursdays, when she goes to the cemetery by way of our shop. She might be as young as sixty, but her hands are wrung with arthritis, and her thin face is chalky with concealer.

"Three rum truffles, in a box."

Madame Luzeron never says "please." That would be too bourgeois, perhaps. Instead she peered at Fat Nico, Alice, the empty cups, and the monkeys. An overplucked eyebrow went up.

"I see you've—redecorated." The slightest of pauses before that last word throws doubt on the wisdom of such a move.

"Fabulous, isn't it?" That was Zozie. She isn't used to Madame's ways, and Madame gave her a piercing look, taking in the overlong skirt, the hair pinned up with a plastic rose, the jangling bracelets on her arms, and the cherry-print wedges on her feet—worn today with a pair of striped stockings in pink and black.

"We fixed up the chairs ourselves," she said, reaching into the display box to select the chocolates. "We thought it would be nice to cheer the place up a bit."

Madame gave the kind of smile you see on the face of ballet dancers whose shoes are hurting them.

Zozie kept talking, oblivious. "Right now. Rum truffles. There you are. What color ribbon? Pink looks nice. Or maybe red. What do you think?"

Madame said nothing, although Zozie seemed not to require an answer. She wrapped the chocolates in their little box, added a ribbon and a paper flower, and placed the confection on the counter between them.

"These truffles look different," said Madame, looking at them suspiciously through the cellophane.

"They are," said Zozie. "Yanne makes them herself."

"Pity," said Madame. "I liked the others."

"You'll like these better," said Zozie. "Try one. It's on the house."

I could have told her she was wasting her time. City people are often suspicious of a free gift. Some refuse automatically, as if unwilling to be beholden to anyone, even to the tune of a single chocolate. Madame gave a little sniff—a well-bred version of Laurent's *mweh*. She put down the coins on the countertop—

And it was then that I thought I saw it. An almost invisible flick of the fingers as her hand brushed against Zozie's. A brief gleam of something in the gray November air. It might have been the flicker of a neon sign across the square—except that Le P'tit Pinson is shut, and it would be hours before the streetlights went on. Besides, I ought to know that gleam. That spark, like electricity, that leaps from one person to the next—

"Go on," said Zozie. "It's been so long since you indulged."

Madame had felt it just as I had. In a moment I saw her expression change. Beneath the refinement of powder and paste, a confusion; a longing; a loneliness; loss—feelings that shifted like clouds across her pinched pale features—

Hastily, I averted my eyes. *I don't want to know your secrets*, I thought. *I don't want to know your thoughts. Take your silly little dog and your chocolates and go home before it's—*

Too late. I'd seen.

The cemetery; a broad gravestone of pale gray marble, shaped like the curve of an ocean wave. I saw the picture set into the stone: a boy of thirteen or so, grinning brashly and toothily at the camera. A school photograph, perhaps, the last one taken before his death, shot in black-and-white but tinted in pastel shades for the occasion. And underneath it there are the chocolates; rows of little boxes, wasted by the rain. One for every Thursday, lying untouched; beribboned in yellow and pink and green. . . .

I look up. She is staring—but not at me. Her frightened, exhausted pale blue eyes are wide and strangely hopeful.

"I'll be late," she says in a small voice.

"You've got time," says Zozie gently. "Sit down awhile. Rest your feet. Nico and Alice were just leaving. Come on," she insists as Madame seems about to protest. "Sit down and have some chocolate. It's raining, and your boy can wait."

And to my amazement, Madame obeys.

"Thank you," she says and sits down in her chair, looking ludicrously out of place against the bright pink leopard print, and eats her chocolate, eyes closed, head resting against the fluffy fake fur.

And she looks so peaceful—and yes, so *happy*.

And outside, the wind rattles the newly painted sign, and the rain sizzles down on the cobbled streets, and December is only a heartbeat away, and it feels so safe and so solid that I can almost forget that our walls are made of paper; our lives of glass; that a gust of wind could shatter us; that a winter storm could blow us away.

Friday, 23 November

I SHOULD HAVE KNOWN SHE'D HELPED THEM ALONG. IT'S WHAT I MIGHT
have done myself, once, in the days of Lansquenet. First, Alice and Nico,
so oddly alike; and I happen to know that he's noticed her before, calls in
at the florist's once a week to buy daffodils (his favorite) but has never yet
found the courage to speak to her or to ask her out.

Now suddenly, over chocolate—

Coincidence, I tell myself.

And now Madame Luzeron, once so brittle and self-contained, releasing her secrets like scent from a bottle that everyone thought had dried up
long ago.

And that sunny glow around the door—even when it's raining—leads
me to fear that someone may have been easing things along; that the stream
of customers we've had over the past few days is not due entirely to our
confectionery.

I know what my mother would say.

Where's the harm? No one gets hurt. Don't they deserve it, Vianne?

Don't we?

I tried to warn Zozie yesterday. To explain why she mustn't interfere.
But I couldn't. The box of secrets, once opened, may never again be closed.
And she finds me unreasonable, I sense that. As mean as she is generous,
like the miserly baker in the old tale who charged for the smell of the baking bread.

What harm is there? I know she'd say. What do we lose from helping them?

Oh, I came so close to telling her. But every time, I stopped myself. Besides, it *might* be coincidence.

But something else happened today. Something that confirmed my doubts. The unlikely catalyst—Laurent Pinson. I've noticed him in Le Rocher de Montmartre several times already this week. That's hardly news; and unless I'm much mistaken, it is not our chocolate that brings him here.

But he was here again this morning; peering at the chocolates in their glass cases; sniffing at the price tags; taking in every detail of our improvements with a sour face and an occasional grunt of barely concealed disapproval.

"*Mweh.*"

It was one of those sunny November days, all the more precious for being so few. Still as midsummer, with that high clear sky, and the vapor trails like scratches against the blue.

"Nice day," I said.

"*Mweh,*" said Laurent.

"Just browsing, or shall I get you a drink?"

"At those prices?"

"On the house."

Some people are incapable of turning down a free drink. Grudgingly Laurent sat down, accepted a cup of coffee and a praline, and began his usual litany.

"To close me down, at this time of year—it's bloody victimization, that's what it is. Someone's out to ruin me."

"What happened?" I said.

He poured out his woes. Someone had complained about him microwaving leftovers; some idiot had fallen ill; they had sent him an environmental health inspector who could barely speak proper French, and although Laurent had been *perfectly* civil to the fellow, he'd taken offense at something he'd said and—

"Bang! Closed! Just like that! I mean, what is the country coming to, when a perfectly decent café—a café that's been here decades—can be shut down by some bloody *pied-noir*. . . ."

I pretended to listen while itemizing in my mind the chocolates that had sold best, and the ones where stock was running low. I pretended too not to notice when Laurent helped himself to another of my pralines without being asked. I could afford it. And he needed to talk.

After a while, Zozie came out of the kitchen, where she'd been helping me with the chocolate logs. Abruptly Laurent ceased his tirade and flushed to the creases in his earlobes.

"Zozie, good day," he said, with exaggerated dignity.

She grinned. It's no secret that he admires her—who wouldn't?—and today she was looking beautiful, in a velvet dress down to the floor and ankle boots in the same shade of cornflower blue.

I couldn't help feeling sorry for him. Zozie's an attractive woman, and Laurent is at that age when a man's head is most easily turned. But it struck me that we'd have him underfoot every day between now and Christmas, cadging free drinks, annoying the customers, stealing the sugar, and complaining about the neighborhood going to the dogs and—

I almost missed it as I turned away and she forked the sign behind her back. My mother's sign, to banish *malchance*.

Tsk-tsk, begone!

I saw Laurent slap at his neck, as if an insect had bitten him there. I drew a breath—too late. It was done. So naturally—as I myself would have done in Lansquenet, if the past four years had never happened.

"Laurent?" I said.

"Must go," said Laurent. "Things to do, you know—no time to waste." And, still rubbing the back of his neck, he hauled himself out of the armchair he had been occupying for the best part of half an hour and almost scuttled out of the shop.

Zozie grinned. "At last," she said.

I sat down heavily on the chair.

"Are you all right?"

I looked at her. This is the way it always begins: with the little things; the things that don't count. But one little thing leads to another, and another, and before you know it, it has started again, and the wind is turning, and the Kindly Ones have picked up the scent and—

And for a second, I blamed Zozie. After all, it was she who had transformed my ordinary *chocolaterie* into this pirates' cave. Before she came, I was quite content to be Yanne Charbonneau—to run a shop like other shops, to wear Thierry's ring, to allow the world to run its course without the slightest interference.

But things have changed. With nothing much more than a flick of the fingers, four whole years are overturned, and a woman who should long since have been dead opens her eyes and seems to breathe. . . .

"Vianne," she said softly.

"That's not my name."

"But it was, wasn't it? Vianne Rocher."

I nodded. "In a past life."

"It doesn't have to be the past."

Doesn't it? It's a dangerously attractive thought. To be Vianne again; to trade in marvels; to show people the magic within themselves . . .

I had to tell her. This has to stop. It isn't her fault; but I cannot allow it to go on. The Kindly Ones are still on our trail, blind as yet but horribly persistent. I can feel them coming through the mists; combing the air with their long fingers, alert to the smallest gleam and glamour.

"I know you're trying to help," I said. "But we can manage on our own. . . ."

She raised an eyebrow.

"You know what I mean." I couldn't quite say it. Instead I touched a chocolate box, traced a mystic spiral on the lid.

"Oh, I see. *That* kind of help." She looked at me curiously. "Why? What's wrong?"

"You wouldn't understand."

"Why not?" she said. "We're the same, you and I."

"We are *not* the same!" My voice was too loud, and I was shaking. "I don't do those things anymore. I'm normal. I'm boring. Ask anyone."

"Whatever." It's Anouk's favorite word at present—punctuated by that whole-body shrug that teenage girls use to signify disapproval. It was deliberately comic—but I didn't feel like laughing.

"I'm sorry," I said. "I know you mean well. But children—they pick these things up. It starts as a game, then it gets out of hand."

"Is that what happened? Did it get out of hand?"

"I don't want to talk about it, Zozie."

She sat down beside me. "Come on, Vianne. It can't be so bad. You can tell me."

And now I could *see* the Kindly Ones; their faces; their grasping hands. I could see them behind Zozie's face, hear their voices, coaxing, reasonable and so very *kind*—

"I'll manage," I said. "I always do."

Oh, you liar.

Roux's voice again, so clear that I almost looked for him. There are too many ghosts in this place, I thought. Too many rumors of other-when, other-where, and worst of all, what-else-might-have-been.

Go away, I told him silently. *I'm someone else now. Leave me be.*

"I'll manage," I repeated, with the ghost of a smile.

"Well, if ever you need me . . ."

I nodded. "I'll ask."

Monday, 26 November

SUZANNE WASN'T IN SCHOOL AGAIN TODAY. SHE'S SUPPOSED TO HAVE FLU, but Chantal says it's because of her hair. Not that Chantal talks to me much, but since I made friends with Jean-Loup, she's been nastier than ever, if that's at all possible.

She talks *about* me all the time. My hair, my clothes, my habits. Today I wore my new shoes (plain, quite nice, but *not* Zozie), and she went on about them all day, asking me where I'd bought them, and how much they'd cost, and sniggering (hers are from someplace along the Champs-Elysées, and I don't believe even her mother would have paid that much), and asking where I had my hair cut, and how much *that* cost, and sniggering again—

I mean, what's the point? I asked Jean-Loup, and he said she must be very insecure. Well, perhaps that's true. But it's been nothing but trouble since last week. Books going missing from out of my desk; my schoolbag knocked over and my things "accidentally" kicked all over the floor. People I've always rather liked suddenly don't want to sit next to me anymore. And yesterday I saw Sophie and Lucie playing a stupid game with my chair, pretending there were bugs on it, trying to sit as far away from where I'd been sitting as possible, as if there was something disgusting there.

And then we had basketball, and I hung all my clothes in the locker room as usual, and when I got there afterward, someone had taken my new shoes, and I looked for them all over the place until at last Faridah pointed them out, all scuffed and dusty behind the radiator, and although I couldn't *prove* it was Chantal, I knew.

I just knew.

Then she started on the chocolate shop.

"I hear it's very nice," she said. That snigger of hers, as if *nice* were some kind of secret code word that only she and her friends could understand. "What's it called?"

I didn't want to say, but I did.

"Ooooo—*nice*," said Chantal, and they sniggered again, that little group of friends she has: Lucie and Danielle and the other hangers-on, like Sandrine, who used to be really nice to me but who only talks to me now when Chantal isn't around.

All of them look a bit like her now; as if being Chantal could be something catching, like a glamorous kind of measles. All of them have the same ironed hair, cut into layers with a little flick at the very ends. All of them wear the same scent (this week it's Angel), and the same shade of pearly pink lipstick. I'll die if they turn up at the shop. I know I will. I'll actually *die*. To have them staring and giggling at me, at Rosette, at Maman with her arms gloved in chocolate to the elbow and that hopeful look—*are these your friends?*

Yesterday, I told Zozie.

"Well, you know what to do. It's the only way, Nanou; you have to confront them. You have to fight back."

I knew she'd say that. Zozie's a fighter. But there are some things you can't do just with attitude. Of course, I know I look a lot better since we talked. Most of it's about standing up straight and practicing that killer smile; but I wear what I like now, rather than what Maman thinks I ought to wear, and although I stand out from the others more, I feel so much better, so much more *me*.

"Well, that's OK as far as it goes. But sometimes, Nanou, it's not enough. I learned that in school. You have to show them once and for all. If they use dirty tricks, then—you'll just have to do the same."

If only I could. "Hide her shoes, you mean?"

Zozie gave me one of her looks. "No, I do *not* mean hide her shoes!"

"Then what?"

"*You* know, Annie. You've done it before."

I thought of that time at the bus queue, and Suze and her hair, and what I'd said—

That wasn't me. I didn't do that.

But then I remembered Lansquenet, and all the games we used to play; and Rosette's Accidents; and Pantoufle; and what Zozie did in the English tea shop; and the colors; and that little village by the Loire, with the little school, and the war memorial, and the sandbanks on the river, and the fishermen, and the café with the nice old couple, and—*what* was its name?

Les Laveuses, whispered the shadow-voice in my mind.

"Les Laveuses," I said.

"Nanou, what's wrong?"

I felt suddenly dizzy, all at once. I sat down on a chair—printed all over with Rosette's little hands and Nico's big ones.

Zozie looked at me closely, her blue eyes narrowed and very bright.

"There's no such thing as magic," I said.

"But there is, Nanou."

I shook my head.

"You know there is."

And—just for a minute—I knew there was. It was exciting but somehow terrifying as well, like walking along a very narrow windy ledge along a cliff face, with the ocean milling and churning below and nothing but empty space between us.

I looked at her. "I can't," I said.

"Why not?"

I yelled: "It was an *accident*!" My eyes felt gritty; my heart was racing; and all the time that wind, that wind—

"OK, Nanou. It's fine." She put her arms around me, and I hid my hot face against her shoulder. "You don't have to do anything you don't want to do. I'll look after you. It's going to be cool."

And it was so good, lying against her shoulder with my eyes closed and the smell of chocolate all around us that for a while I really believed her—that things would be cool, that Chantal and Co. would leave me alone, and that with Zozie around, nothing too bad would ever happen.

———✺———

I suppose I knew they'd turn up one day. Maybe Suze told them where to find me—or maybe I did it myself, in the days when I thought it might help me make friends. All the same, it was a kind of shock. To see them all in there like that—they must have come by Métro, *raced* up the Butte to beat me to it, and—

"Hey, Annie!" It was Nico, just leaving, with Alice at his side. "It's quite a little party in there—some friends of yours from school, I think."

I noticed he was looking a bit red. He's big, of course, and too much exercise leaves him breathless, but that was when I started to feel uneasy; that redness in his colors as well as on his face told me something bad was about to happen.

I nearly turned round there and then. It had been a rotten day: Jean-Loup had to go home at lunchtime—some kind of doctor's appointment, I think—and to make it worse, Chantal had been getting at me all day, sneering at me and saying *where's your boyfriend?* and talking about money, and all the things she was getting for Christmas.

Perhaps it was her idea to come. In any case, there she was, waiting for me when I got home. There they all were—Lucie, Danielle, Chantal, and Sandrine—sitting down with four Cokes in front of them and giggling like maniacs.

I had to go in. There was nowhere to hide, and besides, what kind of person runs away? I muttered *I'm fabulous* under my breath, but to tell you the truth, I didn't feel fabulous at all; just tired, dry mouthed, and a bit sick. I wanted to sit in front of the television, watch some silly kids' thing with Rosette, maybe read a book—

Chantal was talking as I came in. "Did you *see* the size of *him?*" she was saying in a high voice. "Like a *truck*—"

She pretended to look surprised when I came in. As if.

"Oooh, Annie. Was that your *boyfriend?*"

Sniggers all round.

"Oooh, *nice.*"

I shrugged. "He's a friend."

Zozie was sitting behind the counter, pretending not to listen. She glanced at Chantal, then flicked me a questioning look with her eyes—*Is this the one?*

I nodded, relieved. I don't know what I expected her to do—send them packing, maybe, or make them spill their drinks, as she had with the waitress in the English tea shop, or just tell them *go away*—

And so I was astonished when, instead of staying to help, she just got up and said, "You sit and talk to your friends. I'll be in the back if you want me. Have a lovely time. OK?"

And with that she left me—with a grin and a wink, as if she thought being thrown to the wolves was my idea of a lovely time.

Tuesday, 27 November

STRANGE, THAT RELUCTANCE TO ACKNOWLEDGE HER SKILLS. YOU WOULD have thought that a child like her would have given anything to be what she is. And that use of the word *accident* . . .

Vianne uses it too, referring to things unwanted or unexplained. As if there were any such thing in our world, where everything is linked to everything else, everything *touching* in small mystic ways, like skeins of silk in a tapestry. Nothing is ever an accident; nobody is ever lost. And we special ones—the ones who can *see*—moving through life collecting the threads, bringing them together, weaving little deliberate patterns of our own in the borders of the big picture—

How fabulous is that, Nanou? How fabulous, and subversive, and beautiful, and grand? Don't you want to be a part of it? To find your own destiny in that tangle of threads—and to shape it—*not* by accident, but by *design*?

She found me in the kitchen five minutes later. By then she was pale with suppressed rage. I know how it feels, that sick-to-the-stomach, sick-to-the-soul, lurching sense of helplessness.

"You have to make them go," she said. "I don't want them here when Maman gets back."

What she meant was *I don't want to give them any more ammunition.*

I looked sympathetic. "They're customers. What can I do?"

She looked at me.

"I mean it," I said. "They're your friends."

"They're *not!*"

"Oh. Then—" I pretended to hesitate. "Then it wouldn't be so much of an Accident if you and I—*interfered* a little."

Her colors flared at the very thought. "Maman says it's dangerous. . . ."

"Maman has her reasons, perhaps."

"What reasons?"

I shrugged. "Well, Nanou, adults sometimes withhold knowledge from their kids when they're trying to protect them. And sometimes they're not so much protecting the child as protecting themselves from the consequences of that knowledge. . . ."

She looked puzzled at that. "You think she lied to me?" she said.

It was a risk, I knew that. But I've taken my fair share of risks—and besides, she *wants* to be seduced. It's the rebel in the soul of every good child; the desire to flaunt authority; to overthrow those little gods that call themselves our parents.

Annie sighed. "You don't understand."

"Oh, yes I do. You're scared," I said. "You're scared of being different. You think it makes you stand out."

She thought about that for a while.

"That's not it," she said at last.

"Then *what*?" I said.

She looked at me. Behind the door to the shop I could hear the glassy, squealing voices of teenage girls up to no good.

I gave her my most sympathetic smile. "You know, they're never going to leave you alone. They know where you are now. They could come back anytime. They've already had a go at Nico—"

I saw her flinch. I know how much she likes him.

"Do you want them back here every night? Sitting there, laughing at you?"

"Maman would make them go away," she said, though she didn't sound too sure.

"And then what?" I said. "I've seen it happen. It happened to my mother and me. First the small things, the things we thought we could cope with— the practical jokes, the shoplifting, the graffiti on the shutters at night. You can live with those things if you have to, you know. It isn't nice, but you can live with them. But it never stops there. They never give up. Dog shit on the doorstep; odd phone calls in the middle of the night; stones through the windows; and then one day, it's petrol through the letter box and everything goes up in smoke. . . ."

I should know. It nearly happened. An occult bookshop attracts attention, especially when it's out of the city center. Letters to the local press; leaflets condemning Hallowe'en; even a small demonstration outside the shop, with handwritten placards and half a dozen right-thinking members of the parish campaigning like mad to close us down.

"Didn't that happen in Lansquenet?"

"Lansquenet was different."

Her eyes flickered toward the door. I could feel her working it out in her mind. It was close, I could feel it, like static in the air—

"Do it," I said.

She looked at me.

"Do it. I promise there's nothing to be afraid of."

Her eyes were bright. "Maman says—"

"Parents don't know everything. And sooner or later you're going to have to learn to look after yourself. Go on. Don't be a victim, Nanou. Don't let them make you run away."

She thought about that, but I could tell my words had not yet struck home.

"There's worse things than running away," she said.

"Is that what your mother says? Is that why she changed her name? Is that why she's made you so scared? Why won't you tell me what happened in Les Laveuses?"

That struck closer. But not close enough. Her face took on the stubborn, self-contained look that adolescent girls do so well; the look that says, *you can talk and talk*—

So I gave her a nudge. Just a little one. Made my colors iridesce; reached for the secret, whatever it was—

And then I saw it—but fleetingly—a series of pictures like smoke on water.

Water. That's it. A river, I thought. *And a silver cat, a little cat charm*—both of them lit with a Hallowe'en light. I reached again, almost touching it now—then—

BAM!

It was like leaning against an electrified fence. A jolt went through me, knocking me back. The smoke dispersed; the image broke up; every nerve in my body seemed to jangle with electricity. I sensed that it was quite unplanned—a release of pent-up energy like that of a child stamping its foot—but if I'd had even half that power when I was her age. . . .

Annie was looking at me, fists clenched.

I smiled at her. "You're good," I said.

She shook her head.

"Oh, yes you are. You're very good. Maybe better than me. A gift—"

"Yeah, right." She spoke in a low, tense voice. "Some gift. I'd rather be good at dancing, or watercolors." A thought occurred to her, and she flinched. "You won't tell Maman?"

"Why should I?" I said. "What? You think you're the only one who can keep a secret?"

She studied my face for a long time.

Outside, I heard the wind chimes ring.

"They've gone," said Annie.

She was right; looking inside, I could see that the girls were gone, leaving only their scattered chairs, their half-empty Coke cans, and a faint aroma of bubble gum and hair spray and the biscuity scent of teenage sweat.

"They'll be back," I said softly.

"They might not," said Annie.

"Well, if you need help . . ."

"I'll ask," she said.

*A*sk, *ask.* What am I, a fairy godmother?

I searched for Les Laveuses, of course, starting with the Internet, and got nothing; not even a tourist information site, not the slightest reference to a festival or a chocolate shop. Looking further, a single mention of a local *crêperie*, quoted in a food magazine. The owner, a widow: Françoise Simon.

Could *she* have been Vianne under another name? It's possible; though there is no mention in the piece of the woman herself. But a phone call later, and the thread has already run out. Françoise herself answers the phone. Her voice on the phone is dry and suspicious; the voice of a woman in her seventies. I tell her I am a journalist. She tells me that she has never heard of Vianne Rocher. Yanne Charbonneau? Likewise. Good-bye.

Les Laveuses is a tiny place, barely a village, I understand. It has a church, a couple of shops, the *crêperie*, the café, the war memorial. The land around is mostly farmland: sunflowers, maize, and fruit trees. The river runs beside it like a long brown dog. A nothing place, or so you'd think—yet there's something about it that resonates. Some gleam of memory—some squib in the news . . .

I went to the library; asked for the archives. They have every issue of *Ouest France*, stored on disk and microfilm. I began last night, at six o'clock. Searched for two hours, then went to work. Tomorrow I'll do the same— and again—until I find whatever it is. That place is the key—Les Laveuses, by the Loire. And once I have it, who knows what secrets that key may unlock?

My mind keeps going back to Annie. *I'll ask*, she promised me last night. But to ask for help, there must be a need—a genuine need far beyond the petty annoyances of the Lycée Jules Renard. Something to throw caution to the wind and to send both of them running into the arms of their good friend Zozie.

I know what they fear.

But what do they *need*?

This afternoon, alone in the shop while Vianne took Rosette for a walk, I went upstairs to explore her things. Delicately, you understand—my object is not simple theft but something infinitely more far-reaching. As it turns out, she doesn't have much: a wardrobe more elementary than my own; a framed picture on the wall (probably bought from the *marché aux puces*); a patchwork bedspread (I'd guess homemade); three pairs of shoes—all black, how dull is that? And finally, under the bed, gold: a wooden box the size of a shoe box, filled with assorted junk.

Not that Vianne Rocher would think it so. I'm used to living out of boxes and bags; and I know that these people gather no moss. The things inside the wooden box are the jigsaw pieces of her life; things she could never leave behind; her past, her life, her secret heart.

I opened it with the greatest of care. Vianne is secretive, which makes her suspicious. She'll know the precise arrangement of every piece of paper, every object, every thread, every scrap, every particle of dust. She'll know if something has been disturbed; but I have an excellent visual memory, and I do not mean to disturb anything.

Out they come, one by one. Vianne Rocher in abridgment. First, a set of Tarot cards—nothing special, just the Marseille pack, but clearly well used and yellowed with age.

Underneath, there are documents—passports in the name of Vianne Rocher and a birth certificate for Anouk of the same surname. So Anouk has become Annie, I thought; as Vianne became Yanne. No papers for Rosette, which is odd, but an out-of-date passport in the name of Jeanne Rocher, that I guess may have belonged to Vianne's mother. From her photograph I can see that she doesn't look a lot like Vianne—but then, Anouk doesn't look much like Rosette. A piece of faded ribbon, on which hangs a lucky charm in the shape of a cat. A couple of photographs come next—barely a dozen in all. In them I recognize a younger Anouk; a younger Vianne; a younger Jeanne in black-and-white. All carefully stored and secured with a ribbon, along with some rather old letters and a thin wedge of newspaper clippings. Carefully flicking through, cautious of yellowed edges and brittle folds, I recognize an account of the chocolate festival in Lansquenet-sous-Tannes, taken from a local paper. Much the same as what I have already seen, but the photograph is larger and shows Vianne with two other people—a man and a woman, she long-haired and wearing some kind of tartan coat, he smiling with discomfort in the camera's eye. Friends, perhaps? There are no names in the article.

Next, a clipping from a Paris newspaper, crisp and brown as a dead leaf.

I'm afraid to open it out, but I can already see that it concerns the disappearance of a young child, a Sylviane Caillou, snatched from her car seat more than thirty years ago. Next, a more recent clipping, an account of a freak tornado in Les Laveuses, a tiny village on the Loire. Strangely trivial things, you might think, but important enough to Vianne Rocher for her to bring them with her all this way, over so many years, and to hide them in this little box—untouched for some time, or so I'd guess from the layer of dust. . . .

So these are your ghosts, Vianne Rocher. Strange, how very modest they seem. My own are more impressive; but then again, I find that modesty is a very second-rate virtue. You could have done so much better, Vianne. With my help, perhaps you still can.

I sat at my laptop for hours last night, drinking coffee, watching the neon lights from outside and going over the question again and again. Nothing more on Les Laveuses; nothing more on Lansquenet. I was beginning to believe Vianne Rocher as elusive a creature as myself, a castaway on the rock of Montmartre; without a past; impregnable.

Absurd, of course. Nothing's impregnable. But with all the direct lines of enquiry exhausted, only one avenue remained, and this was what kept me wondering until late into the night.

It's not that I was afraid, of course. But these things can be so unreliable, raising more questions than they answer—and if Vianne suspected what I'd done, then any chance I had of getting close to her was gone.

Still, taking risks is part of the game. It's been a long time since I did any scrying—my System relies more on practical methods than bell, book, and candle, and nine times out of ten you get quicker results from the Internet. But this is a time for creativity.

A dose of cactus root, dried and powdered and infused in hot water, helps to achieve the required state of mind. This is pulque, the divine intoxicant of the Aztecs, reinvented a little for my own purpose. Then comes the sign of the Smoking Mirror, scrawled on the dusty floor at my feet. I sit down cross-legged with my laptop in front of me, turn on the screen saver to a suitably abstract theme, and wait for illumination.

My mother certainly wouldn't have approved. She always favored the traditional crystal ball in divination, though at a pinch she would accept the cheaper alternatives—magic mirrors or Tarot cards. Then again, she would—she stocked the things, after all—and if she ever experienced a genuine revelation from any of them, then I certainly never heard anything about it.

There are a number of popular myths about scrying. One is that you need special apparatus. You don't. Just closing your eyes can be enough; although I rather like the images that come from watching a television set between stations, or the fractal patterns of my computer's screen saver. It's just a system like any other; a means of keeping the analytical left brain occupied with trivia, while the creative right brain looks for clues.

Then—

Just drift.

It's a rather pleasant sensation, enhanced as the drug begins to take. It starts as a faint sense of dislocation; the air yawns around me, and although I do not avert my gaze from the screen I am aware that the room feels much larger than usual, the walls receding into the middle distance and booming, ballooning—

Breathing deeply, I think of Vianne.

Her face on the screen in front of me; sepia, like newsprint. Around me, a circle of lights, glimpsed out of the corner of my eye. They draw me in, like fireflies.

What's your secret, Vianne?

What's your secret, Anouk?

What do you need?

The Smoking Mirror seems to shimmer. Perhaps this is the effect of the drug; a visual metaphor made real. A face appears on the screen ahead: Anouk, as clear as a photograph. Then Rosette, a paintbrush in hand. A faded postcard of the Rhône. A silver bangle, far too small for an adult to wear, with a dangling charm in the shape of a cat.

Now there comes a rush of air; a smash of applause; a swooping of invisible wings. I feel very close to something important. And now I can see it—the hull of a boat. A long, low boat, slow as they come. And a line of script, carelessly scrawled—

Who? I ask. Who, damn it?

No answer from the luminous screen. Only the sound of water, the *hisshhh* and hum of engines under the waterline, resolving slowly back into the dim whine of the laptop, the scroll of the screen saver, the incipient headache.

Double, double, toil and trouble—

As I said, as a method, it's often unsound.

And yet, I have learned something, I think. Someone's coming. Someone's getting closer. Someone from the past. Someone who means trouble.

One more strike should do it, Vianne. One more weakness to identify. Then the piñata will release its contents, and its treasures and secrets, Vianne Rocher's life—not to mention that very talented child—will finally belong to me.

8

Wednesday, 28 November

THE FIRST LIFE I STOLE BELONGED TO MY MOTHER. YOU ALWAYS REMEM-
ber your first, you know, however inelegant the theft. Not that I thought of
it as theft at the time; but I needed to escape, and my mother's passport was
lying unused, and her savings were wasting away in the bank—

I was barely seventeen. I could look older—and frequently did—or
younger, if I needed to. People rarely see what they think they see. They see
only what we *want* them to see—beauty, age, youth, wit, even forgettability,
when the need arises—and I'd practiced the art almost to perfection.

I took the hovercraft to France. They hardly glanced at my stolen passport. I'd planned it that way. A dab of makeup, a change of hairstyle, and
a coat belonging to my mother completed the illusion. The rest was all in
the mind, as they say.

Of course in those days, security was lax. I crossed over with nothing
of my own but a coffin and a pair of shoes—the first two charms on my
bracelet—and found myself on the other side, speaking hardly any French,
with no money but the six thousand pounds I'd managed to remove from
my mother's account.

I approached it as a challenge. I found myself a job in a small textiles
factory on the outskirts of Paris. I shared a room with a coworker: Martine Matthieu, from Ghana, aged twenty-four and awaiting her six-months'
work permit. I told her I was twenty-two; that I was Portuguese. She believed me—or I thought she did. She was friendly; I was alone. I trusted
her. I dropped my guard. That was the one mistake I made. Martine

was curious; went through my things and discovered my mother's documents, hidden in my bottom drawer. I don't know why I'd kept them at all. Carelessness, perhaps; or laziness, or some misplaced sense of nostalgia. I certainly hadn't meant to use that identity again. It was too closely linked to St. Michael's-on-the-Green—and it was my bad luck that Martine remembered it from some newspaper she'd read, and linked the photograph with me.

I was young, you understand. The very threat of the police was enough to send me into a panic. Martine knew it—and exploited the fact, to the tune of half my salary per week. It was extortion, pure and simple. I endured it—what else could I have done?

Well, I could have run away, I suppose. But even then I was stubborn. And most of all, I wanted revenge. So I paid Martine her weekly dues; was docile and cowed; bore her tempers; made her bed; cooked her dinner; and generally bided my time. Then when her papers came through at last, I called in sick to work and, in her absence, cleared the flat of everything that might be of use to me (including money, passport, and ID), before reporting her, the sweatshop (and my other coworkers) to the Immigration Services.

Martine gave me my third charm. A silver pendant in the shape of a solar disc, which I easily adapted to my bracelet. By then I had the beginnings of a collection, and for every life I've collected since, I've added a new ornament. It's a small vanity that I allow myself—a reminder of how far I've come.

I burned my mother's passport, of course. Quite apart from the unpleasant memories it brought back, it was far too incriminating for me to do otherwise. But that was my first recorded success, and if it taught me one thing, it's this. There's no room for nostalgia when lives are at stake.

Since then, their ghosts have pursued me in vain. Spirits can only move in straight lines (or so the Chinese believe), and the Butte de Montmartre is an ideal refuge, with its steps and stairways and little winding streets, through which no phantom could find its way.

At least, that's what I'm hoping. Once again last night's evening paper showed a picture of Françoise Lavery. The picture was enhanced, perhaps;

in any case it looks less grainy, although it still bears little resemblance to Zozie de l'Alba.

Enquiries, however, have since revealed that the "real" Françoise died some time last year, in circumstances that now seem suspicious. Clinically depressed after her boyfriend left her, she died of an overdose that was judged accidental, but which may of course have been otherwise. Her flatmate, a girl by the name of Mercedes Desmoines, vanished soon after Françoise's death, but she'd been gone for quite a long time before anyone suspected foul play.

Well, you know. There's no helping some people. And really, I'd thought better of her. Those mousy types can often show unexpected inner strength—though not in her case. Poor Françoise.

Still, I don't miss her. I like being Zozie. Everyone likes Zozie, of course—she is so much *herself*, you see—she doesn't care what anyone thinks. So different from Miss Lavery that you could sit next to her on the Métro and never even see a hint of resemblance.

Still, just to be sure, I've dyed my hair. Black hair suits me, anyway. It makes me look French—or perhaps Italian—gives my skin a pearly quality and emphasizes the color of my eyes. It's a good look for who I am now—and it doesn't hurt that men like it too.

Passing the artists huddled beneath their umbrellas on the rainy Place du Tertre, I waved at Jean-Louis, who greeted me in his usual style.

"Hey, it's you!"

"You never give up, do you?" I said.

He grinned. "Would you? You're gorgeous today. How about a quick profile? It'd look nice on the wall of your chocolate shop."

I laughed. "Well, for one, it isn't my shop. And for another—I might just consider sitting for you—but only if you try my hot chocolate."

Well, that was that, as Anouk might say. Another victory for the *chocolaterie*. Jean-Louis and Paupaul both came in, bought chocolate, and stayed for an hour, during which time Jean-Louis had not only finished my portrait, but also two more—one of a young woman who came in to buy truffles and quickly succumbed to his blandishments, the second a portrait of Alice, commissioned on impulse by Nico, dropping in for his usual.

"Any room for an artist in residence?" said Jean-Louis as he stood up to leave. "This place is amazing. It's changed so much."

I smiled. "I'm glad you like it, Jean-Louis. I hope everyone feels the same."

Well, of course, I haven't forgotten that Thierry comes back from his trip on Saturday. I'm afraid he'll find things very different—poor, romantic Thierry, with his money and his quaint ideas about women.

It's the orphan quality in Vianne that first attracted him, you know; the brave young widow fighting alone. Fighting, but not successfully; spirited, but ultimately vulnerable, Cinderella waiting for her prince to come.

That's what he loves about her, of course. He fantasizes about rescuing her—from what, exactly? Does he know? Not that he would ever say so, or admit it, even to himself. It's there in his colors: a supreme self-confidence—a good-natured but unshakable belief in the combined power of his money and his charm—that Vianne mistakes for humility.

I wonder what he'll make of it, now that her *chocolaterie* is a success?

I hope he won't be disappointed.

Saturday, 1 December

I'VE SEEN 100 FIREPLACES, BUT NOT 1 OF THEM HAS
WARMED MY HEART.
COULD IT B THAT I'M MISSING U?
SEE YOU TOMORROW,
LOVE, T XX

It's raining today; a fine ghostly rain turning to mist on the skirts of the Butte, but Le Rocher de Montmartre looks almost fairylike, gleaming out from the still, wet streets. Sales today surpassed all expectations, topping a dozen customers in a single morning, most of them occasionals, but with a few of our regulars as well.

It's happened so fast—barely a fortnight—and already the change is astonishing. Perhaps it's just the shop's new look; or the scent of melting chocolate; or the window display that catches the eye.

In any case, our clientele has multiplied, bringing in locals and tourists alike, and what began as an exercise to keep myself in practice is starting to become a serious occupation as Zozie and I try to meet the growing demand for my range of handmade chocolates.

We made close to forty boxes today. Fifteen of truffles (still selling well), but also a batch of coconut squares, some sour cherry gobstoppers, some bitter-coated orange peel, some violet creams, and a hundred or so *lunes de miel*, those little discs of chocolate made to look like the waxing moon, with her profile etched in white against the dark face.

It's such a delight to choose a box, to linger over the shape—will it be heart shaped, round, or square? To select the chocolates with care; to see them nestled between the folds of crunchy mulberry-colored paper; to smell the mingled perfumes of cream, caramel, vanilla, and dark rum; to choose a ribbon; to pick out a wrapping; to add flowers or paper hearts; to hear the silky *whisssh* of rice paper against the lid—

I've missed it so much since Rosette was born. The heat of the copper on the stove. The scent of melting *couverture*. The ceramic molds, their shapes as familiar and well loved as a family's Christmas ornaments, passed down over generations. This star; this square; this circle. Each object has significance; each action, so many times repeated, contains a world of memories.

I have no photographs. No albums, no keepsakes, except for the few things in my mother's box: the cards, some papers, the little cat charm. My memories are kept elsewhere. I can remember every scar, every scratch on a wooden spoon or a copper pan. This flat-sided spoon is my favorite; Roux carved it from a single piece of wood, and it fits my hand perfectly. This red spatula—it's only plastic, but I've had it since I was a child—was a gift from a greengrocer in Prague; this small enamel pan with the chipped rim is the one I always used for Anouk's hot chocolate, in the days when we could no more have forgotten that twice-daily ritual than curé Reynaud could have missed communion.

The slab that I use for tempering is cross-hatched with tiny blemishes. I can read them better than the lines on my own hand, although I refrain from doing so. I'd rather not see the future there. The present is already more than enough.

"Is there a *chocolatière* in the house?"

Thierry's voice is unmistakable; big, bluff, and friendly. I heard him from the kitchen (I was making liqueurs, the most awkward of my chocolates to make). A jangle of bells; a stamping of feet—a silence as he looked around.

I came out of the kitchen, wiping melted chocolate on my apron.

"Thierry!" I said and gave him a hug, hands splayed out to spare his suit.

He grinned. "My God. You've really made some changes to this place."

"Do you like it?"

"It's—different." I may have imagined the trace of dismay in his voice as he took in the bright walls, the stenciled shapes, the fingerpainted furniture, the old stuffed armchairs, the chocolate pot and cups on the three-legged table, and the window display with Zozie's red shoes among the mountains of candied treasure. "It looks—" He broke off, and I caught the arc of his gaze, that little flick toward my hand. His mouth tightened a little, I thought, as it does when he doesn't like something. But his voice was warm as he said, "It looks terrific. You've worked wonders in this place."

"Chocolate?" said Zozie, pouring a cup.

"I—no—well, OK then, just the one."

She handed him an espresso cup, with one of my truffles on the side. "It's one of our specials," she told him, smiling.

He looked round once more at the piled boxes, glass dishes, fondants, ribbons, rosettes, cracknels, violet creams, *mocha blanc*, dark rum truffle, chilli squares, lemon parfait, and coffee cake on the countertop with an expression of slightly blank amazement.

"You made all these?" he said at last.

"Don't look so surprised," I said.

"Well, for Christmas, I guess . . ." He frowned a little as he looked at the price tag on a box of chilli chocolate squares. "People really do buy them, then?"

"All the time," I said with a smile.

"Must have cost you a fortune," he said. "All this painting and decorating."

"We did it ourselves. All of us."

"Well, that's great. You've worked so hard." He tried his chocolate, and once more I saw his mouth tighten.

"You know, you don't have to drink it if you don't like it," I said, trying not to sound impatient. "I can make you a coffee if you'd prefer."

"No, this is great." He sipped it again. He's a terrible liar. His transparency should please me, I know; but instead it gives me a twitch of unease.

He is so vulnerable beneath his self-assurance, so unaware of the ways of the wind. "I'm just surprised, that's all," he said. "Everything seems to have changed practically overnight."

"Not everything," I said, smiling.

I noticed Thierry didn't smile back.

"How was London? What did you do?"

"I went to see Sarah. Told her about the wedding. Missed you like crazy."

I smiled at that. "And Alan? Your son?"

That made him smile. He always does when I mention his son, although he rarely speaks of him. I've often wondered how well they get on—that smile is a little too broad, perhaps—but if Alan is anything like his father, then it's quite possible that their personalities are too similar to make them friends.

I noticed he wasn't eating his truffle.

He looked slightly abashed when I pointed it out. "You know me, Yanne. Sweets aren't my thing." And he gave me that big, brash smile again—the one he gives when he speaks of his son. It's really quite funny when you think about it—Thierry's sweet tooth is quite pronounced, but he feels slightly ashamed of it, as if admitting to a taste for milk chocolate places his manliness in doubt. But my truffles are too dark, too rich, and their bitterness is strange to him—

I handed him a milk chocolate square.

"Go on," I said. "I can read your mind."

But just at that moment Anouk came in from the rainy street, all tousled and smelling of wet leaves, with a paper twist of hot chestnuts in one hand. For the past few days, there has been a vendor selling them in front of the Sacré-Coeur, and Anouk has taken to buying a packet every time she passes by. Today, she was in high spirits, looking like a stray Christmas bauble in her red coat and green trousers, with her curly hair all spangled with rain.

"Hey there, *jeune fille!*" said Thierry. "Where have you been? You're soaking wet!"

Anouk gave him one of her grown-up looks. "I've been to the cemetery with Jean-Loup. And I'm not soaking. This is an anorak. It keeps out the rain."

Thierry laughed. "The necropolis. You know what *necropolis* means, Annie?"

"Of course I do. City of the dead." Anouk's vocabulary—always good— has improved with proximity to Jean-Loup Rimbault.

Thierry made a comic face. "Isn't that rather a gloomy spot to hang out with your friends?"

"Jean-Loup was taking photographs of the cemetery cats."

"Really?" he said. "Well, if you can bear to drag yourself away, then I've booked a table for lunch at La Maison Rose—"

"Lunch? But the shop—"

"I'll hold the fort," said Zozie. "You enjoy your afternoon."

"Annie? Are you ready?" said Thierry.

I saw Anouk give him a look. Not quite of contempt—though perhaps of resentment. That doesn't surprise me very much—Thierry, though well meaning, has a rather old-fashioned attitude toward children, and Anouk must sense that some of her habits—running about with Jean-Loup in the rain, spending hours in the old cemetery (where tramps and undesirables congregate), or playing noisy games with Rosette—do not meet entirely with his approval.

"Perhaps you should wear a dress," he said.

The look of resentment intensified. "I like my clothes."

To tell the truth, so do I. In a city where elegant conformity is the primary rule, Anouk dares to be imaginative. Perhaps this is Zozie's influence; but the clashing colors she prefers and her recent habit of customizing her clothes—with a ribbon, a badge, a piece of braid—give everything of hers an exuberance I haven't seen since Lansquenet.

Perhaps this is what she's trying to recapture—a time when things were simpler. In Lansquenet, Anouk ran wild; played down by the river all day long; talked incessantly to Pantoufle; led pirate games and crocodile games and was always in disgrace at school.

But that was a very different world. Barring the river gypsies—disreputable, perhaps, even sometimes dishonest, but certainly not dangerous—there were no strangers in Lansquenet. No one bothered to lock their door; even the dogs were familiar.

"I don't like wearing a dress," she said.

Beside me I could sense Thierry's unvoiced disapproval. In Thierry's world, girls wear dresses—in fact, over the past six months he has bought several for both Anouk and Rosette, in the hope that I will take the hint.

Thierry was watching me, tight-mouthed. "You know, I'm not really hungry," I said. "Why don't we just go for a walk and grab something to eat from a café on the way? There's the Parc de la Turlure, or there's—"

"But I booked," said Thierry.

I couldn't help laughing at his expression. Everything in Thierry's world has to be done according to plan. There are rules for everything; schedules to be met; guidelines to be followed. A lunch table, booked, cannot be un-booked, and even though we both know that he is happiest in a place like Le P'tit Pinson, today he has chosen La Maison Rose, for which Anouk must wear a dress. That's the way he is, of course—rock solid, predictable, in control—but sometimes I wish he wasn't *quite* as inflexible, that he could find room for a little spontaneity—

"You're not wearing your ring," he said.

Instinctively I looked down at my hands. "It's the chocolate," I said. "It gets on everything."

"You and your chocolate," said Thierry.

It was not one of our most successful outings. Perhaps it was the sullen weather, or the crowds, or Anouk's lack of appetite, or Rosette's continuing refusal to use a spoon. Thierry's mouth tightened as he watched Rosette hand-arranging her peas into a spiral pattern on her plate.

"Manners, Rosette," he said at last.

Rosette ignored him, all her attention fixed on the pattern.

"Rosette," he said in a sharper tone.

Still she ignored him, although a woman at an adjoining table looked round at his tone of voice.

"It's all right, Thierry. You know what she's like. Just leave her alone, and—"

Thierry made a sound of exasperation. "My God, what is she, nearly four years old?" He turned to me, his eyes alight. "It isn't normal, Yanne," he said. "You'll have to face up to it. She needs help. I mean, *look* at her." He glared at Rosette, who was eating her peas one by one, using her fingers, and with a look of intense concentration.

He reached out across the table and grabbed Rosette's hand. She looked up at him, startled. "Here. Take the spoon. Hold it, Rosette." He forced the spoon into her hand. She dropped it. He picked it up again.

"Thierry—"

"No, Yanne, she has to learn."

Once more he tried to give Rosette the spoon. Rosette clenched her fingers into a small fist of denial.

"Look, Thierry." I was getting annoyed. "Let me decide what Rosette—"

"*Ouch!*" He broke off abruptly, pulling away his outstretched hand. "She bit me! The brat! She bit me!" he said.

From the edge of my field of vision, I thought I glimpsed a golden gleam; a beady eye; a curly tail—

Rosette fingered the sign for *come here*.

"Rosette, please don't—"

"Bam," said Rosette.

Oh no. Not now—

I stood up to leave. "Anouk, Rosette . . ." I looked at Thierry. Small bite marks stood out against his wrist. Panic bloomed in me like a rose. An Accident in the shop was one thing. But in public, with so many people there—

"I'm sorry," I said. "We have to go."

"But you haven't finished," said Thierry.

I saw him struggling between anger and outrage and the overwhelming need to keep us there, to prove to himself that it was all right, that the situation could be averted, that things could go back to the original plan.

"I can't," I said and picked up Rosette. "I'm sorry—I have to get out of here."

"Yanne," said Thierry, grabbing my arm, and my own rage—that he should dare to interfere with my child, with my life—dissolved as I saw the look in his eyes.

"I wanted it to be perfect," he said.

"It's all right," I told him. "It's not your fault."

He paid the bill and walked us home. At four o'clock, it was already dark, and the streetlights shone against the wet cobbles. We walked in near silence, Anouk holding Rosette's hand, both very careful to avoid the cracks. Thierry said nothing; his face set, his hands jammed deeply into his pockets.

"Please, Thierry. Don't be like this. Rosette missed her nap, and you know how she gets." In fact, I wonder if he does know. His son must be in his twenties now, and maybe he has forgotten what it's like to have a child: the tantrums; the tears; the noise; the fuss. Or maybe Sarah coped with all that, leaving Thierry to play the generous role: the football matches; the walks in the park; the pillow fights; the games.

"You've forgotten what it's like," I said. "It's hard for me to manage sometimes. And you make it worse when you get in the way—"

He turned to me then, his face pale and tense. "I haven't forgotten as much as you think. When Alan was born—" He stopped abruptly, and I could see him struggling for control.

I put my hand on his arm. "What's wrong?"

He shook his head. "Later," he said in a thick voice. "I'll tell you all about it later."

We had arrived in Place des Faux-Monnayeurs, and I paused on the threshold of Le Rocher de Montmartre, the newly painted sign creaking a little, and took a deep breath of the chilly air.

"I'm sorry, Thierry," I told him again.

He shrugged, a bear in his cashmere coat, but I thought his face had softened a little.

"I'll make it up to you," I said. "I'll cook you dinner, and we'll put Rosette to bed, and then we can talk about all this."

He sighed. "OK."

I opened the door.

And saw a man standing inside, a man in black standing very still, whose face was more familiar to me than my own and whose smile, rare and brilliant as summer lightning, was already beginning to fade from his lips. . . .

"Vianne," he said.

It was Roux.

PART FIVE

Advent

1

Saturday, 1 December

THE MOMENT HE WALKED INTO THE SHOP I KNEW HE WAS GOING TO BE my kind of trouble. Some people carry a charge, you know—you can see it in their colors, and his were the pale yellow-blue flare of a gas jet turned very low that could explode at any time.

Not that you'd know it to look at him. Nothing special, so you'd think. Paris swallows up a million just like him every year. Men in jeans and engineer boots; men who seem ill at ease in the city; men who take their wages in cash. I've been there often enough myself to recognize the type; and if he was there to buy chocolate, I thought, then I was the Virgin of Lourdes.

I was standing on a chair, hanging a picture. My portrait, in fact; the one that Jean-Louis drew of me. I heard him come in. A tinkle of bells; the sound of his boots on the parquet floor.

Then he said *Vianne*—and there was something in the tone of his voice that made me turn around. I looked at him. A man in jeans and a black T-shirt; red hair, tied back. As I said, nothing special.

But there was something about him, nevertheless, something that seemed familiar. And his smile was bright as the Champs-Elysées on Christmas Eve, making him extraordinary—but only for a moment, that dazzling smile dropping into a look of confusion as he realized his mistake.

"I'm sorry," he said. "I thought you were—" He stopped abruptly. "Are you the manager?" His voice was quiet, accented with the rolling *rs* and sharp vowels of the Midi.

"No, I just work here," I told him, smiling. "The manager's Madame Charbonneau. Do you know her?"

For a moment he seemed uncertain.

"Yanne Charbonneau," I prompted.

"Yeah. I know her."

"Well, she's out right now. But I'm sure she'll be back soon."

"All right. I'll wait." He sat down at a table, glancing around as he did so at the shop, the pictures, the chocolates—with pleasure, I thought, and some unease, as if unsure of his reception.

"And you are . . . ?" I said.

"Oh. Just a friend."

I smiled at him. "I meant your *name*."

"Oh." Now I was sure he looked ill at ease. Hands in his pockets to hide his discomfort, as if my presence had disrupted some plan too intricate for him to change.

"Roux," he said.

I thought of the postcard, signed *R*. Name or nickname? Probably the latter. *Heading north. I'll drop by if I can.*

And now I knew where I'd recognized him. I'd seen him last at Vianne Rocher's side, in a newspaper photo from Lansquenet-sous-Tannes.

"Roux?" I said. "From Lansquenet?"

He nodded.

"Annie talks about you all the time."

At that his colors lit up like a Christmas tree, and I began to understand what Vianne might see in a man like Roux. Thierry never lights up—unless it's one of his cigars—but then, Thierry has money, which makes up for most things.

"Relax, why don't you, and I'll make you some hot chocolate."

Now he grinned. "My favorite."

I made it strong, with brown sugar and rum. He drank it, then turned restless again, moving from one room to the other, looking around him at the pans, the jars, the dishes and spoons that make up Yanne's chocolate-making paraphernalia.

"You look just like her," he said at last.

"Really?"

As a matter of fact I look nothing like her; but then, I've noticed that most men rarely see exactly what's in front of them. A dash of perfume; long, loose hair; a scarlet skirt; and my high-heeled shoes—glamours so simple a child could see through them, but a man will be fooled every time.

"So—how long has it been since you last saw Yanne?"

He shrugged. "Too long."

"I know how it is. Here. Have a chocolate."

I put one by the side of his cup; a truffle, rolled in cocoa powder prepared to my own special recipe, and marked with the cactus sign of Xochipilli, the ecstatic god, always good for unleashing the tongue.

He didn't eat the chocolate but instead rolled it aimlessly around his saucer. It was a gesture I recognized somehow but couldn't quite identify. I waited for him to start talking—people generally do talk to me—but he seemed content to remain silent, fiddling with his uneaten truffle and watching the darkening street.

"Are you staying in Paris?" I said.

He shrugged. "Depends."

I looked at him enquiringly, but he didn't seem to take the hint. "Depends on what?" I said at last.

He shrugged again. "I get tired of places."

I poured him another demitasse. His reserve—a reserve that seemed closer to sullenness than anything else—was starting to annoy me. He'd been in the *chocolaterie* for nearly half an hour. Unless I'd lost the knack, I thought, I ought to have known everything there was to know about him by now. And yet, there he was—trouble incarnate, and seemingly impervious to all my advances.

I began to feel increasingly impatient. There was something associated with this man, something that I needed to know. I could feel it, so close that it raised the hairs on the back of my neck, and yet—

Think, damn it.

A river. A bangle. A silver cat charm. No, I thought. That wasn't quite right. A river. A boat. Anouk, Rosette—

"You haven't eaten your chocolate," I said. "You should try it, you know. It's one of our specials."

"Oh. Sorry." He picked it up. The cactus sign of Xochipilli gleamed invitingly between his fingers. He lifted the truffle to his mouth; paused a moment, frowning, perhaps at the acrid scent of the chocolate, the dark, woodsy perfume of seduction—

Try me.
Test me.
Taste—

And then, just then as he was almost mine, there came a sound of voices at the door.

He dropped the chocolate and stood up.

The wind chimes rang. The door opened.

"Vianne," said Roux.

And now it was she who just stood and stared, the color slipping from her face, her hands held out, as if to avert some terrible collision.

Behind her, Thierry stood bewildered, sensing perhaps that something was wrong but too self-absorbed to see the obvious. At her side, Rosette and Anouk, hand in hand, Rosette staring with fascination, Anouk's face suddenly alight—

And Roux—

Taking everything in—the man, the child, the look of dismay, the ring on her finger—and now I could see his colors again, fading, dwindling, going back to that gas-jet blue of something turned down to its lowest flame.

"Sorry," he said. "I was just passing through. You know. My boat . . ."

He isn't accustomed to lying, I thought. His pretense at lightness sounded forced, and his fists were clenched deep in his pockets.

Yanne just stared, her face a blank. No movement, no smile; just a mask, behind which I could glimpse the turbulence of her colors.

Anouk saved it. "Roux!" she yelled.

That broke the tension. Yanne stepped forward, the smile on her face now part fear, part fake, part something else that I didn't quite recognize.

"Thierry, this is an old friend." She was flushing now, quite prettily, and the pitch of her voice might well have been excitement at meeting an old acquaintance (though her colors told me otherwise), and her eyes were bright and anxious. "Roux, from Marseille—Thierry, my—hm—"

The unspoken word hung between them like a bomb.

"Pleased to meet you—Roux."

Another liar. Thierry's dislike of this man—this interloper—is immediate, irrational, and wholly instinctive. His overcompensation takes the form of a terrible heartiness not unlike that which he adopts toward Laurent Pinson. His voice booms like Santa Claus; his handshake cracks bone; in a moment he will be calling the stranger *mon pote.*

"So you're a friend of Yanne's, eh? Not in the same business, though?"

Roux shakes his head.

"No, of course not." Thierry grins, taking in the other man's youth and balancing it against everything he himself has to offer. The moment of jealousy subsides; I can see it in his colors, the blue-gray thread of envy taking on the burnished coppery hue of self-satisfaction.

"You'll have a drink, won't you, *mon pote?*"

There. You see. I told you so.

"How about a couple of beers? There's a café just down the road."

Roux shakes his head. "Just chocolate, thanks."

Thierry shrugs his cheery contempt. Pours chocolate—a gracious host—never taking his eyes from the interloper's face.

"So exactly what business are you in?"

"No business," says Roux.

"You do work, don't you?"

"I work," says Roux.

"In what?" says Thierry, grinning a little.

Roux shrugs. "Just work."

Thierry's amusement now knows no bounds. "And you're living on a boat, you say?"

Roux just nods. He smiles at Anouk—the only one here who seems genuinely happy to see him—while Rosette watches him in continued fascination.

And now I can see what I missed before. Rosette's small features are still unformed, but she has her father's coloring—his red hair, his green-gray eyes—as well as his troublesome temperament.

Nobody else seemed to notice, of course. Least of all the man himself. At a guess, I'd say that Rosette's physical and mental lack of development has led him to think that she is much younger than she really is.

"Staying long in Paris?" says Thierry. "Because some might say we've got enough boat people here already." He laughs again, a little too loudly.

Roux just looks at him, empty-faced.

"Still, if you're looking for a job round here, I could use some help doing up my flat. Rue de la Croix, down there . . ." He nods to indicate the direction. "Nice big flat, but it needs gutting—plastering—flooring—decorating—and I'm hoping to finish it all in the next three weeks, so that Yanne and the kids don't need to spend another Christmas in this place."

He puts a protective arm around Yanne, who shrugs it off in quiet dismay.

"You'll have gathered we're getting married, of course."

"Congratulations," says Roux.

"You married yourself?"

He shakes his head. Nothing in his face betrays the slightest emotion. A flicker in the eyes, perhaps, though his colors flame with unrestrained violence.

"Well, if you decide to try it," Thierry said, "just come and see me. I'll find you a house. You can get something surprisingly decent for half a million or so—"

"Listen," says Roux. "I have to go."

Anouk protests. "But you just got here!" She shoots an angry look at Thierry, who does not notice in the least. His dislike of Roux is visceral, rather than reasonable. No thought of the truth has crossed his mind, and yet he suspects the stranger of *something*—not because of anything he has said or done, but simply because he looks the type.

What type? Well, you know the look. It has nothing to do with his cheap clothes or his too-long hair, or his lack of social skills. There's just something about him; a left-handed look, like that of a man from the wrong side of the tracks. A man who might do anything: clone a credit card or set up a bank account using nothing but a stolen driver's license or acquire a birth certificate (maybe even a passport) on behalf of some person long deceased, or steal away a woman's child and vanish like the Pied Piper, leaving nothing but questions in his wake.

Like I said.

My kind of trouble.

Saturday, 1 December

OH, BOY. WELL, HELLO, STRANGER. STANDING THERE IN THE CHOCOLATE shop, just like he'd been away for an afternoon and not for four whole years of time; four years of birthdays and Christmases with hardly a word, never a visit and now—

"Roux!"

I wanted to be angry with him. I really did; but my voice wouldn't let me, somehow.

I shouted out his name, louder than I'd intended.

"Nanou," he said. "You're all grown-up."

There was a kind of sadness in the way he said it, as if he was sorry that I'd changed. But he was just the same old Roux—hair longer, boots cleaner, different clothes, but just the same, slouching with his hands in his pockets, the way he does when he doesn't want to be somewhere, but smiling at me to show that it wasn't my fault, and that if Thierry hadn't been there, he would have picked me up and swung me around, just like the old days in Lansquenet.

"I'm not," I said. "I'm eleven and a half."

"Eleven and a half sounds pretty grown-up to me. And who's the little stranger?"

"That's Rosette."

"Rosette," said Roux. He waved at her, but she didn't wave back, or sign anything. She rarely does with strangers; instead she just stared at him with those big cat's eyes until even Roux had to look away.

Thierry offered him chocolate. Roux always liked it, way back when. Drank it black, with sugar and rum, while Thierry talked to him about business, and London, and the *chocolaterie*, and the flat—

Oh yes. The flat. Turns out Thierry's fixing it up, making it nice for when we move in. He told us about it while Roux was there; how there'd be a new bedroom for me and Rosette, and new decorations, and how he wanted it all to be ready by Christmas, so that his girls would be comfortable—

But all the same there was something mean about the way he said it. He was smiling, you know, but not with his eyes; the way Chantal does when she's talking about her new iPod, or her new outfit, or her new shoes, or her Tiffany bracelet, and I'm just standing there listening.

Roux was there, looking as if he'd been hit.

"Listen," he said, when Thierry shut up. "I've got to go. I just wanted to see how you were, you know, just passing by on my way somewhere—"

Liar, I thought. *You cleaned your boots.*

"Where are you staying?"

"On a boat," he said.

Well, that makes sense. He's always liked boats. I remembered the one in Lansquenet; the one that was burned. I remember his face when it happened too; that look you get when you've worked hard for something you really care about, and then someone mean takes it all away.

"Where?" I said.

"On the river," said Roux.

"Well, *duh*," I said, which should have made him smile. And I realized then that I hadn't even kissed him, hadn't even hugged him since I arrived, and that made me feel bad, because if I did it now it would look like I'd just remembered and didn't really mean it at all.

Instead I took his hand. It was rough and scratchy from working.

I thought he looked surprised; then he smiled.

"I'd like to see your boat," I said.

"Maybe you will," said Roux.

"Is it as nice as the last one?"

"You'll have to decide that for yourself."

"When?"

He shrugged.

Maman looked at me in that way that she has when she's annoyed but won't say so because other people are around. "I'm sorry, Roux," she told him. "If you'd called before—I wasn't expecting . . ."

"I wrote," he said. "I sent a card."

"I never got it."

"Oh." I could tell he didn't believe her. And I knew she didn't believe him. Roux is the world's worst letter writer. He means to write but rarely does; and he doesn't like to talk on the phone. Instead, he sends little things in the post—a carved oak leaf on a string; a striped stone from the seaside; a book—sometimes with an accompanying note, but often with no word at all.

He looked at Thierry. "I've got to go."

Yeah, right. Like there was anywhere he had to be; Roux, who always pleases himself; who never lets anyone tell him what to do. "I'll be back."

Oh, you liar.

I was suddenly so angry with him that I almost spoke the words aloud. *Why did you come back, Roux? Why did you bother to come back at all?*

I told him so, but in my mind, in my shadow-voice, as hard as I could, the way I'd spoken to Zozie on that first day outside the *chocolaterie.*

Coward, I said. *You're running away.*

And Zozie heard. She looked at me. But Roux just stuck his hands even deeper into the pockets of his jeans and didn't even wave as he opened the door and walked away without looking back. Thierry went right after him—just like a dog chasing off an intruder. Not that Thierry would ever fight Roux—but even the thought of it made me want to cry.

Maman was going to go after them both, but Zozie stopped her. "I'll go," she said. "They'll be all right. You wait here with Annie and Rosette."

And off she went into the dark.

"Go upstairs, Nanou," said Maman. "I'll be with you right away."

And so we went upstairs, and waited. Rosette fell asleep, and in a while I heard Zozie come up, then Maman a few minutes later, walking very quietly so as not to disturb us. And after a while I went to sleep, but the sound of the creaky floorboard in Maman's room woke me up a couple of times, and I knew she was still awake in there, standing by the window in the dark, listening to the sound of the wind and hoping—*just once*—it would leave us alone.

Sunday, 2 December

THE CHRISTMAS LIGHTS WENT ON LAST NIGHT. NOW THE WHOLE QUAR-
tier is illuminated; not in colors, but in simple white, like a hedge of stars
over the city. In the Place du Tertre, where the artists stand, the traditional
Nativity scene has been erected, with the Christ child smiling in the straw
and the mother and father looking into the crib, and the Magi standing by
with gifts. It fascinates Rosette, who asks to see it again and again.

Baby, she signs. *Go see baby.* So far she has seen it twice with Nico; once
with Alice; countless times with Zozie; with Jean-Louis and Paupaul; and
of course, with Anouk, who seems almost as fascinated by it as she is, repeating the story to Rosette of how the baby (who has changed sex in Anouk's
version) was born in a stable in the snow, and how the animals came to see
her, and the three wise men, and how even a star stopped overhead—

"Because she was a special baby," Anouk says, to Rosette's delight. "A
special baby, just like you, and soon it'll be *your* birthday too. . . ."

Advent. Adventure. Both words suggest the coming of some extraordinary event. I'd never considered the similarity before; never celebrated the
Christian calendar; never fasted, repented, or confessed.

Almost never, anyway.

But when Anouk was little, we celebrated Yule: lit fires against the
coming dark; made wreaths of holly and mistletoe; drank spiced cider and
wassails and ate smoking-hot chestnuts from an open brazier.

Then Rosette was born, and things changed again. Gone were the
wreaths of mistletoe, the candles, and the frankincense. Nowadays we go

to church and buy more presents than we can afford, and leave them under the plastic tree, and watch TV, and get anxious about the cooking. The Christmas lights may *look* like stars, but closer inspection shows them to be fake: heavy garlands of wires and cables fix them across the narrow streets. The magic has gone—*and isn't that what you wanted, Vianne?* says that dry voice inside my head, the voice that sounds like my mother, like Roux, and now just a little like Zozie; who reminds me of the Vianne I was, and whose patience is a kind of reproach.

But this year again will be different. Thierry loves the traditional ways. The church, the goose, the chocolate log—a celebration, not only of the season, but also of the seasons we have shared together, and will continue to share—

No magic, of course. Well, is that so bad? There's comfort and safety and friendship—and love. Isn't that enough for us? Haven't we been down the other road? Brought up on folktales all my life, why do I find it so hard to believe in the happy-ever-after? Why is it, when I know where he leads, that I still dream of following the Pied Piper?

I sent Anouk and Rosette to bed. Then I went after Roux and Thierry. A small enough delay—three minutes, perhaps, or five at most—but as I stepped out into the still-crowded street I already half knew that Roux would be gone, vanished into the warren of Montmartre. All the same, I had to try. I started toward the Sacré-Coeur—and then among the groups of visitors and tourists I caught sight of Thierry's familiar figure walking down toward Place Dalida, hands in pockets, head thrust forward like a fighting cock's.

I held back, took a left up a cobbled street, and into Place du Tertre. Still no sign of Roux. He was gone. Of course he was—why would he stay?—and yet I lingered at the edge of the square, shivering (I'd forgotten my coat) and listening to the sounds of nighttime Montmartre: music from the clubs below the Butte, laughter, footsteps, children's voices from the Nativity scene across the square, a busker playing the saxophone, fragments of talk snatched on the wind—

It was his stillness that finally caught my attention. Parisians are like shoals of fish—if they stop moving, even for a moment, they die. But he was just standing there, half-hidden in the harlequin light of the red neon sign in a café window. Watching in silence, waiting for something. Waiting for me—

I ran across the square to him. Threw my arms around him and for a moment feared he would not respond. I could feel the tension in his body, see the crease between his brows—and in that harsh light he looked like a stranger.

And then he put his arms around me, reluctantly at first, I thought, then with a fierceness that belied his words. "You shouldn't be here, Vianne," he said.

There's a place in the curve of his left shoulder that matches my forehead perfectly. I found it again, and rested my head. He smelled of the night, and of engine oil, and cedarwood and patchouli and chocolate and tar and wool and the simple unique scent of *him*, something as elusive and familiar as a recurring dream.

"I know," I said.

And yet I couldn't let him go. A word would have done it; a warning; a frown. *I'm with Thierry now. Don't mess things up.* To try to suggest anything else would be pointless and painful and doomed from the start. And yet—

"It's good to see you, Vianne." His voice, though soft, was curiously charged.

I smiled. "You too. But why now? After all this time?"

A shrug from Roux conveys many things. Indifference, contempt, ignorance, even humor. In any case it dislodged my forehead from its cradle and brought me back to earth with a jolt.

"Would knowing make a difference?"

"It might."

He shrugged again. "No reason," he said. "Are you happy here?"

"Of course." It's all I've ever wanted. The shop; the house; schools for the children. The view from my window every day. And Thierry—

"It's just that I never imagined you here. I thought it was just a matter of time. That one day, you'd—"

"What? See sense? Give up? Live on the move, from day to day, from place to place, like you and the other river rats?"

"I'd rather be a rat than a bird in a cage."

He was getting angry, I thought. His voice was still soft, but his Midi accent had become more pronounced, as it often does when his temper is roused. It struck me that perhaps I *wanted* to make him angry, to force him into a confrontation that would leave neither of us with any choice. It hurt to think it, but perhaps it was true. And perhaps he sensed it too, because he looked at me then, and shot me a grin.

"What if I told you I'd changed?" he said.

"You haven't changed."

"You don't know that."

Oh, but I do. And it hurts my heart to see him so very much the same. But *I* have changed. My children have changed me. I can't just do what I want anymore. And what I want is—

"Roux," I said. "I'm happy to see you. I'm glad you came. But it's too late. I'm with Thierry. And he's really nice when you get to know him. He's done so much for Anouk and Rosette—"

"And do you love him?"

"Roux, please—"

"I said, do you love him?"

"Of course I do."

Again, that shrug of deliberate contempt. "Congratulations, Vianne," he said.

I let him go. What else could I do? He'll be back, I thought. He'll have to come back. But so far he hasn't; leaving nothing, not an address, not a phone number—though it would surprise me if Roux had a phone. As far as I know, he has never even had a television set, preferring to watch the sky, he says, a spectacle that never bores him and that never runs repeats.

I wonder where he's staying now. On a boat, he told Anouk. A barge, I thought, was the most likely, carrying cargo up the Seine. Or perhaps another riverboat, assuming he'd managed to find one cheap. A hulk, perhaps; a derelict; working on it between jobs, patching it up, making it his. Roux has endless patience with boats. With people, however—

"Will Roux be back today, Maman?" said Anouk over breakfast.

She'd waited until morning to speak. But then Anouk rarely speaks impulsively; she broods, she reflects, and then she speaks, in that solemn, rather guarded way, like a TV detective just getting to the truth.

"I don't know," I told her. "It's up to him."

"Would you *like* him to come back?" Persistence has always been one of Anouk's most enduring characteristics.

I sighed. "It's difficult."

"Why? Don't you like him anymore?" I heard the challenge in her voice.

"No, Anouk. That's not why."

"Then why is it?"

I almost laughed. She makes it all sound so very straightforward; as if our lives were not a house of cards; every decision, every choice carefully balanced against a multitude of other choices and decisions, precariously stacked against one another and leaning, tilting with every breath—

"Listen, Nanou. I know you like Roux. So do I. I like him a lot. But you have to remember—" I searched for the words. "Roux does what he wants, he always has. Never stays in the same place for long. And that's OK, because he's alone. But the three of us need more than that."

"If we lived with Roux, he wouldn't be alone," said Anouk reasonably.

I had to laugh, though my heart was aching. Roux and Anouk are so strangely alike. Both of them think in absolutes. Both stubborn, secretive, and frighteningly resentful.

I tried to explain. "He *likes* being alone. He lives on the river year-round, he sleeps outside, he's not even comfortable in a house. We couldn't live like that, Nanou. He knows that. And so do you."

She gave me a dark, appraising look. "Thierry hates him. I can tell."

Well, after last night, I don't suppose anyone could fail to see that. His booming, trollish cheeriness; his open contempt; his jealousy. But that's not Thierry, I told myself. Something must have upset him. The little scene at La Maison Rose?

"Thierry doesn't know him, Nou."

"Thierry doesn't know *any* of us."

She went back upstairs with a croissant in each hand and a look that promised further discussion at a later time. I went into the kitchen; made chocolate; sat down and watched it go cold. Thought of February in Lansquenet, with the mimosa in bloom on the banks of the Tannes and the river gypsies with their long narrow boats, so many and so closely packed that you could almost have walked to the other side—

And one man sitting there on his own, watching the river from the roof of his boat. Not so different from the rest of them, and yet somehow I'd known almost straightaway. Some people shine. He's one of them. And even now, after all this time, I can feel myself drawn to that flame again. If it hadn't been for Anouk and Rosette I might have followed him last night. After all, there are worse things than poverty. But I owe my children something more. That's why I'm here. And I can't go back to being Vianne Rocher, to Lansquenet. Not even for Roux. Not even for me.

I was still sitting there when Thierry came in. It was nine o'clock and still quite dark; outside I could hear the distant, dampened sounds of traffic and the chiming of the bells from the little church on Place du Tertre.

He sat down in silence opposite me; from his overcoat I could smell cigar smoke and Paris fog. He sat there for thirty seconds in silence, then reached out a hand to cover mine.

"I'm sorry about last night," he said.

I picked up my cup and looked inside. I must have let the milk boil; there was a puckered skin over the cold chocolate. Careless of me, I thought to myself.

"Yanne," said Thierry.

I looked at him.

"I'm sorry," he said. "I was under stress. I wanted everything to be perfect for you. I was going to take us all out to lunch, then I was going to tell you about the flat, and how I've managed to get us a wedding slot—get this—at the very same church my parents were married in—"

"What?" I said.

He squeezed my hand. "Notre-Dame des Apôtres. Seven weeks' time.

There was a cancellation, and I know the priest—I did some work for him some time back—"

"What are you talking about?" I said. "You bully my children, you're rude to my friend, you walk off without a word, and then you expect me to get all excited about flats and wedding arrangements?"

Thierry gave a rueful grin. "I'm sorry," he said. "I don't mean to laugh, but you really haven't got used to that phone yet, have you?"

"What?" I said.

"Just turn on your phone."

I did and found a new text message, sent by Thierry at eight-thirty the previous night.

LOVE YOU TO DISTRACTION. MY ONLY EXCUSE.
SEE YOU TOMORROW AT 9.
THIERRY. XX

"Oh," I said.

He took my hand. "I'm really sorry about last night. That friend of yours—"

"Roux," I said.

He nodded. "I know how ridiculous it must sound. But seeing him with you and Annie—talking as if he'd known you for years—it reminded me of all the things I don't know about you. All the people in your past, the men you've loved—"

I looked at him in some surprise. As far as my previous life is concerned, Thierry has always shown a remarkable lack of concern. It's one of the things I've always liked about him. His lack of curiosity.

"He's sweet on you. Even I could tell that."

I sighed. It always comes to this. The questions; the enquiries; kindly meant but laden with suspicion.

Where are you from? Where are you heading? Are you visiting relatives here?

Thierry and I had a deal, I thought. I don't mention his divorce; he doesn't talk about my past. It works—or it did, until yesterday.

Nice timing, Roux, I thought bitterly. But then again, that's what he's like. And now his voice in my mind is like that of the wind. *Don't fool yourself, Vianne. You can't settle here. You think you're safe in your little house. But like the wolf in the fairy tale, I know better.*

I went into the kitchen to brew a fresh pot of chocolate. Thierry followed me, clumsy in his big overcoat among Zozie's little tables and chairs.

"You want to know about Roux?" I said, grating chocolate into the pan. "Well, I knew him when I lived in the South. For a while I ran a *chocolaterie* in a village near the Garonne. He lived on a riverboat, moving among towns, doing casual work. Carpentry, roofing, picking fruit. He did a couple of jobs for me. I haven't seen him for over four years. Satisfied?"

He looked abashed. "I'm sorry, Yanne. I'm ridiculous. And I certainly didn't mean to interrogate you. I promise I won't do it again."

"I never thought you'd be jealous," I said, adding a vanilla pod and a pinch of nutmeg to the hot chocolate.

"I'm not," said Thierry. "And to prove it to you—" He put both hands on my shoulders, forcing me to look at him. "Listen, Yanne. He's a friend of yours. He obviously needs the cash. And given that I really want the flat finished by Christmas, and you know how hard it is trying to get anyone at this time of year, I've offered him the job."

I stared at him. "You have?"

He smiled. "Call it a penance," he said. "My way of proving to you that the jealous guy you met last night isn't the real me. And there's something else." He reached into his overcoat pocket. "I got you a little something," he said. "It was going to be an engagement present, but . . ."

Thierry's little somethings are always lavish. Four dozen roses at a time; jewelry from Bond Street; scarves from Hermès. A little too conventional, maybe—but that's Thierry. Predictable to the core.

"Well?"

It was a slim package, barely thicker than a padded envelope. I opened it and found a leather travel wallet containing four first-class plane tickets to New York, dated 28 December.

I stared at them.

"You'll love it," he said. "It's the only place to bring in the New Year. I've booked us into a great hotel—the kids'll love it—there'll be snow—music—fireworks. . . ." He gave me an exuberant hug. "Oh, Yanne, I can't *wait* to show you New York."

As a matter of fact, I've been there before. My mother died there, on a busy street, in front of an Italian deli on Independence Day. It was hot and sunny then. In December it will be cold. People die of the cold in New York in December.

"But I don't have a passport," I said slowly. "At least, I did—but—"

"Out-of-date? I'll see to that."

Well, in fact it's more than out-of-date. It's in the wrong *name*—that of Vianne Rocher—and how could I tell him that, I thought, that the woman he loves is someone else?

But how could I hide it now? Last night's scene has taught me this: Thierry is not quite as predictable as I had assumed. Deceit is an invasive weed, which if not dealt with early enough, forces its tendrils into everything, gnawing, spreading, stifling until at last there's nothing left but a tangle of lies—

He was standing very close, his blue eyes bright—with anxiety, perhaps. He smelled of something vaguely comforting, like cut grass or old books or pine sap or bread. He came a little closer, and now his arms were around me, my head on his shoulder (though where was that little hollow, I thought, that seemed to be made for me alone?), and it felt so familiar, so very *safe*—and yet this time there was a tension too. I could feel it, like live wires about to touch—

His lips found mine. That charge again. Like static between us, half-pleasure, half-not. I found myself thinking of Roux. *Damn you. Not now.* That lingering kiss. I pulled away.

"Listen, Thierry. I need to explain."

He looked at me. "Explain what?"

"The name on my passport—the name I'll have to give at the registry office—" I took a breath. "It's not the name I'm using now. I changed it. It's a long story. I should have told you before, but—"

Thierry interrupted me. "It doesn't matter. No need to explain. We all have things we'd rather not talk about. What do I care if you changed your name? It's who you *are* that interests me, not whether you're a Francine or a Marie-Claude or even, God help us, even a Cunégonde."

I smiled. "You don't mind?"

He shook his head. "I promised I wouldn't interrogate you. The past is the past. I don't need to know. Unless you're about to tell me you used to be a man, or something. . . ."

I laughed at that. "You're safe enough."

"I suppose I could check. Just to be sure." His hands locked in the small of my back. His kiss was harder, more demanding. Thierry never makes demands. His old-fashioned courtesy is one of the things that has always appealed to me, but today he is slightly different—there's a hint of passion long contained; impatience; a thirst for something more. For a moment I am submerged in it; his hands move to my waist, my breasts. There is something almost childishly greedy in the way he kisses my mouth, my face, as if he's trying to lay claim to as much of me as possible, and all the time he is whispering—*I love you, Yanne, I want you, Yanne. . . .*

Half laughing, I came up for air. "Not here. It's past nine-thirty—"

He gave a comic bear's growl. "You think I'm going to wait seven weeks?" And now his arms were bearish too, holding me in a close lock, and he smelled of musk sweat and stale cigars, and all at once and for the first time in our long friendship I could imagine us making love, naked and sweating between the sheets, and I felt a jolt of sudden surprise at the sense of revolt the thought provoked—

I pushed my hands against his chest. "Thierry, please—"

He showed his teeth.

"Zozie's going to be here in a minute—"

"Then let's go upstairs before she arrives."

Already I was gasping for breath. The reek of sweat intensified, mingled with the scent of cold coffee, raw wool, and last night's beer. No longer such a comforting scent, it calls up images of crowded bars and narrow escapes and drunken strangers in the night. Thierry's hands are slablike and eager, spattered with age spots, tufted with hair.

I found myself thinking of Roux's hands. His deft pickpocket's fingers; machine oil under the fingernails.

"Come *on*, Yanne."

He was pulling me across the room. His eyes were bright with anticipation. Suddenly I wanted to protest, but it's too late. I've made my choice. There can be no going back, I thought. I followed him toward the stairs—

A lightbulb blew with a sound like a firecracker going off.

Pulverized glass showered us.

A sound from upstairs. Rosette was awake. Relief made me tremble.

Thierry swore.

"I have to see to Rosette," I said.

He made a sound that was not quite laughter. A final kiss—but the moment had passed. From the corner of my eye I could see a golden something gleaming in the shadows—sunlight, perhaps, or some kind of reflection—

"I have to see to Rosette, Thierry."

"I love you," he said.

I know you do.

It was ten o'clock and Thierry had just left when Zozie came in, wrapped up in an overcoat, wearing purple platform boots and carrying a large cardboard box in both hands. It looked heavy, and Zozie was a little flushed as she put it down carefully on the floor.

"Sorry I'm late," she said. "This stuff is heavy."

"What is it?" I said.

Zozie grinned. She went to the window display and took out the red shoes that have been sitting there for the past couple of weeks.

"I've been thinking we're due for a bit of a change. How about a new display? I mean, this was never meant to be a permanent thing, and to be honest, I miss these shoes."

I smiled at that. "Of course," I said.

"So I picked up this stuff from the *marché aux puces.*" She indicated the cardboard box. "I've got an idea I'd like to try out."

I looked at the box, then at Zozie. Still reeling from Thierry's visit, Roux's reappearance, and the complications that I knew it would bring, the unexpected kindness of the simple gesture left me suddenly close to tears.

"You didn't have to do that, Zozie."

"Don't be silly. I like it." She looked at me closely. "Is anything wrong?"

"Oh, it's Thierry." I tried to smile. "He's been acting strange these past few days."

She shrugged. "I'm not surprised," she said. "You're doing well. Business is good. At last things are looking up for you."

I frowned at her. "What do you mean?"

"What I mean," said Zozie patiently, "is that Thierry still wants to be Santa Claus and Prince Charming and Good King Wenceslas all rolled into one. It was fine while you were struggling—he bought you dinner, dressed you up, showered you with presents—but you're different now. You don't need saving anymore. Someone took away his Cinderella doll and put a real live girl there instead, and he's having trouble coping with it."

"Thierry's not like that," I said.

"*Isn't* he?"

"Well . . ." I grinned. "Maybe a bit."

She laughed at that, and I laughed with her, though I couldn't help feeling a little abashed. Zozie is very observant, of course. But shouldn't I have seen those things myself?

Zozie opened the cardboard box.

"Why not take it easy today? Have a lie-down. Play with Rosette. Don't worry. If he comes, I'll call."

That startled me. "If who comes?" I said.

"Oh, really, Vianne—"

"Don't call me that!"

She grinned. "Well, Roux, of course. Who did you think I meant, the pope?"

I gave a wan smile. "He won't come today."

"What makes you so sure?"

So I told her what Thierry had said: about the flat, and how determined he was to see us there by Christmas, and about the plane tickets to New York, and how he'd offered Roux a job at Rue de la Croix—

Zozie looked surprised at that. "He has?" she said. "Well, if Roux takes it, he must need the money. I can't see him doing it for love."

I shook my head. "What a mess," I said. "Why didn't he say he was coming here? I would have handled it differently. At least I would have been prepared—"

Zozie sat down at the kitchen table. "He's Rosette's father, isn't he?"

I didn't say anything but turned to switch on the ovens. I was planning a batch of gingerbread biscuits, the sort you hang on the Christmas tree, gilded and iced and tied with colored ribbon—

"Of course, it's your business," Zozie went on. "Does Annie know?"

I shook my head.

"Does anyone know? Does *Roux* know?"

Suddenly my strength had gone, and I sat down quickly in one of the chairs, feeling as if she had cut my strings, leaving me in a sudden tangle, voiceless, helpless, and still.

"I can't tell him now," I whispered at last.

"Well, he's no fool. He'll work it out."

Silently I shook my head. It's the first time that I have had any cause to feel grateful for Rosette's differences—but at nearly four years old she still looks and behaves like a child of two and a half, and who would believe the impossible?

"It's too late for all that," I said. "Four years ago, maybe—but not now."

"Why? Did you quarrel?"

She sounds like Anouk. I found myself trying to explain to her too, that things are not simple, that houses must be made of stone, because when the wind comes howling by, only solid stone will keep us from blowing away—

Why pretend? he says in my mind. *What is it that makes you try to fit in? What is it about these people that makes you want to be like them?*

"No, we didn't quarrel," I said. "We just—went different ways."

A sudden, startling image in my mind—the Pied Piper with his flute, all the children following—but for the lame one, left behind as the mountain closes in his wake—

"So what about Thierry?" she said.

Good question, I thought. Does he suspect? He's no fool, either; and yet there's a kind of blindness in him, which might be arrogance or trust or a little of both. And yet he's still suspicious of Roux. I saw it last night—that measuring look—the instinctive aversion of the solid city dweller for the drifter, the gypsy, the traveler. . . .

You choose your family, Vianne, I thought.

"Well, I guess you've made your choice."

"It's the right one. I know it is."

But I could tell she didn't believe me. As if she could see it in the air around me like cotton candy gathering on a spindle. But there are so many kinds of love; and when the hot, selfish, angry kind has long since burned itself out, thank all the gods for men like Thierry, those safe and unimaginative men who think *passion* is just a word from books, like *magic* or *adventure.*

Zozie was still watching me with that patient half-smile, as if she expected me to say something more. When I didn't, she simply shrugged and held out a dish of *mendiants.* She makes them as I do myself: the chocolate thin enough to snap but thick enough to satisfy; a generous sprinkle of fat raisins; a walnut, an almond; a violet; a crystallized rose.

"Try one," she said. "What do you think?"

The gunpowder scent of chocolate arose from the little dish of *mendiants,* smelling of summer and lost time. He had tasted of chocolate when I first kissed him; and the scent of damp grass had come from the ground where we had lain side by side; and his touch had been unexpectedly soft, and his hair like summer marigolds in the dying light—

Zozie was still holding out the dish of *mendiants.* It's made of blue Murano glass, with a little gold flower on the side. It's only a bauble, and yet I'm fond of it. Roux gave it to me in Lansquenet, and I have carried it with me ever since, in my luggage, in my pockets, like a touchstone.

I looked up and saw Zozie looking at me. Her eyes were a distant, fairytale blue, like something you might see in dreams.

"You won't tell anyone?" I said.

"Of course not." She picked up a chocolate between delicate fingers and held it out for me to take. Rich, dark chocolate, rum-soaked raisins, vanilla, rose, and cinnamon . . .

"Try one, Vianne," she said with a smile. "I happen to know they're your favorites."

Monday, 3 December

A GOOD DAY'S WORK, IF I SAY SO MYSELF. SO MUCH OF MY WORK HERE IS A juggling act; a series of balls and blades and flaming torches to be kept in the air for as long as it takes—

It took some time to be sure of Roux. He's sharp enough to cut, that one, and needs careful handling, and it was all I could do to make him stay. But I managed to hold him on Saturday night, and with the help of a few encouraging words, I've managed to keep him in check so far.

It wasn't easy, I have to say. His first impulse was to head straight back to where he'd come from, never to be seen again. I didn't need to look at his colors to know; I could see it in his face as he marched down the Butte with his hair in his eyes and his hands stuck fiercely into his pockets. Thierry was following him too, and I was forced to clear the way with a little cantrip to make him slip, and in the seconds that he was delayed, caught up with Roux and took his arm.

"Roux," I told him. "You can't just leave. There are things you don't know about all of this."

He shook off my arm without slowing down. "What makes you think I want to know?"

"Because you're in love with her," I said.

Roux just shrugged and kept on walking.

"And because she's having second thoughts, but she doesn't know how to tell Thierry."

Now he was listening. He slackened his pace. I seized the opportunity and made the claw sign of One Jaguar right at his back—a cantrip that should have stopped him dead but which Roux just shook off instinctively.

"Hey, stop it," I said, more in frustration than anything else.

He shot me a look of feral curiosity.

"You need to give her time."

"What for?"

"To make up her mind about what she really wants."

He had stopped walking altogether now and was watching with new intensity. I felt a twitch of annoyance at that—he was so obviously blind to anyone who wasn't Vianne—but there'd be time for that later, I told myself. For the moment, I just needed him here. After that, I could make him pay at leisure.

Meanwhile, however, Thierry had picked himself up and was heading toward us down the street. "We don't have time for this now," I said. "Meet me Monday, after work."

"Work?" he said. He began to laugh. "You think I'm going to work for *him?*"

"You'd better," I said. "If you want my help."

After that, I had just enough time to rejoin Thierry as he approached. Barely a few dozen yards away, and hulking in his cashmere coat, he glared at me, and at Roux behind me, with the black-button-eyed ferocity of a big plush bear gone suddenly rogue.

"You've blown it now," I told him softly. "What possessed you to behave like that? Yanne's very upset—"

He bridled at that. "What did I do? It was—"

"Never mind *what did I do.* I can help you, but you have to be nice." Savagely I made the sign of Lady Blood Moon with my fingertips. That seemed to calm him; he looked dismayed. I shot him again, this time with the masterful sign of One Jaguar, and saw his colors subside a little.

He's so much easier than Roux, I thought. So much more cooperative. In a few words, I told him the plan. "It's simple," I said. "There's no way you can lose. It makes you look magnanimous. You'll have the help you need in the flat. You'll see more of Yanne. And what's more"—I lowered my voice again—"you can keep an eye on *him*."

Well, that did it. I knew it would. That delightful combination of vanity, suspicion, and supreme self-confidence—I hardly needed glamours at all, he did it all so well himself.

Yes, I'm almost getting to like Thierry. So comfortable, so predictable, with no sharp edges on which to be cut. Best of all, he's so easily charmed—a smile, a word, and he's all mine. Unlike Roux, with his sullen mouth and look of permanent suspicion.

Damn him, I thought. What's wrong with me? I look like Vianne, I talk like Vianne—he should have been a pushover. But some people are just tougher than others, and my timing so far has been all wrong. Still, I can wait—for a few days, at least. And if glamours won't work, then chemicals will.

Today I waited for closing time impatiently, with an eye to the clock. It seemed to me like a very long day, but I spent it pleasantly enough while outside the rain turned slowly to mist and the people went by like folk in a dream, occasionally stopping to stare blurrily at the half-finished window display that shines out now from Le Rocher de Montmartre like a magic-lantern show.

Never underestimate the power of a window display. The eyes are the windows of the soul, they say, and a display window should be the eyes of the shop, gleaming with promise and delight. The old display was pretty enough, with my red shoes filled with chocolates, but I'm aware that with Christmas approaching in giant strides, we must think of something more enchanting than mere footwear if we are to bring the customers in.

And so our window has become an Advent calendar, draped with scrap silk and lit with a single yellow lantern. The calendar itself is made out of an antique dollhouse that I found in the *marché aux puces*. Too old to attract a child, too decrepit to be of any interest to a collector—its roof badly glued together, its front cracked and mended with masking tape—it was precisely what I had been looking for.

It is large—large enough to fill the window—with a sloping, beveled roof and a painted facade with four lift-out panels to spy inside. For the present, all the panels are shut, and I have placed blinds in the windows, under which we can just glimpse the comforting golden light from inside.

"Wow," said Vianne when she saw me at work. "What is it, a Nativity?"

I grinned. "Not quite. It's a surprise."

So today I worked as fast as I could, shielding the window from prying eyes with the help of a large piece of red-and-gold sari silk behind which the transformation was to occur.

I started with the scenery. Around the house, I constructed a miniature garden: a lake made from a swatch of blue silk with chocolate ducks floating across it; a river; a path made from colored sugar crystals, lined with trees and bushes made from tissue paper and pipe cleaners; everything dusted with icing-sugar snow, and with multicolored sugar mice running out of the Advent house like something out of a fairy tale. . . .

It took me the best part of the morning to put all the scenery in place. Just before twelve Nico came in with Alice—they seem to be inseparable now—and stayed to admire the window. He bought another box of his macaroons while Alice watched wide-eyed as I piped the repairs and improvements to the house's facade with a thin-nozzled icing-sugar bag.

"It's gorgeous," said Alice. "It's better than the Galeries Lafayette."

I have to admit it's a splendid confection. Part house, part cake, with sugar fluting around the windows, sugar gargoyles on the roof, sugar pillars around the doors, and a neat little cap of snow on each window ledge and on the beveled chimney tops.

At lunchtime, I called Vianne in to look.

"D'you like it?" I said. "It's not finished yet, but—what do you think?"

For a while, she said nothing at all. But her colors had already told me everything I needed to know, flaring so bright they almost filled the room. And were there tears in her eyes? Yes. I thought perhaps there were.

"Fabulous," she said at last. "Just—fabulous."

I feigned modesty. "Oh, you know . . ."

"I mean it, Zozie. You've helped me so much." I thought she looked troubled. As well she might; the sign of Ehecatl is a powerful one—speaking of journeys, change, the wind—and she must sense it working around her, maybe even *in* her now (my *mendiants* are special in so many ways), its chemistries mingling with her own, changing, becoming volatile—

"And I don't even pay you a decent wage," she said.

"Pay me in kind," I suggested, grinning. "All the chocolates I can eat."

Vianne shook her head, frowning, seeming to listen for something outside; but the fog had swallowed any sound. "I owe you so much," she went on at last. "And I've never done a thing for you—"

She stopped, as if she'd heard a noise, or had an idea so arresting that it temporarily robbed her of speech. That'll be the *mendiants* again; her favorites; reminding her of happier times. . . .

"I know," she said, her face brightening. "You could move in here. Move in with us. There's Madame Poussin's old rooms. No one's using them just now. It isn't much, but it's better than a bed-and-breakfast. You could stay with us, eat with us—the kids would love it—we don't need the space—and at Christmas, when we move out . . ."

Her face fell, but just a little.

"I'd be in the way," I said, shaking my head.

"You wouldn't. I promise. We'd work all hours. You'd be doing us a favor."

"What about Thierry?" I said.

"What about him?" said Vianne with a touch of defiance. "We're doing what he wants, aren't we? Moving into Rue de la Croix? Why shouldn't you stay with us till then? And when we move out, you can look after the shop. Make sure everything's all right. He practically suggested it anyway—he said I'd need a manager."

I seemed to consider it awhile. *Is* Thierry getting impatient? I thought. Has he shown her his wilder side? I have to say I'd suspected as much—and now that Roux has turned up again, she needs to keep them both at arm's length, at least until she makes up her mind. . . .

A chaperone. That's what she needs. And what better choice than her friend Zozie?

"But you've only just met me," I told her at last. "I could be anyone."

She laughed. "No, you couldn't."

Shows what you know.

"All right," I said. "We've got a deal."

Once more, I was in.

Tuesday, 4 December

So there it is. she's moving in. *how cool is that?*—as jean-loup would say. She brought her stuff round yesterday—what there was of it, anyway. I've never seen anyone travel so light, except maybe for me and Maman, in the days when we were on the road. Two suitcases—one of shoes, the other filled with everything else. Ten minutes to unpack, and already it feels like she's been here forever.

Her room is still full of Madame Poussin's old furniture: old-lady furniture, with a skinny armoire that smells of mothballs and the chest of drawers full of big scratchy blankets. The curtains are brown and cream, with a pattern of roses, and there's a saggy bed with a horsehair bolster, and a speckled mirror that makes everyone look like they have the plague. An old lady's room; but trust Zozie to make it cool again in no time at all.

I helped her unpack her things last night and gave her one of the sandalwood sachets from my wardrobe to help get rid of the old-lady smell.

"That's all right," she said, smiling as she hung up her clothes in the old armoire. "I've brought some things to cheer the place up."

"What things?"

"You'll see."

And we did. While Maman prepared dinner and I took Rosette to see the Nativity again, Zozie worked on the room upstairs. It didn't take her more than an hour; but when I went up later to see, you wouldn't have recognized the place. The old-lady brown-patterned curtains were gone, replaced by a couple of big loose squares of sari material, one red, one blue.

She'd used another one (this one was purple, with silver thread) to cover the fluffy old-lady bedspread, and there was a double string of little colored lights over the mantelpiece, where she'd lined up her shoes pair by pair, like ornaments above the fire.

There was a rag rug too, and a lamp where she'd hung all her earrings like danglers from the bottom of the shade, and one of her hats was pinned to the wall where a picture used to be; and there was a Chinese silk dressing gown hanging behind the door, and a row of jeweled butterflies, like the ones she sometimes wears in her hair, clipped all around the edges of the plaguey mirror.

"Wow," I said. "I love this room."

And there was a scent too, something very sweet and churchy that reminded me somehow of Lansquenet.

"That's frankincense, Nanou," she said. "I always burn it in my rooms."

It was proper incense too, the kind you burn over hot coals. We used to burn it, Maman and I, though nowadays we never do. Too messy, perhaps; but it smells so good, and besides, Zozie's kind of disorder seems to make more sense than anyone else's idea of tidiness.

Then Zozie brought out a bottle of grenadine from somewhere at the bottom of her suitcase, and we all had a kind of party downstairs, with chocolate cake and ice cream for Rosette, and by the time I was ready for bed, it was nearly midnight, and Rosette was asleep on a beanbag, and Maman was clearing the dishes away. And as I looked at Zozie then, Zozie with her long hair and her bracelet with all the little charms, and her eyes lit up like fairy lights, it was just like seeing Maman again, but the way she was in Lansquenet, in the days when she was still Vianne Rocher.

"So what do you think of my Advent house?"

That's the new display, you know, to make up for losing the lollipop shoes. It's a house, and at first I thought it was going to be a crèche, like in the Place du Tertre, with the Jesus baby and the kings and all his family and friends. But actually it's better than that. It's a magical house in a fairy wood, just like in the storybooks. And every day there's going to be a different scene opening up behind one of the doors. Today it's the Pied Piper, and the story's mostly outside the house, with sugar mice instead of rats in pink and white and green and blue, and the Piper made from a wooden clothes peg, with painted red hair and a matchstick in his hand for a flute, piping all the sugar mice into a river made of silk. . . .

And inside the house, there's the mayor of Hamelin, the one who wouldn't pay the Piper, looking out of a bedroom window. He's a peg-doll too, of course, with a nightgown made from a handkerchief and a paper nightcap on his head, and his face drawn on in felt-tip pen, with his mouth wide open in surprise.

And I don't know why, but somehow the Pied Piper reminds me of Roux, with his red hair and shabby clothes, and the greedy old mayor makes me think of Thierry, and I couldn't help thinking that, like the Nativity in Place du Tertre, it wasn't just a window display, that it had to mean something more—

"I love it," I said.

"I hoped you would."

On the beanbag, Rosette made a sleepy little snuffling noise and reached for her blanket, which had fallen on the floor. Zozie found it and put it over her. She stopped for a moment to touch Rosette's hair.

And then I had a weird thought. More than that—an *inspiration*. I guess it was the Advent house, but I was thinking about the Nativity, and the way everyone comes to the stable at once—the animals and the Magi and the shepherds and angels and the star—without anyone having to invite them or anything, as if they'd been summoned there by magic—

I almost told Zozie right then. But I needed time to sort myself out, to make sure I wasn't about to do anything stupid. You see, I'd remembered something too. Something that happened a long time ago, back in the days when we were still different. Something to do with Rosette, perhaps. Poor Rosette, who cried like a cat and who never seemed to feed at all, and sometimes stopped breathing without any reason, for seconds, even minutes at a time. . . .

The baby. The crib. The animals—

The angels and the Magi—

What is a Magus, anyway? And why do I think I've met one before?

Tuesday, 4 December

MEANWHILE, I STILL HAD TO DEAL WITH ROUX. MY PLANS FOR HIM DO not involve contact with Vianne, but I do need him to stay close, and so, as planned, at half past five, I went down to Rue de la Croix and waited for him to come out.

It was closer to six when he left the house. Thierry's taxi had already arrived—he's staying in a nice hotel while work on the flat is under way—but Thierry had not yet left the flat, and I was able to watch from a discreet little vantage point on the corner as Roux waited with his hands in his pockets and his collar turned up against the rain.

Now Thierry has always rather prided himself on being a man of no pretensions, a real man who isn't afraid to get his hands dirty, and who would never make another man feel inferior for lack of money or social status. This is quite untrue, of course. Thierry's a snob of the worst kind—he just doesn't know it, that's all. But it's in his manner all the same: in the way he always calls Laurent *mon pote*; and I could see it now in the careless way he took his time locking up the flat, checking, setting the security alarm, then turning to Roux with a look of surprise—as if to say, *ah yes, I forgot*—

"How much did we call it? A hundred?" he asked.

A hundred euros a day, I thought. Not an especially generous sum. But Roux just gave that shrug of his—the shrug that so infuriates Thierry and makes him want to force a reaction. Roux, in contrast, is very cool, a gas jet turned to its lowest flame. But I noticed that he kept his eyes slightly lowered throughout, as if afraid of what he might reveal.

"Check all right?" Thierry said.

Nice touch, I thought. Of course he must know that Roux has no bank account, that Roux pays no taxes, that Roux may not even be his name.

"Or would you rather have cash?" he said.

Roux shrugged again. "Whatever," he said. Willing to forfeit a whole day's wages rather than concede a point.

Thierry gave his broadest smile. "All right, I'll give you a check," he said. "I'm a bit tight on cash today. Sure you don't mind?"

Roux's colors flared, but he kept stubbornly silent.

"Who shall I make it to?"

"Leave it blank."

Still smiling, Thierry took his time writing the check, then gave it to Roux with a cheery wink. "See you same time tomorrow, then. Unless you've had enough, that is."

Roux shook his head.

"All right, then. Eight-thirty. Don't be late."

And then he was off in his taxicab, leaving Roux with his useless check, apparently too lost in his thoughts to notice me as I approached.

"Roux," I said.

"Vianne?" He turned and shot me that Christmas-tree smile. "Oh, it's you." His face fell.

"The name's Zozie." I gave him a look. "And you could work on your charm a bit."

"Sorry?"

"I mean you could at least *pretend* to be pleased to see me."

"Oh. Sorry." He looked abashed.

"So how's the job?"

"Not bad," he said.

I smiled at that. "Come on," I said. "Let's find somewhere dry to talk. Where are you staying?"

He named a backstreet dive off Rue de Clichy—just the kind of place I'd expect.

"Let's go there. I don't have long."

I knew the place—it was cheap and grubby-looking, but it did take cash, which matters a lot to someone like Roux. There was no key to the front door, but an electronic keypad with a code. I watched him enter it—825436—his profile lit sharply in the crude orange of the streetlight. File that away for later use. Codes of all kinds are useful, I thought.

We went inside. I saw his room. A dark interior; a carpet that felt slightly sticky beneath my feet; a square cell the color of old chewing gum with a single bed and not much else; no window; no chair; just a sink, a radiator and a bad print on the wall.

"Well?" said Roux.

"Try these," I said. I took out a small gift-wrapped box from my coat and handed it to him. "I made them myself. On the house."

"Thanks," he said sourly and dropped the box onto the bed without giving it a second glance.

Once more I felt a sting of annoyance.

One truffle, I thought, *is that too much to ask?* The symbols on the box were powerful (I'd used the red circle of Lady Blood Moon, the seductress, the Eater of Hearts), but just one taste of what was inside would make him so much easier to persuade—

"So when can I call?" said Roux impatiently.

I sat down on the end of the bed. "It's complicated," I began. "You took her by surprise, you know. Turning up the way you did—out of the blue, especially when she's with someone else."

He laughed at that, a bitter sound. "Ah, yes. Le Tresset. Mr. Big."

"Don't worry. I'll cash the check for you."

He looked at me. "You know about that?"

"I know Thierry. He's the kind of man who can't even shake another man's hand without seeing how many bones he can break. And he's jealous of you."

"Jealous?"

"Of course."

He grinned, looking genuinely amused for a second. "Because I've got everything, haven't I? The money, the looks, the place in the country—"

"You've got more than that," I told him.

"What?"

"She loves you, Roux."

For a second he didn't say anything. He didn't even look at me, but I could see the tension in his body and the accompanying flare of his colors—from gas-jet blue to neon red—and I knew that I had shaken him.

"She told you that?" he said at last.

"No, not quite. But I know it's true."

There was a Pyrex glass beside the sink. He filled it with water and drank it in one gulp, then took a deep breath and filled it again. "So if that's the way she feels," he said, "then why's she marrying Le Tresset?"

I smiled and held out the little box, from which the red circle of Lady Blood Moon lit his face with a carnival glow.

"Sure you won't have a chocolate?"

Impatiently, he shook his head.

"All right," I said. "Just tell me this. When you first saw me, you called me Vianne. Why was that?"

"I told you before. You looked like her. Well, at least—the way she used to be."

"Used to be?"

"She's different now," he said. "Her hair, her clothes . . ."

"That's right," I said. "That's Thierry's influence. He's a total control freak; insanely jealous; always wanting things his way. At first he was great. He helped with the kids. He gave her presents, expensive ones. Then he began to pressure her. Now he tells her what to wear, how to behave, even how to raise her children. Of course it doesn't help that he's her landlord and could throw her out at any time."

Roux frowned, and I could tell that I was finally getting to him. I could see doubt in his colors, and, more promisingly, the first flowering of anger.

"So why didn't she tell me? Why didn't she write?"

"Maybe she was afraid," I said.

"Afraid? Of *him*?"

"Perhaps," I said.

Now I could see him thinking hard, head lowered, eyes creased in concentration. For some strange reason, he doesn't trust me; and yet I know he'll take the bait. For her sake, for Vianne Rocher.

"I'll go and see her. Talk to her—"

"That would be a big mistake."

"Why?"

"She doesn't want to see you yet. You have to give her time. You can't just turn up out of the blue and expect her to make a choice."

His eyes told me that was precisely what he'd expected.

I put a hand on his arm. "Listen," I said. "I'll talk to her. I'll try and make her see things your way. But no more visits, no letters, no calls. Trust me on this."

"Why should I?" he said.

Well, I knew he wouldn't be easy, but this was getting ridiculous. I allowed an edge to enter my voice. "Why? Because I'm her friend, and I care what happens to her and the kids. And if you'd just stop thinking about your wounded feelings for a minute, you'd see why she needs some time to think. I mean, where have you been for the past four years? And how does she know you won't take off again? Thierry isn't perfect, of course, but he's here, and he's dependable, which is more than can be said of you."

Some folk respond better to abrasiveness than to charm. Roux is obviously one of these, because then he sounded more civil than at any other time he'd spoken to me.

"I see," he said. "I'm sorry, Zozie."

"So you'll do as I say? Otherwise, there's no point in me even trying to help you."

He nodded.

"You mean it?"

"Yeah."

I gave a sigh. The hard part was done.

A pity, in a way, I thought. In spite of everything, I find him rather attractive. But for every favor the gods bestow, there has to be a sacrifice. And, of course, by the end of the month I'll be asking for a significant favor. . . .

Wednesday, 5 December

S<small>UZE WAS BACK AGAIN TODAY. WEARING A BEANIE HAT INSTEAD OF THAT</small> scarf and trying to make up for lost time. Heads together with Chantal at lunch, and after that it was all out with the lame comments and the *where's your boyfriend* and the stupid *Annie's It* games.

Not that there's anything remotely fun about *that* anymore. Now it's not just halfway mean: it's mean all the way, with Sandrine and Chantal telling everybody about last week's visit to the shop, making it sound like a cross between a hippie den and a junkyard, and laughing like crazy at everything.

To make it worse, Jean-Loup was ill, and I was back to being It on my own. Not that I care about that, of course. But it isn't fair; we've worked so hard, Maman and Zozie and Rosette and me—and now there's Chantal and Co. making us sound like a bunch of losers.

Normally I wouldn't have cared. But things are getting so much better for us, with Zozie moving in with us, and business so good, and the shop full of customers every day, and Roux coming back like that, out of the blue—

But it's been four days, and he hasn't made an appearance yet. I couldn't stop thinking about him at school and wondering where he's keeping his boat, or whether he lied to us about that and he's just sleeping under a bridge somewhere, or in some old deserted house, the way he did in Lansquenet after Monsieur Muscat burned his boat.

And in lessons I couldn't concentrate; and Monsieur Gestin shouted at me for daydreaming, and Chantal and Co. giggled at that, and I didn't even have Jean-Loup to talk to.

And it got a lot worse; because after school as I stood in the queue next to Claude Meunier and Mathilde Chagrin, Danielle came up to me with that fake-concerned expression she puts on so often and said: "Is it true your little sister's retarded?"

Chantal and Suze were standing nearby, looking nicely poker-faced. I could see it in their colors, though, the way they were trying to set me up; and I could see they were so close to laughing that they were nearly bursting with it—

"I don't know what you're talking about." I made my voice expressionless. No one knows about Rosette—or so I thought until today. And then I remembered one day with Suze, playing with Rosette in the shop. . . .

"That's what I've heard," said Danielle. "Your sister's a retard. Everyone knows."

Well, so much for BEST FRIENDS, I thought. And the pink enameled pendant, and the promise she'd made never to tell, cross your heart and hope to—

I glared at Suze in her hot-pink beanie (redheads should *never* wear hot pink).

"Some people ought to mind their own business," I said, loud enough for them all to hear.

Danielle smirked. "It's true, then," she said, and her colors brightened greedily, like hot coals in a sudden draught.

Something in me flared as well. *Don't you dare*, I told her fiercely. *Anyone says another word*—

"Sure it's true," said Suze. "I mean, she's like, what is she, four, or something, and she can't even talk yet, or eat properly. My mum says she's a mong. She *looks* like a mong, anyway."

"No she doesn't," I said quietly.

"Yes she does. She's an ugly retard, just like you."

Suze just laughed. Chantal joined in. Soon they were chanting—*retard, retard*—and I could see Mathilde Chagrin staring at me with those pale, anxious eyes and suddenly—

BAM!

I don't quite know what happened then. It was so fast, like a cat that suddenly goes from purring asleep to hissing and scratching in the space of a second. I know that I forked my fingers at her, as Zozie did in the English tea shop. I don't quite know what I meant to do; but I felt it fly from my hand, somehow, as if I'd actually *thrown* something, a little stone, or a spinning disc of something that burned.

In any case, it acted fast: I heard Suzanne give a scream; then suddenly she was grabbing at her hot-pink beanie, pulling it off her head.

"Ow! Ow!"

"What's wrong?" said Chantal.

"It itches!" wailed Suze. She was scratching her head furiously; I could see pink patches of skin beneath what was left of her hair. "God, it *itches*!"

I felt sick all of a sudden, weak and sick, the way I felt the other night with Zozie. But the worst of it was, I wasn't sorry; instead I felt a kind of thrill, the kind you get when something bad happens, and it's your fault, but no one knows.

"What is it?" Chantal was saying.

"I don't know!" said Suzanne.

Danielle was looking all concerned, but fake, the way she'd looked at me before asking if Rosette was retarded, and Sandrine was making little squeaking noises—of sympathy or excitement, I couldn't tell.

Then Chantal began to scratch *her* head.

"G-got n-nits, Chantal?" said Claude Meunier.

The back of the queue laughed at that.

Then Danielle began to do the same.

It was as if a cloud of itching powder had suddenly descended upon the three of them. Itching powder, or something worse. Chantal looked angry, then alarmed. Suzanne was almost in hysterics. And for a moment it felt so *good*—

A memory came back to me then, of a time when I was very small. A day by the sea; paddling in my swimsuit; Maman sitting with a book on the sand. A boy who splashed me with seawater and made my eyes sting. As he passed by, I threw a stone—a small one; a pebble—expecting to miss.

It was just an accident—

The little boy crying, holding his head. Maman running toward me, dismay in her face. That sick sense of shock—*an accident—*

Images of broken glass; a scraped knee; a stray dog yelping under a bus.

Those are accidents, Nanou.

Slowly, I started to back away. I didn't know whether to laugh or to cry. It was funny—funny in the way a horrible thing can still be funny. And it still felt good, in that horrible way—

"What the hell is it?" yelled Chantal.

Whatever it was, it was potent, I thought. Even itching powder wouldn't have worked as dramatically. But I couldn't quite see what was happening. There were too many people in the way, and the queue had dissolved into a kind of mass, everyone wanting to see what was going on.

I didn't even try. I knew.

Suddenly I needed to see Zozie. She'd know what to do, I thought, and she wouldn't give me the third degree. I didn't want to wait for the bus, so I took the Métro back instead, and ran all the way from Place de Clichy. I was completely out of breath when I got in; Maman was in the kitchen, fixing Rosette's snack, and I swear Zozie knew before I even said a word.

"What's wrong, Nanou?"

I looked at her. She was wearing jeans and her lollipop shoes, looking redder and higher and shinier than ever with their sparkly stack heels. Seeing them made me feel better somehow, and I collapsed into one of the pink leopard chairs with an enormous sigh of relief.

"Chocolate?"

"No thanks."

She poured me a Coke. "That bad?" she said, watching me drink it all in one go, so fast that bubbles came out of my nose. "Here, have another, and tell me what's wrong."

I told her then, but quietly enough for Maman not to overhear. I had to stop twice, once when Nico came in with Alice, and once more when Laurent came in for a coffee and sat for nearly half an hour complaining about all the work to be done on Le P'tit Pinson, and how impossible it was to get a plumber at this time of year, and the immigrant problem, and all the usual things Laurent complains about.

By the time he'd gone it was time to close, and Maman was cooking dinner. Zozie put out the lights in the shop so I could see the Advent house. The Pied Piper has gone now, replaced by a choir of chocolate angels singing in the sugar snow. It looks so beautiful, I thought. But the house is still a mystery. Doors shut, curtains drawn; only a single fairy light shining out from an attic room.

"Can I see inside?" I said.

"Maybe tomorrow," Zozie said. "Why don't you come to my room? Then we can finish our little talk."

Slowly I followed her upstairs. On each narrow step in front of me, the lollipop shoes went *tak-tak-tak* on their fabulous heels, like someone knocking at a door, asking me, begging me to let them in.

Thursday, 6 December

THIS MORNING, FOR THE THIRD DAY RUNNING, THE MIST HANGS LIKE A sail over Montmartre. They're promising snow in a day or two; but for today the silence is eerie, swallowing the usual sounds of traffic and the footsteps of the pedestrians on the cobbles outside. It might be a hundred years ago, with frock-coated ghosts looming out of the fog—

Or it might be the morning of my last day of school, the day of my emancipation from St. Michael's-on-the-Green, the day I first realized that life—that *lives*—are nothing but dead letters on the wind, to be picked up, collected, burned or thrown away whenever the opportunity demands.

You'll learn that soon enough, Anouk. I know you better than you know yourself; there's a complex potential for anger and hate behind that good-little-girl facade, just as there was in the Girl Who Was It—the girl who was I—all those years ago.

But everything needs a catalyst. Sometimes it's a little thing; a featherweight; a flick of the fingers. Some piñatas are tougher than others. But everyone has a pressure point; and the box, once opened, cannot be shut.

Mine was a boy. His name was Scott McKenzie. He was seventeen, blond, athletic, unblemished. He was new to St. Michael's-on-the-Green; otherwise he would have known better from the start and would have avoided the Girl Who Was It in favor of some more worthy candidate for his affections.

Instead, he chose me—at least for a time—and that was how it all began. Not the most original start, though it ended in flames, as these things should. I was sixteen, and with the aid of my System, I had made the most of myself. I was a little mousy, perhaps—the legacy of so many years of being the freak. But I had potential even then. I was ambitious, resentful, nicely underhanded. My methods were mainly practical, rather than occult. I had a working knowledge of poisons and herbs; I knew how to inflict violent stomachaches on those who incurred my displeasure; and I soon learned that a dash of itching powder in a fellow pupil's socks, or a squeeze of chilli oil in a mascara bottle, could have a more instant and dramatic effect than any number of incantations.

As for Scott, he was easy to snare. Teenage boys, even the brightest ones, are one-third brain to two-thirds testosterone, and my recipe—a mixture of flattery, glamour, sex, pulque, and very small doses of a powdered mushroom available to only a select few of my mother's clientele—made him my slave in no time at all.

Don't get me wrong. I never loved Scott. Almost, perhaps—but not quite enough. But Anouk doesn't need to know that; nor does she need to know the more sordid details of what happened at St. Michael's-on-the-Green. Instead I gave her the sanitized version; made her laugh; painted a picture of Scott McKenzie that would have cast Michelangelo's *David* into the shade. Then told her the rest in language she understands: the graffiti; the gossip; the spite; and the dirt.

Small miseries—at least at first. Clothes stolen, books ripped, locker plundered, gossip spread. I was used to that, of course. Petty annoyances that I could hardly be bothered to avenge. Besides, I was almost in love; and there was a certain vicious pleasure to be had in the knowledge that, for the first time, other girls envied me: they looked at me and wondered what on earth it was that a boy like Scott McKenzie found to admire in the Girl Who Was It.

I made a fine tale of it for Anouk. I drew her a list of small vengeances— just naughty enough to make us alike, yet harmless enough to spare her tender heart. The truth is less winsome; but then of course the truth usually is.

"They asked for it," I told Anouk. "You only gave them what they deserved. It wasn't your fault."

Her face was still pale. "If Maman knew . . ."

"Don't tell her," I said. "Besides, where's the harm? It's not as if you hurt anyone. Although," I added, looking thoughtful, "if you don't learn to use those skills of yours, then maybe one day, by accident—"

"Maman says it's just a game. That it isn't real. That it's all just my imagination playing tricks."

I looked at her. "Do you think that's true?"

She muttered something, not meeting my eyes, and leveled her gaze at my shoes instead.

"Nanou," I said.

"Maman doesn't lie."

"Everyone lies."

"Even you?"

I grinned. "I'm not everyone. Am I, Nanou?" I kicked my foot at a slight angle, throwing out light from a jeweled red heel. I imagined its counterpart in her eyes, a tiny reflection in ruby and gold. "Don't worry, Nanou. I know how you feel. What you need is a System, that's all."

"A System?" she said.

And now she told me, hesitantly at first but with a growing eagerness that warmed my heart. They'd had their own System once, I saw: a motley collection of tales, tricks, and glamours; medicine bags to keep out the spirits; songs to quiet the winter wind to keep it from blowing them away.

"But why would the wind blow you away?"

Anouk shrugged. "It just does."

"What song did you sing?"

She sang it to me. It's an old song—a love song, I think—wistful, just a little sad. Vianne sings it still—I hear her sometimes as she talks to Rosette or works at her tempering in the kitchen.

> *V'là l'bon vent, v'là l'joli vent*
> *V'là l'bon vent, ma mie m'appelle—*

"I see," I said. "And now you're afraid you'll raise the wind."

Slowly, she nodded. "It's stupid. I know."

"No it isn't," I said. "Folk have believed it for hundreds of years. In English folklore, witches raised the wind by combing their hair. The Aborigines believe the good wind Bara is held captive for half the year by the bad wind, Mamariga, and every year they have to sing it free. As for the Aztecs . . ." I smiled at her. "They knew the power of the wind, whose breath moves the sun and drives away rain. Ehecatl was his name, and they worshipped him with chocolate."

"But—didn't they make human sacrifices as well?"

"Don't we all, in our own way?"

Human sacrifice. Such a loaded phrase. But isn't that just what Vianne Rocher has done, sacrificing her children to the fat gods of contentment? Desire demands a sacrifice—the Aztecs knew it; and the Maya. They knew the terrible greed of the gods; their insatiable greed for blood and death. And they understood the world a lot better, you might say, than those worshippers in the Sacré-Coeur, the big white hot-air balloon at the top of the Butte. But scratch the icing on the cake, and underneath there's the same dark, bitter center.

Because wasn't every stone of the Sacré-Coeur built upon the fear of death? And are the pictures of Christ exposing his heart so very dissimilar to the images of hearts being cut out of sacrificial victims? And is the ritual of communion, where the blood and the flesh of the Christ is shared, any less cruel or gruesome than these?

Anouk was watching me, wide-eyed.

"It was Ehecatl who gave mankind the ability to love," I said. "It was he who breathed life into the world. Wind was important to the Aztecs; more so than rain, even more important than the sun. Because wind means change; and without change, the world will die."

She nodded like the bright pupil she was, and I felt a startling swell of affection for her, something almost tender—dangerously maternal—

Oh, I'm in no danger of losing my head. But there's an undeniable pleasure in being with Anouk; in teaching her; in telling her the old tales. I remember my own excitement at that first trip to Mexico City; at the colors; the sun; the masks; the chants; the sense of coming home at last—

"You've heard of that phrase—*a wind of change?*"

Again, she nodded.

"Well, that's what we are. People like us. People who can raise the wind."

"But isn't that wrong?"

"Not always," I said. "There are good winds and bad winds. You just have to choose what you want, that's all. *Do what thou wilt*. It's as simple as that. You can be bullied or you can fight back. You can ride the wind like an eagle, Nanou—or you can choose to let it blow you away."

For a long time she said nothing but sat very quietly, looking at my shoe. Finally she raised her head.

"How do you know all this?" she said.

I smiled. "Born in a bookshop, raised by a witch."

"And you'll teach me how to ride the wind?"

"Of course I will. If that's what you want."

Silence as she watched that shoe. A bead of light flicked from the heel and scattered into prisms that laddered the wall.

"Do you want to try them on?"

She looked up at that. "D'you think they'd fit?"

I hid a smile. "Try them and see."

"Oh, wow. Oh, *wow*! How cool is that?"

Teetering like a newborn giraffe on those heels; eyes alight; hands held out in a blind man's fumble and grinning, oblivious of the sign of Lady Blood Moon scratched in pencil against the sole—

"D'you like them?"

She nodded, smiling, suddenly shy. "I love them," she said. "They're lollipop shoes."

Lollipop shoes. That made me smile. And yet there's a rightness to that phrase. "So they're your favorites, are they?" I said.

She nodded again, her eyes like stars.

"Well, you can have them, if you like."

"Have them? To keep?"

"Why not?" I said.

For a moment she was beyond speech. She lifted her foot in a way that managed to be adolescent-gawky and heartbreakingly beautiful all at the same time, and gave me a smile that almost stopped my heart.

Suddenly her face fell. "Maman would never let me wear these. . . ."

"Maman doesn't need to know."

Anouk was still watching her foot, watching the way the light reflected from the spangled red heels onto the floor. I think even then she knew my price; but the lure of those shoes was too much to resist. Shoes that could take you anywhere; shoes that could make you fall in love; shoes that could make you someone else—

"And nothing bad will happen?" she said.

"Nanou." I smiled. "They're only shoes."

Thursday, 6 December

THIERRY HAS BEEN WORKING HARD THIS WEEK. SO HARD THAT I'VE barely spoken to him; between our work in the shop and his refurbishments in the house, there seems to have been no time at all. He phoned today to talk to me about parquet flooring (do I prefer light oak or dark?) but has warned me against dropping by. The place is a mess, he tells me. Plaster dust everywhere; half the floor taken up. Besides, he says, he wants it to be perfect before I see it again.

I dare not ask after Roux, of course, though I know from Zozie that he is there. Five days since he arrived here so unexpectedly, and so far he has not returned. That surprises me a little—though perhaps it should not. I tell myself it's better this way, that seeing him again would only make things even more difficult. But the damage is done. I've seen his face. And outside I can hear a tinkle of chimes, as the wind begins to stir again. . . .

"Perhaps I should just drop by," I said, in a casual tone that fools no one. "It seems so wrong not to see him at all, and. . . ."

Zozie shrugged. "Sure—if you want to get him sacked."

"Sacked?"

"Well, *duh*," she said impatiently. "I don't know if you've noticed, Yanne, but I think Thierry might be just a *little* bit squiggle-eyed about Roux already, and if you start just dropping by, there'll be a scene, and before you know it—"

It made sense, as always, I thought. Trust Zozie to point it out. But I must have looked disappointed, because she grinned and put her arm around my shoulders. "Look, if you like, *I'll* check on Roux. I'll tell him he's more than welcome to come by here whenever he wants to. Hell, I'll even bring him sandwiches if you like."

I laughed at her exuberance. "I don't think that will be necessary."

"Just don't worry. Things'll work out."

I'm beginning to think perhaps they will.

M adame Luzeron was in today, on her way to the cemetery with her little fluffy peach-colored dog. She bought, as always, three rum truffles but seems less distant nowadays; more inclined to sit and stay, to taste a cup of mocha and a slice of my three-layer chocolate cake. She stays, but still she rarely talks, although she likes to watch Rosette drawing under the counter, or looking at one of her storybooks.

Today she was watching the Advent house, now open to show the tableau inside. Today's scene is set in the hallway, with guests arriving at the door of the house, and the hostess in her party dress standing there to welcome them.

"That's a most original display," said Madame Luzeron, moving her powdered face closer to the window. "All the little chocolate mice. And the little dolls—"

"Clever, aren't they? Annie made those."

Madame sipped at her chocolate. "Perhaps she's right," she said at last. "There's nothing so sad as an empty house."

The dolls are all made of wooden pegs, carefully colored and painstakingly dressed. Much time and effort has gone into making them, and I recognize myself in the lady of the house. At least, I recognize Vianne Rocher, her dress made from a scrap of red silk; her long black hair—at Anouk's request—made from a snip of my own hair, glued on and tied up with a bow.

"Where's your doll?" I asked Anouk later.

"Oh, I haven't finished making it yet. But I will," she said, looking so earnest that I smiled. "I'll make a doll for everyone. And by Christmas Eve,

they'll all be done, and all the doors in the house will be open, and there'll
be a big party for everyone—"

Ah, I thought. *The point emerges.*

It's Rosette's birthday on the twentieth. We've never had a party for her.
A bad time, and always was, too close to Yule and not far enough away from
Les Laveuses. Anouk always mentions it every year, though Rosette doesn't
seem to mind. To Rosette, all days are magical, and a handful of buttons
or a piece of scrunched-up silver paper can be every bit as marvelous as the
most exquisite of toys.

"Could *we* have a party too, Maman?"

"Oh, Anouk. You know we can't."

"Why not?" she said stubbornly.

"Well, you know, it's a busy time. And besides, if we're moving to Rue
de la Croix—"

"Well, *duh*," said Anouk. "That's exactly my point. We shouldn't just
move without saying good-bye. We should have a party on Christmas Eve.
For Rosette's birthday. For our friends. Because you know that as soon as
we move into Thierry's place, everything's going to be different, and we'll
have to do everything Thierry's way, and—"

"That's not fair, Anouk," I said.

"But it's true, isn't it?"

"Maybe," I said.

A party on Christmas Eve, I thought. As if I didn't have enough to do
in the *chocolaterie* at the very busiest time of the year. . . .

"Well, I'd help, of course," said Anouk. "I could write out invitations,
and plan the menu, and put up the decorations, and I could make a cake
for Rosette. You know she likes chocolate orange best. We could make
her a cake in the shape of a monkey. Or it could be a fancy dress party,
with everyone dressed like animals. And we could have grenadine—and
Coke—and chocolate, of course."

I had to laugh. "You've thought about this a lot, haven't you?"

She made a face. "Well, maybe a bit."

I sighed.

Why not? Perhaps it's time.

"All right," I said. "You can have your party."

Anouk gave a gleeful wriggle. "Cool! D'you think it'll snow?"

"Well, it might."

"And could people come in fancy dress?"

"If they wanted to, Nanou."

"And could we invite whoever we liked?"

"Of course."

"Even Roux?"

I should have guessed. "Why not?" I said. "If he's still here."

I have not really spoken of Roux to Anouk. I have not mentioned that he is working for Thierry only a couple of blocks away. Lying by omission doesn't quite count; and yet I'm sure that if she knew—

Last night I read the cards again. I don't know why, but I took them out, still fragrant with my mother's scent. I do this so seldom—I barely believe—

And yet, here I am, shuffling the cards with the expertise of many years. Laying them out in the Tree of Life pattern my mother favored; seeing the images flicker by.

Outside the shop, the wind chimes are still, but I can hear it even so: a resonance like that of a tuning fork that makes my head ache and the hairs on my arms stand on end.

Turn over the cards, one by one.

Their faces are more than familiar.

Death; the Lovers; the Hanged Man; Change.

The Fool; the Magus; the Tower.

I shuffle the cards and try again.

The Lovers. The Hanged Man. Change. Death.

Again, the same cards, in a different order, as if what pursues me has subtly altered.

The Magus; the Tower; the Fool.

The Fool has red hair and is playing a flute. He reminds me somehow of the Pied Piper in his feathered hat and patchwork coat—gazing up into the sky, heedless of the dangerous ground. Has he opened the chasm at his feet himself, a trap for whoever might follow him? Or will he go recklessly over the edge?

I hardly slept at all after that. The wind and my dreams conspired to wake me, and on top of that Rosette was restless, less cooperative than at any time in the past six months, and I spent three hours trying to get her to sleep. Nothing worked: not hot chocolate in her special cup; not any of her favorite toys; not her monkey night-light or her special blanket (an oatmeal-colored disaster upon which she dotes); not even my mother's lullaby.

I thought she seemed excited rather than upset, only wailing and hiccuping when I was about to leave, but otherwise perfectly happy for both of us to be wide awake.

Baby, signed Rosette.

"It's nighttime, Rosette. Go to sleep."

Go see baby, she signed again.

"We can't now. Tomorrow, maybe."

Outside, the wind rattled the window frames. Inside, a row of small objects—a domino, a pencil, a piece of chalk, two plastic animal figurines—skittered down from the mantelpiece onto the floor.

"Please, Rosette. Not now. Go to sleep, and tomorrow, we'll see."

At two-thirty I finally managed to get her to sleep, closing the door between us and lying down on my sagging bed. Not quite a double bed, though too large for a single one, it was already old when we moved in, and the random percussion of its broken springs has been the cause of many a sleepless night. Tonight it was an orchestra, and at just after five I gave up on sleep and went downstairs to make coffee.

Outside, it was raining; a fat, heavy rain that sluiced down the alleyway and spouted exuberantly from the guttering. I picked up a blanket that had been lying on the stairs and took it, with my coffee, into the front of the shop. Then I sat down in one of Zozie's armchairs (so much more comfortable than the ones upstairs), and, with only the soft yellow light from the kitchen filtering out through the half-closed door, I curled up and waited for morning to come.

I must have dozed off—a sound awoke me. It was Anouk, barefoot in her red-and-blue-checked pajamas, a blurry shimmer at her heels that could only be Pantoufle. I have noticed over the past few years that although by day Pantoufle can disappear for weeks, and sometimes months on end, he is a stronger and more persistent presence at night. As I suppose he has to be; all children are afraid of the dark. Anouk came over, slid under the blanket, and curled up against me with her hair in my face and her cold feet tucked up behind my knees, as she used to when she was much younger, in the days when things were simple.

"I couldn't sleep. The ceiling drips."

Ah, yes. I'd forgotten. There's a leak in the roof, which no one so far has quite managed to fix. That's the problem with these old buildings. However much work is done on them, there's always something new to address: a rotten window frame; a broken gutter; woodworm in the joist; a cracked slate. And though Thierry has always been generous, I don't like to ask him too often for help. It's nonsense, I know; but I don't like to ask.

"I was thinking about our party," she said. "Does Thierry really have to come? You know he'll ruin everything."

I gave a sigh. "Oh, please. Not now." Anouk's violent enthusiasms usually amuse me, but not at six in the morning.

"Go on, Maman," she said. "Couldn't we just not invite him this time?"

"We'll be fine," I said. "You'll see." I was quite aware that it wasn't an answer, and Anouk shifted restlessly, pulling the blanket over her head. She smelled of vanilla and lavender and the faint, sheepy scent of her tangled hair, grown coarser over the past four years, like uncarded wild wool.

Rosette's hair is still baby fine, like milkweed and marigolds, rubbed thin at the back where her head rests against the pillow at night. Four years old in less than two weeks, and she still has the look of a much younger child: arms and legs like little pipes, eyes too large for her small face. My Cat Baby, I used to call her, back in the days when it was still a joke.

My Cat Baby. My changeling.

Under the blanket, Anouk moved again, tucking her face into my shoulder and her hands into my armpit.

"You're cold," I said.

She shook her head.

"How about a cup of hot chocolate?"

She shook her head, more violently. I found myself marveling at the way these little things can tear at the heart—the forgotten kiss, the discarded toy, the unwanted story, the look of annoyance where once there would have been a smile. . . .

Children are knives, my mother once said. *They don't mean to, but they cut.* And yet we cling to them, don't we, we clasp them until the blood flows. My summer child, grown stranger as the year turns, and it struck me how long it had been since she had let me hold her this way, and I wished it could be longer, but the clock on the wall said six-fifteen—

"Get into my bed, Nanou. It's warmer there, and the ceiling won't drip."

"What about Thierry?" she said.

"We'll talk about it later, Nanou."

"Rosette doesn't want him," said Anouk.

"How on earth can you know that?"

Anouk shrugged. "I just know."

I sighed and kissed the top of her head. Again, that sheepy-vanilla scent—and with it, something stronger and more adult, which I finally identified as frankincense. Zozie burns it in her rooms. I know Anouk spends a lot of time there, talking and trying on her clothes. It's good for her to have someone like Zozie; an adult—not me—in whom to confide.

"You ought to give Thierry a chance. I know he's not perfect, but he really likes you—"

"*You* don't really want him either," she said. "You don't even miss him when he's not there. You're not in *love*."

"Now don't start that," I said, exasperated. "There are lots of different ways of loving. I love *you*; and I love Rosette; and just because what I feel for Thierry isn't the same, it doesn't mean that I—"

But Anouk wasn't listening. She struggled out from under the blanket, shaking herself free of my arms. I know what this is about, I thought. She liked Thierry well enough before Roux came back, and when he's gone—

"I know what's best. I'm doing this for you, Nanou."

Anouk shrugged, looking very like Roux.

"Trust me. We're going to be fine."

"Whatever," she said and went upstairs.

10

Friday, 7 December

OH DEAR. IT'S SO SAD WHEN COMMUNICATIONS BREAK DOWN BETWEEN a mother and her daughter. Especially a pair as close as these two. Today Vianne was tired; I could see it in her face. I don't think she slept very much last night. Too tired, in any case, to notice the growing resentment in her daughter's eyes, or the way she turns to me for approval.

Still, Vianne's loss can be my gain; and now I am on the scene, so to speak, I can make my influence felt in a hundred inconspicuous new ways. Let's start with the skills that Vianne has so cleverly subverted: those wonderful weapons of will and desire—

So far I have still not found out what Anouk fears from using them. Something happened, certainly; something for which she feels responsible. But weapons are meant to be used, Nanou. For good or for ill. It's your choice.

For the moment she still lacks confidence, but I have assured her that no possible harm can come of a little working or two. She may even use them on behalf of others—it rankles, of course, but we can cure her of selflessness later on—and by then, it won't be a novelty, and we can work on essential things.

So what is it you want, Anouk?

What is it that you really want?

Well, of course, those things that every good child wants. To do well at school; to be popular; to gain petty revenge on her enemies. Those things are easily dealt with, and we can move on to working with people.

There's Madame Luzeron, so like a sad old porcelain doll with her pale, powdered face and her precise, brittle movements. She needs to buy more chocolate; three rum truffles a week is hardly enough to justify our attention.

Then there's Laurent, who comes every day and sits for hours over a single cup. He's more of a nuisance than anything. His presence can discourage the rest—especially Richard and Mathurin, who would otherwise call round every day—and he steals the sugar lumps from the bowl, filling his pockets with the air of a man who means to get his money's worth.

Then there's Fat Nico. An excellent customer, buying up to six boxes a week. But Anouk worries about his health; has noticed him walking up the Butte and is alarmed at the effort it takes him even to climb a flight of steps. He shouldn't be so fat, she says. Is there a way to help him too?

Well, you and I know that you don't get far by granting wishes. But the way to her heart is a tortuous one, and if I'm not wrong, the returns will be more than worth my while. Meanwhile I let her amuse herself—as a kitten may sharpen its claws on a ball of wool in readiness for its first mouse.

And so our curriculum begins. Lesson One, sympathetic magic.

In other words, dolls.

We make the dolls out of wooden clothes pegs—it's far less messy than using clay—and she carries them around with her, two in each pocket, awaiting the moment to test them out.

Peg-doll one: Madame Luzeron. Tall and stiff in a dress made from a stray piece of taffeta tied with rusty ribbon. Hair made out of cotton wool; little black shoes and dusky shawl. Features drawn on in felt pen—Nanou pulling a dreadful face as she concentrates on getting the expression just right—there's even a cotton-wool replica of her fuzzy little dog, attached to Madame's belt with a twist of pipe cleaner. It will do; and a strand of Madame's hair, carefully picked from the back of her coat, will complete the figure in no time at all.

Peg-doll two is Anouk herself. There is an uncanny accuracy to the small figures she creates: this one has Anouk's curly hair and is dressed in a piece of yellow cloth, with Pantoufle in gray wool, perched on her shoulder.

Peg-doll three is Thierry le Tresset, complete with his mobile phone.

Peg-doll four is Vianne Rocher, dressed in a bright red party frock, rather than her usual black. In fact I've only seen her wear red on one occasion. But in Anouk's mind, Mother wears red—the color of life and love and magic. That's interesting. I can use that. But later, perhaps, when the time is right.

Meanwhile, I have other work to do. Not least in the *chocolaterie*; with Christmas approaching in giant strides, it's time to really build up that clientele; to find out who has been naughty or nice; to try, test, taste our winter stock—and perhaps add a few special little extras of our own.

Chocolate can act as a medium for many things. Our handmade truffles—still a favorite—are rolled in a mixture of cocoa powder, icing sugar, and a number of additional substances of which my mother would certainly not have approved, but which ensure that our customers are not only satisfied, but also refreshed, energized, and eager for more. Today we sold thirty-six boxes of the truffles alone, with orders left for a dozen extra. At this rate we could top a hundred a day by Christmas.

Thierry called round at five today to report on the progress of the flat. He seemed slightly bewildered at the unusual level of activity in the shop and, I would say, not entirely pleased.

"It's like a factory in there," he remarked, with a nod at the kitchen door, where Vianne was making *mendiants du roi*—thick slices of candied orange dipped in dark chocolate and scattered with edible gold leaf—so pretty it's almost a shame to eat them, and perfect for the season, of course. "Doesn't she ever take any time off?"

I smiled. "You know. The Christmas rush."

He grunted. "I'll be glad when it's all over with. I've never been so pushed with a job. Still, it's going to be worth it—assuming I get it done on time. . . ."

I saw Anouk shoot him a look as she sat at the table with Rosette.

"Don't worry," he said. "A promise is a promise. It's going to be the best

Christmas ever. Just the four of us, at Rue de la Croix. We can go to midnight mass at the Sacré-Coeur. Wouldn't that be great, eh?"

"Maybe." Her voice was expressionless.

I saw him suppress an impatient sigh. Anouk can be very hard work, and her resistance to him is palpable. Perhaps this is because of Roux, still absent but always in her thoughts. I've seen him regularly, of course, a couple of times on the Butte itself, once crossing Place du Tertre, once going down the stairs by the funicular—moving fast and with a knitted cap to cover his hair, as if he's afraid to be recognized.

I've also met up with him at the hostel in which he is staying, to check on his progress, to feed him lies, to cash his checks, and to ensure that he stays docile and obedient. He's getting understandably impatient by now, and a little hurt that Vianne has not yet asked for him. Plus he's working all hours for Thierry, of course, beginning at eight in the morning and often finishing late at night, and when he leaves Rue de la Croix he's sometimes too tired even to eat, but goes back to his hostel and sleeps like the dead.

As for Vianne, I sense her concern—and her disappointment too. She has not been to Rue de la Croix. Anouk too is under strict instructions to stay away. If Roux wants to see them, he'll come, Vianne says. If not—well. It's his choice.

Thierry was looking more impatient than ever. He stepped into the kitchen, where Vianne was carefully laying out the finished *mendiants* onto a sheet of baking paper. I thought there was something furtive in the way he pulled the door half-closed, and I noticed his colors were brighter than usual, edged with jittery reds and purples.

"I've hardly seen you all this week." His voice carries; I could hear it quite clearly from the front of the shop. Vianne's is less easy to hear; a murmur of something like protest, perhaps. The sound of a scuffle. His giant laughter. "Come on. One kiss. I've missed you, Yanne."

That murmur again, her voice rising. "Thierry, be careful. The chocolates—"

I hid a smile. The old goat. Getting frisky, is he? Well, that doesn't surprise me at all. That chivalrous facade may have fooled Vianne, but men, like dogs, are predictable, Thierry le Tresset more than most. Beneath his apparent self-confidence, Thierry is deeply insecure, and the arrival of Roux has made him more so. He has become territorial, both at Rue de la Croix, where his hold on Roux gives him a strange, unacknowledged thrill, and here at Le Rocher de Montmartre.

I heard Vianne's voice faintly through the door. "Thierry, please. This isn't the time."

Meanwhile Anouk was listening. Her face showed no expression at all, but her colors gleamed. I smiled at her. She didn't smile back. Instead she glanced at the door and made a little beckoning movement with her fingers. Anyone else would have missed it. She might not even have known she was making it. But at the same moment, a draft seemed to catch at the kitchen door, and it swung open sharply, slamming against the painted wall.

A small interruption, but it was enough. I caught a flash of annoyance from Thierry's colors, a kind of relief from Vianne herself. Of course this impatience is new to her; she is so used to thinking of him as an avuncular figure: dependable; safe; if a little dull. His new possessiveness is slightly overwhelming, and for the first time she is dimly aware of a feeling, not just of alarm, but of distaste.

It's all because of Roux, she thinks. All her doubts will leave with him. But for now the uncertainty makes her nervous, unreasonable. She kisses Thierry on the mouth—guilt is sea green, in the language of colors—and gives him a smile that is overbright.

"I'll make it up to you," she says.

With two fingers of her right hand, Anouk makes a tiny gesture of dismissal.

Opposite, on her little chair, Rosette is watching her, bright-eyed. She copies the sign—*tsk-tsk, begone!*—and Thierry slaps a hand to the back of his neck, as if an insect has stung him there. The wind chimes ring—

"I have to go."

Indeed he does; clumsy in his big overcoat, he almost trips as he opens the door. Anouk's hand is in her pocket now, where she keeps his peg-doll safe. She pulls it out and goes to the display window, where she places it carefully outside the house.

"Bye, Thierry," says Anouk.

Rosette signs with her fingers. *Bye-bye.*

The door slams shut. The children smile.

It's really very drafty today.

11

Saturday, 8 December

WELL, IT'S A START. THE BALANCE IS SHIFTING. NANOU MAY NOT SEE IT, but I do. Little things, benign at first, that will make her mine in no time at all.

She stayed in the shop for most of today, playing with Rosette, helping out—and waiting for another chance to use those new peg-dolls of hers. She found one in Madame Luzeron, who came in midmorning—though it wasn't her day—with her fluffy little dog in tow.

"Back so soon?" I smiled at her. "We must be doing something right."

I saw that her face looked rather drawn; and she was wearing her cemetery coat, which meant that she must have called there again. Perhaps a special day, I thought—a birthday or an anniversary—in any case, she looked tired and vaguely brittle, and her gloved hands were shaking with cold.

"Sit down," I suggested. "I'll bring you some chocolate."

Madame hesitated.

"I shouldn't," she said.

Anouk gave me a furtive glance, and I saw her pull out Madame's peg-doll, marked with the seductive sign of Lady Blood Moon. A plug of modeling clay serves as a base, and in a second Madame Luzeron—or at least, her double—stands inside the Advent house, looking out at the lake with its skaters and its chocolate ducks.

For a moment she seemed not to notice; and then her eye was strangely drawn—perhaps to the child with her bright, rosy face; perhaps to the object in the window, now glowing with a curious light.

Her disapproving mouth softened a little.

"You know, I had a dollhouse when I was a girl," she said, peering into the display window.

"Really?" I said, smiling at Anouk. It's rare that Madame volunteers information.

Madame Luzeron sipped her chocolate. "Yes. It was my grandmother's, and although it was supposed to come to me when she died, I was never allowed to play with it."

"Why not?" said Anouk, fixing the little cotton-wool dog more firmly to the peg-doll's dress.

"Oh, it was too valuable—an antiquarian once offered me a hundred thousand francs for it—and besides, it was an heirloom. Not a toy."

"So you never got to play with it. That's not fair," said Anouk, now carefully placing a green sugar mouse under a tissue-paper tree.

"Well, I was young," said Madame Luzeron. "I might have damaged it or—"

She stopped. I looked up and saw her frozen.

"What a funny thing," she said. "I haven't thought of it in years. And when Robert wanted to play with it—"

She put down her cup with a sudden brisk mechanical movement.

"It *wasn't* fair, was it?" she said.

"Are you all right, madame?" I said. Her thin face was the color of icing sugar, sculpted into sharp little wrinkles like the frosting on a cake.

"I'm fine, thank you." Her voice was cool.

"Would you like a piece of chocolate cake?" That was Anouk, looking concerned, always wanting to give things away. Madame gave her a hungry look.

"Thank you, my dear. I'd love one," she said.

Anouk cut a generous slice. "Robert—was that your son?" she said.

Madame pecked out a silent *yes*.

"How old was he when he died?"

"Thirteen," said Madame. "A little older than you, perhaps. They never found out what was wrong with him. Such a healthy boy—I never let him eat sweets, even—then, suddenly, dead. You wouldn't think it was possible, would you?"

Anouk shook her head, wide-eyed.

"Today's his anniversary," she went on. "Eighth of December, 1979. Long before you were born. In those days you could still get a plot in the big cemetery—if you were prepared to pay enough. I've lived here forever. My family has money. I could have let him play with the dollhouse if I'd wanted to. Have *you* ever had a dollhouse?"

Once more, Anouk shook her head.

"I have it still, somewhere in the attic. I even have the dolls it came with, and the little furniture. All handmade in original materials. Venetian mirrors on the walls. Crafted before the Revolution. I wonder if any child *ever* got to play with the damn thing."

She was looking slightly flushed now, as if her use of a forbidden word had infused her bloodless face with something approaching animation.

"Perhaps *you* might like to play with it."

Anouk's eyes lit up at once. "Wow!"

"You're very welcome, little girl." She frowned. "You know, I don't think I actually know your names. I'm Isabelle—and my little dog is Salammbô. You can stroke her if you like. She doesn't bite."

Anouk bent to touch the little dog, which frisked and licked enthusiastically at her hands. "She's so sweet. I love dogs."

"I can't believe I've been coming here for years and I never even asked your names."

Anouk grinned. "I'm Anouk," she said. "And this is my good friend Zozie." And she went on fussing with the little dog, and such was her absorption that she never even noticed that she'd given Madame the wrong name, or that the sign of Lady Blood Moon was shining out from the Advent house, shining with a radiance that filled the room.

Sunday, 9 December

THE WEATHERMAN LIED. HE SAID THERE'D BE SNOW. HE SAID THERE'D BE a cold snap, but all we've had so far is mist and rain. It's better in the Advent house—it's proper Christmas *there*, at least, and outside it's all frost and ice, like something in a story, with icing-sugar icicles hanging down from the roof and a fresh scatter of sugar snow over the lake. Some of the peg-dolls are skating there, all muffled up in hats and coats, and some children (they're supposed to be Rosette, Jean-Loup, and me) are building an igloo out of sugar cubes, while someone else (Nico, in fact) is dragging the Christmas tree up to the house on a matchbox sledge.

I've been making a lot of peg-dolls this week. I'm putting them round the Advent house, where everyone can see them without really noticing what they're for. They're really cool to make, you know; you can draw on the faces with felt-tip pen, and Zozie brought me a box of scraps of ribbon and cloth for making the clothes and the other stuff. So far I've got Nico, Alice, Madame Luzeron, Rosette, Roux, Thierry, Jean-Loup, Maman, and me.

Some of them aren't finished, though. You have to finish them with something that belongs to the person: a strand of hair; a fingernail; or something they've touched or worn. It isn't always easy getting those things; and then you have to give them a name and a sign and whisper a secret into their ear.

With some people, that's easy to do. Some secrets are easy to guess: like Madame Luzeron, who feels so sad about her son, even though he died so long ago; or Nico, who wants to lose weight but can't; or Alice, who can, but really shouldn't.

As for the names and the symbols we use—Zozie says they're Mexican. They could be anything, I guess, but we use these because they're interesting, and the symbols are not too hard to remember.

There are a lot of symbols, though, and it may take a while to learn them all. Plus I don't always remember which names to use—they're so long and complicated, and of course I don't know the language. But Zozie says that's OK, as long as I can remember what the symbols mean. There's the Ear of Maize, for good luck; Two Rabbit, who made wine from the maguey cactus; Eagle Snake, for power; Seven Macaw, for success; One Monkey, the trickster; the Smoking Mirror, which shows you things that regular people don't always see; Lady Green Skirt, who looks after mothers and children; One Jaguar, for courage and to protect you from bad things; and Lady Moon Rabbit—that's my sign—for love.

Everyone has a special sign, she says. Zozie's sign is One Jaguar. Maman's is Ehecatl, the Changing Wind. I suppose they're like the totems we had, back in the days before Rosette was born. Rosette's sign, Zozie says, is Red Tezcatlipoca, the Monkey. He's a mischievous god, but a powerful one; and he can change his shape to that of any animal.

I like the old stories Zozie tells. But I can't help feeling nervous sometimes. I know she says we don't do any harm—but what if she's wrong? What if there's an Accident? What if I use the wrong kind of sign and make something bad happen without meaning to?

The river. The wind. The Kindly Ones.

Those words keep coming into my mind. And they're all tied up somehow with the Nativity scene in Place du Tertre—the angels and the animals and the Magi—though I still don't know what they're doing there. Sometimes I think I can almost see, but never quite enough to be sure, like one of those dreams that makes perfect sense until the minute you wake up, when it just dissolves into nothing at all.

The river. The wind. The Kindly Ones—

What does that mean? Words in a dream. But I'm still so afraid, though I don't know why. What is there to be afraid of? Perhaps the Kindly Ones are like the Magi: wise men bearing gifts. It feels right, but it doesn't stop me feeling scared, that something bad's about to happen. That it's somehow my fault—

Zozie says I shouldn't worry. We can't hurt anyone unless we want to, she says. And I don't ever want to hurt anyone—not even Chantal, not even Suze.

I made Nico's doll the other night. I had to pad it to make it look real, and I made his hair from the wiry brown stuff that was inside Zozie's old armchair, upstairs in her room with her other things. Then you have to give it a symbol—I chose One Jaguar, for courage—and whisper a secret in its ear. So I said: *Nico, you need to take control*—which ought to do it, don't you think?—and I'll put it behind one of the doors in the Advent house and wait until he comes along.

And then there's Alice, who's his opposite. I had to make her a bit fatter than she really is, because peg-dolls can only be so thin. I tried taking some wood off the sides of the doll, and that worked OK until I cut my finger with the penknife, and Zozie had to bandage it up. Then I made her a pretty little dress out of a piece of old scrap lace, and whispered, *Alice, you're not ugly and you need to eat more*, and gave her the fish sign of Chantico the Fast Breaker, and put her next to Nico in the Advent house.

Then there's Thierry, wrapped in gray flannel and with a wrapped sugar lump painted to look like his mobile phone. I couldn't get hold of a strand of his hair, so instead I took a petal from one of the roses that he gave Maman and hoped that might work instead. Of course I don't want anything bad to happen to him. I only want him to stay away.

So I gave him the sign of One Monkey and put him *outside* the Advent house, with his coat and scarf on (I made them out of brown felt), just in case it gets cold out there.

And then, of course, there's Roux. His doll isn't finished yet, because I need something of his, and there isn't anything I can use—not even a thread—that belongs to him. But I've made it look like him, I think, all in black, with a piece of orange furry stuff glued on to look like his hair. I gave him the sign of the Changing Wind, and whispered *Roux, don't go away*—though so far we haven't seen him at all.

Not that it matters. I know where he is. He's working for Thierry at Rue de la Croix. I don't know why he hasn't come back, or why Maman doesn't want to see him, or even why Thierry hates him so much.

I talked to Zozie about it today, as we sat in her rooms as usual. Rosette was there, and we'd been playing a game—quite a noisy, silly game, and Rosette was excited and laughing like mad, with Zozie being a wild horse and Rosette riding on her back, and then suddenly, for no reason, the hairs stood up on the back of my neck, and I looked up and saw a yellow monkey sitting on the mantelpiece, as clear as I sometimes see Pantoufle.

"Zozie," I said.

She looked up. She didn't seem all that surprised; it turns out she's seen Bam before.

"That's a clever little sister you've got," she said, smiling at Rosette, who had got down from her back and was playing with the sequins on a cushion. "You don't look at all alike, but I guess looks aren't everything."

I hugged Rosette and gave her a kiss. Sometimes she reminds me of a rag doll, or a flop-eared bunny, she's so soft. "Well, we don't have the same dad," I told her.

Zozie smiled. "I guessed," she said.

"But that doesn't matter," I went on. "Maman says you choose your family."

"She does?"

I nodded. "It's better that way. Our family could be anyone. It's not about birth, Maman says. It's about how you feel for someone else."

"So—even I could be family?"

I smiled at her. "You already are."

She laughed at that. "Your evil aunt. Corrupting you with magic and shoes."

Well, that set me off. Rosette joined in. And above us, the yellow monkey danced and made everything on the mantelpiece dance too—all Zozie's shoes, lined up like ornaments, but so much cooler than china figurines— and I thought how natural it seemed, the three of us, all together like that. And I felt a sudden pang of guilt about Maman downstairs, and about how, when we're up here, it can sometimes be easy to forget she's there at all.

"Did you never wonder who Rosette's father was?" said Zozie suddenly, looking at me.

I shrugged. I've never seen the point. We always had each other, of course. We never wanted anyone else—

"It's just that you probably knew him," she said. "You would have been six or seven at the time, and I just wondered. . . ." She looked down at her bracelet, playing with the charms on it, and I got the feeling she was trying to tell me something, but something she didn't want to say.

"What?" I said.

"Well—look at her hair." She put a hand on Rosette's head. Her hair is the color of sliced mango, very curly and very soft. "Look at her eyes." Her eyes are a very pale green-gray, just like a cat's, and as round as pennies. "Doesn't that remind you of someone?"

I thought about that for a little while.

"Think, Nanou. Red hair, green eyes. Can sometimes be a pain in the arse."

"Not Roux?" I said, and began to laugh, but all at once I was feeling jittery inside and I wished she wouldn't say any more.

"Why not?" said Zozie.

"I just know."

As a matter of fact I've never really thought much about Rosette's dad. I suppose that at the back of my mind there's still the idea she never had one at all; that the fairies brought her, just like the old lady always said.

Fairy baby. Special baby.

I mean, it's not fair what people think—that she's stupid, or retarded, or slow. *Special baby*, we used to say. Special, as in different. Maman doesn't like us to be different—but Rosette just is, and is that so bad?

Thierry talks about getting help for her. Therapy, speech coaching, and all kinds of specialists—as if there might be a cure for being special that a specialist would be bound to know.

But there's no cure for being different. Zozie's taught me that already. And how could Roux be Rosette's dad? I mean, he's never seen her before. Didn't even know her name—

"He *can't* be Rosette's dad," I said, although by then I wasn't sure.

"Well, who else could it be?" she said.

"I don't know. Not Roux, that's all."

"Why not?"

"Because he'd have stayed with us, that's why. He wouldn't have let us go away."

"Well, maybe he didn't know," she said. "Maybe your mother never told him. After all, she never told *you*."

I started to cry then. Stupid, I know. I hate it when I have to cry, but I couldn't make it stop, somehow. It was like an explosion inside of me, and I couldn't figure out if I hated Roux now, or whether I loved him even more—

"Shhh. Nanou." Zozie put her arms around me. "It's OK."

I put my face into her shoulder. She was wearing a big old chunky sweater, and the cable knit pressed into my cheek hard enough to leave marks. It isn't OK, I wanted to tell her. That's just what adults always say when they don't want kids to know the truth; and most of the time it's a lie, Zozie.

Adults always seem to lie.

I gave a great big shuddery sob. How can Roux be Rosette's dad? She doesn't even know him. She doesn't know that he takes his hot chocolate black, with rum and brown sugar. She hasn't seen him make a fish trap out of willow, or a flute out of a length of bamboo, or know that he hears the call of every bird on the river and can copy them so that even the birds can't tell the difference—

He's her father, and she doesn't even know.

It's not fair. It should have been *me*—

But now I could feel something else coming back. A memory—a familiar sound—a scent of something far away. It was getting closer now, moving in like the pointing star in a Nativity scene. And I could almost remember now—except that I didn't *want* to remember. I closed my eyes. I could hardly move. I was suddenly sure that if I moved even a little bit, then all of it would come rushing out, like a fizzy drink when someone's been shaking the bottle, and that once opened, there'd be no going back—

I started to tremble.

"What's wrong?" said Zozie.

I couldn't move. I couldn't speak.

"What are you afraid of, Nanou?"

I could hear the charms on her bracelet moving, and the sound was almost exactly the same as that of the wind chimes above our door.

"The Kindly Ones," I said in a whisper.

"What does that mean? The Kindly Ones?" I could hear the urgency in her voice. She put her hands on my shoulders then, and I could *feel* how much she wanted to know; it was trembling all through her, like lightning in a jar.

"Don't be afraid, Nanou," she said. "Just tell me what it means, OK?"

The Kindly Ones.

The Magi.

Wise men bearing gifts.

I made the kind of noise you make when you're trying to wake up from a dream but can't. There were too many memories crowding me, pushing me, all wanting to be seen at once.

That little house by the side of the Loire.

They'd seemed so kind, so interested.

They'd even brought gifts.

And at that moment I opened my eyes very suddenly and very wide. I didn't feel afraid anymore. At last I remembered. I understood. I knew what had happened to change us; to make us run away, even from Roux; to make us pretend we were regular people when we knew at heart we could never be.

"What is it, Nanou?" said Zozie. "Can you tell me now?"

"I think so," I said.

"Then tell me," she said, beginning to smile. "Tell me everything."

PART SIX

The Kindly Ones

Monday, 10 December

AND NOW AT LAST, HERE IT COMES, THAT DECEMBER WIND, SCREAMING down the narrow streets, stripping the year-end rags from the trees. *December, beware; December, despair*, as my mother always said. And once again, as the year draws in, it feels as if a page has turned.

A page—a card—the wind, perhaps. And December was always a bad time for us. The last month; the dregs of the year; slouching toward Christmas with its skirt of tinsel dragging in the mud. The dead-end part of the year looms; the trees are stripped three-quarters bare; the light is like scorched newspaper; and all my ghosts come out to play like fireflies in the spectral sky—

We came on the wind of the carnival. A wind of change, of promises. The merry wind, the magical wind, making March hares of everyone, tumbling blossoms and coattails and hats; rushing toward summer in a frenzy of exuberance.

Anouk was a child of that wind. A summer child; her totem, the rabbit—eager, bright-eyed, and mischievous.

My mother was a great believer in totems. Much more than just an invisible friend, a totem reveals the secret heart; the spirit; the secret soul. Mine was a cat, or so she said—thinking perhaps of that baby bangle and its little silver charm. Cats are secretive by nature. Cats have split personalities. Cats run scared at a breath of wind. Cats can see the spirit world and walk the line between light and dark.

The wind blew stronger, and we fled. Not least because of Rosette, of course. I'd known from the start I was carrying a child, and like a cat, I bore her in secret, far away from Lansquenet—

But by December the wind had turned, taking the year from light into dark. I'd carried Anouk with no difficulty. My summer child came with the sun, at four-fifteen on a bright June morning, and from the moment I set eyes on her I knew she was mine, and mine alone.

But Rosette was different from the start. A small, limp, fretful baby who wouldn't feed and who looked at me as if I were a stranger. The hospital was on the outskirts of Rennes, and as I waited beside Rosette, a priest dropped by to counsel me, and to express surprise that I would not have my daughter baptized in the hospital.

He seemed a calm and kindly man, but too like so many of his kind, with his well-worn words of comfort and his eyes that saw all of the next world, but none of this one. I gave him the usual litany. I was a widow, Madame Rocher, on my way to live with relatives. He clearly did not believe this; looked at Anouk with suspicious eyes and upon Rosette with growing concern. She might not live, he told me earnestly; could I bear to have her die unbaptized?

I sent Anouk to a hostel nearby while I recovered slowly and watched over Rosette. It was in a very small village—a place called Les Laveuses, on the Loire. And it was to there that I fled from the kind old priest as Rosette's strength dwindled and his demands became more insistent.

For kindness can kill as readily as cruelty; and the priest—whose name was Père Leblanc—had begun to make independent enquiries regarding any relatives I might have in the region, including who might be looking after my eldest daughter, where she had received her schooling, and the fate of the imaginary Monsieur Rocher—enquiries that I did not doubt would eventually lead him to the truth.

So one morning I took Rosette and fled by taxi to Les Laveuses. The hostel was cheap and impersonal; a single room with a gas fire and a double bed with a mattress that sagged almost to the floor. Rosette was still reluctant to feed, and her voice was a pitiful plaintive mew that seemed to echo the wail of the wind. Worse still, her breathing would sometimes falter, stopping for five or ten seconds at a time, then hitching back with a hiccup and a snuffle, as if my baby had decided—if only temporarily—to rejoin the land of the living.

We stayed in the hostel for two more nights. Then, as New Year approached, the snow arrived, dusting the black trees and the sandbanks along the Loire with bitter sugar. I looked for somewhere else to stay and was offered a flat above a little *crêperie* run by an elderly couple called Paul and Framboise.

"It's not very big, but it's warm," Framboise said—a fierce little lady with berry-black eyes. "You'll be doing me a favor, keeping an eye on the place. We're closed in winter—no tourists here—so you needn't be afraid of getting in the way." She looked at me closely. "That baby," she said. "It cries like a cat."

I nodded.

"Hm." She sniffed. "You should get it seen to."

"What does she mean?" I asked Paul later as he showed us our little two-room flat.

Paul, a gentle old man who rarely spoke, looked at me and shrugged. "She's superstitious," he said at last. "Like a lot of old people round here. Don't take it to heart. She means well."

I was too tired then to enquire further. But after we had settled in, and Rosette had begun to feed a little—though she remained very restless and barely slept—I asked Framboise what she had meant.

"They say a cat baby's bad luck," said Framboise, who had come in to clean the already spotless kitchen.

I smiled. She sounded so very like Armande, my dear old friend from Lansquenet.

"Cat baby?" I said.

"Hm," said Framboise. "I've heard of them but never seen one. My father used to tell me the fairies would sometimes come in the night and put a cat in place of the real baby. But the Cat Baby won't feed. The Cat Baby cries all the time. And if anyone upsets the Cat Baby, then the fairies will sort them out for sure."

She narrowed her eyes menacingly, then just as suddenly smiled. "Of course, it's only a story," she said. "All the same, you should see a doctor. Cat Baby doesn't look well to me."

That at least was true enough. But I've never been easy with doctors and priests, and I hesitated to follow the old lady's advice. Three more days elapsed, with Rosette mewing and gasping throughout, and eventually I overcame my reluctance and called to see the doctor in nearby Angers.

The doctor examined Rosette with care. She needed tests, he said at last. But that cry confirmed it in his mind. It was a genetic condition, he said, most commonly known as cri du chat, thus named for that eerie, mewing cry. Not fatal, but incurable; and with symptoms that, at this early stage, the doctor was hesitant to predict.

"So she *is* a Cat Baby," said Anouk.

It seemed to delight her that Rosette was different. She'd been an only child for so long; and now, at seven, she seemed at times weirdly adult. Caring for Rosette; coaxing her to feed from a bottle; singing to her; rocking her in the chair Paul had brought from their old farmhouse.

"Cat Baby," she crooned, rocking the chair. "Rock-a-Cat Baby, on the treetop." And Rosette did seem to respond to her. The crying stopped—at least some of the time. She gained weight. She slept up to three or four hours at night. Anouk said it was the air of Les Laveuses, and put down saucers of milk and sugar for the fairies, in case they called by to see how the Cat Baby was doing.

I had not returned to the doctor in Angers. Further tests would not improve Rosette. Instead we watched her, Anouk and I; we bathed her in herbs; we sang to her; we massaged her thin little pipe-stick limbs with lavender and tiger balm and fed her milk from an eyedropper (she would not take a bottle).

A fairy baby, Anouk said. She certainly was a pretty one; so delicate with her small shapely head and her wide-spaced eyes and pointed chin.

"She even *looks* like a cat," said Anouk. "Pantoufle says so. Don't you, Pantoufle?"

Ah, yes. Pantoufle. At first I'd thought maybe Pantoufle would disappear, once Anouk had a baby sister to care for. The wind was still blowing across the Loire, and Yule, like midsummer, is a time of change; an uncomfortable time for travelers.

But with the arrival of Rosette, Pantoufle seemed, if anything, to get stronger. I found I now saw him with increasing clarity—sitting beside the baby's crib; watching her with button-black eyes as Anouk rocked her and talked to her and sang songs to quiet her.

V'là l'bon vent, v'là l'joli vent

"Poor Rosette doesn't have an animal," said Anouk as we sat together by the fire. "Maybe that's why she cries all the time. Maybe we should ask one to come. To look after her, the way Pantoufle looks after me."

I smiled at that. But she was in earnest; and I should have known that if I didn't address the problem, she would. And so I promised we'd give it a try. Just this once, I'd play the game. And we'd been so good for the past six months: no cards, no charms, no rituals. I missed it, and so did Anouk. What harm could come of a simple game?

We'd been living in Les Laveuses for nearly a week, and things were beginning to get better for us. We'd already made some friends in the village; I'd grown very fond of Framboise and Paul. We were comfortable in the flat above the *crêperie*. With Rosette's birth we had more or less missed Christmas, but the New Year was approaching, full of the promise of new beginnings. The air was still cold, but it was clear and frosty, and the sky was a vibrant, piercing blue. Rosette continued to worry me; but we were slowly learning her ways, and with the help of the eyedropper, we were able to give her the nourishment she needed.

Then Père Leblanc caught up with us. He arrived with a woman he said was a nurse, but whose questions, repeated to me by Anouk, led me to suspect that perhaps she was some kind of social worker. I was out when they called—Paul had driven me to Angers to pick up some nappies and milk for Rosette—but Anouk was there, and Rosette was in her crib upstairs. And they'd brought a basket of groceries for us, and they were so kind and interested—asking after me, implying we were friends—that my trusting Anouk, in her innocence, told them far more than was wise.

She told them about Lansquenet-sous-Tannes and about our travels along the Garonne with the river gypsies. She told them about the chocolate shop, and the festival we had organized. She told them about Yule and Saturnalia, and the Oak King and the Holly King, and the two great winds that divide the year. When they expressed interest in the red good-luck sachets over the door and the saucers of bread and salt on the step, she spoke of fairies, and little gods, and animal totems, and candlelit rituals, and drawing down the moon, and singing to the wind, and Tarot cards, and cat babies—

Cat babies?

"Oh yes," replied my summer child. "Rosette's a cat baby, which is why she likes milk. And that's why she cries like a cat all night. But it's all right. She just needs a totem. We're still waiting for it to arrive."

I can only imagine what they made of that. Secrets and rites; unbaptized infants; children left with strangers, or worse—

He asked her if she would come with him. Of course, he had no authority. He told her she'd be safe with him; that he would keep her safe throughout the investigation. He might even have taken her away, but for Framboise, who came in to check on Rosette and found them sitting there in her kitchen, with Anouk close to tears and the priest and the woman talking earnestly to her, telling her that they knew she was afraid, that she wasn't alone, that hundreds of children were just like her, that she could be saved if she trusted them—

Well, Framboise put an end to that. She sent them both packing with a flick of her tongue, made tea for Anouk and milk for Rosette. She was still there when Paul brought me home; and she told me of the visit from the woman and the priest.

"Those folk just don't know how to mind their business," she said scornfully over her tea. "Looking for devils under the bed. I told them—all you have to do is look at her face." She nodded toward Anouk, now playing quietly with Pantoufle. "Is that the face of a child in danger? Does she look afraid to you?"

I was grateful to her, of course. But I knew in my heart that they'd be back. Perhaps with official papers next time, some kind of a warrant to search or to question. I knew Père Leblanc would not give up; that given the chance, that kindly, well-meaning, dangerous man—or someone just like him, one of his kind—would follow me to the ends of the earth.

"We'll leave tomorrow," I said at last.

Anouk gave a wail of protest. "No! Not again!"

"We have to, Nanou. Those people—"

"Why us? Why does it always have to be us? Why doesn't the wind blow *them* away, for a change?"

I looked at Rosette, asleep in her crib. At Framboise, with her wrinkled old winter-apple face; at Paul, who had listened in a silence that said more than he could have said with words. And then a flicker of something caught my eye; something that might have been a trick of the light, or a spark of static, or a stray ember from the fire.

"Wind's up," said Paul, listening by the chimney breast. "Wouldn't be surprised if we had a storm."

Sure enough, I could hear it now: the last assault of the December wind. *December, despair.* Throughout the night I heard its voice, keening and wailing and laughing. Rosette was fretful all night long, and I slept fitfully as the wind squalled and ratcheted the slates on the roof and rattled the windows in their frames.

At four o'clock I heard the sound of something moving in Anouk's room. Rosette was awake. I went to see. And I found Anouk sitting on the floor in a badly drawn circle of yellow chalk. There was a candle burning beside her bed, and another one over Rosette's crib, and in the warm yellow light she looked rosy and flushed.

"We fixed it, Maman," she told me, bright-eyed. "We fixed it so that we could stay."

I sat down beside her on the floor. "How?" I said.

"I told the wind we were staying here. I told it to take someone else instead."

"It isn't that easy, Nanou," I said.

"Yes it is," said Anouk. "And there's something else." She gave me a smile of heartbreaking sweetness. "Can you see him?" She pointed to something in the corner of the room.

I frowned. There was nothing. Well, almost nothing. A fugitive gleam—a flicker of candlelight on the wall—a shadow, something like eyes, a tail—

"I don't see anything, Nanou."

"He belongs to Rosette. He came on the wind."

"Oh, I see." I smiled. Sometimes Anouk's imagination is so infectious that I find myself almost carried away, seeing things that cannot be there.

Rosette stretched out her arms and mewed.

"He's a monkey," said Anouk. "His name is Bamboozle."

I had to laugh. "I don't know how you think of these things." And yet even then I felt uneasy. "You know it's just a game, right?"

"Oh no, he's real," said Anouk with a smile. "Look, Maman. Rosette sees him too."

In the morning, the wind had dropped. An evil wind, a tornado, the locals said, felling trees and leveling barns. The newspapers called it a tragedy and spoke of how, on New Year's Eve, a branch from a tree had dropped onto a passing car as it drove through the village early that evening. Both driver and passenger had been killed—one of them a priest from Rennes.

An act of God, the papers said.

Anouk and I knew otherwise.

It was just an Accident, I repeated as she woke up crying night after night in our tiny flat in Boulevard de la Chapelle. *Anouk, those things aren't real*, I said. *Accidents happen. That's all it was.*

And as the year turned she began to believe. The nightmares stopped. She seemed happy again. But still there was something in her eyes—a shift from the summer child she was—something older, wiser, stranger. And now Rosette—my winter child—seeming more like Anouk day by day, imprisoned in her own little world, refusing to grow like other children; not speaking, not walking, but watching with those animal eyes. . . .

Were we responsible? Logic says not. But logic goes only so far, it seems. And now that wind is here again. And if we do not obey its call, then whom will it choose to take in our place?

There are no trees on the Butte de Montmartre. For that at least I am grateful. But the December wind still smells of death, and no amount of frankincense can sweeten its dark seduction. December was always a time of darkness; of ghosts holy and unholy; of fires lit in defiance against the dying of the light. The gods of Yule are stern and cold; Persephone is trapped underground, and spring is a dream, a lifetime away.

V'là l'bon vent, v'là l'joli vent
V'là l'bon vent, ma mie m'appelle—

And in the bare streets of Montmartre, the Kindly Ones still roam abroad, shrieking their defiance to the season of goodwill.

Tuesday, 11 December

AFTER THAT IT CAME EASILY. SHE TOLD ME THEIR LITTLE STORY IN FULL: the chocolate shop in Lansquenet; the scandal that followed; the woman who died; then Les Laveuses, the birth of Rosette, and the Kindly Ones who had tried and failed to take her away.

So that's what she fears. Poor little girl. Don't think that because there's something in this for me that I am entirely heartless. I listened to her disjointed tale; held her when it became too much; stroked her hair; and dried her tears—which is more than anyone did for me when I was sixteen and my world collapsed.

I reassured her as well as I could. Magic, I said, is a tool of Change; of the tides that keep the world alive. Everything is linked together; an evil done on one side of the world is balanced by its opposite on the other. There is no light without dark; no wrong without right; no injury without revenge.

As for my own experience—

Well, I told her as much as she needed to know. Enough to make us conspirators; to link us in remorse and guilt; to sever her from the world of light and draw her gently into the darkness—

In my case, as I said, it began with a boy. It ended with one too, as it happens; for if hell has no fury like a woman scorned, then there's nothing on earth like a cheated witch.

It went pretty well for a week or two. I queened it over the other girls, enjoying my newfound conquest and the sudden status I had achieved. Scott and I were inseparable; but Scott was weak and rather vain—it's what had made him so easy to enslave. And very soon the temptation to confide in his locker-room friends—to boast, to strut, and finally, to mock—became too much for him to resist.

I sensed it at once—the change of balance. Scott had talked a little too much, and the rumors chased one another like dead leaves from one end of the school to another. Graffiti appeared on shower-room walls; people nudged one another as I passed by. My greatest enemy was a girl named Jasmine—scheming, popular, and picture-pretty modest—who launched the first wave of rumors. I fought them with every dirty trick at my disposal, but once a victim, always a victim, and I soon returned to my usual role, a target for every snide comment and joke. Then Scott McKenzie joined the other side. After a series of increasingly halfhearted excuses, he was seen out openly in town with Jasmine and her friends; and finally was pushed, cajoled, shamed, and taunted into a direct assault. On my mother's shop, no less; long since the butt of ridicule with its displays of crystals and books on sex-magic, now once more the target of their attack.

They came by night. A group of them, half-drunk and laughing and shushing and pushing one another. A little too early for Mischief Night; but the shops were already full of fireworks, and Hallowe'en was beckoning with long skinny fingers that smelled of smoke. My room looked out onto the street. I heard them approach, heard sounds of mirth and tautened nerves; heard a voice—*go on, do it!*—a muttered response, another voice saying urgently—*go on, go on*—then ominous silence.

It lasted almost a minute. I checked. Then came the sound of something exploding, very close by, in a confined space. For a moment I thought they had put firecrackers in the garbage bin—then the scent of smoke reached me. I looked out the window and saw them scatter—six of them, like frightened pigeons—five boys and a girl, whose walk I recognized. . . .

And Scott. Of course. Running ahead of the pack, his blond hair very pale in the streetlight. And as I watched, he looked back at me—and just for a moment, our eyes might have met—

But the glare from the shop window must have made it impossible. That red-orange flare as the fire spread, leaping and tumbling and somersaulting like an evil acrobat from a rail of silk scarves to a trapeze of dream catchers and finally to a stack of books—

Shit. I saw his lips move. He halted—the girl at his side pulled him on. His friends joined in—he turned and ran. But not before I had marked them all; those sleek and stupid teenage faces, fire blushed and grinning in the orange light—

It wasn't much of a fire, in the end; out before the fire brigade came. We even managed to salvage most of the stock, though the ceiling was blackened and the place stank of smoke. It had been a rocket, the firemen said; a Standard rocket poked through the letter box and set alight. The policeman asked me if I'd seen anything. I said no.

But the next day, I began my revenge. Claiming sickness, I stayed at home, and plotted, and worked. I made six little dolls from wooden pegs. I made them as realistically as I could, with hand-stitched clothes and faces carefully cut out of that year's class photograph and glued into place below the hair. I named them all, and as the Día de los Muertos approached, I worked and schemed to have them ready.

I collected stray hairs from coats on pegs. I stole clothing from the locker room. I tore pages out of exercise books, ripped tags from satchels, raided bins for used tissues, and removed well-chewed pen lids from desktops when no one was looking. By the end of the week I had enough material of one kind or another to invest in a dozen peg-dolls, and on Hallowe'en, I called in the debt.

It was the night of the half-term school disco. Nothing had been said to me officially, but it was well known that Scott was taking Jasmine to the disco, and that if I was there, there would be trouble. I didn't intend to go to the dance, but I *certainly* intended trouble; and if Scott or anyone stood in my way, then I could guarantee that they would get it.

You have to remember, I was very young. Naïve too in many ways, though not as naïve as Anouk, of course, or indeed as prone to guilt. But I came up with a two-pronged revenge, one that satisfied the demands of my System while providing a solid underpinning of practical chemistry that would add authority to my occult experimentation.

At sixteen, my knowledge of poisons was not as advanced as it might have been. I knew the obvious ones, of course; but so far I'd had little chance to see them in action. I intended to change that. And so I made up a compound of all the most virulent substances I could lay my hands on: mandrake, morning glory, yew. All on sale in my mother's shop and, if dissolved or infused into a quantity of vodka, rather difficult to spot. I bought the vodka from the corner shop; used half of it for the tincture, then added a few extras of my own—including the juice of an agaric mushroom that I had the good luck to discover under a hedge on the school grounds. I then strained the tincture carefully back into the bottle—marked now with the sign of Hurakan the Destroyer—and left it in my open schoolbag, where I was certain karma would do the rest.

Sure enough, by break it had gone, and Scott and his friends had acquired a collective smirk and a furtive manner. I went home that night almost happy and completed all of my six peg-dolls with a long, sharp needle through the heart as I whispered a little secret to each.

Jasmine—Adam—Luke—Danny—Michael—Scott—

Of course I couldn't possibly have known that for sure, just as I could not have known that instead of drinking the vodka themselves, they would use it to spike the bowl of fruit punch at the disco, thereby spreading karma's bounty even more generously than I could have hoped.

The effects, I heard, were spectacular. My brew induced projectile vomiting, hallucination, stomach cramps, paralysis, kidney dysfunction, and incontinence—affecting over forty pupils, including the six original perpetrators.

It could have been worse. Nobody died. Well, not directly, anyway. But poisoning on such a grand scale rarely passes unseen. There was an enquiry; someone talked; and at last the guilty parties confessed, incriminating themselves—and me—as each tried to put the blame elsewhere. They admitted to pushing the rocket through our letter box. They admitted to stealing the bottle from my bag. They even admitted to spiking the drinks—but denied all knowledge of the bottle's contents.

Predictably, the police came to our house next. They expressed a good deal of interest in my mother's herbal supplies and questioned me rather closely—with no success. I was an expert in stonewalling by then, and nothing—not their kindness, nor their threats—could make me change my story.

There *had* been a bottle of vodka, I said. I'd bought it myself—reluctantly—and on Scott McKenzie's express instructions. Scott had big plans for the disco that night and had suggested bringing a few *little extras* to (as he said) *liven up the party a bit.* I'd taken this to mean drugs and alcohol; which was why I'd chosen not to go rather than betray my lack of enthusiasm for his plan.

I admitted that I'd known it was wrong. I should have spoken up at the time; but I'd been afraid after the rocket incident, and had gone along tacitly with their plan, fearing possible repercussions.

As it happened, something must have gone wrong. Scott didn't know very much about drugs, and I guessed he must have overdone it. I wept a few crocodile tears at the thought; listened earnestly to the officer's lecture; then looked relieved at my lucky escape and promised never to get involved in anything like that, ever again.

It was a good performance, and it convinced the police. But my mother had her doubts all along. Her discovery of the peg-dolls did much to confirm this, and she knew enough about the properties of the substances in which she dealt to have more than an inkling of whom and what.

I denied it all, of course. But it was clear she didn't believe me.

People could have died, she kept saying. As if that hadn't been my plan. As if I cared, after what they'd done. And then she began to talk about *getting help*—about counseling and anger management and maybe a child psychiatrist—

"I never should have taken you to Mexico City that year," she kept saying. "You were fine till then—a good little girl—"

Crazy as a coot, of course. Believing in every crackpot notion that came her way, and now, this growing delusion that somehow the obedient little girl she'd taken to Mexico for the Día de los Muertos had been taken over by some evil force—something that had changed her and made her capable of these terrible things.

"The black piñata," she kept repeating. "What was inside? What was inside?"

But by then she'd grown so hysterical that I hardly knew what she was trying to say.

I didn't even remember a black piñata—it was such a long time ago, and besides, there were so many in the carnival. As for what was inside—well, sweets, I suppose, and little toys, and charms, and sugar skulls, and all the usual things you'd find inside a piñata on the Day of the Dead.

To suggest that it might have been anything else—that perhaps some spirit or little god (perhaps even Santa Muerte, greedy old Mictecacihuatl herself) had entered me during that Mexican trip—

Well, if anyone needed help, I said, it was the person who'd dreamed up *that* fairy tale. But she insisted; dared call me *unstable*; quoted her Creed and finally told me that if I didn't own up to what I'd done, then she would have no other choice—

That finally decided it. That night I packed for a one-way journey. I took her passport and my own; some clothes; some money; her credit cards, checkbook, and keys to the shop. Call me sentimental; I also took one of her earrings—a little pair of shoes—as a charm to add to my bracelet. I've added to it a lot since then. Every charm here is a trophy of sorts, a reminder of the many lives I have collected and used to enrich my own. But that's where it really started. With a single pair of silver shoes.

Then I crept softly downstairs, lit a couple of fireworks I'd bought that day, and dropped them among the stacks of books before very quietly letting myself out.

I never looked back. There was no need. My mother always slept like the dead, and besides, the dose of valerian and wild lettuce that I'd slipped in her tea would surely have quietened the most restless of sleepers. Scott and his friends would be suspects at first—at least until my disappearance was confirmed—by which time I fully intended to be over the seas and far away.

I toned it down for Anouk, of course, omitting all mention of the bracelet, the black piñata, or of my fiery farewell. I painted a touching picture of myself, alone and misunderstood, friendless upon the Parisian streets; racked with guilt, sleeping rough, living on nothing but magic and wits.

"I had to be tough. I had to be brave. It's hard, being alone at sixteen, but I managed to fend for myself somehow, and in time I learned that there are two forces that can drive us. Two winds, if you like, blowing in opposite directions. One wind takes you to what you want. The other one drives you from what you fear. And people like us have to make a choice. To ride the wind, or to let it ride you."

And now at last as the piñata splits open, lavishing bounty on the faithful, here comes the prize I have waited for, the ticket to not one life, but two—

"Which one will you choose, Nanou?" I say. "Fear or desire? The Hurakan, or Ehecatl? The Destroyer, or the Wind of Change?"

She fixes me with that blue-gray gaze, the color of a storm cloud's edge just as it begins to break. Through the Smoking Mirror I can see her colors shifting in the most turbulent of purples and blues.

And now I can see something else. An image, an icon, presented here with more clarity than an eleven-year-old child could possibly articulate. I see it for less than a second, but even so it is enough. It's the Nativity scene on Place du Tertre, the mother, the father, and the crib.

But in this version of the scene, the mother is wearing a red dress, and the father's hair is the same color—

And at last, I begin to understand. That's why she wants this party so much; that's why she lavishes so much attention on the little peg-dolls in the Advent house, grouping, positioning them with as much care and attention as she would have given the real thing.

Look at Thierry outside the house. He has no role to play in this strange reenactment. Then there are the visitors—the Magi, the shepherds, the angels. Nico, Alice, Madame Luzeron, Jean-Louis, Paupaul, Madame Pinot. They serve as the Greek chorus: to give encouragement and support. Then there is the central group. Anouk, Rosette, Roux, Vianne—

What was the first thing she said to me?

Who died? My mother. Vianne Rocher.

I took it as a kind of joke, a child's attempt to be provocative. But knowing Anouk a little better now, I begin to see how serious those seemingly flippant words might be. The old priest and the social worker were not the only casualties of that December wind, four years ago. Vianne Rocher and her daughter Anouk died just as surely on that day, and now she wants to bring them back—

How alike we are, Nanou.

You see, I too need another life. Françoise Lavery dogs me still. To-night's local paper showed her again, now otherwise known as Mercedes Desmoines and Emma Windsor, among other aliases, and showing two blurry pictures taken from CCTV. You see, Annie, I have Kindly Ones of my own, and they may be slow, but they are unwavering, and their pursuit of me now goes beyond irksome into something that almost threatens me.

How did they find out about Mercedes? And how did they catch up with Françoise so soon? And how long do you think it will be before even Zozie falls to their relentlessness?

Perhaps it's time, I tell myself. Perhaps I've exhausted Paris at last. Glamours aside, perhaps the time has come for me to take to another set of roads. But not as Zozie. Not anymore.

If someone offered you a whole new life, wouldn't you take it?

Of course you would.

And if that life could offer you adventure, riches, and a child—not just any child, but this beautiful, promising, talented child, untouched as yet by the hand of karma, that sends every bad thought and questionable deed straight back at you with threefold strength—something to toss to the Kindly Ones when at last there's nothing else—

Wouldn't you, if you had the chance?

Wouldn't you?

Of course you would.

Wednesday, 12 December

WELL, THAT'S MORE THAN A WEEK OF LESSONS SO FAR, AND ALREADY she says she can see a change. I've been learning more of the Mexican stuff—names and stories and symbols and signs. Now I know how to raise the wind with Ehecatl, the Changing One; and how to invoke Tlaloc, for rain, and even how to call down the Hurakan to bring revenge on my enemies.

Not that I'm thinking of revenge. Chantal and Co. have been out of school ever since that day at the bus stop. Apparently they've all got it now. Some kind of ringworm, Monsieur Gestin says, but anyway, they have to stay at home until it gets better, in case they infect anyone else. You'd be amazed at the difference it makes to a class of thirty kids when the four nastiest people are away. But without Suzanne, Chantal, Sandrine, and Danielle, it's actually *nice* to be at school. No one's It; no one laughs at Mathilde for being fat; and Claude actually answered a question in math today without stuttering.

Today, in fact, I've been working on Claude. He's really nice when you get to know him, although he stammers so badly most of the time that he hardly ever talks to anyone. But I managed to slip a piece of paper marked with a symbol into his pocket—One Jaguar, for bravery—and it might just be that the others are away, but already I think I can see a difference.

He's more relaxed now; he sits up instead of slouching, and although his stammer hasn't actually gone, it didn't sound too bad today. Sometimes it gets so bad that his words jam up completely and he goes red in the face and almost cries—and everyone's embarrassed for him—even the teacher—and can't look (except for Chantal and Co., of course), but today he talked more than he ever does normally, and that didn't happen, not even once.

I talked to Mathilde as well today. She's very shy, and she doesn't talk much; wears big black sweaters to hide her shape; tries to be invisible, hoping that people will leave her alone. They never do; and she moves around with her head down, as if she's afraid to catch someone's eye, and it makes her look tubby and awkward and sad, so that no one sees that she's got great skin—unlike Chantal, who's getting spots—and her hair is really thick and beautiful, and with the right attitude, she could be too—

"You should try it," I told her. "Surprise yourself."

"Try what?" said Mathilde, as if to say: *why are you wasting your time on me?*

So I told her some of what Zozie told me. She listened, forgetting to look at the floor.

"I couldn't do *that*," she said at last, but I noticed a hopeful look in her eyes, and this morning at the bus stop I thought she looked different: straighter and more confident, and for the first time since I'd known her, she was wearing something that wasn't black. It was just an ordinary top, but dark red and not too baggy, and I said, *that's nice*, and Mathilde looked confused but pleased, and for the first time ever, went smiling to school.

All the same, it feels kind of weird. To be suddenly—well, not *popular*, exactly, but something like it, anyway; to have people look at you differently; be able to change the way they think. . . .

How could Maman ever give that up? I wish I could ask her; but I know I can't. I'd have to tell her about Chantal and Co.; and about the peg-dolls; and Claude and Mathilde; and Roux; and Jean-Loup—

Jean-Loup was back in school today, looking a bit pale, but cheerful enough. Turns out his illness was only a cold, but his heart thing makes him delicate, and even a cold can be serious. Still, today he was back, taking pictures again, watching the world through his camera. Jean-Loup takes pictures of everyone: teachers, the janitor, pupils, me. He takes them very fast, so that no one has time to change what they're doing, and sometimes this gets him into trouble—especially with the girls, who want to be able to primp and pose—

"And wreck the picture," said Jean-Loup.

"Why?" I said.

"Because a camera sees more than the naked eye."

"Even ghosts?"

"Those too."

Well, it's funny, I thought; but he's totally right. He's talking about the Smoking Mirror and how it can show you things that you might not see in the normal way. He doesn't know the old symbols, of course. But perhaps he's been taking pictures for so long that he's learned Zozie's trick of focusing—of seeing things as they really are, and not the way people want them to be. That's why he likes the cemetery; he's looking for things the eye doesn't see. Ghost-lights, the truth, or something like that.

"So what do I look like, according to you?"

He flicked through his gallery of pictures and showed me a shot of myself, taken that break just as I was running out into the yard.

"It's a bit blurry," I said—my arms and legs were all over the place—but my face was all right, and I was laughing.

"It's you," said Jean-Loup. "It's beautiful."

Well, I couldn't figure out whether he was being bigheaded or whether he'd paid me a compliment, so I just ignored it and looked at the rest.

There was Mathilde, looking sad and fat but really quite pretty underneath; and Claude talking to me without the slightest bit of a stammer; and Monsieur Gestin with a funny, unexpected look, as if he was trying to look stern when actually he was laughing inside; and then some pictures of the *chocolaterie* that Jean-Loup hadn't downloaded yet, that he flicked through too fast to see.

"Wait a minute," I said. "Isn't that Maman?"

It was, with Rosette. I thought she looked old, and Rosette had moved, so that you couldn't really see her face. And now I could see Zozie at her side—not looking like herself at all, with her mouth turned down, and an odd kind of something in the eyes—

"Come on! We'll be late!" he said.

And then we were running for the bus, and off to the cemetery as usual, to feed the cats and to stroll in the lanes under the trees with the brown leaves falling and the ghosts all around.

It was getting dark by the time we got there, with the tombs just shapes against the sky. Not much good for photographs—unless you use flash, which Jean-Loup calls "lame"—but weird and gorgeous all the same with the Christmas lights farther up the Butte strung out in a spiderweb of stars.

"Most people never see all this."

He was taking pictures of the sky, yellow and gray with the tombs against it like hulks in a derelict boatyard.

"That's why I like it now," he went on. "When it's nearly dark, and folk have gone home, and you can really see that it's a cemetery, and not just a park filled with famous people."

"They'll close the gates pretty soon," I said.

They do that, you know, to stop vagrants sleeping there. Some still do, though. They climb the wall, or they hide away where the *gardien* doesn't see them.

That's what I thought he was, at first. A vagrant, getting ready to bunk down for the night, just a shadow behind one of the tombs, wearing one of those big overcoats and a woolly hat pulled over his hair. I touched Jean-Loup's arm. He nodded at me.

"Get ready to run."

Not that I was really scared, or anything. I don't think you're in any more danger from a homeless person than from someone with a regular house. But no one knew where we were; it was dark; and I knew Jean-Loup's mother would have a fit if she knew where he went after school most nights.

She thinks he goes to the chess club.

I don't think she really knows him at all.

So anyway. There we were, ready to run if the man showed any sign of coming at us. And then he turned and I saw his face—

Roux?

But before I could call out his name, he was gone, slipping away among the tombs, quick as a cemetery cat and quiet as a ghost.

Thursday, 13 December

MADAME LUZERON CAME IN TODAY, BRINGING SOME THINGS FOR THE Advent window. Toy furniture from her old dollhouse, packed carefully in shoe boxes lined with tissue paper. There's a four-poster bed with embroidered hangings, and a dining table and six chairs. There are lamps and rugs and a tiny gilt mirror, and several small china-faced dolls.

"I can't let you part with these," I said as she spread the objects out onto the counter. "These are antiques."

"They're only toys. Keep them just as long as you like."

And so I put them in the house, where another door has opened today. It's a sweet little scene, depicting a small redheaded girl (one of Anouk's peg-dolls) standing admiring an enormous pile of matchboxes, each painstakingly wrapped in colored paper and tied with the very tiniest of bows.

Of course, it's Rosette's birthday soon. The party that Anouk has planned so very meticulously is in part a celebration of this and partly, I sense, an attempt to re-create some (possibly imaginary) time when Yule meant more than just tinsel and presents, and real life was closer to the intimate, imaginary scenes around the little Advent house than the tawdrier truth of our Paris streets.

Children are such sentimentalists. I've tried to curb her expectations; to explain to her that a party is just a party, and that, however lovingly planned, a party cannot bring back the past, or change the present, or guarantee even the smallest shower of snow.

But my comments have had no effect on Anouk, apart from the fact that she now discusses all party matters with Zozie, rather than with me. In fact I've noticed that since Zozie moved in, Anouk spends most of her free time with her, up in her rooms, trying on her shoes (I've heard the sound of high heels on wood), sharing private jokes, and talking—interminably—of what, I wonder?

It's touching, in a way, I think. But there's a part of me—an envious, ungrateful part—that still feels slightly left out in this. Of course it's wonderful that Zozie is here; she has been such a good friend; has looked after the children; has helped us reinvent the shop and begin to make a living at last—

But don't think I'm blind to what's going on. If I look, I can see behind the scenes—the subtle gilding of the place; the cluster of bells in the window; the charm that I mistook for a Christmas ornament dangling above the threshold; the signs, the symbols, the figures in the Advent house, the everyday magic I had thought long since abandoned springing to life in every corner—

What harm can there be? I ask myself. It's hardly really magic at all, just a few little charms, a good-luck sign or two; the kind of thing to which my mother would not have given a second thought. . . .

But I can't help feeling uneasy now. Nothing comes entirely free. Like the boy in the tale who sold his shadow for a promise, if I close my eyes to the terms of the sale; if I buy on credit from the world, soon I'll have to pay the price—

And what is it, Zozie?

What's your price?

I felt increasingly troubled throughout the rest of the afternoon. Something in the air, perhaps; something in the winter light. I found myself wishing for someone—though who it was I could not say. My mother, perhaps; Armande, Framboise. Someone simple. Someone to trust.

Thierry phoned twice, but I screened his calls. He could not begin to understand. I tried to concentrate on work, but for some reason everything went wrong. I heated the chocolate too much or too little; let milk boil; put pepper instead of cinnamon into a batch of hazelnut rolls. By midafternoon my head was aching, and at last I left Zozie in charge and went out for a breath of air.

I walked at random, with nowhere in mind. Certainly not Rue de la Croix; although that was where I found myself less than twenty minutes later. The sky was brittle and china blue, but the sun was too low to cast any warmth. I was glad of my coat—mud brown, like my boots—and pulled it tighter around my body as I entered the shadows of the lower Butte.

It was a coincidence, that's all. I hadn't thought of Roux all day. But there he was, outside the flat, in workboots and overalls, a black knitted cap to cover his hair. He had his back to me, but I knew him at once—it's something about the way he moves, deftly, but without great haste, the lean, tough muscles in his back and arms flexing as he throws boxes and crates of builders' rubbish into the Dumpster that stands on the curb.

I stepped instinctively behind a parked van. The suddenness of seeing Roux; surprise at finding myself there when Zozie had warned me to stay away; these things conspired to make me cautious, and I watched him now from behind the van, invisible in my drab coat, heart punching like a pinball machine. Should I speak to him? I thought. Did I *want* to speak to him? What was he doing here, anyway? A man who hates the city; hates noise; despises wealth and prefers the open sky to a roof—

Just then Thierry came out of the house. I sensed tension between them straightaway. Thierry looked annoyed; his face was red; he spoke to Roux in a sharp voice and gestured for him to go inside.

Roux pretended not to hear.

"What are you, deaf or daft?" said Thierry. "We're on a bloody schedule, in case you forgot. And check the levels before you start. Those boards are oak, not half-inch pinewood."

"Is that the way you talk to Vianne?"

Roux's accent comes and goes with his moods. Today it was almost exotic, a burr of lazy gutturals. Thierry, with his Parisian twang, can barely understand a word.

"What?"

Roux made his voice insolently slow. "I said, do you talk to Vianne like that?"

I saw Thierry's face darken a little. "*Yanne* is the person I'm doing this for."

"Now I can see what she sees in you."

Thierry gave an unpleasant laugh. "I'll ask her about it tonight, shall I? As it happens, I'm seeing her then. I'm thinking of asking her out for a meal. Somewhere that *doesn't* serve pizza by the slice."

And at that he set off up the street, leaving Roux to make an obscene gesture at his retreating back. Quickly I ducked round the side of the van, feeling foolish, but not wanting either of them to know I was there. Thierry passed by within six feet, features compressed between anger, dislike, and a kind of spiteful satisfaction. It made him look older, a stranger somehow; and for a moment I felt like a child caught looking through a forbidden door. Then he was gone, and Roux was alone.

I watched him for a few minutes more. Unobserved, people tend to show unexpected aspects of themselves—I'd seen that already in Thierry as he strode past me up the street. But Roux sat down on the side of the curb and stayed there, not moving, eyes on the ground, looking more tired than anything else, although it's hard to tell with Roux.

I ought to go back to the shop, I thought. Anouk would be home in less than an hour, Rosette would need her afternoon snack, and if Thierry was coming round—

Instead I stepped out from behind the van.

"Roux."

He jumped to his feet, briefly unguarded, lit up with that radiant smile of his. Then wariness took over again. "Thierry's not here, if that's what you want."

"I know," I said.

The smile returned.

"Roux—" I began. But he held out his arms, and I found myself there as I had before, with my head against his shoulder, and the warm soft scent of him—something quite separate from the smell of cut wood, or polish, or sweat—like an eiderdown over us both.

"Come inside. You're shivering."

I followed him in and went upstairs. The flat was unrecognizable.

Draped in white sheets, still as snow, the furniture piled into corners, the floor a drift of fragrant dust. Freed of Thierry's clutter I could see how large the flat really was; the high ceilings with their plaster moldings; the wide doorways; the intricate balconies on the street side.

Roux saw me noticing. "Rather pleasant, as cages go. Mr. Big spares no expense."

I looked at him. "You don't like Thierry."

"And you do?"

I ignored the gibe. "He isn't always so abrupt. He's usually very nice, you know. He must be under stress, or maybe you were winding him up—"

"Or maybe he's nice to important people, and says what he likes to those who don't matter."

I gave a sigh. "I hoped you'd get on."

"Why do you think I haven't walked out? Or hit the bastard in the face?"

I looked away and did not answer. The charge between us intensified. I was very conscious of him standing close to me, of the streaks of paint on his overalls. He was wearing a T-shirt underneath, and on a cord around his neck hung a small piece of green river-glass.

"So what are you doing here?" he said. "Hanging around with the hired help?"

Oh, Roux, I thought. What can I say? That it's because of that secret place just above your collarbone where my forehead fits so perfectly? That it's because I know, not just your favorites, but every twist and turn of you? That you have a tattoo of a rat on your left shoulder that I've always pretended not to like? That your hair is the color of fresh paprika and marigolds and that Rosette's quick little drawings of animals remind me so much of the things you make from wood and stone that often it hurts me to look at her and to think of her never knowing you—

Kissing him would just make it worse. And so I kissed him, little soft kisses all over his face, pulling off his cap and my overcoat, finding his mouth with such scalding relief—

For the first few minutes I was blind, beyond thought. Only my mouth existed just then; only my hands on his skin were real. The rest of me was imaginary; coming to life at the touch of him, little by little, like melting snow. And in a daze we kissed again, standing in that empty room with the scent of oil and sawdust in the air and the white sheets spread like the sails of a ship—

Somewhere at the back of my mind I was aware that this had not been the plan; that this would complicate everything beyond measure. But I couldn't stop. I'd waited so long. And now—

I froze. *Now what?* I thought. Now we were back together? What then? Would that help Anouk and Rosette? Would that banish the Kindly Ones? Would our love put even a single meal on the table, or still the wind for even a day?

Better you'd stayed asleep, Vianne, said my mother's voice inside my head. *And better, if you care for him—*

"This isn't what I came for, Roux." With an effort, I pushed him away. He did not try to hold me back but watched me instead as I pulled on my coat and straightened my hair with shaking hands.

"Why are you here?" I said fiercely. "Why did you stay in Paris at all, with everything that's happening?"

"You didn't tell me to leave," he said. "Besides, I wanted to know about Thierry. I wanted to make sure you were OK."

"I don't need your help," I said. "I'm fine. You saw that in the chocolate shop."

Roux smiled. "Then why are you here?"

Over the years I have learned to lie. I've lied to Anouk; lied to Thierry; and now I have to lie to Roux. If not for him, then for myself—because I knew that if any more of that sleeping part of me were to awaken, then Thierry's embraces would not only be unwelcome, but wholly intolerable, and that all my plans of the past four years would blow away like leaves on the wind.

I looked at him. "I'm asking you now. I want you to leave. This whole thing isn't fair on you. You're waiting for something that can't possibly happen, and I don't want you to get hurt anymore."

"I don't need help," he mocked. "I'm fine."

"Please, Roux."

"You *said* you loved him. This proves you don't."

"It isn't that easy. . . ."

"Why not?" said Roux. "Because of the shop? You'd marry him for a *chocolate shop?*"

"You make it sound so ridiculous. But where were you four years ago? And what makes you think you can come back now, expecting to find that nothing's changed?"

"You haven't changed so much, Vianne." He put out a hand to touch my face. The static between us was gone now, to be replaced by a dull, sweet ache. "And if you think I'm leaving *now*—"

"I have to think of my children, Roux. This isn't just about me." I took his hand and squeezed it hard. "If today proves anything, then it's this. I can't be alone with you anymore. I don't trust myself. I don't feel safe."

"Is safety so very important, then?"

"If you had children, you'd know it was."

Well, that was the greatest lie of all. But I had to say it. He has to leave. For my own peace of mind, if not for his; for the sake of Anouk and Rosette. They were both upstairs when I got in, Anouk already tearing up to Zozie's room in a clatter of excitement about something that had happened at school. For once, I was glad to be left alone, and I went to my own room for half an hour, to read my mother's cards again and to calm my agitated nerves.

The Magus; the Tower; the Hanged Man; the Fool.

Death. The Lovers. Change.

Change. The card shows a wheel, turning remorselessly round and round. Popes and paupers, commoners and kings hold on desperately to its spokes, and through the primitive design, I can make out their expressions, the open mouths, the complacent smiles turning to wails of terror as the wheel runs its course—

I look at the Lovers. Adam and Eve, standing naked, hand in hand. Eve's hair is black. Adam's is red. There is no great mystery to this. The cards are printed in three colors only: yellow, red, and black, which, with the background of white, make up the colors of the four winds—

Why have I drawn these cards again?

What message do they hold for me?

At six, Thierry phoned to ask me out. I told him I had a migraine, and by then it was almost true; my head throbbed like a sick tooth, and the thought of eating made it worse. I promised I'd see him tomorrow instead and tried to put Roux out of my mind. But whenever I tried to get to sleep, I felt the touch of his lips on my face, and when Rosette awoke and began to cry, I heard his accents in her voice, and saw shadows of him in her green-gray eyes. . . .

Friday, 14 December

TEN DAYS TO GO BEFORE CHRISTMAS EVE. TEN DAYS BEFORE THE BIG bang, and what I thought would be simple enough is actually turning out to be kind of complicated.

First, there's Thierry. Then there's Roux.

Oh boy. What a mess.

Ever since Sunday's talk with Zozie, I've been trying to think of the best thing to do. My first impulse was to go to Roux straightaway and tell him everything, but Zozie says that would be a mistake.

In a story it would be easy enough. Tell Roux he's a father, get rid of Thierry, then things can go back to the way they were and everyone can get together on Christmas Eve for a massive celebration. End of story. Piece of cake.

In real life, it's not so simple. In real life, Zozie says, some men can't cope with fatherhood. Especially with a child like Rosette—what if he just can't handle that? What if he's ashamed of her?

I hardly slept at all last night. Seeing Roux in the cemetery made me wonder if Zozie was right, and that he didn't want to see us at all. But then, why keep working for Thierry? Does he know, or doesn't he? I went over and over it, and still it wouldn't make sense to me. And so today I made up my mind and went to find him at Rue de la Croix.

I arrived at the house at about half past three, feeling all wound up and shivery inside. I'd skipped the last lesson of school—it was a study period, and if anyone mentions it, I'll just say I was in the library. Jean-Loup would have known if he'd been there, but Jean-Loup was ill again today, and with the sign of One Monkey drawn on my hand, I slipped away without anyone noticing.

I took the bus to Place de Clichy and walked from there to Rue de la Croix, a broad, quiet street overlooking the cemetery, with big old stucco houses like a row of wedding cakes all along one side, and a high brick wall on the other.

Thierry's apartment is on the top floor. He actually owns the whole building: two whole floors and a basement flat. It's the biggest apartment I've ever seen, though Thierry doesn't think it's big at all and complains about the size of the rooms.

When I got there the place looked empty. There was scaffolding on one side of the building, and cellophane sheets over the doors. There was a man in a hard hat sitting outside, having a smoke, but I could tell it wasn't Roux.

I went in. I took the stairs. From the first landing I could hear machine sounds and smell the sweet and somehow horsy scent of freshly cut wood. Now I could hear voices too: well, *one* voice—Thierry's voice—raised above the sound of work. I went up the last few stairs, snowy with sawdust and shavings of wood. The door was shielded in cellophane, and I parted it and looked inside.

Roux was wearing a filter-mask and using the machine to sand down the bare floorboards. The smell of raw wood was everywhere. Thierry was standing above him in a gray suit and a yellow hard hat, and that look he gets when Rosette won't use a spoon, or spits out her food at table. As I watched, Roux turned off the machine and pulled down his mask. He looked tired and not too happy.

Thierry looked at the floorboards and said: "Vac up the dust and get the polisher. I want you to get at least one coat of varnish down before you leave."

"You must be joking. I'd be here till midnight."

"I don't care," said Thierry. "I'm not going to waste another day. We need to be finished by Christmas Eve."

And then he walked straight out and past me down the stairs to the first floor. I was standing behind the dust sheet, and he didn't see me as he went by; but I saw him quite close up, and there was a look on his face I didn't like at all. It was a kind of *smug* look; not quite a smile, with too many teeth. As if Santa Claus, instead of giving out presents for all the kids, had decided to keep them all for himself this year. And just then I hated Thierry. Not just because he'd shouted at Roux, but also because he thought he was *better* than Roux. You could see it in the way he looked at him; in the way he stood over him, like someone getting a shoeshine; and in his colors there was something more—something that might have been envy, or worse—

Roux was sitting cross-legged on the floor, the filter-mask around his neck and a bottle of water in his hand.

"Anouk!" He grinned. "Is Vianne here?"

I shook my head. His face fell.

"Why didn't you come? You said you would."

"I've been busy, that's all." He jerked his chin up at the room, all gift-wrapped in builders' cellophane. "Do you like it?"

"Meh," I said.

"No more moving. Room of your own. Near the school, and everything."

Sometimes I wonder why adults make such a big deal out of education when it's obvious that kids know far more about life than they do. Why do they make it so complicated? Why can't they keep it simple, for once?

"I heard what Thierry said to you. He shouldn't talk to you like that. He thinks he's so much better than you. Why don't you tell him to get lost?"

Roux shrugged. "I'm getting paid. Besides"—I saw the gleam in his eyes—"I may get my own back some time soon."

I sat down next to him on the floor. He smelled of sweat and of the sawdust he'd been working in; his arms and hair were dusted with it. But something about him was different. I couldn't quite figure it out. A kind of funny, bright, *hopeful* look that hadn't been there at the *chocolaterie*.

"So what can I do for you, Anouk?"

Tell Roux he's a father. Yeah. Right. Like so many things, it sounds easy. But when it comes to the practical—

I wet the tip of my finger and drew the sign of Lady Moon Rabbit in the dust on the floor. That's my sign, Zozie says. A circle with a rabbit inside. It's supposed to look like the new moon, and it's the sign of love and new beginnings, and I thought that since it's my sign, then perhaps it would work better on Roux.

"What's wrong?" He smiled. "Cat got your tongue?"

Perhaps it was that word, *cat*. Or perhaps it's because I've never been much good at lying, especially not to the people I love. In any case, I blurted it out. The question that had been burning a hole in the roof of my mouth ever since my talk with Zozie—

"Do you know you're Rosette's dad?"

He stared at me. "Say *what*?" he said. There was no mistaking the shock in his eyes. So he hadn't known; but from his face he wasn't what you'd call pleased either.

I looked down at the sign of Lady Moon Rabbit and drew the broken cross of Red Monkey Tezcatlipoca next to it in the floury dust.

"I know what you're thinking. She's kind of small for a four-year-old. She dribbles a bit. She wakes up at night. And she's always been slow with some things, like learning to talk and using a spoon. But she's really funny—and really sweet—and if you give her a chance—"

Now his face was the color of the sawdust. He shook his head, like it was a bad dream or something that he could just shake away.

"Four?" he said.

"It's her birthday next week." I smiled at him. "I knew you didn't know. I said, 'Roux would never have left us like that. Not if he'd known about Rosette.'" And I told him then about when she was born, and about the little *crêperie* in Les Laveuses, and how ill she had been at first, and how we'd fed her from an eyedropper, and about our move to Paris, and everything that happened there. . . .

"Wait a minute," said Roux. "Does Vianne know you're here? Does she know you're telling me this?"

I shook my head. "No one knows."

He thought about that one for a while, and slowly his colors went from quiet blues and greens to splashy reds and oranges, and his mouth turned down, hard, not like the Roux I know at all.

"So—all this time she never said a thing? I had a daughter, and I never even knew?" He always sounds more from the Midi when he's angry, and right then his accent was so thick that it could have been a foreign language altogether.

"Well, maybe she didn't get the chance."

He made an angry sound in his throat. "Maybe she thinks I'm not cut out to be a father."

I wanted to hug him, to make him feel better, to tell him we loved him—*all* of us. But he was too crazy to listen just then—I could see that even without the Smoking Mirror—and all at once I thought that it might have been a mistake to tell him like that, that I should have listened to Zozie's advice—

Then suddenly he stood up, as if he'd come to a decision, scuffing the sign of Red Monkey Tezcatlipoca in the dust at his feet.

"Well, I hope you all enjoyed the joke. Pity you couldn't have made it last a bit longer—at least until I'd finished the flat—" He pulled the filter-mask from around his neck and threw it savagely at the wall. "You can tell your mother I'm through. She's safe. She's made her choice, she can stick with it. And while you're at it, you can tell Le Tresset that he can do his own decorating from now on. I'm off."

"Where?" I said.

"Home," said Roux.

"What, back to your boat?"

"What boat?" he said.

"You said you had a boat," I reminded him.

"Yeah, well." He looked at his hands.

"You mean you *don't* have a boat?" I said.

" 'Course I do. It's a terrific boat." He was looking away, and his voice was flat. I made the Smoking Mirror with my fingers, and saw his colors, all mixed up in angry reds and cynical greens, and thought—*Oh, please, Roux. Just this once.*

"Where is it?" I said.

"Port de l'Arsenal."

"How come you're there?"

"I was just passing through."

Well, *that* was another lie, I thought. It takes a long time to bring a boat upriver from the Tannes. Months, even. And you don't just *pass through* Paris, either. You have to book with the Port de Plaisance. You have to pay for a mooring. And that made me wonder, if Roux *had* a boat, why he'd be working here for Thierry.

But if he was going to lie, I thought, then how could I tell him anything? The whole of my plan (such as it was) had been kind of based on the assumption that Roux would be really pleased to see me, and that he'd say how much he'd missed me and Maman, and how hurt he'd been to find out she was marrying Thierry, and then I'd tell him about Rosette, and he'd understand then how he couldn't leave, and he'd live with us in the *chocolaterie*, so that Maman wouldn't have to marry Thierry, and we could be a family—

Come to think of it, it sounded kind of cheesy now.

"But what about me and Rosette?" I said. "We're having a party on Christmas Eve." I took out his card from my schoolbag and held it out. "You've just *got* to be there," I told him desperately. "Look, you've got an invitation and everything."

He gave a nasty laugh. "Who, me? You must be thinking of someone else's father."

Oh boy, I thought. What a mess this is. It seemed like the more I tried to talk to him, the angrier he seemed to get, and my new System, which has already worked changes for Nico and Mathilde and Madame Luzeron, doesn't work on Roux at all.

If only I'd just finished his doll—

And then I had an inspiration.

"Look," I said. "You've got dust in your hair." I reached up to brush it off.

"Ouch!" said Roux.

"Sorry," I said.

"Please can I see you tomorrow?" I said. "Even if it's only to say good-bye?"

He paused for such a long time that I was sure he was going to refuse.

Then he sighed. "I'll meet you in the cemetery at three o'clock. By Dali-da's tomb."

"OK," I said, and smiled to myself.

Roux saw the smile. "I'm not staying," he said.

Well, that's what you think, Roux, I thought.

And I opened my hand, where three red hairs had caught between my fingers.

Because this time, Roux, who pleases himself, is going to do what *I* want for a change. This time it's my turn. *I* decide. He'll be at our party on Christmas Eve, whatever it takes. Whatever it costs. He may not want to, I thought, but he'll come—even if I have to call up the Hurakan to drag him here.

Friday, 14 December

INVOCATION TO THE WIND.

First, light your candles. Red ones are good, for luck and stuff; though white ones are OK too, of course. But if you really want to do the thing properly, make them black candles, because black's the color of the year's end, the slow dark time between Día de los Muertos and December full moon, when the dead year begins to turn again.

Now draw a yellow chalk circle on the floor. Move the bed and the blue rag rug so we can use the wooden floor. Put them back when it's over, so Maman doesn't see the marks we've left. Maman wouldn't understand; but then . . .

Maman doesn't need to know.

You'll see I'm wearing my red shoes. I don't know why—they feel lucky, somehow, like nothing bad could ever happen when I'm wearing them. And carry some colored powder paint or sand (you'll see I'm using sugar crystals) to mark the points around the circle. Black, north; white, south; yellow, east; red, west. Scatter the sand all around the circle to pacify the little wind gods.

Now for the sacrifice—frankincense and myrrh. That's what the Magi brought, you know, for the Jesus-baby in his crib. I guess if it was good enough for the Jesus-baby, then it's good enough for us. And gold—well, I've got some chocolate squares wrapped in gold paper, which ought to be OK, don't you think? Zozie says the Aztecs always used to offer chocolate to the gods. And blood, of course—though I'm hoping they won't want much of that. A pinprick—*ouch*—OK, that's all—light the incense and we're ready to go.

Now sit in the circle, legs crossed, and take your peg-dolls one in each hand. You'll need a bag of red sugar crystals to scatter on the floor for drawing in.

First comes the sign of Lady Moon Rabbit. Pantoufle can keep that sign for me, here at the edge of the chalk circle. Then we draw Blue Hummingbird Tezcatlipoca, for the sky on my left side, and Red Monkey Tezcatlipoca, for the earth, on yours. Bam stands guard on that side, with the sign of One Monkey next to him.

There. That's ready. Isn't it fun? We did this once before, remember? But something went wrong. It won't this time. This time we're calling the right wind. Not the Hurakan, but the Changing Wind, because there's something here we need to change.

OK? Now draw the spiral sign in the red sugar on the floor.

Now for the invocation. I know you don't know the words, but you can join in the song all the same if you'd like. Sing—

V'là l'bon vent, v'là l'joli vent

That's right. Softly, though.

Good. Now the peg-dolls. That one's Roux. You don't know Roux, but you will soon. And that's Maman, see? Maman in her pretty red dress. Her real name is Vianne Rocher. That's what I whispered in her ear. And who's this, with the mango hair and the big green eyes? That's you, Rosette. That's you. And we'll stand them all here in the circle together, with the candles burning and the sign of Ehecatl in the middle. Because they belong together, like the people in the Nativity house. And soon they'll be together again, and we can be a family—

And this—who's this outside the yellow circle? That's Thierry, with his mobile phone. We don't want the wind to hurt Thierry, but he can't be here with us anymore, because you can only have one father, Rosette, and he's not the one. So he has to go. Sorry, Thierry.

Can you hear the wind outside? That's the Wind of Change on its way.

Zozie says you can ride the wind; that it's like a wild horse that can be tamed and trained to do just what you want it to. You can be a kite, a bird; you can grant wishes; you can find your heart's desire—

If wishes were horses, beggars would ride.

Come on, Rosette. Let's ride.

Saturday, 15 December

IT'S AMAZING, ISN'T IT, HOW DECEITFUL A CHILD CAN BE? LIKE A DOMESTIC cat, purring on the sofa by day, but by night, a strutting queen, a natural killer, disdainful of her other life.

Anouk is no killer—at least, not yet—but she does have that feral side to her. I'm delighted to know that, of course—I'm not in the market for a household pet—but I'll need to keep a close eye on her, if she's going to take action behind my back.

First, she invoked Ehecatl without me. I do not resent this at all—in fact I'm rather proud of her. She's imaginative; ingenious; making up rituals where existing ones do not satisfy—a natural Chaoist, in short.

Second, however—and rather more important—she went to see Roux yesterday, in secret and against my advice. Fortunately she wrote it all down in her diary, which I monitor on a regular basis. It's easy to do: like her mother, she keeps her secrets in a shoe box at the back of her wardrobe— predictable, but convenient—and I've been checking both since I arrived.

And a good thing too, as it turns out. She's meeting him today, she says, in the cemetery at three o'clock. In a way, it couldn't be better; my plans for Vianne are nearing completion, and it's nearly time for the next stage. But stealing a life is so much easier on paper than in the flesh—a few discarded household bills, a passport lifted from a handbag at the airport, even the name on a fresh gravestone, and the job's practically done for me. But this time I want more than a name, more than credit details, much more than money.

It's a game of strategy, of course. Like so many games of strategy, it's based on putting the pieces in place without letting the opponent suspect what's happening, then deciding which pieces to sacrifice in order to emerge the winner. After that, it's one-on-one—a battle of wills between Yanne and me—and I have to say I'm looking forward to it even more than I could have imagined. To face her at last in the final round, knowing what's at stake for both of us—

Now *that* will be a game worth playing.

Let's recap the moves so far. Between my other interests, I have been working very hard on the contents of Yanne's *piñata*, and I have discovered a number of things.

One, she is not Yanne Charbonneau.

Well, we already knew that, of course. But more interestingly, she is not Vianne Rocher—or so the contents of her box would suggest. I knew there was something important I'd missed, and the other day, when she was out, I eventually found what I'd been looking for.

Actually, I'd seen it before and overlooked its importance as I focused on Vianne Rocher. But it's there in the box, tied with a piece of faded red ribbon: a silver charm that might equally have come from a cheap bracelet or a Christmas cracker; shaped like a cat and blackened with time. It's there in Vianne's shoe box, with a packet of sandalwood and some Tarot cards that have seen better days.

Like myself, Vianne travels light. Nothing she keeps is trivial. Every item in this box has been kept for a reason, and none less so than this silver charm. It's mentioned in the newspaper clipping, so brittle and brown that I'd not dared to unfold it completely: the account of the disappearance of eighteen-month-old Sylviane Caillou from outside a chemist's, more than thirty years ago.

Did she ever try to go back? Instinct tells me she did not. *You choose your family,* as she says, and that girl, her mother, whose name does not even appear in the clipping—is nothing to her but DNA. To me, however—

Call me curious. I looked her up on the Internet. It took a little time—children vanish every day, and this was an old case, long since closed and without great interest—but I found it at last, and with it the name of

Sylviane's mother, twenty-one when the baby was taken, now forty-nine according to her school reunion website; divorced, no kids, still living in Paris near Père Lachaise and managing a little hotel.

It's called Le Stendhal, and you can find it on the corner of Avenue Gambetta and Rue Matisse. No more than a dozen bedrooms in all; a balding tinsel Christmas tree and an extravagantly overchintzed interior. By the fireplace there is a small round table upon which a china doll in a pink silk dress stands stiffly under a glass cloche. Another doll, this one dressed as a bride, stands watch at the foot of the stairs. A third—blue-eyed, in a red fur-trimmed coat and hat—is perched on the reception desk.

And there, behind the desk, Madame herself: a big-bodied woman with the drawn face and thinning hair of the habitual dieter and a look of her daughter in the eyes—

"Madame?"

"Can I help you?"

"I'm from Le Rocher de Montmartre. We're doing a special promotion on handmade chocolates, and I wonder if I could give you these samples to try—"

Madame's face went sour at once. "I'm not interested," she said.

"There's no obligation. Just try a few, and—"

"Thank you, no."

Of course, I'd been expecting that. Parisians are deeply suspicious folk, and it did sound rather too good to be true. All the same, I took out a box of our specials and opened it on the desktop. Twelve truffles, rolled in cocoa powder, each nestled in its bassinet of crinkly gold paper, a yellow rose on the corner of the box; the symbol of the Lady Blood Moon was scratched onto the side of the lid.

"There's a calling card inside," I said. "If you like them, you can order direct. If not—" I shrugged. "They're on the house. Go on. Try one. See what you think."

Madame hesitated. I could see her natural suspicion at war with the scent that came from the box: the smoky, espresso scent of cacao; the hint of clove; of cardamom; of vanilla; the fleeting aroma of Armagnac—a fragrance like lost time; a bittersweetness like childhood's end.

"So, are you giving these out to every hotel in Paris? You're not going to make much of a profit if you are."

I smiled. " 'Speculate to accumulate,' that's what I say."

She picked a truffle from its bed.

Bit into it.

"Hm. Not bad."

In fact, I think it's more than that. Her eyes half-close; her thin mouth moistens.

"You like it?"

She should; the seductive sign of Lady Blood Moon lights up her face with its rosy glow. I can see Vianne in her more clearly now; but a Vianne grown old and tired somehow; embittered by the pursuit of wealth; a child-less Vianne with no outlet for her love but her hotel and her china dolls.

"It's certainly something," said Madame.

"The card's inside. Come visit us."

Eyes closed, Madame nodded dreamily.

"Merry Christmas," I said.

Madame did not answer.

And beneath the cloche, the blue-eyed doll in the fur coat and hat smiled serenely out at me, like a child frozen in a bubble of ice.

Saturday, 15 December

I COULD HARDLY WAIT TO SEE ROUX TODAY. TO SEE IF THINGS WERE different; to see if I'd managed to change the wind. I'd expected a sign. Snow or something, or northern lights, or a weird weather change, but when I got up this morning it was the same yellow sky and the same wet road, and although I kept an eye on Maman, she didn't look any different, but worked in the kitchen like she always does, with her hair tied back sensibly and an apron over her black dress.

Still, you have to give these things time to work. Things don't change so quickly, and I guess it wasn't reasonable for me to expect everything to happen—for Roux to come back, and Maman to wake up to the truth about Thierry, *and* for it to snow—all at once in a single night. And so I stayed cool; went out with Jean-Loup; all the time waiting for three o'clock.

Three o'clock, by Dalida's tomb. You can't miss it—it's a life-size sculpture, though I'm not quite sure who Dalida was—some kind of actress, probably. I got there a few minutes late, and Roux was waiting for me. At ten past three it was already quite dark, and as I ran up the steps toward the tomb, I could just see him sitting on a gravestone nearby, looking a bit like a sculpture himself, very still in his long gray coat.

"I thought you weren't coming."

"I'm sorry I'm late." I gave him a hug. "I had to get rid of Jean-Loup, you see."

He grinned at that. "You make it sound so sinister. Who's he?"

I explained, feeling a bit embarrassed. "A friend from school. He loves this place. He likes to take photographs here. Thinks he's going to see a ghost someday."

"Well, he's in the right place," said Roux. He looked at me. "So. What's going on?"

Oh, boy. Well, I didn't even know where to start. So many things have happened over the past few weeks, and—

"Actually, we had a fight."

Stupid, I know, but my eyes were watering. Nothing to do with Roux, of course, and I hadn't meant to mention it, but now that I had—

"What about?" he said.

"Something stupid. Nothing," I said.

Roux gave me the kind of smile you sometimes see on the faces of church statues. Not that he looks anything like an angel, of course. But—kind of patient, if you know what I mean—a kind of *I-can-wait-all-day-here-if-I-have-to* smile.

"Well, he won't come round to the *chocolaterie*," I said, feeling cross and a bit weepy, and especially cross that I'd told Roux. "Says he doesn't feel comfortable."

Actually, that's not all he said. But the rest of it was so stupid and so wrong that I couldn't bear to say it again. I mean, I really like Jean-Loup. But Zozie's my best friend—apart from Roux and Maman, of course—and it bothers me that he's so unfair.

"He doesn't like Zozie?" said Roux.

I shrugged. "He doesn't know her really," I said. "It's because of that time she snapped at him. She's not at all uptight usually. She just hates having her picture taken."

But it wasn't just that. He showed me today two dozen pictures he'd printed off from his computer and taken that day in the *chocolaterie*; pictures of the advent house; of Maman and me; of Rosette; and lastly, four pictures of Zozie, all of them taken at funny angles, as if he were trying to catch her in secret—

"That's not fair. She told you to stop."

Jean-Loup looked stubborn. "Look at them, though."

I looked at them. They were terrible. All of them blurred and looking nothing like her at all—just a pale oval for a face and a mouth that twisted like barbed wire—and in all of them, the same printing flaw: a darkish smudge around her head, with a yellow circle surrounding it—

"You must have messed the prints up," I said.

He shook his head. "That's just how they came out."

"Well, it must have been the light, or something."

"Maybe," he said. "Or something else."

I looked at him. "What do you mean?"

"You know," he said. "Ghost-lights."

Oh, boy. Ghost-lights. I guess Jean-Loup's been wanting to see his weird phenomena for such a long time that he's totally flipped out this time. I mean, *Zozie*, of all people. How wrong can you be?

Roux was watching me with that carved-angel look. "Tell me about Zozie," he said. "You sound like you're pretty good friends."

So I told him about the funeral, and the lollipop shoes, and Hallowe'en, and the way Zozie had suddenly blown into our lives like something from a fairy tale, and made everything fabulous—

"Your mother looks tired."

I thought—*you can talk*. He looked exhausted; his face even paler than usual, and his hair in desperate need of a wash. I wondered if he was getting enough to eat, and whether I ought to have brought some food.

"Well, it's a busy time for us. With Christmas, and everything—"

Hang on a minute, I thought to myself.

"Have you been spying on us?" I said.

Roux shrugged. "I've been around."

"Doing what?"

He shrugged again. "Call me curious."

"Is that why you stayed? Because you were curious?"

"That, and because I thought your mother was in some kind of trouble."

I jumped at that. "But she *is*," I said. "We all are." And I told him again about Thierry, and his plans, and how nothing was the same anymore, and how I missed the old days when everything was simple.

Roux smiled. "It was never simple."

"At least we knew who we were," I said.

Roux just shrugged and said nothing. I put my hand in my pocket. There was his peg-doll, the one from last night. Three red hairs, and a whispered secret, and the spiral sign of Ehecatl, the Changing Wind, drawn in felt pen over the heart.

I closed my hand around it, hard, as if that could make him stay.

Roux shivered and pulled his coat tighter around him.

"So—you're not really leaving, are you?" I said.

"I was going to. Perhaps I should. But there's still something bothering me. Anouk, have you ever had the feeling there's something going on, that somebody's using you, manipulating you somehow, and that if only you knew how and why . . ."

He looked at me and I was relieved to see no anger in his colors, just reflective blues. He went on in a quiet voice, and I thought that it was the most I'd ever heard him say all at once, Roux being a man of not many words.

"I was angry yesterday. So angry that Vianne could have hidden such a thing from me that I couldn't see straight—couldn't listen—couldn't think. Since then I've been doing some thinking," he said. "I've been wondering how the Vianne Rocher I knew could have turned into someone so different. At first I thought it was just Thierry—but I know his type. And I know Vianne. I know she's tough. And I know that there's no way she's going to let someone like Le Tresset take over her life, not after everything she's been through. . . ." He shook his head. "No, if she's in trouble, it's not from him."

"Then who?" I said.

He looked at me. "There's something about your friend Zozie. Something I can't put my finger on. But I can't help feeling it when she's around. There's something too perfect. Something not right. Something almost—dangerous."

"What d'you mean?"

Roux just shrugged.

Now I was starting to feel annoyed. First Jean-Loup, and now Roux. I tried to explain.

"She's helped us, Roux—she works in the shop, looks after Rosette, she teaches me things."

"What kind of things?"

Well, if he didn't like Zozie, I was hardly going to tell him *that*. I put my hand in my pocket again, where the peg-doll felt like a little bone wrapped up in wool. "You don't know her, that's all. You should give her a chance."

Roux looked stubborn. When he makes up his mind, it's hard to change it. It's so unfair—my two best friends—

"You'd like her. Really. I know you would. She looks after us—"

"If I believed that, I'd be gone by now. As it is—"

"You'll stay?"

I forgot about being mad at Roux and threw my arms around his neck. "You'll come to our party on Christmas Eve?"

"Well . . ." He sighed.

"Fabulous! That way you can really get to know Zozie. And you can meet Rosette properly—oh, Roux, I'm so glad you're staying."

"Yeah. Me too."

But he didn't sound glad. In fact he sounded worried as hell. Still, the plan worked, which is what counts. Rosette and I managed to change the wind—

"So, how are you doing for cash?" I said. "I've got . . ." I looked in my pocket. "Sixteen euros and some change, if it helps. I was going to buy Rosette a birthday present, but. . . ."

"No," he said, a bit sharply, I thought. He's never been good at taking money, so perhaps it was the wrong thing to say. "I'm fine, Anouk."

Well, he didn't look fine. I could see that now. And if he wasn't getting paid—

I made the sign of the Ear of Maize and pressed my palm against his hand. It's a good-luck sign that Zozie taught me; for wealth and riches and food and stuff. I don't know how it works, but it does; Zozie used it in the *chocolaterie*, to make more customers buy Maman's truffles, and though obviously that won't help Roux, I'm hoping it'll work some other way, like getting him another job, or a Lotto win, or finding some money in the street. And I made it glow in my mind's eye, so that it shone against his skin like sparkly dust. That ought to do it, Roux, I thought. That way it won't be charity.

"Will you come round before Christmas Eve?"

He shrugged. "I don't know. I've got—a few things to sort out before then."

"But you'll come to the party? Promise?" I said.

"I promise," said Roux.

"Cross your heart and hope to die?"

"Cross my heart. And hope to die."

Sunday, 16 December

ROUX DIDN'T COME TO WORK TODAY. IN FACT, HE HASN'T BEEN THERE ALL weekend. It turns out that he left early on Friday, checked out of the hostel in which he was staying, and hasn't been seen by anyone since.

I suppose I should have expected as much. After all, I asked him to leave. So why do I feel so strangely bereft? And why do I keep looking out for him?

Thierry is incandescent with rage. In Thierry's world, to walk off a job is both shameful and dishonest, and it was clear that he would accept no possible excuse. There's something about a check, too; a check Roux cashed, or didn't cash—

I didn't see much of Thierry this weekend. Some trouble with the flat, he'd said, when he dropped in briefly on Saturday night. He'd mentioned Roux's absence only in passing—and I hadn't dared ask for too many particulars.

Today, he told me the whole thing, calling in at the end of the day. Zozie was just closing up; Rosette was playing with a jigsaw—she makes no attempt to link the pieces but instead seems to enjoy making complicated spiral patterns with them on the floor—and I was just starting a last batch of cherry truffles when he came into the shop, clearly furious, red in the face and ready to explode.

"I knew there was something about him," he said. "Those people. They're all the bloody same. Shiftless, thieving—*travelers*." He gave the word the filthiest inflection, making it sound like an exotic oath. "I know he's supposed to be a friend of yours. But even you can't be blind to this. To walk off a job without a word—to mess up my schedule. I'll sue him for that. Or perhaps I'll just beat the crap out of the ginger bastard—"

"Thierry, please." I poured him a coffee. "Try to calm down."

But where the subject of Roux is concerned, it seems that this is impossible. Of course, they're very different people. Solid, unimaginative Thierry, who has never lived outside Paris in his life; whose disapproval of single mothers, "alternative lifestyles," and foreign food has always rather amused me—till now.

"What is he to you anyway? How come he's such a friend of yours?"

I turned away. "We've been through this."

Thierry glared. "Were you lovers?" he said. "Is that it? Were you sleeping with the bastard?"

"Thierry, please—"

"Tell me the truth! *Did you fuck him?*" he yelled.

Now my hands were trembling. Anger, all the more violent for being suppressed, came rushing to the surface.

"And what if I did?" I snapped at him.

Such simple words. Such *dangerous* words.

He stared at me, suddenly gray-faced, and I realized that the accusation, for all its violence, had just been another of Thierry's big gestures; dramatic, predictable, but ultimately meaningless. He'd needed an outlet for his jealousy, his need for control, his unspoken dismay at the speed at which our trade has improved—

He spoke again, in a shaky voice. "You owe me the truth, Yanne," he said. "I've let this go for much too long. I don't even know who you *are*, for God's sake. I just took you on trust, you and your kids—and have you ever heard me complain? A spoiled brat and a retard—"

Abruptly he stopped.

I stared at him blankly. Finally, he'd crossed a line.

On the floor, Rosette looked up from the jigsaw she was playing with. A light flickered overhead. The plastic shapes that I use for making biscuits began to rattle against the tabletop, as if an express train were going by.

"Yanne, I'm sorry. I'm so sorry." Thierry was trying to regain lost ground, like a door-to-door salesman who still sees a chance of nailing that elusive deal—

But the damage was done. The house of cards, so carefully built, now swept away at a single word. And now I can see what I'd missed before. For the first time, I can *see* Thierry. I've already seen his pettiness. His gloating contempt of the underling. His snobbery. His arrogance. But now I can see his colors too; his hidden vulnerabilities; the uncertainty behind his smile; the tension in his shoulders; the odd stiffening of his posture whenever he has to look at Rosette.

That ugly word.

Of course I have always been aware that Rosette makes him slightly uncomfortable. As always, he overcompensates, but his cheeriness is a forced thing, like someone petting a dangerous dog.

And now I can see that it's not just Rosette. This *place* makes him uncomfortable; this place we made without his help. Every batch of chocolates; every sale; every customer greeted by name; even the chair on which he sits—all of these things remind him that we three are independent, that we have a life outside of him, that we have a past in which Thierry le Tresset played no part at all—

But Thierry has a past of his own. Something that makes him what he is. All his fears are rooted there. His fears, his hopes, his secrets—

I look down at the familiar granite slab on which I temper my chocolates. It's a very old piece, black with age, already worn when I acquired it and bearing the scars of repeated use. There are flecks of quartz in the stone that catch the light unexpectedly, and I watch them shine as the chocolate cools, ready to be heated and tempered again.

I don't want to know your secrets, I think.

But the granite slab knows different. Spackled with mica, it winks and gleams, catching my eye, holding my gaze. I can almost see them now, images mirrored in the stone. As I watch, they take shape, they begin to make sense, glimpses of a life, a past that makes Thierry the man he is.

That's Thierry in the hospital. Younger by twenty years or more, he's waiting outside a closed door. He has two gift packs of cigars in his hand, each tied with a ribbon—one pink, one blue. He has covered every base.

Now it's another waiting room. There are murals of cartoon characters on the walls. A woman sits close, with a child in her arms. The boy is maybe six years old. He stares vacantly at the ceiling throughout, and nothing—not Pooh or Tigger or Mickey Mouse—brings the smallest gleam to his eye.

A building, not quite a hospital. And a boy—no, a young man—on the arm of a pretty nurse. The young man looks about twenty-five. Bulky like his father, he stoops, his head too heavy for his neck, his smile as vacant as a sunflower's.

And now at last I understand. This is the secret he has tried to hide. I understand that broad, bright smile, like a man selling false religion door to door; the way he never speaks of his son; his intense perfectionism; the way he sometimes looks at Rosette—or rather, how he *doesn't* look at her—

I gave a sigh.

"Thierry," I said. "It's all right. You don't have to lie to me anymore."

"*Lie* to you?"

"About your son."

He stiffened then, and even without the granite slab I could see the agitation growing in him. His face was pale; he started to sweat, and the anger that his fear had displaced came rushing back like an evil wind. He stood up, bearlike suddenly, knocking over his coffee cup and scattering the chocolates in their brightly colored wrappers all over the tabletop.

"There's nothing wrong with my son," he said, rather too loudly for the room. "Alan's in the building trade. A real chip off the old block. I don't see him much, but that doesn't mean he doesn't respect me—doesn't mean I'm not proud of him." He was shouting now, making Rosette cover her ears. "Who's been saying anything else? Was it Roux? Has that bastard been snooping around?"

"It's nothing to do with Roux," I said. "If you're ashamed of your own son, then how can you ever care for Rosette?"

"Yanne, please. It's not like that. I'm not ashamed. But he was my son, Sarah couldn't have any more children, and I just wanted him to be . . ."

"Perfect. I know."

He took my hands. "I can live with it, Yanne. I promise I can. We'll get a specialist on the case. She'll have everything she could ever want. Nannies, toys—"

More gifts, I thought. As if that would change the way he feels. I shook my head. The heart doesn't change. You can lie, hope, pretend to yourself—but in the end, can you ever escape the element to which you were born?

He must have seen it in my face; his own face fell, his shoulders slumped.

"But everything's arranged," he said.

Not *I love you*, but *everything's arranged*.

And for all the bitter taste in my mouth I felt a sudden, soaring rush of joy. As if something poisoned in my throat had managed to dislodge itself—

Outside the wind chimes sounded, once, and without thinking I forked the sign against bad luck. Old habits die hard, of course. I haven't made that sign in years. But I couldn't help feeling uncomfortable, as if even such a small thing might reawaken the changing wind. And when Thierry had gone, and I was alone, I thought I heard voices on the wind, the voices of the Kindly Ones, and the distant sound of laughter.

Monday, 17 December

So there it is. It's off. Yippee. Some quarrel about Roux, I think, and I could hardly wait to tell him after school, except that I couldn't find him anywhere.

I tried the hostel in Rue de Clichy, where Thierry says he's been staying till now, but no one opened the door when I knocked, and there was an old man with a bottle of wine who shouted at me for making a noise. Roux wasn't at the cemetery, and no one's seen him at Rue de la Croix, so finally I had to give up, although I did leave a note marked URGENT for him at the hostel, so I guess he'll see it when he gets back. *If* he goes back there, of course. Because by then, the police had arrived, and no one was going anywhere.

At first I thought they'd come for me. It was after dark—nearly seven o'clock—and Rosette and I were having dinner in the kitchen. Zozie had gone out somewhere, and Maman was wearing her red dress, and it was just the three of us for a change—

Then they came round, two officers, and my first stupid thought was that something awful had happened to Thierry, and that it was somehow my fault because of what we did on Friday night. But Thierry was with them, and he looked fine, except that he was even louder and cheerier and more *salut-mon-pote* than ever, but there was something in his colors that made me think that perhaps he was only *pretending* to be cheery, something to fool those people he was with, and that made me nervous all over again.

Turns out it was Roux they were looking for. They stayed in the shop about half an hour, and Maman sent me upstairs with Rosette, but all the same I managed to hear quite a lot of what was going on, though I'm not sure of all the details.

Apparently it's about a check. Thierry says he gave it to Roux—he kept the stub and everything—and Roux tried to alter it before putting the money into his account, so that he'd get a lot more money than the check was actually for.

A thousand euros, they said. This is called *fraud*, Thierry says, and you can go to prison for it, especially if you use a different name to open the account and take out the money before anyone finds out, then disappear without a trace, not even leaving a forwarding address.

So that's what they're saying about Roux. Which is stupid, because everyone knows Roux doesn't *have* a bank account and would never steal anything, even from Thierry. But he *has* vanished without a trace. Apparently he hasn't been seen in the hostel since Friday, and obviously he hasn't been to work. That means I might be the last person to have seen him. It also means he can't come back here, because if he does, he'll be arrested. Stupid Thierry. I hate him. I wouldn't put it past him to have made all this up just to get at Roux.

Maman and he quarreled about it when the two policemen had gone. I could hear Thierry shouting all the way up the stairs. Maman was being reasonable—saying *there must have been some mistake*. And I could hear Thierry getting more and more worked up, saying: *I don't see how you can still take his side*, and calling Roux a criminal and a *degenerate*—which means a layabout and not-to-be-trusted—and saying *Yanne, it's not too late*. Until at last Maman told him to go, and he did, leaving a blurry cloud of his colors behind him in the front of the shop, like a bad smell.

Maman was crying when I came back downstairs. She said she wasn't, but I knew. And her colors were all confused and dark, and her face was white except for two red spots under her eyes, and she said not to worry, that things were going to be OK, but I knew she was lying. I always know.

It's funny, isn't it, what adults tell kids? *There's nothing wrong. It's going to be fine. I don't blame you, it was an Accident*—but all the time that Thierry was here I was thinking about the time I'd met Roux by Dalida's tomb, and how grungy he'd looked, and how I'd given him the Ear of Maize to give him wealth and good fortune—

And now I wonder what I did. I can almost see it in my mind's eye: the last check from Thierry's bank, and Roux saying *I've got a few things to sort out first*, and just adding zero to the sum—

It's stupid, of course. Roux isn't a thief. A few potatoes from the edge of a field, apples from an orchard, maize from a verge, a fish from someone's private pond—but never money. Not like this.

But now I'm beginning to wonder again. What if it was a kind of revenge? What if he was trying to get back at Thierry? Worse still, *what if he did it for me and Rosette?*

A thousand euros is a lot of money for someone like Roux. You could buy a boat with that perhaps. You could settle down. Start an account. Put money aside for a family—

And then I remembered what Maman said. *Roux does what he wants, he always has. He lives on the river year-round, he sleeps outside, he's not even comfortable in a house. We couldn't live like that.*

And then I knew. It is my fault. With peg-dolls and wishing and symbols and signs, I've made Roux a criminal. And what if he's arrested? What if he has to go to jail?

There's a story Maman used to tell, about three fairies called Pic Blue, Pic Red, and Colégram. Pic Blue looks after the sky, the stars, the rain, the sun, and the birds of the air. Pic Red looks after the earth and everything that grows there: plants and trees and animals. And Colégram, who is the youngest, is supposed to look after the human heart. But Colégram can never get it right; whenever he tries to give anyone their heart's desire, someone always gets hurt. One time he tries to help a poor old man by turning autumn leaves to gold, but the old man is so excited at seeing the money that he tries to get too much into his knapsack and is crushed to death beneath the weight. I don't remember how the story ends, just that I felt sorry for Colégram, who tries so hard and always gets it so wrong. Maybe I'm like that too. Maybe I just can't do hearts.

Boy, what a mess. It was going so well. But a lot can happen in seven days, and the wind hasn't stopped changing yet. And anyway it's too late. We can't stop now. We've come too far to turn and run. Just one more working should do it, I think. One more call to the Changing Wind. Perhaps we got something wrong last time: a color, a candle, a mark in the sand. This time we're going to put it right, Rosette and me. Once and for all.

Tuesday, 18 December

THIERRY WAS HERE FIRST THING THIS MORNING, ASKING AFTER ROUX again. He seems to think that this business will change things between us; that to discredit Roux will somehow restore my faith in *him*.

Things are not so easy, of course. I've tried to explain—this is not about Roux. But Thierry is immovable. He has several friends in the police force and has already used his influence to bring more attention than it deserves to this rather minor case of fraud. But Roux has vanished, as he always does, like the Pied Piper into the side of the hill.

As he left, Thierry threw me one last, poisonous scrap of information, presumably from his friend in the gendarmerie—

"That account he used to cash the check. It's in a woman's name," he said. He gave me a sly, triumphant smile. "Looks like your friend isn't alone."

Today I wore my red dress again. Not my usual, I know, but the scene with Thierry, Roux's disappearance, and the weather—still dull and charged with snow—made me long for a touch of something bright.

And maybe it was the dress itself, or maybe some wild trace on the wind, but for all my anxiety, in spite of everything—Thierry's words; the ache in my heart when I think about Roux; my sleepless nights; my fears— I found myself singing as I worked.

It's as if a page has somehow turned. I feel free for the first time in years, I think; free of Thierry; free even of Roux. Free to be whoever I want—though who that is, I do not know.

Zozie had gone out for the morning. I was alone for the first time in weeks, except for Rosette, fully occupied with her box of buttons and her drawing book. I'd almost forgotten what it was like to stand behind the counter in a crowded *chocolaterie*, to talk to the customers, to find out their favorites.

It was startling, in a way, to see so many regulars. Of course I'm aware of comings and goings as I work in the kitchen at the back of the shop, but I hadn't really noticed how many people come in here now. Madame Luzeron—though it isn't her day. Then Jean-Louis and Paupaul, drawn by the promise of a warm place to sketch as well as their increasing appetite for my coffee-mocha layer cake. Nico—on a diet, now, but a diet that seems to involve eating lots of macaroons. Alice, with a bunch of holly for the shop and a request for her favorite, chocolate fudge. Madame Pinot, asking after Zozie—

She was not the only one. All of our regulars asked after Zozie, and Laurent Pinson, who came in all brushed and gleaming and greeted me with an exuberant bow, seemed to wilt when he saw who I was, as if that red dress had led him to expect someone else behind the till.

"I hear you're having a party," he said.

I smiled. "Just a small one. On Christmas Eve."

He gave me that fawning smile of his, the one he uses when Zozie is around. I know from Zozie that he is alone—no family, no children on Christmas Eve. And although I don't especially like the man, I can't help feeling sorry for him, with his starched yellow collar and hungry-dog smile.

"You're welcome to join us, of course," I said. "Unless you've got other plans."

He frowned a little, as if trying to recall the details of his frenetic social calendar.

"I *might* be able to make it," he said. "There's a lot to do, but—"

I hid a smile behind my hand. Laurent is the kind of man who needs to feel that he's doing you a tremendous favor by accepting one himself.

"We'd love to see you, Monsieur Pinson."

He shrugged magnanimously. "Well, if you insist. . . ."

I smiled. "That's nice."

"And that's a very becoming dress, if I may say so, Madame Charbon-neau."

"Call me Yanne."

He bowed again. I caught the scent of hair oil and sweat. And I won-dered—is this what Zozie does, every day while I make chocolates? Is this why we have so many customers?

A lady in an emerald coat, shopping for presents for Christmas. Her favorites are caramel swirls, and I tell her so without hesitation. Her hus-band will enjoy my apricot hearts, and their daughter will love my gilded chocolate chilli squares—

What's happening? What's changed in me?

A new sense of recklessness seems to have caught me, a feeling of hope, of confidence. I am no longer quite myself but something closer to Vianne Rocher, to the woman who blew into Lansquenet on the tail of the carnival wind—

Outside the chimes are totally still, and the sky is dark with unshed snow. This week's unnatural mildness has lifted, and it's cold enough to make breath plume as, in the square, the passersby like gray columns blur past. There's a musician on the corner; I can hear the sound of a saxophone playing "Petite Fleur" in its lingering, almost-human voice.

I think to myself—*he must be cold.*

It's a strange thought for Yanne Charbonneau. Real Parisians cannot afford such thoughts. There are so many poor people here in this city; homeless people; old people bundled up like Salvation Army parcels in shop doorways and back alleys. All of them are cold; all hungry. Real Pari-sians do not care. And I do want to be a real Parisian. . . .

But the music keeps playing, reminding me of another place, another time. I was someone else then, and the houseboats across the Tannes were crowded so close that you might almost have walked from one side of the river to the other. There was music then: steel drums and fiddles and whis-tles and flutes. The river people lived on music, it seemed, and though some villagers called them beggars I never actually saw them beg. In those days there would have been no hesitation—

You have a gift, my mother used to say. *And gifts are meant to be given away.*

I make a pot of hot chocolate. I pour a cup and I take it to the saxophone player—who is surprisingly young, no more than eighteen—with a slice of chocolate cake on the side. It's a gesture that Vianne Rocher would have made without thinking.

"On the house."

"Hey, thanks!" His face lights up. "You must be from the chocolate shop. I've heard about you. You're Zozie. Right?"

I begin to laugh, a little wildly. The laughter feels as bittersweet and strange as everything else on this strange day, but the saxophone player doesn't seem to notice.

"Got any requests?" he says to me then. "Anything you like, I'll play. On the house," he adds with a grin.

"I—" I faltered. "Do you know 'V'là l'bon vent'?"

"Yeah. Sure." He picks up his sax. "Just for you, Zozie," he says.

And as the sax begins to play, I shiver with something more than the cold as I walk back to Le Rocher de Montmartre, where Rosette is still playing quietly on the floor among a hundred thousand spilled buttons.

Tuesday, 18 December

I worked in the kitchen for the rest of today, while Zozie dealt with the customers. We're getting more customers than ever now; more than I can deal with alone, and it's good that she is still happy to help, because as Christmas approaches it seems that half Paris has developed a sudden appetite for handmade chocolates.

The supplies of *couverture* that I thought might last me until the New Year were exhausted within a couple of weeks, and we are getting deliveries every ten days just to keep up with increasing demand. The profits are above anything I could have dared to hope for, and all Zozie can say is: *I knew business would look up before Christmas,* as if such miracles happened every day. . . .

And once more I find myself wondering at how very quickly things have changed. Three months ago, we were strangers here; castaways on this rock of Montmartre. Now we are part of the scenery, just like Chez Eugène or Le P'tit Pinson; and locals who would never have thought to set foot in a tourist shop now pass here once or twice a week (and in some cases almost every day) for coffee, cake, or chocolate.

What has changed us? The chocolates, of course; I know that my handmade truffles are far better than anything out of a factory. The decor, too, is more welcoming; and with Zozie here to help me, there is time to sit and talk awhile.

Montmartre is a village within the city—and remains deeply if dubiously nostalgic, with its narrow streets and old cafés and country-style cottages, complete with summer whitewash and fake shutters at the windows and bright geraniums in their terra-cotta pots. To the folk of Montmartre, marooned above a Paris simmering with change, it sometimes feels like the *last* village; a fleeting fragment of a time when things were sweeter and simpler; when doors were always left unlocked and any ills and injuries could be cured with a square of chocolate—

It's all an illusion, I'm afraid. For most people here, those times never existed. They live in a world that is part fantasy, where the past is so deeply buried beneath wishful thinking and regret that they have almost come to believe their own fiction.

Look at Laurent, who speaks so bitterly against immigrants, but whose father was a Polish Jew who fled to Paris during the war, changed his name, married a local girl, and became Gustave Jean-Marie Pinson, Frencher than the French, sound as the stones of the Sacré-Coeur.

He does not speak of it, of course. But Zozie knows—he must have told her. And Madame Pinot, with her silver crucifix and her tight-lipped disapproving smile and shop window full of plaster saints—

She was never a Madame in her life. In her younger days (so says Laurent, who knows these things), she was a cabaret dancer at the Moulin Rouge and would sometimes perform in a nun's wimple, high heels, and a black satin corset so tight it would make your eyes water—hardly what you'd expect of a seller of religious memorabilia, and yet—

Even our handsome Jean-Louis and Paupaul, who work the Place du Tertre with such expertise, seducing the ladies into parting with their money with swashbuckling compliments and broad innuendo. You'd think at least they were what they seemed. But neither one has ever set foot in a gallery, or been to art school, and for all their masculine appeal, both of them are quietly though sincerely gay and are planning a civil ceremony— perhaps in San Francisco, where such things are more common and less harshly judged.

So says Zozie, who seems to know everything. Anouk too knows more than she tells me, and I find myself increasingly worrying about her. She used to tell me everything. But recently, she has grown restless and secretive; hiding for hours at a time in her room; spending most of her weekends in the cemetery with Jean-Loup, and her evenings talking with Zozie.

It's natural, of course, for a child her age to want a little more independence than she has. But there's a kind of watchfulness in Anouk—a coldness of which even she may be unaware—that makes me uneasy. It's as if some pivot has shifted between us, some relentless mechanism that has begun to move us slowly apart. She used to tell me everything. Now everything she says seems oddly guarded; her smiles are too bright, too forced for comfort.

Is this because of Jean-Loup Rimbault? Don't think I haven't noticed the way she hardly mentions him now; the cautious look when I speak of him; the careful way she dresses for school when once she hardly brushed her hair. . . .

Is it because of Thierry, perhaps? Is she anxious because of Roux?

I've tried asking her outright if there's something wrong; something at school, perhaps, some trouble I don't know about. But she always says *no, Maman*, in that clipped little good-girl voice, and trots off upstairs to do her homework.

But in the kitchen later that night, I hear laughter coming from Zozie's room, and I creep to the bottom of the stairs to listen, and I hear Anouk's voice, like a memory. And I know that if I open the door—to ask, perhaps, if she wants a drink—then the laughter will stop, and her eyes turn cool, and the Anouk I heard from far away will be gone like something in a fairy tale. . . .

Zozie was rearranging the Advent window, where a new door has opened today. A Christmas tree, cleverly made from sprigs of pine, now stands in the hallway of the little house. The mother stands at the door of the house, looking out into the garden, where a choir of carolers (she has used chocolate mice) are gathered in a semicircle, looking in.

As it happens, we put up our tree today. It's only a small one, from the florist's down the road, but it smells wonderfully of needles and sap, like a story of children lost in the woods, and there are silver stars to hang on the branches, and white fairy lights to drape all around. Anouk likes to dress the tree, and so I have deliberately left it bare so that when she gets home from school, we'll be able to decorate it together.

"So, what's Anouk up to these days?" The lightness in my tone is forced. "Seems like she's always running off somewhere."

Zozie smiled. "It's nearly Christmas," she said. "Kids are bound to get excited around Christmas."

"She hasn't said anything to you? She's not upset about Thierry and me?"

"Not that I know of," Zozie said. "If anything, she seems relieved."

"So there's nothing on her mind?"

"Just the party," Zozie said.

That party. I still don't know what she expects to achieve. Since the day she first mentioned it, my little Anouk has been willful and strange; making plans; suggesting dishes; inviting all comers with lavish disregard for the practicalities of seating and space.

"Can we invite Madame Luzeron?"

"Of course, Nanou. If you think she'll come."

"And Nico?"

"All right."

"And Alice, of course. And Jean-Louis and Paupaul—"

"Nanou, these people have homes of their own—families—what makes you think—"

"They'll come," she says, as if she has arranged it personally.

"How do you know?"

"I just do."

Maybe she does, I tell myself. She seems to know a great many things. And there's something else—some secret in her eyes—a hint of something from which I am excluded.

I look into the *chocolaterie*. It looks warm in there, almost intimate. Candles are burning on the tables; the Advent window is lit with a rose glow. It smells of orange and clove from the pomander hanging above the door; of pine from the tree; of the mulled wine that we are serving alongside our spiced hot chocolate; and of fresh gingerbread straight out of the oven. It draws them in—three or four at a time—regulars and strangers and tourists alike. They stop at the window, catch the scent, and in they come, looking a little dazed, perhaps, at the many scents and colors and all their favorites in their little glass boxes—bitter orange cracknel; *mendiants du roi*; hot chilli squares; peach brandy truffle; white chocolate angel; lavender brittle—all whispering inaudibly—

Try me. Taste me. Test me.

And Zozie at the center of it all. Even at the busiest times—laughing, smiling, teasing, giving out chocolates on the house, talking to Rosette, making everything a little brighter just because she is there. . . .

It feels as if I'm watching myself, the Vianne I was in another life.

But who am I now? I lurk behind the kitchen door, unable somehow to look away. A memory of another time; a man standing in a similar door-way, peering suspiciously inside. Reynaud's face; his hungry eyes; the hate-ful, haunted look of a man half disgusted by what he sees—but who must look in, nevertheless.

Could this be what I have become? Another version of the Black Man? Another Reynaud, tormented by pleasure, unable to bear the joy of others, crushed beneath his envy and guilt?

Absurd. How could I be envious of Zozie?

Worse still, how is it that I am afraid?

At four-thirty Anouk blows in from the misty streets, a light in her eyes and a telltale glimmer at her heels that might be Pantoufle, if he existed. She greets Zozie with an exuberant hug. Rosette joins in. They spin her round, shouting *bam-bam-bam*! It becomes a game, a kind of wild dance that ends with the three of them collapsing, laughing and breathless, onto the furry pink armchairs.

And as I watch from the kitchen door, a sudden thought occurs to me. There are too many ghosts in this place, of course. Dangerous ghosts; laughing ghosts; ghosts from a past we cannot afford to see reborn. And the strange thing is, they look oddly alive; as if I, Vianne Rocher, might be the ghost and the little threesome in the shop the real thing, the magic number, the circle that cannot be broken—

That's nonsense, of course. I know I'm real. Vianne Rocher is just a name I wore, perhaps not even my real name. She can have no purpose beyond that; she can have no future outside of me.

But I still can't stop thinking about her, like a favorite coat, or a pair of shoes, given on impulse to some charity shop, to be loved and worn by someone else. . . .

And now I can't help wondering—

How much of myself have I given away? And if I am no longer Vianne—who is?

PART SEVEN

The Tower

Wednesday, 19 December

WHY, HELLO, MADAME. YOUR FAVORITE? LET ME SEE—CHOCOLATE truffles, to my special recipe, marked with the sign of Lady Blood Moon and rolled in something that teases the tongue. A dozen? Or shall we make it two? Packed in a box of crinkly gold paper and tied with a ribbon of brightest red—

I knew she'd come eventually. My specials tend to have that effect. She came just before closing time; Anouk was upstairs doing her homework, and Vianne was in the kitchen again, working on tomorrow's sales.

First, I see her catch the scent. It's a combination of many things; the Christmas tree in the corner; the musty aroma of old house; orange and clove; ground coffee; hot milk; patchouli; cinnamon—and chocolate, of course; intoxicating, rich as Croesus, dark as death.

She looks around, sees wall hangings, pictures, bells, ornaments, a doll-house in the window, rugs on the floor—all in chrome yellow and fuchsia-pink and scarlet and gold and green and white. *It's like an opium den in here*, she almost says, then wonders at herself for being so fanciful. In fact she has never seen an opium den—unless it was in the pages of the *Arabian Nights*—but there's something about the place, she thinks. Something almost—magical.

Outside, the yellow-gray sky is luminous with the promise of snow. Forecasters have been announcing it for several days, though to Anouk's disappointment it has so far remained too mild for anything but sleet and this interminable mist.

"Lousy weather," says Madame. Of course, she would think so; see-ing, not magic in the clouds, but pollution; not stars, but lightbulbs in the Christmas lights; no comfort, no joy but the endless, anxious grind of peo-ple rubbing together without warmth, searching for last-minute gifts that will be opened without pleasure, and in a rush to go to some meal that they will not enjoy, with folk they have not seen for a year, and would not choose to see at all—

Through the Smoking Mirror I look at her face. It's a hard face in many ways, the face of a woman whose personal fairy tale never had a chance of happily-ever-after. She has lost parents, lover, and child; she has made good through sheer hard work; she wept herself dry years ago and has no pity now for herself or for anyone else. She hates Christmas, despises New Year's—

All this I see through the Eye of Black Tezcatlipoca. And now, with an effort, I can just glimpse what stands behind the Smoking Mirror—the fat woman sitting in front of the television, eating *choux* from a white patisserie box while her husband works late for the third night running; the window of an antiques shop, and a china-faced doll under a cloche; the chemist's where she once stopped to buy nappies and some milk for her baby girl; her mother's face, broad and harsh and unsurprised, when she came to tell her the terrible news—

But she has come so far since then. So very far—and yet there's some-thing inside her, this void, still wailing for something to fill it again—

"Twelve truffles. No. Make it twenty," she says. As if truffles could make a difference. But somehow these truffles are different, she thinks. And the woman behind the counter, with her long dark hair with the crys-tals braided into it and the emerald shoes with the shining stack heels— shoes made for dancing all night, for leaping, for flying, for anything but walking—*she* looks somehow different too, not like everyone else around here, but strangely more alive, more real—

There's a scatter of dark powder on the counter where the truffles have shed cacao onto the glass. It's easy, with a fingertip, to sketch the sign of One Jaguar—the feline Aspect of Black Tezcatlipoca—into the powdered chocolate. She stares at it, half mesmerized by the colors and scent as I wrap the box, taking my time with ribbons and paper.

Then Anouk comes in—right on cue—all wild-haired and laughing at something Rosette has done, and Madame looks up, her face going suddenly slack.

Does she recognize something, perhaps? Could it be that the vein of talent that runs so richly in Vianne and Anouk has left some vestige here at the source? Anouk gives her beaming smile. Madame smiles back, hesitantly at first, but as the conjunction of Blood Moon and Rabbit Moon joins the pull of One Jaguar, her doughy face becomes almost beautiful in its longing.

"And who's this?" she says.

"It's my little Nanou."

That's all I need to say. Whether or not Madame can see something familiar in the child, or whether it is simply Anouk herself, with her Dutch-doll face and Byzantine hair, that has captured her, who can say? But Madame's eyes have grown suddenly bright, and when I suggest that she stay for a cup of chocolate (and perhaps one of my special truffles on the side), she accepts the invitation without a murmur, and sitting at one of the handprinted tables, she stares with an intensity that is far beyond mere hunger at Anouk as she goes in and out of the kitchen; greets Nico as he passes the door and calls him in for a cup of tea; plays with Rosette and her box of buttons; talks about the birthday tomorrow; runs outside to check for snow; runs back inside; peers at the changes to the Advent house; rearranges a key figure or two; then checks for snow again—it will come, it *must* come at least for Christmas Eve, because she loves snow almost more than anything. . . .

It's time to close the shop. In fact, it's twenty minutes past our closing time when Madame seems to shake herself free of some daze.

"What a sweet little girl you have," she says as she stands up, brushes the chocolate crumbs from her lap, and looks wistfully at the kitchen door, through which Anouk has already gone, taking Rosette with her at last. "She plays with the other one just like a sister."

That makes me smile, but I don't put her right.

"Got any kids of your own?" I say.

She seems to hesitate. Then she nods. "A daughter," she says.

"Going to see her this Christmas?"

Oh, the anguish such a question may inadvertently cause—I see it in her colors, a pure streak of brilliant white that cuts like lightning across the rest.

She shakes her head, not trusting the words. Even now, after so many years, the feeling still has the power to surprise her with its immediacy. When will it fade, as so many people have promised it will? So far it has not—that grief that overrides everything else, sending lover, mother, friend, plunging into insignificance in the face of the desolate chasm that is the loss of a child—

"I lost her," she says in a quiet voice.

"I'm so sorry." I put my hand on her arm. I'm wearing short sleeves, and my charm bracelet, laden with its tiny figures, makes its heavy chinking sound. The shine of silver catches her eye—

The little cat charm has gone black with age, more like the One Jaguar of Black Tezcatlipoca than the cheap shiny bauble it once was.

She sees it and stiffens, thinking almost at once that it's absurd, that such coincidences do not happen, that it's only a cheap charm bracelet and that it could have nothing at all to do with the long-lost baby bangle and its little silver kitty-cat—

But oh! What if it could, she thinks. You hear about these things some-times—not always in movies, but sometimes in life—

"That's a-an interesting b-bracelet." Her voice is shaking so much now that she can hardly say the words.

"Thanks. I've had it for years."

"Oh, really?"

I nod. "Each of these charms is a reminder of something. This was when my mother died. . . ." I point out a charm shaped like a coffin. It's from Mexico City, in fact—I must have got it in some piñata or other—and there's a little black cross on the coffin lid.

"Your mother?"

"Well, I called her that. I never knew my birth parents. This key was for my twenty-first. And this cat is my oldest, luckiest charm. I've had it all my life, I think, even before I was adopted."

She stares at me now, almost paralyzed. It's impossible, and she knows it—but something less rational in her insists that miracles happen, magic exists. It's the voice of the woman she used to be, the one who—aged barely nineteen—fell in love with a man of thirty-two who told her he loved her, and whom she believed.

And what about that little girl? Didn't she recognize something in her? Something that pulls and tears at her heart like a kitten tormenting a ball of string.

Some people—myself, for instance—are born to be cynics. But once a believer, always a believer. I sense that Madame is one of these; have known it, in fact, from the moment I saw those porcelain dolls in the lobby of Le Stendhal. She's an aging romantic, embittered, disappointed, and therefore all the more vulnerable, and her piñata needs only a word from me to open up like a flower.

A word? I meant a *name*, of course.

"I have to shut up shop, Madame." I propel her gently toward the door. "But if you'd like to come again—we're having a party on Christmas Eve. If you don't have any other plans, perhaps you'd like to drop in for an hour?"

She looks at me with eyes like stars.

"Oh, yes," she whispers. "Thank you. I will."

Wednesday, 19 December

THIS MORNING ANOUK LEFT FOR SCHOOL WITHOUT SAYING GOOD-BYE. I should not be too surprised at this—it's what she has done every day this week, coming late to breakfast with a *Hey, everyone!* grabbing her croissant in one hand and racing off into the dark.

But this is Anouk, who used to lick my face in sheer exuberance and shout *I love you!* across crowded streets—now silent and so self-absorbed that I feel bereft and icy with fear; the doubts that have dogged me since she was born now waxing as the weeks march on.

She is growing up, of course. Other things preoccupy her. Friends at school. Homework. Teachers. Maybe a boyfriend (Jean-Loup Rimbault?), or the sweet delirium of a first crush. There are other things, perhaps; secrets whispered; great plans made; things that she may tell her friends, but which if her mother knew, would make her cringe with embarrassment—

All perfectly normal, I tell myself. And yet the sense of exclusion is almost more than I can bear. We are not like other people, I think. Anouk and I are different. And whatever discomfort that may bring, I cannot ignore it anymore—

With that knowledge I find myself changing—becoming snappish and critical at the slightest thing, and how is my summer child to know that the note in my voice is not anger, but fear?

Did my own mother feel the same? Did she feel that sense of loss, that fear even greater than the fear of death, as she tried in vain, as all mothers do, to freeze the remorseless passage of time? Did she follow me, as I follow

Anouk, picking up markers on the road? The toys outgrown; clothes cast off; bedtime stories left untold; all abandoned in her wake as the child runs ever eagerly into the future, away from childhood, away from *me*—

There was a story my mother used to tell. A woman desperately wanted a child but being unable to conceive, one winter's day made a child of snow. She made it with exquisite care, clothed it, and loved it, and sang to it, until the Winter Queen took pity on the woman and brought the child of snow to life.

The woman—the mother—was overcome. She thanked the Winter Queen with tears of joy and swore that her new daughter would never want for anything, or ever know sorrow as long as she lived.

"But be careful, lady," the Winter Queen warned. "Like calls to like; and change to change; and the world turns, for good or for ill. Keep your child well out of the sun; keep her obedient as long as you can. For a child of desire is never content—not even with a mother's love."

But the mother was barely listening. She took her child home and loved her and cared for her, just as she had promised the Winter Queen. Time passed; the child grew with magical speed; snow white and sloe black and beautiful as a clear winter's day.

Then spring approached; the snow began to melt; and the Snow Child grew increasingly dissatisfied. She wanted to go outside, she said; to be with other children; to play. The mother refused at first, of course. But the child would not be cajoled. She cried, grew wan, refused to eat, so that finally, reluctantly, the mother gave way.

"Stay out of the sun," she warned the child. "And never take off your hat and coat."

"All right," said the child and skipped away.

All that day, the Snow Child played. It was the first time she had ever seen other children. She played hide-and-seek for the first time; learned singing games and clapping games and running games and more. When she came home she looked unusually tired but happier than her mother had ever seen her before.

"May I go out again tomorrow?"

With a heavy heart, her mother agreed—as long as she kept on her hat and coat—and once more the Snow Child was out all day. She made secret friendships and solemn pacts; skinned her knees for the very first time; and once more came home with a gleam in her eye and demanded to go out again on the morrow.

Her mother protested—the child was exhausted—but finally agreed once more. And on the third day the Snow Child discovered the exhilarating joys of disobedience. For the first time in her short life she broke a promise; broke a window; kissed a boy; and took off her hat and coat in the sun.

Time passed. When night fell and the Snow Child had still not returned, the mother went in search of her. She found her coat; she found her hat; but of the Snow Child there was no sign, nor ever again, but a silent pool of water where no pool had been before.

Well, I never liked that story much. Of all the stories my mother used to tell, that was the one that frightened me most; not for the tale itself, but for the expression on her face and the tremor in her voice and the way she held me painfully tight as the wind blew wild in the winter dark.

Of course then I had no idea of why she seemed so afraid. Now I know better. They say that childhood's greatest fear is that of being abandoned by one's parents. So many children's stories reflect it: Hansel and Gretel; the Babes in the Wood; Snow White pursued by the evil queen—

But now it is I who am lost in the woods. Even in the heat of the kitchen stove, I shiver and pull my thick cable-knit sweater tighter around my shoulders. Nowadays I feel the cold; but Zozie might still be dressed for summer, with her bright print skirt and ballet shoes, her hair tied up in a yellow bow.

"I'm going out for an hour or so. Is that OK?"

"Of course it is."

How can I refuse, when she still won't accept a proper wage?

And once again, silently I ask myself—

What's your price?

What do you want?

The December wind still blows outside. But the wind has no power over Zozie. I watch as she turns out the lights in the front of the shop, and she hums as she closes the shutters over the window display, where the wooden peg-dolls in the stucco house are gathered around the birthday scene, while outside, under the porch lantern, a choir of chocolate mice with tiny hymn sheets pinned to their paws sings silently in the crystal-sugar snow.

Thursday, 20 December

THIERRY WAS BACK HERE AGAIN TODAY, BUT ZOZIE DEALT WITH HIM—I'M
not sure how. I owe her so much, a fact that disturbs me most of all. But
I have not forgotten what I saw the other day in the *chocolaterie*, or that
uncomfortable feeling of watching myself—the Vianne Rocher I used to
be—reborn in the person of Zozie de l'Alba, using my methods, speaking
my lines, daring me to challenge her.

I watched her covertly all today, as I did yesterday and the day before.
Rosette was playing quietly; the mingled scents of clove and marshmallow and cinnamon and rum drifted across the warm kitchen; my hands
were floured in icing sugar and cocoa powder; the copper glowed; the kettle
warbled on the hearth. It was all so familiar—so absurdly *comfortable*—and
yet some part of me could not rest. Every time the doorbell rang, I looked
into the shop to check.

Nico dropped by with Alice at his side, both of them looking absurdly
happy. Nico tells me he has lost weight, in spite of his addiction to coconut
macaroons. A casual observer might not notice the difference (he still looks
as large and cheery as ever); but Alice says that he has lost five kilos and can
wear his belt three notches tighter.

"It's, like, being in love," he told Zozie. "It's gotta burn calories, or something. Hey, great tree. Triffic tree. You want a tree like that, Alice?"

Alice's voice is less easy to hear. But at least she *is* speaking; and her
small, pointed face seems to have taken some color today. She looks like a

child next to Nico, but a happy one, no longer lost; and her eyes never seem to leave his face.

I thought of the Advent house, and of the two little figures with their pipe-cleaner hands joined beneath the Christmas tree.

Then there's Madame Luzeron, who has started to call in more frequently, and who plays with Rosette while she sips her mocha. She too is looking more relaxed; and today she was wearing a bright red twinset under her black winter coat, and she actually got down on her knees as she and Rosette rolled a wooden dog solemnly to and fro across the tiles—

Then Jean-Louis and Paupaul joined the game, and Richard and Mathurin on their way to *pétanque*; and Madame Pinot, who would never have come in six months ago, but who Zozie calls by her first name (Hermine) and who casually asks for *my usual.* . . .

As the busy afternoon sped on, I was touched to see so many customers bringing in presents for Rosette. I'd forgotten that they must see her with Zozie, while I am in the back making chocolates, but even so, it was unexpected, reminding me of all the friends we have gained since Zozie joined us a month ago.

There was the wooden dog from Madame Luzeron; a painted green eggcup from Alice; a stuffed rabbit from Nico; a jigsaw from Richard and Mathurin; a drawing of a monkey from Jean-Louis and Paupaul. Even Madame Pinot dropped round with a yellow hairband for Rosette—and to put in an order for violet creams, for which she has an enthusiasm bordering on greed. Then Laurent Pinson came in as usual, to steal the sugar and to inform me with gleeful despondency that business was terrible everywhere, and that he'd just seen a Muslim woman in a full veil walking down the Rue des Trois Frères; and as he went out he dropped a package on the table, which, when opened, was found to contain a pink plastic charm bracelet that probably came with a teen magazine, but that Rosette loves uncritically, and refuses to remove, even at bathtime.

And then, just as we were about to close, the odd woman who was here yesterday came round again, bought another box of truffles, and left a present for Rosette. That surprised me first of all—she isn't a regular of ours, and even Zozie doesn't know her name—but when we opened the gift wrapping, our surprise was greater still. Inside there was a box containing a baby doll, not large but clearly antique, with a soft body and a porcelain face framed in a bonnet lined with fur. Rosette loves it, of course, but I couldn't accept such a lavish gift from a stranger, and I packed the doll into its box, meaning to give it back to the woman when—and if—she returns.

"Don't worry about it," said Zozie. "It probably belonged to her kids, or something. Look at Madame Luzeron and her dollhouse furniture."

I pointed out, "Those things are only on loan."

"Come on, Yanne," said Zozie. "You have to stop being so suspicious about everything. You have to give people a chance—"

Rosette pointed at the box. *Baby*, she signed.

"All right. Just for tonight."

Rosette gave a silent crow.

Zozie smiled. "See? It's not so hard."

All the same I can't help feeling uneasy. Rarely does anything ever come free—there's not a gift or a kindness that doesn't have to be paid for in full in the end. Life has taught me that, at least. That's why I am more cautious now. That's why I keep the wind chimes over my door, to warn me of the Kindly Ones, those messengers of credit due—

Tonight Anouk came in from school as usual, with no indication of her presence but the scampering sound of her feet on the wooden stairs as she went to her room. I tried to remember the last time it was that she greeted me as she used to do, coming to find me in the kitchen with a hug and a kiss and a barrage of chatter. I tell myself that I'm being too sensitive. But there was a time when she could no more have forgotten my kiss than she could have forgotten Pantoufle—

Yes, right now I'd welcome even that. A glimpse of Pantoufle; a casual word. Some sign that the summer child I knew has not entirely disappeared. But for days now I have not seen him, and she has hardly spoken to me—not about Jean-Loup Rimbault, not about her friends from school, not about Roux, Thierry, or even about the party anymore; though I know how hard she has worked on it, writing invitations on pieces of card, each one decorated with a sprig of holly and a picture of a monkey, copying out menus, planning games.

And now I find myself watching her across the dinner table and wondering at how adult she looks, and how suddenly, troublingly beautiful, with her dark hair and her stormy eyes and the promise of cheekbones in her vivid face.

I find myself watching her with Rosette, seeing the graceful, studious way she bends her head over the yellow-iced birthday cake and the oddly touching smallness of Rosette's hands in her bigger ones. *Blow the candles, Rosette*, she says. *No, don't dribble. Blow. Like this.*

I find myself watching her with Zozie—

And oh, Anouk—it happens so fast—that sudden switch from light to shade, from being the center of someone's world to being nothing but a detail in the border, a figure in the shadows, seldom studied, barely seen—

Back in the kitchen, late that night, I put her school clothes in the washing machine. For a moment I hold them to my face, as if they might retain some part of her that I have lost. They smell of the outside, and of the incense smoke from Zozie's rooms, and of the malt-biscuity scent of her sweat. I feel like a woman searching her lover's clothes for signs of infidelity—

And in the pocket of her jeans, I find something that she has forgotten to take out. It's a doll made from a wooden clothes peg, the same kind of doll that she has been making for the window display. But looking at this one more closely, I can recognize who it's meant to be; I can see the marks drawn on it in felt-tip pen, and the three red hairs tied around the waist, and if I narrow my eyes, then I can see the glow that surrounds it, so faint and so very familiar that I might almost have missed it otherwise. . . .

Once more I go to the Advent window, where tomorrow's scene is already set. The door opens into the dining room, and everyone is gathered around the table, where a chocolate cake stands ready to be cut. There are tiny candles on the table, and tiny plates and glasses, and now that I look more carefully I can recognize almost everyone there—Fat Nico, Zozie, little Alice in her big boots, Madame Pinot with her crucifix, Madame

Luzeron in her funeral coat, Rosette, myself, even Laurent—and Thierry, who has not been invited, standing under the snow-covered trees.

And all of them marked with that golden gleam—

Such a small thing—

Such a *huge* thing.

But there's surely no harm in a game, I think. Games are how children make sense of the world; and stories, even the darkest of them, are the means with which they learn to cope—with loss, with cruelty, with death—

But there is more to this little tableau. The family-and-friends-at-the-table scene—the candles; the tree; the chocolate log—are all contained *inside* the house. Outside, the scene is different. Heavy snow in the form of icing sugar has gathered on the ground and the trees. The lake with its ducks is frozen now; the sugar mice with their hymn sheets have gone, and long, murderous icicles—sugar-spun, but glassy-sharp—now hang from the branches of the trees.

Thierry is standing right under them, and a dark chocolate snowman, big as a bear, is watching him menacingly from the forest close by.

I look more closely at the little peg-doll. Uncannily, it *looks* like Thierry; his clothes, his hair, his mobile phone, even his expression somehow, depicted by an ambivalent line and a couple of dots for eyes.

And there is something else too. A spiral symbol in the sugar snow, drawn with the tip of a small finger. I've seen it before, in Anouk's room, chalked up on her notice board; drawn in crayon on a pad; reproduced a hundred times with buttons and jigsaw pieces on this floor, now lustrous with that undeniable glamour—

And now I begin to understand. Those signs scratched under the countertop. The medicine bags hanging over the door. The new influx of customers; the friends we have made; all the changes that have occurred here over the past few weeks. This is far more than a child's game. This is more like a secret campaign over a territory I was not even aware was in dispute.

And the general behind this campaign?

Do I even need to ask?

Friday, 21 December
WINTER SOLSTICE

IT'S ALWAYS MAD ON THE LAST DAY OF TERM. LESSONS ARE MOSTLY GAMES
and tidying up; there are form parties, cakes, and Christmas cards; teachers
who haven't smiled all year go around wearing novelty Christmas bauble
earrings and Santa hats and sometimes even giving out sweets.

Chantal and Co. have been keeping their distance. Since they got back
some time last week, they haven't been half as popular as they used to be.
Maybe it's a ringworm thing. Suze's hair is coming back, though she still
wears her beanie all the time. Chantal looks OK, I guess, but Danielle,
who was the first to call Rosette those names, has lost most of her hair *and*
her eyebrows as well. They can't possibly know that *I* did that—but all
the same, they keep out of my way, like sheep around an electric fence. No
more *It* games. No more pranks. No more jokes about my hair, or visits to
the *chocolaterie*. Mathilde heard Chantal tell Suze I was "creepy." Jean-Loup
and I just laughed like crazy. "Creepy." I mean, how lame can you get?

But now there's only three days to go, and there's still no sign at all of
Roux. I've been looking out for him all week, but he hasn't been seen by
anyone. I even went round to the hostel today, but there was no sign of
anyone there at all, and Rue de Clichy isn't somewhere you'd want to hang
around—especially not now when it's getting dark, with sick splattered on
the pavements and sleeping drunks bundled into the steel-shuttered doorways.

But I thought he'd be here last night, at least—for Rosette's birthday, if

nothing else—and of course he wasn't. I miss him so much. But I can't help
thinking there's something wrong. Did he lie about having a boat? Did he
forge that check? Has he gone for good? Thierry says he'd better be gone, if
he knows what's good for him. Zozie says he might still be around, hiding
out somewhere nearby. Maman doesn't say anything.

I've told Jean-Loup about it all. Roux, Rosette, and the whole mess. I
told him Roux was my best friend, and now I'm afraid he's gone for good,
and he kissed me and said *he* was my friend—

It was just a kiss. Not anything gross. But now I feel all shivery and
tingly, like there's a triangle playing inside my stomach or something, and
I think perhaps—

Oh, boy.

He says I should talk to Maman, and try to sort things out with her,
but she's always so busy nowadays, and sometimes at dinner she's so quiet
and she looks at me in a sad kind of disappointed way, as if there's something I ought to have done, and I don't know what to say to make things
better—

Maybe that's why I slipped tonight. I'd been thinking of Roux and the
party again, and whether I can trust him to come after all. Because missing Rosette's birthday's bad enough, but if he's not there on Christmas Eve,
then it won't work out the way we planned, like he's some special secret
ingredient to a recipe that can't be finished otherwise. And if it doesn't happen right, then things will never go back to the way they were before, and
they need to, they need to, especially now. . . .

Zozie had to go out tonight, and Maman was working late again. She's
getting so many orders now that she can hardly handle all of them; and so
for dinner I made a pot of spaghetti, then took mine up to my room so Maman could have space to work.

It was ten o'clock when I went to bed, but even then I couldn't sleep, so
I went down to the kitchen for a drink of milk. Zozie still wasn't back and
Maman was making chocolate truffles. Everything smelled of chocolate:
Maman's dress; her hair; even Rosette, who was playing on the kitchen
floor with a pat of dough and some pastry cutters.

It all looked so safe, so familiar. I ought to have known it was a mistake.

Maman looked tired and kind of stressed; she was pounding away at the truffle paste like it was bread dough or something, and when I came down for my glass of milk she hardly looked at me at all.

"Hurry up, Anouk," she said. "I don't want you staying up too late."

Well, Rosette's only four, I thought, and she's allowed to stay up late—

"It's the holidays," I said.

"I don't want you falling ill," said Maman.

Rosette pulled on my pajama leg, wanting to show me her pastry shapes.

"That's nice, Rosette. Shall we cook them now?"

Rosette grinned and signed: *yum, yum.*

Thank goodness for Rosette, I thought. Always happy; always smiling. Not like everyone else round here. When I grow up, I'll live with Rosette; we could stay on a boat on the river, like Roux, and eat sausages right out of the can, and light bonfires at the side of the river, and maybe Jean-Loup could live nearby—

I lit the oven and took out a baking tray. Rosette's pastry shapes were a bit grubby, but that wouldn't matter when they were cooked. "We'll bake them twice, like biscuits," I said. "Then we can hang them on the Christmas tree."

Rosette laughed and hooted at the pastry shapes through the glass oven door, signing for them to cook fast. That made me laugh, and for a minute it felt OK, as if a cloud had gone from overhead. Then Maman spoke, and the cloud was back.

"I found something of yours," she said, still pounding away at the truffle paste. I wondered what she'd found, and where. In my room, or my pockets, perhaps. Sometimes I think she spies on me. I can always tell when she's been through my things: books left out of place; papers moved; toys put away. I don't know what she's looking for—but so far she hasn't found my secret special hiding place. It's a shoe box, hidden at the bottom of my wardrobe, with my diary, and some pictures, and some other stuff that I don't want anyone to see.

"This is yours, isn't it?" She reached into the kitchen drawer and pulled out Roux's peg-doll, which I'd left in the pocket of my jeans. "Did you make this?"

I nodded.

"Why?"

For a while I didn't say anything. What could I say? I don't think I could have explained even if I'd wanted to. To have everything right back in its place; to bring Roux back, and not just Roux—

"You've seen him, haven't you?" she said.

I didn't answer. She already knew.

"Why didn't you tell me, Anouk?" she said.

"Well, why didn't you tell *me* he was Rosette's dad?"

Now Maman went very still. "Who told you that?"

"No one," I said.

"Was it Zozie?"

I shook my head.

"Then who?"

"I just guessed."

She put down the spoon on the side of the dish and sat down very slowly on the kitchen chair. She sat there in silence for such a long time that I could smell the pastry shapes beginning to burn. Rosette was still playing with the pastry cutters, stacking them up on top of one another. They are made of plastic, six of them, all in different colors: a purple cat, a yellow star, a red heart, a blue moon, an orange monkey, and a green diamond. I used to like playing with them when I was small, making chocolate biscuits and gingerbread shapes, and decorating them with yellow and white icing from a squeezy bag.

"Maman?" I said. "Are you OK?"

For a moment she didn't say anything, just looked at me, eyes dark as forever. "Did you tell him?" she said at last.

I didn't answer. I didn't need to. She could see it in my colors just as I could see it in hers. I wanted to say that it was all right, that she didn't have to lie to me, that I knew all kinds of things now, that I could help *her*—

"Well, now at least we know why he's gone."

"You think he's gone?"

Maman just shrugged.

"He wouldn't go because of that!"

Now she gave a tired smile and held out the peg-doll, all gleaming with the sign of the Changing Wind.

"It's just a doll, Maman," I said.

"Nanou, I thought you trusted me."

I could see her colors then, all sad grays and anxious yellows, like old newspapers kept up in an attic somewhere that somebody wanted to throw away. And now I could see what Maman was thinking—flashes of it, anyway—like flicking through a scrapbook of thoughts. A picture of me, six years old, sitting beside her at a chrome-topped counter, both of us grinning like mad, with a tall glass of creamy hot chocolate between us and two little spoons. A storybook, with pictures, left open on a chair. A drawing of mine, with two shaky people that might have been me and Maman, both with smiles as big as summer watermelons, standing under a lollipop tree. Me fishing from Roux's boat. Me now, running with Pantoufle, running toward something I can never reach—

And something—a shadow—over us.

It frightened me to see her so afraid. And I wanted to trust her, to tell her that it was OK, and how nothing was ever really lost, because Zozie and I were bringing it back—

"Bringing what back?"

"Don't worry, Maman. I know what I'm doing. This time there won't be an Accident."

Her colors flared, but her face stayed calm. She smiled at me, speaking very slowly and patiently, as if she were talking to Rosette. "Listen, Nanou. This is very important. I need you to tell me everything."

I hesitated. I'd promised Zozie—

"Trust me, Anouk. I need to know."

So I tried to explain about Zozie's System; and the colors, and the names, the Mexican symbols, and the Changing Wind, and our lessons up in Zozie's room, and the way I'd helped Mathilde and Claude, and how we'd helped the chocolate shop to break even at last, and Roux, and the peg-dolls, and how Zozie had said there were no such things as Accidents, only regular people and people like us.

"You said it wasn't real magic," I said. "But Zozie says we should use what we've got. We shouldn't just pretend we're like everyone else. We shouldn't have to hide anymore. . . ."

"Sometimes hiding's the only way."

"No, sometimes you can fight back."

"Fight back?" she said.

So then I told her what I'd done at school; and how Zozie had told me about riding the wind, and using the wind, and how we shouldn't be afraid. And finally I told her about Rosette and me, and how we'd called the Changing Wind to bring Roux back, so we'd be a family—

She flinched at that, like she'd burned herself.

"And Thierry?" she said.

Well, he had to go. Surely Maman could see that. "Nothing bad happened, did it?" I said. Except that—

Maybe it did, I thought. Maybe if Roux really did forge that check, then maybe *that* was the Accident. Maybe it's what Maman says: that nothing comes without a price, and even magic has to have an equal and opposite reaction, like Monsieur Gestin tells us in physics at school—

Maman turned to the kitchen stove. "I'm making hot chocolate. Do you want some?"

I shook my head.

She made the chocolate anyway, grating it into the hot milk, adding nutmeg and vanilla and a cardamom pod. It was getting late—eleven o'clock—and Rosette was nearly asleep on the floor.

And for a moment I thought it was all right, and I was happy I'd cleared the air, because I hate having to hide from Maman, and I was thinking that perhaps now she knew the truth she wouldn't be afraid anymore, and she could be Vianne Rocher again, and fix it so we'd be all right—

She turned, and I knew I'd made a mistake.

"Nanou, please. Take Rosette to bed. We'll deal with this tomorrow."

I looked at her. "You're not angry?" I said.

She shook her head, but I could see she was. Her face was white and very still, and I could see her colors, all mixed up in reds and angry oranges and panicky zigzags of gray and black.

"It isn't Zozie's fault," I said.

Her face told me she didn't agree.

"You won't tell her, will you?"

"Just go to bed, Nou."

So I did, and lay awake for a long time, listening to the wind and rain in the eaves and watching the clouds and the stars and the white Christmas lights, all jumbled up against the wet windowpane, so that after a while there was no way to tell which were the real stars and which were the fake.

Friday, 21 December

It's been a long time since i did any scrying. An accidental glimpse; a spark, like static from a stranger's hand—but nothing more deliberate. I can see their favorites, that's all. Whatever their secrets, I don't want to know.

Tonight, however, I must try again. Anouk's account, though incomplete, is enough to make me see that, at least. I managed to keep calm until she left; to maintain the illusion of control. But now I can hear the December wind, and the Kindly Ones are at the door. . . .

My Tarot deck is no help to me. It just keeps showing me the same thing, the same cards in a different order, however much I shuffle them.

The Fool; the Lovers; the Magus, Change.

Death; the Hanged Man; the Tower.

So this time, I'm using chocolate, a technique I haven't tried in years. But I need to keep my hands busy tonight, and making truffles is such a simple thing that I could do it blind, by touch, with only the scent and the sound of the melted *couverture* with which to gauge the temperature.

It is a kind of magic, you know. My mother despised it—called it trivial, a waste of time—but it's *my* kind of magic, and my tools have always worked better for me than hers. Of course, all magic has consequences; but I think we've gone too far to worry about that. I was wrong to try to lie to Anouk—more so for trying to lie to myself.

I work very slowly, eyes half-closed. I smell the hot copper in front of me; the water boils with a scent of age and metal. These pans have been with me many years; I know their contours, the dents that time has put upon them, and in some places they bear the bright burnished marks of my hands against the darker patina.

Everything around me seems to have taken on a sharper kind of definition. My mind is free; the wind is up; outside the solstice moon is only a few days' waxing to full, and it rides the clouds like a buoy in a storm.

The water simmers but must not boil. Now into the small ceramic pan I grate the block of *couverture*. Almost at once the scent rises, the dark and loamy scent of bitter chocolate from the block. At this concentration it is slow to melt; the chocolate is very low in fat, and I will have to add butter and cream to the mixture to bring it to truffle consistency. But now it smells of history; of the mountains and forests of South America; of felled wood and spilled sap and campfire smoke. It smells of incense and patchouli; of the black gold of the Maya and the red gold of the Aztec; of stone and dust and of a young girl with flowers in her hair and a cup of pulque in her hand.

It is intoxicating; as it melts, the chocolate becomes glossy; steam rises from the copper pan, and the scent grows richer, blossoming into cinnamon and allspice and nutmeg; dark undertones of anise and espresso; brighter notes of vanilla and ginger. Now it is almost melted through. A gentle vapor rises from the pan. Now we have the true *Theobroma*, the elixir of the gods in volatile form, and in the steam I can almost see—

A young girl dancing with the moon. A rabbit follows at her heels. Behind her stands a woman with her head in shadow, so that for a moment she seems to look three ways—

But now the steam is getting too thick. The chocolate must be no warmer than forty-six degrees. Too hot, and the chocolate will scorch and streak. Too cool, and it will bloom white and dull. I know by the scent and the level of steam that we are close to the danger point. Take the copper off the heat and stand the ceramic in cold water until the temperature has dropped.

Cooling, it acquires a floral scent; of violet and lavender *papier poudré*. It smells of my grandmother, if I'd had one, and of wedding dresses kept carefully boxed in the attic, and of bouquets under glass. I can almost see the glass now, a round cloche under which a doll stands, a blue-eyed doll in a fur-trimmed red coat that reminds me strangely of someone I know....

A woman with a tired face looks longingly at the blue-eyed doll. I think I've seen her before somewhere. And behind her, another woman stands, with her head half hidden behind the curved glass. I seem to know this woman, somehow, but her face is distorted through the cloche and she could be almost anyone—

Return the pan to the simmering water. Now it must reach thirty-one degrees. It is my last chance to make sense of this, and I can feel a tremor in my hands as I look down into the melted *couverture*. Now it smells of my children: of Rosette with her birthday cake and Anouk, sitting in the shop, six years old, talking and laughing and planning—what?

A festival. A Grand Festival du Chocolat—with Easter eggs and chocolate hens and the pope in white chocolate—

It is a wonderful memory. That year, we faced down the Black Man and won—we rode the wind, at least, for a while—

But this is no time for nostalgia. Banish the steam from the dark surface. Try again.

And now we are in Le Rocher de Montmartre. A table is set, all our friends are here. Another kind of festival now—I see Roux at the table, smiling, laughing, with a holly crown on his red hair, holding Rosette in his arms and drinking a glass of champagne—

But that's just wishful thinking, of course. We often see what we want to see. For a moment I am shaken almost to tears—

Once more I pass my hand through the steam.

And now the festival is different again. There are firecrackers and marching bands and people dressed as skeletons—the Day of the Dead, with children dancing in the streets and paper lanterns with demon faces painted on them, and sugar skulls on sticks, and Santa Muerte parading through the streets with her three faces watching every which way—

But what can it have to do with me? We never got as far as South America, although my mother longed to see the place. We never even got to Florida—

I reach out a hand to disperse the steam. And it's then that I see her. A mouse-haired girl of eight or nine, hand in hand with her mother among the crowds. I sense they are different from the rest—something about their skin, their hair—and they look around in half-lost wonderment at every-thing: the dancers; the demons; the painted piñatas on long pointed sticks with firecrackers tied to their tails. . . .

Once again, I move my hand across the surface of the chocolate. Little tendrils of steam rise up, and now I can smell gunpowder, a dangerous scent, all smoke and fire and turbulence—

And now I see the girl again, playing with a group of other children in a back alley outside a darkened little shopfront. There is a piñata hanging above the doorway, a striped and fabulous tiger-thing in red and yellow and black. The others are shouting—*Hit it! Hit it!*—and showering it with sticks and stones. But the little girl holds back. There is something inside the shop, she thinks. Something—*more*—*attractive.*

Who *is* the girl? I really don't know. But I want to follow her inside. There is a curtain across the door, made up of long strips of multicolored plastic. She holds out a hand—a thin silver bracelet circles her wrist—and looks back to where the children are still trying to dislodge the tiger piñata, then ducks through the curtain into the shop.

"Don't you like my piñata?"

The voice comes from the corner of the shop. It belongs to an old woman, a grandmother, no, a *great-great-*grandmother—so old she might be a hundred, or even a thousand, to the little girl. She looks like a witch from a storybook, all wrinkles and eyes and clutching hands. In one of these she holds a cup; and from it, an odd scent reaches the little girl, something heady, intoxicating.

All around her on the shelves are bottles and jars and pots and gourds; dried roots hang from the ceiling, giving out a cellar smell; and there are lighted candles everywhere, making the shadows grin and dance.

A skull looks down from a high shelf.

At first the girl thinks it's a sugar skull, like the others at the carnival, but now she isn't so sure anymore. And in front of her, on the counter, is a black object about three feet long—the size of a baby's coffin, perhaps.

It looks like a papier-mâché box, painted a dull and uniform black except for the sign—which looks almost like a cross, but not quite—painted in red across the lid.

Why, it's a kind of piñata, she thinks.

The great-grandmother smiles and hands her a knife. It's a very old knife, rather blunt, and looks as if it's made of stone. The girl looks curiously at the knife, then back at the old woman and her strange piñata.

"Open it," urges the great-grandmother. "Open it. It's all for you."

The scent of chocolate intensifies. It's reaching the correct temperature now; the thirty-one-degree threshold beyond which the *couverture* must not rise. The vapor thickens; the vision blurs; quickly I move the chocolate away from the heat and try to recapture what I have seen—

Open it.

It smells of age. But from inside, something calls to her; not quite a voice, but coaxing, promising . . .

It's all for you.

What, exactly?

Strike one. The piñata echoes flatly, like a crypt door, like an empty cask, like something much larger than this small black box.

Strike two. It cracks; a split appears along its length. The girl smiles, half-seeing the hoard of tinfoil and trinkets and chocolates inside—

Nearly there now. One more strike—

And now at last the child's mother appears, pushing the plastic curtain aside and looking in with widening eyes. She calls a name. Her voice is shrill. The little girl does not look up, too absorbed in the black piñata, which needs only one more strike to release its secrets—

The mother cries out again. Too late. The child is too absorbed in her task. The grandmother leans forward eagerly, almost tasting it now, she thinks; rich as blood and chocolate.

The stone knife falls with a hollow sound. The split widens—

She thinks: *I'm in.*

Aand now the last of the vapor has gone. The chocolate will set correctly, with a good sheen and a pleasing snap. And now I know where I've seen her before, that little girl with the knife in her hand—

I've known her all my life, I suppose. We fled her for years, my mother and I, running like gypsies from town to town. We have met her before in fairy tales: she's the Wicked Witch in the gingerbread house; she's the Pied Piper; she's the Winter Queen. For a while we knew her as the Black Man—but the Kindly Ones have so many disguises, and their kindness spreads like wildfire, calling the tune, ringing the changes, charming us out of Hamelin, sending all of our troubles racing and tumbling in the wake of those enticing red shoes—

And now I can see her face at last. Her real face, hidden behind a lifetime of glamours, variable as the moon and hungry, *hungry*—as she steps through the door in her bayonet heels and stands watching me with a radiant smile. . . .

6

Friday, 21 December

SHE WAS WAITING FOR ME WHEN I CAME IN. CAN'T SAY I WAS ALTO-gether surprised. I'd been expecting a reaction for some days now, and to tell the truth, it's overdue.

Time, at last, to set things right. I've played the tabby cat too long. Time to show my feral side, to face my opponent on her home ground.

I found her in the kitchen, wrapped in a shawl, with a cup of chocolate long since gone cold. It was past midnight; it was still raining outside, and there was a lingering smell of something burned.

"Hello, Vianne."

"Hello, Zozie."

She looked at me.

Once more, I was in.

If I have a single regret regarding the lives I have stolen, it's this: that so much of it was done in stealth, and that my adversaries never knew or appreciated the poetry of their downfall.

My mother—not the brightest spark—may have come close to it once or twice, though I don't think she ever believed it, really. In spite of her occult interests, she really wasn't all that imaginative, preferring meaning-less rituals to anything closer to the bone.

Even Françoise Lavery, who, with her background, must have caught a glimpse of it at the end, was still unable to grasp the elegance of it all; the way that her life had been neatly reclaimed and repackaged. . . .

She'd always been a bit unstable. Like my mother, a mousy type—natural prey to one such as myself. She was a teacher of classical history, living in a flat off Place de la Sorbonne, and she'd taken to me (as most people do) the day we met, not quite by chance, in a lecture at the Institut Catholique.

She was thirty-two; overweight; a borderline depressive; friendless in Paris, plus she'd recently split up with her boyfriend and was looking for a female flatmate in town.

It sounded perfect—I got the job. Under the name of Mercedes Desmoines I became her protector, her confidante. I shared her affection for Sylvia Plath. I sympathized with her over the stupidity of men and took an interest in her very dull thesis on the role of women in pre-Christian mysticism. It's what I do best, after all; and little by little I learned her secrets, nurtured her melancholy tendencies, then when the time came, collected her life.

It wasn't much of a challenge, of course. There are half a million just like her: milk-faced, mousy-haired girls with neat handwriting and bad dress sense, hiding their disappointments beneath a veil of academia and common sense. You might even say I did her a favor; and when she was ready, I slipped her a dose of something reasonably painless to help her along.

After that, it was just a question of tying up a few loose ends—suicide note, identification, cremation, and the like—before I was able to junk Mercedes, gather up what was left of Françoise—bank details, passport, birth certificate—and take her on one of those foreign trips she was always planning but never booked, while at home, people may have wondered how it could be that a woman could vanish so completely and efficiently, leaving nothing in her wake—no family, no papers, not even a grave.

Some time later, she was to reappear as an English teacher at the Lycée Rousseau. By then, of course, she'd been largely forgotten, lost in a mound of paperwork. The truth is, most people don't care. Life goes on at such a pace that it's easier to forget the dead.

I tried, at the end, to make her understand. Hemlock is such a useful drug; so easy to come by in summer, of course, and it makes the victim so manageable. In a matter of minutes paralysis sets in, and after that it's all good, with plenty of time for discussion and exchange of views—or rather *view*, in my case, as Françoise seemed incapable of speech.

Frankly, that disappointed me. I'd been looking forward to seeing her reaction when I told her, and although I wasn't exactly expecting approval, I'd hoped for something more from a person of her intellectual caliber.

But all I got was disbelief, and that rictus in her staring face—never pretty at the best of times—so that if I'd been a susceptible person I might have seen her again in my dreams, and heard the choking sounds she made as she struggled vainly against the draft that did in Socrates.

Nice touch, I thought. But wasted on my poor Françoise, who sadly discovered her zest for life only minutes before its end. And I was left, once again, with a sense of regret. Once more, it had been too easy for me. Françoise was no challenge at all. A silver mouse charm on my bracelet. Natural prey to one such as myself.

Which brings me to Vianne Rocher.

Now there's an opponent worthy of me—a witch, no less, and a powerful one, for all her silly scruples and guilt. Perhaps the *only* worthy opponent that I have ever encountered thus far. And here she is, waiting for me with that quiet knowledge in her eyes, and I know she sees me clearly at last, sees me in my true colors, and there's no sensation quite as fine as that first true moment of intimacy—

"Hello, Vianne."

"Hello, Zozie."

I sit down at the table opposite her. She looks cold, bundled up in her shapeless dark sweater, her white lips pinched with unsaid words. I smile at her, and her colors shine out—strange, how much affection I feel, now that the knives are drawn at last.

Outside, the wind is riding high. A killer wind, charged with snow. Sleepers in doorways will die tonight. Dogs will howl; doors slam. Young lovers will look into each other's eyes and for the first time will silently question their vows. Eternity is *such* a long time—and here, at the dead end of the year, Death seems suddenly very close.

But isn't that what it's all about, this festival of winter lights? This little defiance in the face of the dark? Call it Christmas if you like, but you and I know it's older than that. And beneath all the tinsel and the carol singing and the glad tidings and the gifts lies a bleaker and more visceral truth.

This is a time of essential loss; of the sacrifice of innocents; of fear, darkness, barrenness, death. The Aztecs knew, and so did the Maya, that, far from wanting to *save* the world, their gods were bent on its destruction, and that only the blood of sacrifice could appease them for a little while. . . .

We sat there in silence, like old friends. I fingered the charms on my bracelet; she stared into her chocolate cup. Finally she looked at me.

"So what are you doing here, Zozie?"

Not too original, but—hey, it's a start.

I smiled. "I'm a—collector," I said.

"Is that what you call it?"

"For want of a name."

"And what do you collect?" she said.

"Debts outstanding. Promises due."

She flinched at that, as I knew she would.

"What do I owe you?"

"Let's see." I smiled. "For assorted workings, glamours, charms, tricks, protection, turning straw into gold, averting bad luck, piping the rats out of Hamelin, and generally giving you back your life—" I saw her begin to protest, but moved on. "I think we agreed you'd pay me in kind."

"In kind?" she repeated. "I don't understand."

In fact, she understood me perfectly. It's a very old theme, and she knows it well. The price for your heart's desire is your heart. A life for a life. A world in balance. Stretch a rubber band far enough and at last it snaps back in your face.

Call it karma, physics, chaos theory, but without it, poles tilt; ground shifts; birds drop from the sky; seas turn to blood; and before you know it, the world's at an end.

By rights I could take her life, you know. Today I'm inclined to be generous. Vianne Rocher has two lives—I only need the one. But lives are interchangeable; in this world identities may be passed around like playing cards; shuffled; reshuffled; and redealt. That's all I'm asking for. Your hand. And you owe me a debt. You said so yourself.

"So what's your name?" said Vianne Rocher.

My *real* name?

Ye gods, it's been so long that I've almost forgotten. What's in a name? Wear it like a coat. Turn it, burn it, throw it away and steal another. The name doesn't matter. Only the debt. And I'm calling it in. Right here, right now.

One small obstacle remains. Her name is Françoise Lavery. Clearly I must have made a mistake somewhere in my calculations, missed something in the general cleanup, because this ghost still won't leave me alone. She's in the papers every week—not on the front page, thankfully, but nevertheless I could do without the publicity, and this week, for the first time, the piece suggests foul play as well as simple fraud. There are posters too showing her face, on billboards and lampposts around the city. Of course I look nothing like her these days. But a combination of bank and surveillance camera footage may yet lead them uncomfortably close, and all it needs then is some random element to be thrown into the mix, and all my elaborate plans are blown.

I need to vanish—and very soon—and (this is where *you* come in, Vianne) the best way of doing that is to leave Paris for good.

This, of course, is where the problem lies. You see, Vianne, I like it here. I never imagined I could get so much fun—so much profit—from a simple *chocolaterie*. But I like what this place has become, and I see its potential as you never did.

You saw it as a hiding place. I see it as the eye of the storm. From here, we can be the Hurakan—we can wreak havoc; shape lives; wield power—which is really the name of the whole ball game, when you come to think about it—as well as making money, of course, always a plus in today's venal world. . . .

When I say we—

I mean *me*, of course.

"But why Anouk?" Her voice was harsh. "Why bring my daughter into this?"

"I like her," I said.

She looked scornful at that. "*Like* her? You used her. Corrupted her. You made her think you were her friend—"

"At least I've always been honest with her."

"And I haven't? I'm her *mother*—" she said.

"You choose your family." I smiled. "You'd better be careful she doesn't choose me."

She thought about that one for some time. She looked calm enough, but I could see the turbulence in her colors, the distress and confusion and something else—a kind of knowledge I didn't quite like.

At last she said, "I could ask you to leave."

I grinned. "Why not try? Or call the police—better still, call the social services. I'm sure they could offer you all kinds of support. They've probably still got your notes in Rennes—or was it Les Laveuses?"

She cut me off. "What exactly do you want?"

I told her as much as she needed to know. My time is short—but she can't know that. Nor can she know about poor Françoise—soon to reappear as someone else. But she knows I am the enemy now; her eyes were bright and cold and aware, and she laughed scornfully (if a little hysterically) as I delivered my ultimatum.

"You're saying *I* should leave?" she said.

"Well," I pointed out reasonably, "is Montmartre really big enough to hold *two* witches?"

Her laughter was like broken glass. Outside, the voice of the wind keened its eerie harmonies. "Well, if you think I'm going to pack up and run away just because you did a few sneak workings behind my back, then you're going to be disappointed," she said. "You're not the first to try this, you know. There was this priest—"

"I know," I said.

"Then what?"

Oh, that's good. I like that defiance. It's what I have been hoping for. Identities are so easy to take. I've taken enough of them in my time. But the opportunity to face another witch on her home ground, with weapons of choice, to collect her life, to add it to my charm bracelet with the black coffin and the silver shoes . . .

How many times do you get *that* chance?

I'll give myself three days, that's all. Three days to win or lose. After that it's so long, good night, and off to pastures green and new. Free spirit, and all that. Go wherever the wind takes me. It's a big world out there, full of opportunities. I'm sure I'll find something to challenge my skills.

For now, however—

"Listen, Vianne. I'll give you three days. Till after the party. Pack up by then, take what you can, and I won't try to stop you. Stay, and I won't answer for the consequences."

"Why? What can you do?" she said.

"I can take it all, piece by piece. Your life, your friends, your children—"

She stiffened. That's her weakness, of course. Those children—especially our little Anouk, already so very talented . . .

"I'm not going anywhere," she said.

Good. That's what I thought you'd say. No one hands over their life like that. Even mousy Françoise fought back a little at the end, and I'm expecting rather more from you. You have three days to make your stand. Three days to placate the Hurakan. Three days to become Vianne Rocher.

Unless, of course, I can get there first.

Saturday, 22 December

TILL AFTER THE PARTY. WHAT DOES SHE MEAN? SURELY THERE CAN BE NO party now, with this strange threat hanging over our heads. That was my first reaction, when Zozie had gone to bed and I was left in the freezing kitchen to think out my plan of defense.

My instincts all tell me to throw her out. I know I could; but the thought of what effect that might have on my customers—let alone on Anouk—makes it quite impossible.

And as for the party—well. I am not unaware that over the past couple of weeks this party has taken on a significance far greater than any of us could have imagined. For Anouk, it is a celebration of us, an expression of hope (and maybe we still share the same perpetual fantasy, that Roux will come back and that everything will be made miraculously new).

As for our customers—no, our *friends*—

So many have contributed over the past few days, bringing food, wine, decorations for the Advent house, the Christmas tree itself donated by the florist for whom little Alice works; champagne offered by Madame Luzeron; glasses and crockery supplied by Nico's restaurant; organic meat by Jean-Louis and Paupaul, who paid for it, I suspect, with flattery and a portrait of the supplier's wife.

Even Laurent brought *something* (mostly sugar lumps, I'll admit), and it's so good to be a community again, to feel included, to be a part of something larger than just the little campfire circle we make for ourselves. I'd always thought Montmartre such a cold place, its people so rude and contemptuous with their *Vieux Paris* snobbery and their mistrust of strangers. But now I can see there's a heart behind the cobblestones. Zozie taught me that, at least. Zozie, who plays my part as well as I ever did myself.

There's a story my mother used to tell. Like all her stories, it's about herself—a fact I came to realize too late, when the doubts I'd had in the long months leading up to her death became too much for me to ignore, and I went in search of Sylviane Caillou.

What I found confirmed what my mother had said in the delirium of her final days. *You choose your family*, she said—and she'd chosen me, eighteen months old and somehow *hers*—like a parcel delivered to the wrong address that she could legitimately claim.

She wouldn't have cherished you, she'd said. *She was careless. She let you go.*

But the guilt of it had followed her across continents, a guilt that eventually turned to fear. That was my mother's real weakness—that fear—and it kept her running all her life. Fear that someone would take me away. Fear that one day I'd learn the truth. Fear that she had been wrong all those years ago, that she had cheated a stranger out of her life, and that in the end she would have to pay—

The story goes like this.

A widow-woman had a daughter whom she cherished above all things. They lived in a cottage in a wood, and though they were poor, they were as happy together as any two people have ever been, before or since.

In fact they were so happy that the Queen of Hearts, who lived nearby, heard of them and was envious, and set out to collect the daughter's heart, for although she had a thousand lovers and more than a hundred thousand slaves, she was always hungry for more, and she knew that she could never rest knowing that there was a single heart out there that had been given to another.

And so the Queen of Hearts made her way quietly to the widow's cottage. As she hid among the trees, she saw the daughter playing alone, for the cottage was a long way from even the nearest village, and there were no playmates to share the daughter's game.

So the Queen, who was no queen at all, but a powerful witch, changed her shape to that of a little black cat and strolled out, tail high, from among the trees.

And all day the child played with the cat, which gamboled and chased pieces of string and climbed trees and came at her call and ate from her hand and was undoubtedly the most playful and picture-perfect of pretty kitty cats any child had ever seen—

But for all its purring and preening, the cat could not steal the daughter's heart, and when night came, the child went indoors to where her mother had laid dinner on the table, and the Queen of Hearts yowled her displeasure to the night, and ripped out the hearts of many small nocturnal creatures, but was not satisfied, and wanted the child's heart even more than before. . . .

So on the second day, she changed into a handsome young man and lay in wait for the widow's daughter as she searched for her kitty cat in the woods. Now the daughter had never seen a young man, except from afar, on market days. And this one was glorious in every way—black hair, blue eyes, fresh as a girl, but all boy—and she forgot about the kitty cat, and they walked, and talked, and laughed, and ran together through the forest like fallow deer in season.

But when night came, and he dared steal a kiss, the daughter's heart still belonged to her mother, and that night the Queen hunted deer and cut out their hearts, and ate them raw—but still she was not satisfied and longed for the child more than ever.

So, on the morning of the third day, the witch did not change her shape but instead stayed close to the house and watched. And as the child went off in vain to search for her friend of the previous day, the Queen of Hearts kept her eyes fixed on the child's mother. She watched as the mother washed clothes in the stream, and knew that she could do it better. She watched as the mother cleaned the house, and knew that she could do it better. And as night fell, she took the shape of the mother herself—her smiling face, her gentle hands—and when the daughter came back home, there were *two* mothers there to greet her. . . .

What on earth could the mother do? The Queen of Hearts had studied her, had copied every gesture, every mannerism too flawlessly to be caught out. Everything she did, the witch could do better, faster, more perfectly—

And so the mother set the table with another place for the visitor.

"*I'll* make dinner," said the Queen. "I know all your favorites."

"We'll *both* make dinner," said the mother. "And then my daughter will decide."

"*My* daughter," said the witch. "And I think *I* know the way to her heart."

Well, the mother was a good cook. And she had never worked harder over a meal—not at Easter, not at Yule. But the witch had magic on her side, and her glamours were very powerful. The mother knew all the child's favorites—but the Queen knew those she had yet to discover, and she set them effortlessly on the table, one by one, throughout the meal.

They began with a winter soup, lovingly cooked in a copper pot with a shinbone left over from Sunday lunch—

But the witch brought in a light bouillon, simmered with the sweetest of baby shallots and scented with ginger and lemongrass and served with croutons so crisp and small that they seemed to vanish in her mouth—

The mother brought in the second course. Sausages and potato mash; a comforting dish the child always loved, with sticky onion marmalade—

But the witch brought in a brace of quail that had been gorged on ripe figs all their lives, now roasted and stuffed with chestnuts and foie gras and served with a coulis of pomegranate—

Now the mother was close to despair. She brought dessert: a stout apple pie, made to her mother's recipe.

But the witch had made a *pièce montée*: a pastel-colored sugared dream of almonds, summer fruit, and pastries like a puff of air, all scented with rose and marshmallow cream, and served with a glass of Château d'Yquem—

And the mother said: "All right. You win," as her heart just snapped clean in two, with a sound like popcorn in the pan. And the witch smiled and reached for her prey—

But the daughter did not return her embrace. Instead she fell to her knees on the floor.

"Mother, don't die. I *know* it's you."

And the Queen of Hearts gave a scream of rage as she realized that even now, in the moment of her triumph, the child's heart was still not hers. And she screamed so loudly and so furiously that her head exploded like a fair-day balloon, and the Queen of Hearts in her terminal wrath became the queen of nothing at all.

As for the ending of the tale—

Well, that depended on my mother's mood. In one version, the mother survives, and she and the child live alone forever in their cottage in the wood. On darker days, the mother dies, and the child is left alone in her grief. And there is a third version, where the impostor, in a final twist, foresees the mother's broken heart and collapses herself, thus prompting a vow of eternal love from the child while the real mother stands by, unable to speak, discarded and powerless as the witch begins to feed—

I never told Anouk that tale. It frightened me then as it frightens me now. In stories we find the truth, and though no one outside of a fairy tale ever died of a broken heart, the Queen of Hearts is very real, though she does not always go by that name.

But we've faced her before, Anouk and I. She's the wind that blows at the turn of the year. She's the sound of one hand clapping. She's the lump in your mother's breast. She's the absent look in your daughter's eyes. She's the cry of the cat. She's in the confessional. She's hiding inside the black piñata. But most of all she is simply Death; greedy old Mictecacihuatl herself, Santa Muerte, the Eater of Hearts, most terrible of the Kindly Ones—

And now it's time to face her again. To pick up my weapons—such as they are—and to stand and fight for the life we have made. But for that I need to be Vianne Rocher, if ever I can find her again. The Vianne Rocher who faced down the Black Man at the Grand Festival du Chocolat. The Vianne Rocher who knows everyone's favorites. The peddler of sweet dreams, small temptations, treats, trinkets, tricks, petty indulgences, and everyday magic—

If only I can find her in time.

Saturday, 22 December

IT MUST HAVE SNOWED DURING THE NIGHT. JUST A THIN SCATTERING for now, turning to gray slush nearly at once. Still, it's a start. There'll be more soon. You can already see it in the clouds; clouds so heavy and dark below the Butte that they're practically touching the church spires. Clouds only *look* lighter than air; actually the water in just one of those clouds could weigh millions of tons, Jean-Loup says; that's a whole multistory full of cars parked up there, just waiting to fall, today or tomorrow, in tiny little flakes of snow.

On the Butte, it's Christmas in a big way. There's a fat Santa Claus sitting at the terrace of Chez Eugène, drinking *café-crème* and scaring the kids. The artists are out in force too, and there's a little band of college students playing hymns and Christmas songs just outside the church. I'd arranged to meet Jean-Loup this morning, and Rosette wanted to see the Nativity (again), so I took her out for a little walk while Maman worked and Zozie went out to do some shopping.

Neither of them mentioned what happened last night, but they both looked OK this morning, so I guess Zozie must have sorted things out. Maman was wearing her red dress, the one that always makes her feel good, and she was talking about recipes, and everything sounded so cheerful and right—

Jean-Loup was waiting in Place du Tertre when I finally got there with Rosette. Everything takes time with Rosette—anorak, boots, hat and gloves—and it was nearly eleven by the time we got there. Jean-Loup had his camera—the big one with the special lens—and he was taking pictures of people going by: foreign tourists; children watching the Nativity; the fat Santa smoking a cigar—

"Hey! It's you!" That was Jean-Louis with his sketch pad, trying to pick up a tourist girl. He chooses them for their handbags, you know—he has a sliding scale of tariffs, based entirely on the style of the bag—and he can always spot a fake.

"Fakes never fork out," he says. "But show me a nice Louis Vuitton and I'm in."

Jean-Loup laughed when I told him that. Rosette laughed too, though I don't think she really understood. She likes Jean-Loup and his camera. *Picture*, she signs, when she sees him now. She means the digital camera, of course; she likes to pose for a photograph and see it at once in the little box.

Then Jean-Loup suggested going down to the cemetery to see what was left of last night's snow, so we went down the steps by the funicular and walked along to Rue Caulaincourt.

"Can you see the cats, Rosette?" I said as we looked down from the metal bridge into the cemetery. Someone must have been feeding them because there were a couple dozen of them, sitting around the entrance, where the lower level of the cemetery leads to a big round flower bed with long, straight avenues of tombs branching out like compass points.

We went down the steps to Avenue Rachel. It's dark down there, with the bridge overhead and the heavy clouds pressing down. Jean-Loup had said there'd be more snow here, and he was right—every tomb had its white beret—though it was wet and pocked with holes, and you could tell it wouldn't last. But Rosette loves snow; she kept picking bits up between her fingers and laughing silently when it disappeared.

And then I saw him waiting for us. I wasn't even really surprised. Sitting very still next to Dalida's tomb, a carved figure all in gray, with only the pale plume of his breath to show that he was alive at all.

"Roux!" I said.

He grinned at me.

"What do you think you're doing here?"

"Well, thanks for the welcome." He smiled at Rosette and pulled out something from his pocket. "Happy birthday, Rosette," he said.

It was a whistle, made from a single piece of wood and polished to a silky shine.

Rosette took it and put it in her mouth.

"Not that way. This way." He demonstrated, blowing into the opening. It made a high *squeeee* sound, much louder than you'd have expected, and Rosette's face opened in a big, happy smile. "She likes it," said Roux. He looked at Jean-Loup. "And you must be the photographer."

"Where have you been all this time?" I said. "People have been looking for you."

"I know," he said. "That's why I checked out." He picked up Rosette and tickled her. She put out a hand to touch his hair.

"Be serious, Roux." I frowned at him. "The police were here, and everything. They're saying you forged a check. I told them it was a mistake, that you'd never do a thing like that—"

Maybe it was the light, or something, but I couldn't make out his reaction to that. The December light, with the streetlamps on early, and that splatter of snow against the stone making everything else look darker still. Anyway, I just couldn't see. His colors were burning very low, and I couldn't tell if he was scared, or angry, or even surprised.

"Is that what Vianne thinks?"

"I don't know."

"Her faith in me is awesome, isn't it?" He shook his head ruefully, but I could see he was grinning. "Still, I hear the wedding's off. Can't say I'm heartbroken about *that*."

"You should have been a spy," I said. "How d'you find all that out so fast?"

He shrugged. "People talk. I listen," he said.

"So where are you staying now?" I asked.

Not the hostel, I knew that already. But he looked, if anything, even worse than last time we'd met—pale and unshaven and very tired. And now I'd found him here again—

People do sleep in the cemetery. The *gardien* turns a blind eye as long as they don't make a mess, but you sometimes find a stash of blankets, or an old kettle, or a trash can packed with fuel for tonight's fire, or a neat little stack of tins hidden away inside some chapel of rest that no one uses anymore, and sometimes at night, so Jean-Loup says, you can see as many as half a dozen little fires in different spots inside the cemetery walls—

"You're sleeping here, aren't you?" I said.

"I'm sleeping on my boat," said Roux.

But he was lying—I could see that at once. And I didn't believe he had a boat. If he had, he wouldn't be here, and he wouldn't have stayed at Rue de Clichy. But Roux wasn't telling; he just kept playing with Rosette, tickling her and making her laugh, while Rosette made wet *squeee* noises with her new whistle and laughed in that silent way she has, with her mouth open as wide as a frog's.

"So what are you going to do now?" I said.

"Well, for a start, I've got a party to go to on Christmas Eve. Or had you forgotten?" He made a face at Rosette, who laughed and hid her face behind her hands.

I was beginning to think that Roux wasn't taking any of this seriously enough. "You're coming?" I said. "Do you think it's safe?"

"I promised, didn't I?" he said. "In fact, I've got a surprise for you."

"A present?"

He grinned. "Just wait and see."

I was dying to tell Maman I'd seen Roux. But after last night I knew I had to be careful. There are things I don't quite dare tell her now, in case she gets angry, or doesn't understand.

With Zozie, of course, it's different. We talk about all kinds of things. In her room I wear my red shoes and we sit on her bed with the furry blanket over our knees, and she tells me stories about Quetzalcoatl and Jesus and Osiris and Mithras and Seven Macaw—the kind of stories Maman used to tell but doesn't have time for anymore. I guess she thinks I'm too old for stories. She's always telling me I should grow up.

Zozie says growing up's overrated. She never wants to settle down. There are too many places she hasn't seen. She won't give them up for anyone.

"Not even for me?" I said tonight.

She smiled, but I thought she looked sad at that. "Not even for you, little Nanou."

"But you're not going away," I said.

She shrugged. "That depends."

"Depends on what?"

"Well, on your mother, for a start."

"What do you mean?"

She gave a sigh. "I wasn't going to tell you," she said. "But your mother and I—we've been talking. And we've decided—well, *she's* decided—that maybe it's time for me to move out."

"Move out?" I said.

"Winds change, Nanou." And that was so close to what Maman might have said that it took me right back to Les Laveuses, and that wind, and the Kindly Ones. But this time I wasn't remembering. I was thinking about Ehecatl, the Changing Wind, and I was seeing things as they would be if Zozie left us: her room deserted, dust on the floor, everything just ordinary again, just a little chocolate shop with nothing special anymore—

"You can't," I said wildly. "We need you here."

She shook her head. "You *needed* me. But look at you now—business is good, you've got lots of friends. You don't need me anymore. As for me—I have to move on. Ride that wind to wherever it goes."

A horrible thought came to me. "This is about me, isn't it?" I said. "It's about what we've been doing here. Our lessons, and the peg-dolls, and everything. She's afraid that if you stay there'll be another Accident—"

Zozie shrugged. "I won't lie to you. But I didn't think she'd be so jealous—"

Jealous? *Maman?*

"Well, of course," said Zozie. "Remember, she used to be like us once. Free to go wherever she liked. But now she's got other responsibilities. She can't just do what she wants anymore. And whenever she looks at you now, Nanou—well, maybe it just reminds her too much of everything she's had to give up."

"But that's not fair!"

Zozie smiled. "No one said it was fair," she said. "It's about control. You're growing up. You're developing skills. You're growing beyond your mother's authority. It makes her anxious; makes her scared. She thinks I'm taking you away from her, giving you things she can't give you herself. And that's why I have to leave, Nanou. Before something happens we'll both regret."

"But what about the party?" I said.

"If you want me, I'll stay till then." She put her arms around me and hugged me tight. "Listen, Nanou. I know it's hard. But I want you to have what I never had. A family. A home. A place of your own. And if the wind needs a sacrifice, then let it be me. I've nothing to lose. Besides—" She gave a little sigh. "I don't want to settle down. I don't want to spend my life wondering what's over the next hill. I would have left sooner or later—and now's as good a time as any—"

She pulled the blanket over us both. I shut my eyes tight, not wanting to cry, but I could feel a lump in the back of my throat like I'd swallowed a little potato whole.

"But I *love* you, Zozie—"

I couldn't see her face (my eyes were still shut), but I felt her let out a long, deep sigh—like air that's been trapped for a long time in a sealed box, or underground.

"I love you too, Nanou," she said.

We stayed like that for a long time, sitting in bed wrapped up in the blanket. Outside, the wind started up again, and I was glad there were no trees on the Butte, because the way I was feeling just then, I think I could have let them all come crash-crashing down if that could have persuaded Zozie to stay and made the wind take someone else.

Sunday, 23 December

WHAT A PERFORMANCE. TOLD YOU SO. IN ANOTHER LIFE I'D HAVE MADE
a fortune in the movie business. It certainly had Anouk convinced—the
seeds of doubt are germinating nicely—which should serve me well come
Christmas Eve.

I don't think she'll mention our talk to Vianne. My little Nanou is secretive; she does not share her thoughts so easily. And her mother has let
her down, of course; has lied to her on several points, and on top of all that,
is evicting her friend—

She too can dissemble, when required. Today she looked a little with-
drawn, though I doubt whether Vianne will have noticed that. She's too
busy planning tomorrow's celebration to wonder at her daughter's sudden
lack of excitement, or to ask herself where she has been all day while cakes
baked and spiced wine simmered.

Of course I too have plans to fulfill. But mine are rather less culinary in
emphasis. Vianne's kind of magic—such as it is—is far too domestic for my
taste. Don't think I can't see what you're doing, Vianne. The place is alive
with petty seductions: rose-scented treats, miracles, and macaroons. And
Vianne herself—in that red dress, with a red silk flower in her hair—

Who do you think you're fooling, Vianne? Why bother, when I do it
so much better?

I was out for most of the day. People to see; things to do. Today I ditched
all that was left of my current identities, including Mercedes Desmoines,
Emma Windsor, and even Noëlle Marcelin. I have to admit, it caused me a

pang. But too much ballast slows you down—and besides, I won't be needing them.

After that it was time for a few social calls. Madame from Le Stendhal, who is coming on nicely; Thierry le Tresset, who has been watching the *chocolaterie* from nearby in the vain hope of a glimpse of Roux; and Roux himself, who has checked out of his digs by the cemetery and into the cemetery itself, where a small chapel of rest serves as his current home.

It's comfortable enough, I daresay. These tombs were built in the days when the wealthy dead were housed in a luxury undreamt of by the living poor. And with the help of regular doses of misinformation, sympathy, rumor, flattery—not to mention cash and a steady supply of my very own specials—I have ensured, if not his trust and affection, at least his presence on Christmas Eve.

I found him at the back of the cemetery, near the wall that divides it from the Rue Jean Le Maistre. It's the farthest place from the entrance lodge, where broken and abandoned graves lie among compost and rubbish bins, and that's where the down-and-outs assemble round a fire that burns in a metal can.

Today there were half a dozen of them, dressed in coats too big for them and boots as scarred and cracked as their hands. Most were old—the young ones can earn their cash in Pigalle, where youth is always in demand—and one of them had a cough that started deep in his lungs and hacked its way out every minute or so.

They looked at me incuriously as I picked my way through the neglected graves toward the little circle of men. Roux met me with his usual lack of enthusiasm.

"You again."

"So glad you're pleased." I handed him a parcel of food—coffee, sugar, cheese, some sausages from the butcher's around the corner, and some buckwheat pancakes to wrap them in. "Don't share it with the cats this time."

"Thanks." At last he deigned to smile. "How's Vianne?"

"She's fine. She misses you." It's a small flattery that never fails.

"And Mr. Big?"

"He's coming round."

I've managed to convince Roux that Thierry calling the police is just a ploy to get Vianne back on his side. I have not gone into details of the charge; but I have led him to believe that it has already been dropped for lack of evidence. The only danger now, I have told him, is that Thierry, in a fit of pique, will evict Vianne from her home in the *chocolaterie* if she transfers her allegiance too quickly to Roux, and so he must be patient awhile, wait for the dust to settle, and trust me to make Thierry see sense.

Meanwhile, I pretend to believe in his boat, moored, he says, in the Port de l'Arsenal. Its existence (even fictional) makes him a man of property, a man of pride who, far from accepting charity from me in the shape of food parcels and loose change, is actually doing us all a favor by staying close by to watch over Vianne.

"Been to check on the boat today?"

He shook his head. "Later, perhaps."

This is another fiction I pretend to believe. That he goes over to the Arsenal every day to check on his boat. Of course I know he does no such thing. But I rather like to see him squirm. "If Thierry won't see sense," I said, "it's a comfort to think that Vianne and the kids could stay with you on the boat for a while. At least till they find another place—never easy at this time of year—"

He glared at me. "That's not what I want."

I gave him my sweetest smile. "Of course not," I said. "It's just nice to know there's the option, that's all. So how are you set for tomorrow, Roux? Need any clothes washed?"

Once more he shook his head, and I wondered how he'd managed so far. There's a laundrette round the corner, of course, and some public showers off the Rue Ganeron. That's probably where he goes, I thought. He must think I'm an imbecile.

Still, I need him—for a little longer. After tomorrow it won't matter anymore. After that he can go to perdition any way he likes.

"Why are you doing this, Zozie?" It's a question he has asked before, with a growing suspicion that only increases with every attempt I make at seduction. Some men are just like that, I think—impervious to my kind of charm. Still, it rankles. He owes me so much, and scarcely a word of gratitude.

"You know why I'm doing it, Roux," I said, allowing a trace of asperity to enter my voice. "I'm doing it for Vianne and the kids. For Rosette, who deserves a father. For Vianne, who has never got over you. And—I'll admit it—for myself, because if Vianne goes, I go, and I've come to like that *choco-laterie*, and I don't see why I should have to leave."

That convinced him. I knew it would. A suspicious type like Roux mistrusts anything close to altruism. Well, he would—Roux, who acts out of self-interest, who is only here now because he sees some profit in it for himself; some share in Vianne's lucrative business, perhaps, now that he knows Rosette is his child—

It was three o'clock when I returned to the *chocolaterie*, and already it was getting dark. Vianne was serving a customer, and she looked at me sharply as I came in, although her greeting was pleasant enough.

I know what she's thinking. Folk *like* Zozie. To advertise her hostility now would be damaging only to Vianne herself. Already she is wondering if my threats of the other night were designed to lure her into an ill-considered attack, to show her colors too soon and thereby lose the safe ground.

The battle begins tomorrow, she thinks. Canapés and frivolities, sweet enough to tempt the saints. *They* will be her weapons of choice—and how naïve of her to imagine that I will respond in kind. Domestic magic is *such* a bore—ask any child, and you'll see how they prefer the villains to the heroes of the books they read, the wicked witches and hungry wolves to the plain-vanilla princes and princesses.

Anouk is no exception, I'll bet. Still, we'll have to wait and see. Go ahead, Vianne. Attend to your pots. See what domestic magic can do while I work on my own recipe. According to popular tradition, the way to the heart is through the stomach.

Personally, I prefer a more direct approach.

PART EIGHT

Yule

Monday, 24 December
CHRISTMAS EVE 11:30 A.M.

IT'S SNOWING AT LAST. IT'S BEEN SNOWING ALL DAY. BIG FAT FAIRY-TALE
flakes like whirligigs from the winter sky. *Snow changes everything*, so says
Zozie, and already the magic's beginning to work: changing shops, houses,
parking meters into soft white sentinels as the snow falls, gray against the
luminous sky, and little by little, Paris disappears; every flake of soot, every
discarded bottle, crisp packet, dog turd, and sweet wrapper reclaimed and
made new again under the snow.

That isn't really true, of course. But all the same it *looks* true, as if things
could really change tonight, and everything be put right, instead of just
covered over like icing on a cheap cake.

The last door in the Advent house opened up today. Behind it, there's
a Nativity scene: mother, father, and baby in the crib—well, not quite a
baby anymore, but sitting up with a smile on her face and a yellow monkey
by her side. Rosette loves it—and so do I—but I can't help feeling a little
sorry for *my* peg-doll, left outside in the party room while the three of them
celebrate alone.

That's stupid, I know. I shouldn't feel bad. You choose your family, Maman says, and it doesn't matter that Roux isn't my real father, or that Rosette is only my half sister, or perhaps not even a sister at all. . . .

Today I've been working on my fancy dress. I'm coming as Little Red
Riding Hood, because all I need for my outfit is a red cape—with a hood,
of course. Zozie helped me finish it, with a piece of cloth from a charity

shop and Madame Poussin's old sewing machine. It looks pretty good for homemade, with my basket with the red ribbons, and Rosette's coming as a monkey in her brown jumpsuit with a tail sewn on.

"What are you coming as, Zozie?" I asked her for the hundredth time.

She smiled. "Wait and see, or you'll spoil the surprise."

Monday, 24 December
CHRISTMAS EVE 3:00 P.M.

THE LULL BEFORE THE HURRICANE. THAT'S HOW IT FEELS NOW, WITH
Rosette upstairs having her nap and the snow outside claiming everything
with its quiet gluttony. Snow comes so relentlessly; it swallows sound, kills
scent, steals light right out of the sky.

It's settling now along the Butte. Of course there's no traffic to challenge its progress. People pass by with hats and scarves all barnacled with
the driving snow, and the bells from St.-Pierre-de-Montmartre come mut-
edly and from afar, like something under an evil charm.

I've hardly seen Zozie all day. Deep in my plans for the party tonight,
between kitchen, costumes, and customers, I have had very little time to
observe my opponent, who keeps to her room, giving nothing away. I wonder when she'll make her move.

My mother's voice, the storyteller, says it will be at dinner tonight, like
in the tale of the widow's daughter; but it unnerves me that so far I have not
seen her make any preparations, or bake even a single cake. Could it be that
I have it wrong? Is Zozie somehow bluffing me, trying to force me to show
a hand she knows will injure my standing here? Could it be that she means
to do nothing at all while I bring down the Kindly Ones all unsuspecting
on my own head?

Since Friday night there has been no apparent conflict between us—
though now I can see the mocking looks and the sly winks she gives me
that no one else sees. Still cheery as ever, still beautiful, still strutting in

her extravagant shoes—but to me she now seems a parody of herself; too knowing beneath that conspicuous charm, enjoying the game in a jaded way, like an elderly whore dressed up as a nun. It is perhaps that enjoyment that offends me most—the way she plays to a balcony of one. There's nothing at stake for her, of course. But I am playing for my life.

One last time, I draw the cards.

The Fool; the Lovers; the Magus, Change.

The Hanged Man; the Tower—

The Tower is falling. Stones tumble from its crown as it topples into darkness. From the parapet, tiny figures hurl themselves, gesticulating, into the void. One is wearing a red dress—or is it a cloak, with a little hood?

I do not look at the final card. I've seen it too many times before. My mother, ever the optimist, interpreted it in many ways—but to me that card means only one thing.

Death grins out from the woodcut design; jealous, joyless, hollow-eyed, hungry—Death the insatiable; Death the implacable; Death the debt we owe to the gods. Outside, the snow has settled thickly, and although the light has begun to fade, the ground is weirdly luminous, as if street and sky had exchanged places. It's a far cry from the pretty picture-book snow of the Advent house, although Anouk loves it and keeps finding excuses to check the street. She's out there now; from my window I can see her bright figure against that baleful white. She looks very small from where I'm standing, a little girl lost in the woods. Of course, that's absurd; there are no woods here. That's one of the reasons I chose this place. But everything changes under snow, and magic comes into its own again. And the winter wolves come slinking down the alleys and streets of the Butte de Montmartre. . . .

Monday, 24 December
CHRISTMAS EVE 4:30 P.M.

JEAN-LOUP CAME ROUND THIS AFTERNOON. HE PHONED THIS MORNING TO
say he was bringing some of the photographs he took the other day. He de-
velops them himself, you know—at least, in black-and-white he does—and
he's got hundreds of prints at home, sorted and labeled in all kinds of files,
and he sounded excited and out of breath, like there was something special
that he wanted to show me.

I thought maybe he'd been in the cemetery, that he'd finally managed to
take a picture of those ghost-lights he's always talking about.

But it wasn't his cemetery pictures he'd brought. Nor was it his prints
from the Butte, the Nativity house and the Christmas lights, and the cigar-
chewing Santa. These were all photos of Zozie—the digital snaps he'd
taken in the *chocolaterie*, plus some new ones in black-and-white, some of
them taken from outside the shop, and some with Zozie in a crowd as she
walked across the square to the funicular, or stood in a queue outside the
bakery on the Rue des Trois Frères.

"What's this?" I said. "You know she doesn't like—"

"Look at them, Annie," he said.

I didn't want to look at them. The only time we ever fell out was over
those stupid pictures of his. I didn't want that to happen again. But why
had he taken them at all? There must have been some reason, I thought—

"Please," said Jean-Loup. "Just look at them. Then if you think there's
nothing weird about them, I promise you I'll throw them away."

Well, looking at them—there were thirty or so—made me feel quite uncomfortable. The thought that Jean-Loup had been spying on Zozie—*stalking* her—was bad enough, but there was something about those photographs; something that made it even worse.

You could see they were all of Zozie, all right. You could see her skirt with the bells on the hem, and her funky boots with the three-inch soles. Her hair was the same, and her jewelry, and the raffia bag she uses to carry her shopping.

But her face—

"You've done something to these prints," I said, pushing them back toward Jean-Loup.

"Cross my heart, I haven't, Annie. And everything else on the film was OK. It's *her. She's* doing it, somehow. How else can you explain this?"

I wasn't sure how to explain it myself. Some people take a good photograph. The word for this is *photogenic*, and Zozie definitely wasn't that. Some people take an OK photograph, and I don't know if there's a word for it, but Zozie wasn't *that*, either. *All* of those pictures were terrible, with her mouth an odd kind of shape somehow, and a look in her eyes, and a sort of smudge around her head, like a halo gone wrong—

"So she isn't photogenic. So what? Not everyone is."

"There's more," said Jean-Loup. "Just look at this." And he pulled out a folded piece of newspaper, a clipping from one of the Paris newspapers with a blurry picture of a woman's face. Her name, it said, was Françoise Lavery. But the picture was just like those prints of Zozie, tiny eyes and twisted mouth, even down to that weird smudge. . . .

"What's it supposed to prove?" I said. It was just a picture, kind of blown up and grainy like most pictures you see in the paper. A woman who might have been any age, with hair in a kind of plain bob and little glasses under her long fringe. Nothing like Zozie at all. Apart from that smudge and the shape of her mouth—

I shrugged. "It could be anyone."

"It's her," said Jean-Loup. "I know it can't be, but it is."

Well, that was just ridiculous. And the clipping didn't make much sense either. It was all about a teacher in Paris who disappeared some time last year. I mean, Zozie was never a teacher, was she? Or is he suggesting she's a ghost?

Even Jean-Loup wasn't sure. "You read about these things," he said, carefully replacing the clipping inside the envelope. "Walk-ins, I think they call them."

"Whatever."

"You can laugh, but there's something wrong. I can feel it when she's around. I'm going to bring my camera tonight. I want some close-ups— some kind of proof—"

"You and your ghosts." I was feeling annoyed. He's only a year older than me—who the hell does he think he is? If he knew half of what I know now—about Ehecatl and One Jaguar or the Hurakan—he'd probably have a seizure, or something. And if he knew about Pantoufle, or about me and Rosette invoking the Changing Wind, or about what happened in Les Laveuses—he'd probably lose his mind.

And so I did something perhaps I shouldn't have done. But I didn't want us to quarrel again, and I knew we would if he kept on talking. So slyly, with my fingers, I drew the sign of One Monkey, the trickster. And then I flicked it out at him like a little pebble from behind my back.

Jean-Loup frowned and touched his head.

"What is it?" I said.

"Dunno," said Jean-Loup. "Just felt—kind of—*blank*. What were we talking about just now?"

I mean, I like him. I really do. I wouldn't want anything bad to happen to him. But he's what Zozie calls *regular people*, as opposed to *people like us*. Regular people follow rules. People like us make new ones instead. There are so many things I can't tell Jean-Loup, things he wouldn't understand. I can tell Zozie anything. She knows me better than anyone.

So as soon as Jean-Loup had gone, I burned the clipping and the photographs—he'd forgotten to take them with him—in the fireplace in my room, and watched the flakes of ash turn white and settle like snow in the grate.

There. All gone. I feel better now. Not that I'd ever suspect Zozie; but that face made me uncomfortable, with its twisted mouth and mean little eyes. I couldn't have seen her before, could I? In the shop, or the street, or perhaps on the bus? And that name—Françoise Lavery. Have I heard it somewhere else? It's quite a common name, of course. But why does it make me think of—

A mouse?

Monday, 24 December
CHRISTMAS EVE 5:20 P.M.

WELL, I NEVER LIKED THAT BOY. A USEFUL TOOL, THAT'S ALL HE WAS, TO
pry her away from her mother's influence and make her more receptive to
mine. But now he has overstepped the mark—has dared to try and under-
mine me—and I'm afraid he'll have to go.

I saw it in his colors as he prepared to leave the shop. He'd been upstairs
with Anouk—listening to music, or playing games, or whatever those two
get up to these days—and he greeted me politely enough as he picked up
his anorak from the coat stand behind the door.

Some people are easier to read than others; and Jean-Loup Rimbault,
for all his guile, is still only a twelve-year-old. There was something too
candid about that smile, something I'd seen more than once in my teaching
days as Françoise. It's the smile of a boy who knows too much and thinks
he can get away with it. And what was in that paper file that he left with
Anouk in her bedroom just now?

Could it perhaps have been—*photographs?*

"Coming to the party tonight?"

He nodded. "Sure. The shop looks great."

Certainly, Vianne has been busy today. There are clusters of silver stars
hanging from the ceiling and branches of candles ready to be lit. There is
no dining table here, so she has pushed the small tables together to make
a single long one, covering them with the customary three tablecloths—

one green, one white, one red. A wreath of holly hangs from the door, and cedarwood and fresh-cut pine fills the air with a foresty scent.

Around the room, the traditional thirteen desserts of Christmas are stacked on glass dishes like pirates' treasure, gleaming and lustrous in topaz and gold. Black nougat for the devil, white nougat for the angels, and clementines, grapes, figs, almonds, honey, dates, apples, pears, quince jelly, *mendiants* all jeweled with raisins and peel, and *fougasse* made with olive oil and split like a wheel into twelve parts—

And of course there is the chocolate—the Yule log cooling in the kitchen; the nougatines, the celestines, the chocolate truffles piled onto the counter in a fragrant scatter of cocoa dust.

"Try one," I say, handing them out. "You'll see, they're your favorites."

He takes the truffle dreamily. Its aroma is pungent and slightly earthy, like mushrooms picked at the full moon. In fact there may actually be some mushroom in there—my specials are full of mysterious things—but this time the cocoa powder has been artfully doctored to deal with importunate little boys, and besides, the sign of the Hurakan scratched in cocoa on the countertop is more than enough to do the trick.

"See you at the party," he says.

Actually, I don't think you will. My little Nanou will miss you, of course; but not for very long, I think. In a very short time, the Hurakan is going to descend on Le Rocher de Montmartre, and when that happens—

Well, who knows? And wouldn't knowing spoil the surprise?

Monday, 24 December
CHRISTMAS EVE 6:00 P.M.

So NOW AT LAST THE *CHOCOLATERIE*'S SHUT, AND THERE'S NOTHING BUT
the poster on the door to suggest that anything's happening here.

CHRISTMAS PARTY 7:30 TONIGHT! it says over a pattern of stars and
monkeys.

FANCY DRESS RECOMMENDED.

I still haven't seen Zozie's fancy dress. I guess it's something fabulous,
but she hasn't told me what it is. So after watching the snow for nearly an
hour, I got impatient and went to her room to see what she was doing.

But when I went in, I got a surprise. It wasn't Zozie's room anymore.
The sari-curtains had been taken down; the Chinese dressing gown was
gone from the back of the door, the ornaments from the lamp shade. Even
her shoes had vanished from the top of the mantelpiece, and that's when it
really sank in, I think.

Seeing them gone.

Her fabulous shoes.

There was a suitcase on the bed, a small one, leather, that looked as if it
had seen a lot of traveling. Zozie was just closing it up, and she looked at me
when I came in, and I knew what she'd say without even having to ask.

"Oh, sweetheart," she said. "I was going to tell you. Really I was. But I
didn't want to spoil your party for you—"

I couldn't believe it. "You're going tonight?"

"I'd have to go some time," she said reasonably. "And after tonight it won't matter so much."

"Why not?"

She shrugged. "Didn't you call the Changing Wind? Don't you want to be a family, you and Roux and Yanne and Rosette?"

"That doesn't mean you have to leave!"

She threw a stray shoe into the case. "You know that's not the way it works. There's a payoff, Nanou. There has to be."

"But *you're* family too!"

She shook her head. "It wouldn't work. Not with Yanne. She disapproves of me too much. And maybe she's right to disapprove. Things don't go as smoothly when I'm around."

"But that's not fair! Where will you go?"

Zozie looked up from her packing and smiled.

"Wherever the wind takes me," she said.

Monday, 24 December
CHRISTMAS EVE 7:00 P.M.

JEAN-LOUP'S MOTHER PHONED JUST NOW TO SAY THAT HER SON HAS FALLEN
ill rather suddenly and won't be coming after all. Anouk is naturally disappointed, and slightly worried about her friend, but the excitement of the
party is too much to keep her down for long.

In her red cape and hood she looks more than ever like a Christmas
bauble, skipping from here to there in a frenzy of activity. "Are they here
yet?" she repeats, although the invitations said seven-thirty and the church
bell has barely rung the hour. "Can you see anyone outside?"

In fact the snow is so dense now that I can barely see the streetlamp
across the square, but Anouk keeps pressing her face to the window, making a ghost of herself on the glass.

"Zozie!" she calls. "Are you ready yet?"

There comes a muffled reply from Zozie, who has been upstairs for the
past two hours.

"Can I come up?" calls Anouk.

"Not yet. I told you. It's a surprise."

There is something fey about Anouk tonight, an animation that is one
part joy and three parts delirium. One moment she looks barely nine years
old; the next she is half-adult and troubling, lovely in her red cloak, her hair
like storm clouds around her face.

"Calm down," I tell her. "You'll wear yourself out."

She hugs me impulsively, the way she used to when she was a child, but before I can hug her back, she has gone, flitting restlessly from dish to dish, glass to glass, rearranging holly leaves, ivy twists, candlesticks, napkins tied with scarlet string, multicolored cushions on chairs, a cut glass bowl from a charity shop now filled with a spiced garnet red winter punch rich with nutmeg and cinnamon, spiked with lemon and a gasp of cognac, and with a clove-studded orange suspended in the crimson depths.

Rosette, by contrast, is unusually calm. Swaddled in her monkey suit, she watches everything with wide eyes but is most fascinated by the Advent house, with her very own Nativity scene with its falling snow lit up in a halo of light, with a group of monkeys standing by (Rosette insists that the monkey is a Christmas animal) in the place of the more customary ox and ass.

"D'you think he'll come?"

Of course she means Roux. Anouk has asked me so many times; and it hurts me to think of her disappointment if he does not. After all, why should he come? Why should he still be in Paris at all? But Anouk seems quite convinced that he is—has she seen him, I ask myself?—and the thought makes me feel dangerously light-headed, as if being Anouk could be catching, somehow, and that snow at Yule might not be a chance weather phenomenon, but a magical event that could wipe out the past—

"Don't you *want* him to come?" she says.

I think of his face; of the patchouli-machine-oil scent of him; the way his head dips when he's working on something; his rat tattoo; his slow smile. I've wanted him now for so long. And I've fought him too—his diffidence, his scorn for convention, his stubborn refusal to conform—

And I think of all the years we fled, as we ran from Lansquenet to Les Laveuses to Paris and Boulevard de la Chapelle with its neon sign and the mosque nearby; to Place des Faux-Monnayeurs and the *chocolaterie*, trying vainly at every stopping place to fit in, to change, to be average—

And I wonder—in all that traveling, in hotel rooms and boarding-houses and villages and towns, across those years of longing and fear—

Who was I really running from? The Black Man? The Kindly Ones? My mother? Myself?

"Yes, Nou. I want him to come."

Such a relief to say the words. To admit it at last, against all reasonable argument. Having tried and failed to find, if not love, then a kind of contentment with Thierry, to admit to myself that some things simply cannot be rationalized; that love is not a matter of choice; that sometimes you can't escape the wind—

Of course Roux never believed I'd settle down. He always said I was fooling myself; expected, in his quiet arrogance, that someday I would admit defeat. I want him to come. But all the same, I won't run away—not if Zozie brings the whole place down in ruins on my head. This time, we stand. Whatever it takes.

"Someone's here!" The wind chimes ring. But the figure at the door in its curly wig is far too bulky to be Roux.

"Careful, folks! Wide load coming through!"

"Nico!" cries Anouk and throws herself at the large figure—frogged coat, knee boots, and jewelry to shame a king. He is carrying an armful of presents, which he drops under the Christmas tree, and although I know the room is not large, he seems to fill it with his giant good cheer.

"Who are you supposed to be?" says Anouk.

"Henri IV, of course," says Nico grandly. "The culinary king of France. Hey—" He stops for a moment to sniff the air. "Something smells good. I mean—really good. What's cooking, Annie?"

"Oh, lots of things."

Behind him, Alice has come as a fairy, complete with tutu and sparkly wings, although traditional fairies don't often wear such big boots. She is vivid and laughing with enjoyment, and although she is still slender, her face seems to have lost some of its sharpness, making her prettier, less fragile—

"Where's Shoe Lady?" says Nico.

"She's getting ready," says Anouk, dragging Nico by the hand to his place at the laden dinner table. "Come on, get a drink, there's everything." She dips a ladle into the punch. "Don't go nuts on the macaroons. There's enough to feed an army here."

Next comes Madame Luzeron. Far too dignified for fancy dress, but festive in her sky blue twinset, she drops her presents under the tree and accepts a glass of punch from Anouk and a smile from Rosette, who is play-ing with her wooden dog on the floor.

The chimes ring again, and it's Laurent Pinson, all shiny shoes and with fresh shaving-marks on his face, then Richard and Mathurin, Jean-Louis and Paupaul—Jean-Louis wearing the most garish yellow waistcoat I have ever seen—then Madame Pinot, who has come as a nun, then that anxious-looking lady who gave Rosette the doll (invited by Zozie, I think), and suddenly we are a jamboree of people, drinks, laughter, canapés, and sweets, and I watch with one eye to the kitchen while Anouk plays host-ess in my place and Alice nibbles a *mendiant*, and Laurent takes a handful of almonds and puts them in his pocket for later, and Nico calls again for Zozie, and I wonder when she will make her move—

Tak-tak-tak come her shoes down the stairs.

"So sorry I'm late," she says, and smiles, and for a moment there's an ebb; a silence as she enters the room, all fresh and glowing in her red dress, and now we can all see that she has cut her hair to shoulder length, exactly like mine, tucked back behind her ears, like mine, with my straight fringe and that little kick at the back that nothing ever seems to tame—

Madame hugs Zozie as she comes down. I must find out her name, I think, although for the moment I cannot take my eyes from Zozie, who now moves into the center of the room, to laughter and applause from the guests.

"So who have you come as?" says Anouk.

But it is to me that Zozie speaks, with that knowing smile that only I see.

"Well, Yanne, isn't this fun? Can't you see? I've come as *you*."

Monday, 24 December
CHRISTMAS EVE 8:30 P.M.

WELL, YOU KNOW, THERE'S NO PLEASING SOME PEOPLE. BUT WASN'T IT
worth it just for the look on her face, that sudden, sorry, stricken pallor,
the tremor that goes through her body as she sees herself coming down the
stairs—

I have to say it's a good job. Dress, hair, jewelry, everything but her
shoes, all reproduced to eerie perfection and worn with just that hint of a
smile. . . .

"Hey, it's like you're twins, or something," says Fat Nico with childish
delight as he helps himself to more macaroons. Laurent twitches nervously,
as if caught out in some private fantasy. Of course people can still tell us
apart—you can do so much with glamours, but outright transformation is
the stuff of fairy tale—and yet it is uncanny, how easily I take to the role.

The irony is not lost on Anouk, whose excitement has reached near-
manic proportions as she flits in and out of the *chocolaterie*—to see the snow,
or so she says, but she and I know she is waiting for Roux—and I guess that
the sudden flashes of iridescence in her colors are born not from pleasure
but from an energy that must be discharged, or risk burning her up like a
paper lantern.

Roux is not here. Not yet, at least—and now it is time for Vianne to
serve dinner.

With some reluctance, she begins. It's early yet, and he may still come—
his place is set at the end of the table, and if anyone asks, she will say that

this is the place set to honor the dead, an old tradition that echoes the Día de los Muertos, quite appropriate for this evening's celebration.

We begin with an onion soup as smoky and fragrant as autumn leaves, with croutons and grated Gruyère and a sprinkle of paprika over the top. She serves and watches me throughout, waiting, perhaps, for me to produce from thin air an even more perfect confection that will cast her effort into the shade.

Instead I eat, and talk, and smile, and compliment the chef, and the chink of crockery goes through her head, and she feels slightly dazed, not quite herself. Well, pulque is a mysterious brew, and the punch is liberally spiked with it, courtesy of Yours Truly, of course, in honor of the joyful occasion. As comfort, perhaps, she serves more punch, and the scent of the cloves is like being buried alive, and the taste is like chillies spiced with fire, and she wonders, *Will it ever end?*

The second course is sweet foie gras, sliced on thin toast with quinces and figs. It's the snap that gives this dish its charm, like the snap of correctly tempered chocolate, and the foie gras melts so lingeringly in the mouth, as soft as praline truffle, and it is served with a glass of ice-cold Sauternes that Anouk disdains, but which Rosette sips in a tiny glass no larger than a thimble, and she gives her rare and sunny smile, and signs impatiently for more.

The third course is a salmon baked *en papillote* and served whole, with a bérnaise sauce. Alice complains she is nearly full, but Nico shares his plate with her, feeding her tidbits and laughing at her minuscule appetite.

Then comes the pièce de résistance: the goose, long roasted in a hot oven so that the fat has melted from the skin, leaving it crisp and almost caramelized, and the flesh so tender it slips off the bones like a silk stocking from a lady's leg. Around it there are chestnuts and roast potatoes, all cooked and crackling in the golden fat.

Nico makes a sound half-lust, half-laughter. "I think I just died and went to calorie heaven," he says, attacking a goose leg with relish. "You know, I haven't tasted anything this good since my ma died. Compliments to the chef! If I wasn't *totally* in love with the stick-insect here, I'd marry you just like *that*—" And he waves his fork in a cheery way, almost putting out

Madame Luzeron's eye in his exuberance (she turns her face away just in time).

Vianne smiles. The punch must be taking effect by now, and she is flushed with her success. "Thank you," she says, standing up. "I'm so glad you're all here tonight so I can thank you for all the help you've given us."

That's rich, I think to myself. Exactly what have *they* done, I ask?

"For your custom, support, and friendship," she says, "at a time when all of us needed it." She smiles again, perhaps dimly aware now of the chemistries coursing freely through her veins, making her strangely talkative, strangely imprudent and almost reckless, like some much younger Vianne from some other half-forgotten life.

"I had what you'd call an unstable childhood. It meant I never really settled down. I didn't feel accepted anywhere I went. I always felt like an outsider. But now I've managed to stay here four years, and I owe it all to people like you."

Yawn, yawn. Speech coming on.

I pour myself a glass of punch and catch my little Anouk's eye. She's looking a little restless, I see, perhaps because of Jean-Loup's absence. He must be very ill, poor boy. They think it might have been something he ate. And with a delicate heart like his, anything can be dangerous. A cold, a chill, a cantrip, even—

Could it be that she feels guilty, somehow?

Please, Anouk. Perish the thought. Why should *you* feel responsible? As if you're not already alert enough to every little negative. But I can see your colors, dear, and the way you've been looking at my little Nativity scene, with its magic circle of three standing under the light of electric stars.

Speaking of which, we're missing one. Late as expected, but approaching fast, sneaking up the backstreets of the Butte as sly as a fox around a henhouse. His place is still set at the head of the table; plates, glasses, all untouched.

Vianne thinks maybe she is a fool. Anouk herself is beginning to think that all her planning and invocations have been for nothing, that even the snow will change nothing, and that nothing is left to keep her here.

But there is time yet as the meal comes to an end, for red wines from the Gers, for *p'tits cendrés* rolled in oakwood ash, for fresh unpasteurized cheeses, for old matured cheeses and aged Buzet and quince paste and walnuts and green almonds and honey.

And now Vianne brings out the thirteen desserts and the Yule log, thick as a strongman's arm and armored in inch-thick chocolate, and everyone who thought they might have had enough by now—even Alice—finds just a *little* more space for a slice (or two, or three, in Nico's case), and although the punch is finished at last, Vianne opens a bottle of champagne and we drink a toast.

Aux absents.

Monday, 24 December
CHRISTMAS EVE 10:30 P.M.

ROSETTE IS GETTING SLEEPY NOW. SHE'S BEEN SO GOOD THROUGHOUT THIS
meal, eating with her fingers, but clean enough, not dribbling much, and
talking (well, signing) a lot to Alice, who's sitting beside her little chair.

She loves Alice's fairy wings, which is good, because Alice has brought
her a pair of her own, wrapped up under the Christmas tree. Rosette's too
little to wait for midnight—she really ought to be in bed by now—and so
we thought she could open her presents now. But she stopped right there
at the fairy wings, which are purple and silver and kind of cool—in fact
I'm hoping Alice might have brought me a pair, which looks kind of likely
from the shape of the package. So now Rosette's a flying monkey, which
she thinks is hilarious, and she's crawling all over the place in her purple
wings and monkey suit, laughing at Nico from under the table, a chocolate
biscuit in her hand.

But now it's late and I'm feeling tired. Where's Roux? Why didn't he
come? I can't think about anything else; not food; not even presents. I'm
too wound up. My heart feels like a clockwork toy spinning around, out of
control. For a minute I close my eyes, and there's the scent of coffee now,
and the spiced hot chocolate that Maman drinks, and the sound of plates
being cleared away.

He'll come, I think. *He has to come.*

But it's so late, and he isn't here. Didn't I do everything right? The can-

dles, and the sugar, and the circle, and the blood? The gold and frankincense? The snow?

So why isn't he here by now?

I don't want to cry. It's Christmas Eve. But it wasn't supposed to be like
this. Is this the payoff Zozie mentioned? Get rid of Thierry—but at what
cost?

Then I hear the chimes, and I open my eyes. There's someone standing
at the door. For a moment I see him quite clearly; all in black, with his red
hair loose—

But I look again, and it isn't Roux. It's Jean-Loup at the door, and the
red-haired woman next to him must be his mother, I guess. She's looking
kind of sour-faced and embarrassed, but Jean-Loup seems OK, a bit pale
perhaps, but then he always looks pale—

I jump out of my chair. "You made it! Hooray! Do you feel all right?"

"Never better," he says, grinning. "How lame would it be if I missed
your party after all the work you've done?"

Jean-Loup's mother tries to smile. "I don't want to intrude," she says.
"But Jean-Loup insisted—"

"You're welcome," I say.

And as Maman and I hurry to find a couple of extra chairs in the
kitchen, Jean-Loup puts a hand in his pocket and pulls out something. It
looks like a present, wrapped in gold paper, but it's small, about the size of
a praline.

He gives it to Zozie. "I guess they're not my favorites, after all."

She's standing with her back to me, so I don't see her face, or what the
little packet contains. But he must have decided to give Zozie a chance, and
I'm so relieved I could almost cry. Things are really working out. All we
need is for Roux to come back, and for Zozie to decide to stay—

Then she turns and I see her face, and for a second it doesn't look like
Zozie at all. Must be a trick of the light, I guess, but just for a moment
there she looked angry—angry? No, *furious*—her eyes like slits, her mouth
full of teeth, her hand clenched so hard around the half-open packet that
chocolate oozes out like blood. . . .

Well, like I said, it's getting late. My eyes must be playing tricks on me. Because half a second later she's back again, all smiling and gorgeous in her red dress and red velvet shoes, and I'm just about to ask Jean-Loup what the little package was when the wind chimes ring again, and another someone comes in, a tall figure in red and white with a furry hood and a big fake beard—

"Roux!" I yell, and I jump to my feet.

Roux pulls away the fake beard. Underneath, he's grinning.

Rosette is almost at his feet. He picks her up and swings her into the air. "A monkey!" he says. "My favorite. Better still, a flying monkey!"

I give him a hug. "I thought you weren't coming."

"Well, I'm here."

A silence falls. He's standing there, Rosette clinging onto one arm. The room's full of people, but they might as well not be there at all, and although he seems relaxed enough, I can tell from the way he's watching Maman—

I look at her through the Smoking Mirror. She's playing it cool, but her colors are bright. She takes a step forward.

"We saved you a place."

He looks at her. "You sure?"

She nods.

And everybody stares at him then, and for a moment I think maybe he's going to say something, because Roux doesn't like it when people stare—in fact Roux isn't too comfortable around people at all—

But then she takes another step and kisses him softly on the mouth, and he puts down Rosette and holds out his arms—

And I don't need the Smoking Mirror to know. No one could ignore that kiss, or the way they fit together like pieces of a jigsaw puzzle, or the light in her eyes as she takes his hand and turns to smile at everyone—

Go on, I tell her in my shadow voice. *Tell them. Say it. Say it now—*

And for a second she looks at me. And I know she's got my message somehow. But then she looks round at our circle of friends, and Jean-Loup's mother still standing up and looking like a sucked lemon, and I can see her hesitate. Everyone is watching her—and I know what she's thinking. It's obvious. She's waiting for them to get the Look; the look we've seen so many times; the look that says: *you don't belong here—you're not one of us— you're different. . . .*

Around the table, no one speaks. They watch her in silence, all rosy-faced and well fed, except for Jean-Loup and his mother, of course, who stares at us like we were a den of wolves. There's Fat Nico holding hands with Alice in her fairy wings; Madame Luzeron, incongruous in her twin-set and pearls; Madame Pinot in her nun's outfit, looking twenty years younger with her hair undone; Laurent with a gleam in his eye; Richard and Mathurin, Jean-Louis and Paupaul sharing a smoke; and none of them—*none* of them has the Look—

And it's *her* face that changes. It softens, somehow. As if a weight has come off her heart. And for the first time since Rosette was born she really *looks* like Vianne Rocher, the Vianne who blew into Lansquenet and never cared what anyone said—

Zozie gives a little smile.

Jean-Loup grabs hold of his mother's hand and forces her to sit down on a chair.

Laurent's mouth drops open a notch.

Madame Pinot goes strawberry pink.

And Maman says, "Folks, I'd like you to meet someone. This is Roux. He's Rosette's father."

Monday, 24 December
CHRISTMAS EVE 10:40 P.M.

I HEAR THE COLLECTIVE SIGH GO ROUND; SOMETHING THAT IN DIFFER-
ent circumstances might have been disapproval, but in this case, after food
and wine, mellowed by the season and the unaccustomed glamour of snow,
seems like the *ahhh!* that follows a particularly spectacular firework.

Roux looks wary, then he grins, accepts a glass of champagne from Madame Luzeron, and raises it to all of us.

He followed me into the kitchen as the conversation started again. Rosette came with him, still crawling in her monkey suit, and I remember now
how fascinated she was the first time he walked into the shop, as if even
then she had recognized him.

Roux bent down to touch her hair. The resemblance between them was
sweetly poignant, like memories and lost time. There are so many things he
hasn't seen; when Rosette first held up her head; her first smile; her animal
drawings; the spoon dance that so angered Thierry. But I already know
from the look on his face that he'll never blame her for being different; that
she will never embarrass him; that he will never compare her to anyone else,
or ask that she be anything other than herself—

"Why did you never tell me?" he said.

I hesitated. Which truth should I tell? That I was too afraid, too proud,
too stubborn to change, that, like Thierry, I'd been in love with a fantasy
that, when it finally came within my grasp, revealed itself to be, not gold,
but nothing more than wisps of straw?

"I wanted us to settle down. I wanted us to be ordinary."

"Ordinary?"

I told him the rest; told of our flight from town to town, the fake wedding ring, the change of name, the end of magic, Thierry; the pursuit of acceptance at any cost, even my shadow, even my soul.

Roux stayed silent for a while, then he laughed softly in his throat. "All this for a chocolate shop?"

I shook my head. "Not anymore."

He always said I tried too hard. Cared too much—and now I can see that I didn't care enough for the things that really matter to me. A *chocolaterie* is, after all, just sand and mortar, stone and glass. It has no heart; no life of its own except for what it takes from us. And when we have given that away—

Roux picked up Rosette, who did not squirm as she usually does when approached by a stranger but gave a silent crow of delight and signed something with both her hands.

"What did she say?"

"She says you look like a monkey," I said, laughing. "From Rosette, that's a compliment."

He grinned at that and put his arms around us both. And for a moment we stood entwined, Rosette clinging to his neck, the soft sound of laughter from the next room, and the scent of chocolate on the air—

And then a silence falls over the room, and the wind chimes ring, and the door blows wide, and through the opening I can see another hooded figure all in red, but bigger, bulkier, and so familiar beneath his false beard that I don't have to see the cigar in his hand—

And in the silence Thierry comes in, with a lurch in his step that speaks of drink.

He fixes Roux with a malevolent stare and says: "Who is she?"

"She?" says Roux.

Thierry crosses the room in three strides, clipping the Christmas tree in his path and scattering presents over the floor. He thrusts his white-bearded face toward Roux.

"You know," he says. "Your accomplice. The one who helped you cash my check. The one the bank's got on CCTV—and who by all accounts has ripped off more than one sucker in Paris this year—"

"I don't have an accomplice," says Roux. "I never cashed your—"

And now I can see something in his face, a dawning of something, but it's too late.

Thierry grabs him by the arm. They're so close now, reflections in a distorted mirror, Thierry wild-eyed, Roux very pale—

"The police know all about her," Thierry says. "But they've never been so close before. She changes her name, see? Works alone. But this time she made a mistake. She hitched up with a loser like you. So who is she?" He's shouting now, his face as red as Santa's own. He fixes Roux with his drunken glare. "Who the hell is Vianne Rocher?"

Monday, 24 December

WELL, ISN'T THAT THE MILLION-DOLLAR QUESTION?

Thierry is drunk. I can see that at once. He reeks of beer and cigar smoke, which clings to his Santa Claus costume and that absurdly festive cotton-wool beard. Beneath it his colors are murky and threatening, but I can tell he's in poor shape.

Across from him, Vianne is white as an ice statue, her mouth half-open, her eyes ablaze. She shakes her head in helpless denial. She knows Roux would not give her away; and Anouk is speechless, twice stricken, first by the touching little family scene she has glimpsed behind the kitchen door, second by this ugly intrusion when everything seemed so perfect at last—

"Vianne Rocher?" Her voice is blank.

"That's right," says Thierry. "Otherwise known as Françoise Lavery, Mercedes Desmoines, Emma Windsor, to name but a few—"

Behind her, I see Anouk recoil. One of those names has struck a chord. Does it matter? I think not. In fact, I think the game is mine—

He fixes her with that measuring stare. "*He* calls you Vianne." Of course, he means Roux.

Silently, she shakes her head.

"You mean you've never heard that name?"

Once more she shakes her head, and *oh!*—

The look on her face as she sees the trap; sees how neatly she has been maneuvered to this very point; understands how her only hope is to deny herself for the third time—

Behind them, no one is watching Madame. Quiet during the festive meal, speaking mostly to Anouk, she now watches Thierry with an expression of stark and uncomplicated horror. Oh, I have prepared Madame, of course. With gentle hints, subtle charm, and good old-fashioned chemistry I have brought her to this moment of revelation, and now all it takes is a single name and the piñata cracks open like a chestnut on the fire. . . .

Vianne Rocher.

Well, that's my cue. Smiling, I stand, and I have time for a last quick celebratory sip of champagne before all eyes are upon me—hopeful, fearful, furious, worshipful—as now at last I claim the prize—

I smile. "Vianne Rocher? That would be me."

Monday, 24 December
CHRISTMAS EVE 11:00 P.M.

SHE MUST HAVE FOUND MY PAPERS, OF COURSE, HIDDEN IN MY MOTHER'S
box. After that, it's easy enough to open an account in my name; to send
off for a new passport, a driving license, everything she requires to become
Vianne Rocher. She even looks just like me now; easy again, using Roux
as bait, to use my stolen identity in a way that will at some time incrimi-
nate us—

Oh, I can see the trap now. Too late, as always in stories like this, I
understand what she wants at last. To force my hand, to trick me into re-
vealing myself, to blow me away like a leaf on the wind, with a new set of
Furies on my tail—

But what's a name? I ask myself. Can't I choose another one? Can't I
change it, as I have done so many times before, call Zozie's bluff, and force
her to leave?

Thierry is staring at her in astonishment. "*You?*" he says.

She shrugs. "Surprised?"

The others are watching her, stupefied.

"*You* stole the money? *You* cashed the checks?"

Behind her, Anouk is very pale.

Nico says: "It can't be true."

Madame Luzeron shakes her head.

"But Zozie's our friend," says little Alice, blushing furiously at making
even such a short speech. "We owe her so much—"

Jean-Louis interrupts. "I know a fake when I see one," he says. "And Zozie isn't a fake. I swear."

But now Jean-Loup speaks up. "It's true. Her picture was in the newspaper. She's really good at changing her face, but I knew it was her. My photographs—"

Zozie gives him a barbed smile. "Of course it's true. It's all true. I've had more names than I can count. I've lived from hand to mouth all my life. I've never had a proper home, or a family, or a business, or any of the things Yanne has here—"

And she shoots me a smile like a falling star, and I can't speak, can't move, captivated like the rest of them. The fascination is so intense that I could almost believe I've been drugged; my head feels like a hive of bees; colors shift around the room, making it spin like a carousel—

Roux puts out his arm to steady me. He alone seems not to share in the general feeling of consternation. I'm vaguely aware of Madame Rimbault—Jean-Loup's mother—staring at me. Her face is pinched with disapproval beneath the dyed hair. She very clearly wants to leave—and yet she too is mesmerized, caught up in Zozie's narrative.

Zozie smiles and carries on. "You might say I'm an adventurer. All my life I've lived on my wits—gambling, stealing, begging, fraud. I've never known anything else. No friends, no place I liked enough to stay . . ."

She pauses, and I can *feel* the glamour in the air, all incense and sparkling dust, and I know that she can talk them round, can twist them round her little finger.

"But here," she says, "I found a home. I found people who like me, people who like me for who I am. I thought I could reinvent myself here—but old habits die hard. I'm sorry, Thierry. I'll pay you back."

And as their voices begin to rise, confused and distressed and wavering, the quiet Madame now faces Thierry; Madame, whose name I don't even know, but whose face is pale now with something she can barely articulate, her eyes like agates in that hard face.

"How much does she owe you, Monsieur?" she says. "I'll pay it myself, with interest."

He stares at her, incredulous. "Why?" he says.

Madame straightens up to her full height. It isn't much; beside Thierry she looks like a quail facing down a bear.

"I'm sure you have a right to complain," she says in her nasal Parisian voice. "But I have good reason to believe that Vianne Rocher, whoever she is, is far more my concern than yours."

"How so?" says Thierry.

"I'm her mother," she says.

Monday, 24 December
CHRISTMAS EVE 11:05 P.M.

AND NOW THE SILENCE THAT HAS BOUND HER IN ITS ICY COCOON SPLITS open in a broken cry. Vianne, no longer pale but flushed with pulque and confusion, steps out to face Madame in the little semicircle that has gathered around her.

A bunch of mistletoe hangs above their heads, and I feel a wild, mad, relentless urge to run up to her and kiss her right there on the mouth. She's so easy to manipulate—like all of them—and now I can almost taste the prize, can feel it in the rhythm of my blood, can hear it like surf on a distant beach, and it tastes so sweet, like chocolate—

The sign of One Jaguar has many properties. True invisibility is, of course, impossible outside of fairy tales, but the eye and the brain can be fooled in ways that cameras and film cannot, and it is easy enough, while their attention is focused on Madame, to creep away—not *quite* unnoticed —to collect the case I have so neatly packed.

Anouk followed, as I knew she would. "Why did you say that?" she demanded. "Why did you say you were Vianne Rocher?"

I shrugged. "What do I have to lose? I change my name like my coat, Anouk. I never stay in one place for long. That's the difference between us. I could never live like that. I could never be respectable. I don't care what they think of me—but your mother has so much to lose. There's Roux, and Rosette, and the shop, of course—"

"But what about that woman?" she said.

So I filled her in on the sorry tale: the child in the car seat; the little cat charm. Turns out Vianne never mentioned it. Can't say I'm really surprised.

"But if she knew who her mother was," said Anouk, "then couldn't she have found her again?"

"Perhaps she was afraid," I said. "Or perhaps she felt closer to her adopted mother. *You choose your family*, Nanou. Isn't that what she always says? And perhaps . . ." I faked a pause.

"And what?"

I smiled. "People like us are different. We have to stick together, Nanou. We have to choose our family. After all," I told her slyly, "if she can lie to you about this, then can you be sure *you* weren't stolen too?"

I left her to think about that for a while. In the other room, Madame was still talking, her voice rising and falling in the rhythms of the natural storyteller. She and her daughter have that in common; but it's not the time to hang around. I have my case; my coat; my papers. As always, I travel light. From my pocket I bring out Anouk's present: a small package wrapped in red.

"I don't want you to go, Zozie."

"Nanou, I really have no choice."

The present gleams among the folds of red tissue paper. It's a bracelet; a slim band made of silver, lustrous and new. By contrast, the single charm that hangs on it is dark with age—a tiny blackened silver cat.

She knows what it means. A sob escapes her.

"Zozie, no—"

"I'm sorry, Anouk."

Quickly I cross the deserted kitchen. Plates and glasses neatly stacked along with the remains of the feast. On the stove, a pot of hot chocolate simmers; its steam is the only sign of life.

Try me. Taste me, it implores.

It's a small enough glamour, an everyday charm, and Anouk has withstood it for the last four years, but all the same it pays to be safe, so I turn off the heat under the pot as I make my way toward the back door.

With one hand I carry my case. With the other I cast the sign of Mictecacihuatl like a handful of cobwebs in the air. Death, and a gift. The essential seduction. More potent by far than chocolate.

And now I turn to smile at her. Outside, and the darkness will swallow me whole. The night wind flirts with my red dress. My scarlet shoes are like blood on the snow.

"Nanou," I say. "We've all got a choice. Yanne or Vianne. Annie or Anouk. Changing Wind or the Hurakan. It's not always easy, being like us. If you want easy, you'd better stay here. But if you want to ride that wind—"

For a moment she seems to hesitate, but I already know I've won.

I won the moment I took on your name, and with it, the call of the Changing Wind. You see, Vianne, I never meant to stay. I never wanted your *chocolaterie*. I never wanted any part of the sad little life you've made for yourself.

But Anouk, with her gifts, is invaluable. So young and yet so talented, and most of all, so easy to manipulate. We could be in New York by tomorrow, Nanou, or London, or Moscow, or Venice, or even good old Mexico City. There are plenty of conquests waiting out there for Vianne Rocher and her daughter Anouk, and won't we both be fabulous; won't we go through them all like the December wind?

Anouk is watching me, mesmerized. It all makes so much sense to her now that she wonders why she never saw it before. A fair exchange; a life for a life.

And am I not your mother now? Better than life and twice as much fun? Why would you need Yanne Charbonneau? Why would you need *anyone*?

"But what about Rosette?" she protests.

"Rosette has a family now."

A moment while she thinks about that. Yes, Rosette will have a family. Rosette does not need to choose. Rosette has Yanne. Rosette has Roux—

Another sob escapes her. *"Please—"*

"Come on, Nanou. It's what you want. Magic, adventure, life on the edge—"

She takes a step, then hesitates. "You promise you'll never lie to me?"

"Never have. Never will."

Another pause, and the lingering scent of Vianne's hot chocolate pulls at me, saying *try me, taste me* in its smoky plaintive dying voice.

Is that the best you can do, Vianne?

But Anouk still seems to hesitate.

She's looking at my bracelet; at the silver charms that are hanging there: coffin, shoes, ear of maize, hummingbird, snake, skull, monkey, mouse—

She frowns, as if she's trying to remember something that's just on the tip of her tongue. And her eyes brim with tears as she looks up at the copper pan cooling on the stove.

Try me. Taste me. A last sad fading perfume, like a ghost of childhood on the air.

Try me. Taste me. A skinned knee; a small damp palm with chocolate dust imprinted into life line and heart line.

Taste me. Test me. A memory of both of them lying in bed, a picture book on the blanket between them, Anouk laughing wildly at something Vianne said . . .

Once more I cast the sign of Mictecacihuatl, old Lady Death, the Gobbler of Hearts, like black fireworks into her path. It's getting late; Madame's tale will be done, and very soon they will miss us both.

Anouk looks dazed, watching the stove with a look of one half in a dream. Through the Smoking Mirror I can now see the cause: a small gray shape sitting by the pan, a blur that might be whiskers, a tail—

"Well?" I ask. "Are you coming or not?"

Monday, 24 December
CHRISTMAS EVE 11:05 P.M.

"I LIVED DOWN THE HALL FROM JEANNE ROCHER." HER VOICE HAD THE typical clipped vowels of the native Parisienne, like stiletto heels rapping out the words. "She was a little older than me, and she earned her money doing Tarot readings and helping people to quit smoking. I went to her once, a couple of weeks before my daughter was taken. She told me I'd been thinking of having her adopted. I called her a liar. All the same, it was true."

She carried on, her expression bleak. "It was a bedsit flat in Neuilly-Plaisance. Half an hour from the center of Paris. I had an old 2CV, two waitressing jobs at local cafés, and the occasional handout from Sylviane's father, who by then I'd realized would never leave his wife. I was twenty-one and my life was over. Child care ate what little I earned; I didn't know what else to do. It wasn't that I didn't *love* her. . . ."

The image of that little cat charm flashes briefly through my mind. There's something touching about it, somehow, the silver charm with its lucky red ribbon. Did Zozie steal that too? Perhaps she did. Perhaps that's how she fooled Madame Caillou, her harsh face softened now with the memory of her loss.

"It was two weeks later that she disappeared. I left her for two minutes, that's all—Jeanne Rocher must have been watching me, biding her time. When I thought to look for her she'd packed up and left, and there was no proof. But I always wondered—" She turned to me, her face alight. "And then I met your friend Zozie, with her little girl, and I knew, I *knew*—"

I looked at the stranger opposite me. An ordinary woman of fifty or so, looking rather older, perhaps, with her heavy hips and penciled brows. A woman I might have passed a thousand times in the street without thinking for a moment that there could be any possible kinship between us, now standing there with that look of terrible hope on her face, and *this* is the trap, I know it is, and my name is not my soul, I know.

But I can't, I just *can't* let her believe—

"Please, Madame." I smiled at her. "Someone has played a cruel joke. Zozie's not your daughter," I said. "Whatever she may have claimed, she's not. And as for Vianne Rocher—"

I paused. Roux's face was expressionless, but his hand found mine and held it tight. Thierry's eyes were on me too. And I knew at that moment I had no choice. A man who casts no shadow, I know, isn't really a man at all, and a woman who gives up her name—

"I remember a red plush elephant. A blanket with flowers. I think it was pink. And a bear with one eye made from a black button. And a little silver cat charm tied with a piece of red ribbon—"

Now Madame was watching me, eyes bright under her penciled brows.

"They traveled with me for years," I said. "The elephant went pink with age. I wore it down to the stuffing inside, and still I wouldn't let her throw it away. They were the only toys I really had, and I carried them in my backpack with their heads sticking out so they could have a chance to breathe—"

A silence. Her breath, a rasp in her throat.

"She taught me how to read palms," I said. "And Tarot cards, and tea leaves, and runes. I've still got her pack in a box upstairs. I don't use it much, and it isn't quite proof, but it's everything I have left of her—"

She was staring at me now, lips parted, mouth drawn in a grimace of some emotion too complex to identify.

"She said you wouldn't have cared for me. She said you wouldn't have known what to do. But she saved the charm with her Tarot cards, and she saved the newspaper clippings, and before she died, I think she meant to tell me, but I couldn't quite believe it then—I didn't *want* to believe it then."

"There was a song I used to sing. A lullaby. Do you remember?"

For a moment I paused. I was eighteen months old. How could I remember such a thing?

Then suddenly it came to me. The lullaby we always sang to turn aside the changing wind; the song that soothes the Kindly Ones—

> *V'là l'bon vent, v'là l'joli vent,*
> *V'là l'bon vent, ma mie m'appelle.*
> *V'là l'bon vent, v'là l'joli vent,*
> *V'là l'bon vent, ma mie m'attend.*

And now she opened her mouth and wailed, a great, torn hopeful cry that cut through the air like beating wings. "That was it. Oh, that was—" Her voice wavered helplessly, and she fell toward me, arms open like a drowning child.

I caught her—she would have fallen otherwise—and the scent of her was like old violets and clothes kept too long unworn, like mothballs and toothpaste and powder and dust; so absurdly unlike the familiar sandalwood scent of my mother that it was all I could do to hold back the tears—

"Vianne," she said. "My Vianne."

And I held her, just as I'd held my mother in the days and weeks before her death, with quiet words of reassurance that she did not hear, but that calmed her a little, and finally she began to sob, with the long exhausted sobs of someone who has seen more than their eyes can bear, felt more than their heart can withstand—

Patiently I let them subside. A minute later those tearing sounds in her chest had settled into a series of low tremors, and her face, ravaged now by the flow of tears, turned to look at the circle of guests. For a long time, no one moved. Some things are just too much to take; and this woman in her naked grief made them shy away, like children from some fierce animal dying in the road.

No one offered a handkerchief.

No one looked her in the eye.

No one spoke.

Then, and to my astonishment, Madame Luzeron got to her feet and spoke up in her cut glass voice. "My poor dear. I know how you feel."

"You do?" Madame's eyes were a mosaic of tears.

"Well, I lost my son, you know." She put her hand on Madame's shoulder and guided her to an armchair nearby. "You've had a shock. Have some champagne. My late husband always used to say that champagne was largely medicinal."

Madame gave a wavering smile. "You're very kind, Madame—"

"Isabelle. And you?"

"Michèle."

So that was my mother's name. Michèle.

At least I can still be Vianne, I thought, and now I began to shake so violently that I almost collapsed into my chair.

"You OK?" said Nico, concerned.

I nodded, trying to smile.

"You look like you could do with something medicinal yourself," he said, handing me a glass of Cognac. He looked so earnest—and so incongruous—in his Henri IV wig and frogged silk coat that I started to cry—absurd, I know—and for a time I quite forgot the little scene that Michèle's story had interrupted.

But Thierry had not forgotten it. Drunk he might have been, but not drunk enough to forget why he had followed Roux here. He'd come in search of Vianne Rocher, and he'd found her at last, perhaps not as he'd imagined her, but here, and with the enemy—

"So *you're* Vianne Rocher." His voice was flat. His eyes were pinpricks in red dough.

I nodded. "I was. But I'm not the person who cashed those checks—"

He cut me off. "I don't care about that. What matters is you lied to me. *Lied. To me.*" Angrily he shook his head, but there was something pitiable in the gesture, as if he couldn't quite believe that, once again, Life had failed to live up to his exacting standards of perfection.

"I was willing to marry you." Now his voice was slurred with self-pity. "I would have given you a home, you and your kids. Another man's kids. One of them—*well*—I mean, *look* at her." He glanced at Rosette in her monkey suit, and the familiar rictus came over his face. "Look at her," he said again. "She's practically an animal. Crawls on all fours. Can't even speak. But I would have taken care of her—I would have got the best specialists in Europe on her case. For your sake, Yanne. Because I loved you."

"*Loved* her?" said Roux.

Everybody turned to look.

He was leaning against the kitchen door, hands in his pockets, eyes bright. He had unzipped his Santa suit, and beneath it he was all in black, and the colors reminded me so much of the Pied Piper on the Tarot card that suddenly I could hardly breathe. And now he was speaking, in that fierce, harsh voice; Roux, who hates crowds, avoids scenes where he can and never, *ever* makes a speech—

"Love her?" he said. "You don't even know her. Her favorite chocolates are *mendiants*; her favorite color is bright red. Her favorite scent is mimosa. She can swim like a fish. She hates black shoes. She loves the sea. She's got a scar on her left hip from when she fell out of a Polish goods train. She doesn't like having curly hair, even though it's gorgeous. She likes the Beatles, but not the Stones. She used to steal menus from restaurants because she could never afford to eat there herself. She's the best mother I've ever met—" He paused. "And she doesn't need your charity. As for Rosette . . ." He picked her up and held her so that her face was almost touching his own. "She's my little girl. And she's perfect."

For a moment Thierry looked puzzled. Then realization began to set in. His face darkened; his eyes went from Roux to Rosette, from Rosette to Roux. The truth is undeniable; Rosette's face may be less angular, her hair a lighter shade of red, but she has his eyes, and his satirical mouth, and at that moment there could be no mistake—

Thierry turned on his polished heel, a crisp maneuver slightly marred by the fact that he struck the table with his hip, sending a champagne glass to smash to the floor, scattering across the tiles in an explosion of fake diamonds. But when Madame Luzeron picked it up—

"Hey, that's lucky," said Nico. "I could have sworn I heard it go—"

Madame gave me a curious look.

"Just lucky, I guess."

Just like the blue glass dish again, the Murano dish I dropped that day, but now I'm not afraid anymore. I just looked at Rosette in her father's arms, and what I felt was not dismay, or fear, or anxiety, but an overwhelming sense of pride—

"Well, you'd better enjoy it while you can." Thierry was standing by the door, massive in his red suit. "Because as of now, I'm giving you notice. A quarter's notice, as per our deal, after which I'm closing you down." He eyed me with malign good cheer. "What, did you think you were going to stay, after everything that's happened here? I own this place, in case you'd forgotten, and I've got plans that don't include you. Have fun with your little chocolate shop. You'll all be gone by Easter."

Well, that's not the first time someone's said that. As the door slammed behind him I felt, not fear, but another astonishing lurch of pride. The worst had happened, and we had survived. The changing wind had won again, but this time I felt no sense of defeat. Instead I felt delirious; ready to face down the Furies themselves—

And then I had a terrible thought. I stood up abruptly, scanned the room. Conversation was starting again, slowly at first but gaining momentum. Madame Luzeron poured champagne. Nico began to talk to Michèle. Paupaul was flirting with Madame Pinot. From what I could hear, the general consensus was that Thierry was drunk, that all of his threats were empty talk, that by next week it would all be forgotten, because the *chocolaterie* was a *part* of Montmartre, and could no more disappear than Le P'tit Pinson—

But someone was missing. Zozie was gone.

Nor was there any sign of Anouk.

Monday, 24 December
CHRISTMAS EVE 11:15 P.M.

IT'S BEEN SO LONG SINCE I LAST SAW PANTOUFLE. I'D ALMOST FORGOTTEN what it was like to have him nearby, watching me with his berry black eyes, or sitting all warm on my knee, or on my pillow late at night in case I got scared of the Black Man. But Zozie's already at the door, and we have to catch that Changing Wind—

I call Pantoufle in my shadow-voice. I can't just leave without Pantoufle. But he doesn't come, just sits by the stove with his whiskers twitching and that look he gets, and it's funny, but I can't remember ever being able to see him so clearly, every hair, every whisker etched in light. And there's a scent of something too, coming from that little pan—

It's only chocolate, I tell myself.

But it smells different, somehow. Like the chocolate I used to drink as a child, all creamy and hot with chocolate curls and cinnamon and a sugar spoon to stir it with.

"Well?" she says. "Are you coming or not?"

Once again, I call Pantoufle. But once again he doesn't hear. And of course I want to go, to see those places she told me about, to ride the wind, to be fabulous—but there's Pantoufle sitting by the copper pan, and somehow I just can't turn away.

I know he's just an imaginary friend, and here's Zozie, so real and alive, but there's something I have to remember somehow, a story Maman used to tell about a boy who gave his shadow away—

"Come *on*, Anouk." Her voice is sharp. The wind feels cold in the kitchen now, and there's snow on the step and on her shoes. Inside the shop there's a sudden noise; I can smell the chocolate and hear Maman calling me—

But now Zozie's taking my hand, and she's dragging me through the open back door. I can feel the snow sliding under my shoes, and the cold of the night creeps under my cloak—

"*Pantoufle!*" I call for the last time.

And finally he comes to me, shadowy across the snow. And for a second I see her face, not through the Smoking Mirror, but through the shadow of Pantoufle—and it's a stranger's face, not Zozie's at all, but twisted and bent like a handful of scrap metal, and old, *old*, like the oldest great-great-grandmother in the world, and instead of the red dress like Maman's, she's wearing a skirt of human hearts, and her shoes are all blood in the drifting snow—

I scream and try to pull away.

She claws at me with the sign of One Jaguar, and I can hear her telling me that we're going to be fine, not to be afraid, that she's chosen me, that she wants me, needs me, that none of the others would understand—

And I know I can't stop her. I have to go. I've gone too far, my magic's nothing next to hers—but the scent of chocolate is still so strong, like the scent of a forest after the rain, and suddenly I can see something else, a hazy picture in my mind. I can see a little girl, only a few years younger than me. She's in some kind of shop, and in front of her there's a kind of black box, like the coffin charm on Zozie's bracelet—

"*Anouk!*"

I can tell that's Maman's voice. But I can't see her now. She's too far away. And Zozie's dragging me into the dark, and my feet are following in the snow. And the little girl's going to open the box, and there's something terrible inside, and if only I *knew*, I could stop her, perhaps—

We're opposite the chocolate shop. We're standing at the corner of Place des Faux-Monnayeurs, looking down the cobbled street. There's a streetlamp there, and it lights up the snow, and our shadows stretch all the way down to the steps. I can see Maman from the corner of my eye, looking out into the square. She looks a hundred miles away, and yet it can't be very far. And there's Roux, and Rosette, and Jean-Loup, and Nico, and their faces are very distant somehow, like something seen through a telescope—

The door opens. Maman steps out.

I can hear Nico's voice from far away, saying, *"What the hell's that?"*

Behind them, the murmur of voices lost in a terminal blur of static.

The wind is rising. The Hurakan—and there's no way Maman can fight that wind, although I can see she's planning to try. She looks very calm. She's almost smiling. And I wonder how I or anyone else could have thought she looked anything like Zozie—

Zozie gives her cannibal smile. "At last, a flash of spirit?" she says. "Too late, Vianne. I've won the game."

"You haven't won anything," says Maman. "Your kind never wins. You may think you do, but the victory's always an empty one."

Zozie snarls. "How would you know? The child followed me of her own accord."

Maman ignores her. "Anouk. Come here."

But I'm pinned to the spot in that frozen light. I *want* to go—but there's something else, a whispering voice, like an icy fishhook in my heart, that's pulling me the other way.

It's too late. You've made your choice. The Hurakan won't go away—

"Please, Zozie. I want to go home—"

Home? What home? Killers don't have a home, Nanou. Killers ride the Hurakan—

"But I'm not a killer—"

Really? You're not?

She laughs like chalk on a blackboard.

I scream: "Let me *go!*"

She laughs again. Her eyes are like cinders, her mouth is a wire, and I wonder how I could ever have thought she was fabulous. She smells of dead crab and gasoline. Her hands are like bunches of bones; her hair is like rotting seaweed. And her voice is the night; her voice is the wind; and now I can hear how hungry she is, how much she wants to swallow me whole—

Then Maman speaks. She sounds very calm. But her colors are like the northern lights, brighter than the Champs-Elysées, and she flicks out her fingers at Zozie in a little gesture I know very well—

Tsk-tsk, begone!

Zozie gives a pitying smile. The string of hearts around her waist flips and flirts like a cheerleader's skirt.

Tsk-tsk, begone! She forks it again, and this time I see a tiny spark skip across the square toward Zozie like a cinder from a bonfire.

Once more, Zozie smiles. "Is that the best you can do?" she says. "Domestic magic and cantrips even a child could learn? What a waste of your skills, Vianne, when you could have been riding the wind with us. Still, some people are too old to change. And some people are just afraid to be free—"

And she takes a step toward Maman, and suddenly she's changed again. It's a glamour, of course, but she's beautiful, and even I can't help but stare. The necklace of hearts has gone now; and she's wearing hardly anything but a linked skirt of something that looks like jade, and a lot of golden jewelry. And her skin is the color of mocha cream, and her mouth is like a cut pomegranate, and she smiles at Maman and says—

"Why don't you come with us, Vianne? It's not too late. The three of us—we could be unstoppable. Stronger than the Kindly Ones. Stronger than the Hurakan. We'd be fabulous, Vianne. Irresistible. We'd sell seductions and sweet dreams, not just here, but everywhere. We'd go global with your chocolates. Branches in every part of the world. Everyone would love you, Vianne, you'd change the lives of millions—"

Maman falters. *Tsk-tsk, begone!* But her heart isn't in it anymore; the little spark dies before it's halfway across the square. She takes a step toward Zozie—she's only a dozen feet away, and her colors are gone, and she looks like she's in some kind of dream—

And I want to tell her it's all a cheat, that Zozie's magic is like a cheap Easter egg, all shiny foil on the outside, but open it up and there's nothing there—and then I remember what Pantoufle showed me: the little girl, and the shop, and the black box, and the great-great-grandmother sitting there grinning like a wolf in disguise—

And suddenly I find my voice, and I shout out as loudly as I can, without quite knowing what the words mean, but knowing they're words of power, somehow, words to conjure with, words to stop the winter wind—

And I shout, "Zozie!"

She looks at me.

And I say, *"What was in the black piñata?"*

Monday, 24 December
CHRISTMAS EVE 11:25 P.M.

IT BROKE THE CHARM. SHE STOPPED. SHE STARED. MOVED CLOSER TO ME across the snow and brought her face up close to mine. And now I could smell that dead-crab stink, but I didn't blink or look away.

"You dare to ask me that?" she snarled.

And now I could hardly bear to look. She'd changed her face and was fearsome again; a giantess; her mouth a cave of mossy teeth. The silver bracelet on her wrist now looked like a bracelet of skulls, and her skirt of hearts was dripping with blood, a curtain of blood in the fallen snow. She was terrible, but she was afraid, and behind her Maman was watching with a funny kind of smile on her face, as if she understood far more about it than I did, somehow—

She gave me the tiniest of nods.

I said the magic words again. "What was in the black piñata?"

Zozie made a harsh sound in her throat. "I thought we were friends, Nanou," she said. And suddenly she was Zozie again, the old Zozie of the lollipop shoes, with her scarlet skirt and her pink-streaked hair and her jangly multicolored beads. And she looked so real and so familiar that it hurt my heart to see her so sad. And her hand on my shoulder was trembling, and her eyes filled with tears as she whispered—

"Please—oh please, Nanou, don't make me tell—"

My mother was standing six feet away. Behind her in the square were Jean-Loup, Roux, Nico, Madame Luzeron, Alice, and their colors were like fireworks on the Fourteenth of July, all gold and green and silver and red—

I caught a sudden scent of chocolate drifting from the open door, and I thought of the copper pan on the hob, and the way the steam had reached out to me like ghostly pleading fingers, and the voice I'd almost thought I heard, my mother's, saying, *Try me, taste me—*

And I thought about all the times she'd offered me hot chocolate, and I'd said no. Not because I don't like it, but because I was angry that she'd changed; because I blamed her for what happened to us; and because I wanted to get back at her, to make her see I was different—

It isn't Zozie's fault, I thought. Zozie's just the mirror that shows us what we want to see. Our hopes; our hates; our vanities. But when you really look at it, a mirror's just a piece of glass—

For the third time, I said in my clearest voice: "*What was in the black piñata?*"

Monday, 24 December
CHRISTMAS EVE 11:30 P.M.

I CAN SEE IT ALL SO CLEARLY NOW, LIKE PICTURES ON A TAROT CARD. THE darkened shop; skulls on the shelves; the little girl; the great-great-grand-mother standing by with a look of appalling greed on her ancient face.

I know that Anouk sees it too. Even Zozie sees it now, and her face keeps changing, going from old to young, from Zozie to the Queen of Hearts, mouth twisting from contempt to indecision and finally to naked fear. And now she's only nine years old, a little girl in her carnival dress with a silver bracelet round her wrist.

"You want to know what was inside? You *really* want to know?" she says.

Monday, 24 December

SO YOU REALLY WANT TO KNOW, ANOUK?

Shall I tell you what I saw?

What was I expecting, you ask? Sweets, perhaps, or lollipops; chocolate skulls; necklaces of sugar teeth; all the tawdry Day of the Dead merchandise ready to explode out of the black piñata like a shower of dark confetti?

Or something else, some occult revelation: a glimpse of God; a hint of beyond; some assurance, perhaps, that the dead are still here, guests at our table; unquiet sleepers; custodians of some essential mystery that will one day be imparted to the rest of us?

Isn't that what we all want? To believe that Christ arose from the dead; that angels guard us; that fish on a Friday is sometimes holy and at other times a mortal sin; that it somehow *matters* if a sparrow falls, or a tower or two, or even an entire race, annihilated in the name of some specious deity or other, barely distinguishable from a whole series of One True Gods—ha!—Lord, what fools these mortals be, and the joke of it is that we're *all* fools, even to the gods themselves, because for all the millions who were slaughtered in their name, for all the prayers and sacrifices and wars and revelations, who *really* remembers the Old Ones now—Tlaloc and Coatlicue and Quetzalcoatl and even greedy old Mictecacihuatl herself—their temples made into "heritage sites," their stones toppled, their pyramids overgrown, all lost in time like blood in the sand?

And what do we really care, Anouk, if a hundred years from now the Sacré-Coeur has become a mosque, or a synagogue, or something else altogether? Because by then we'll *all* be sand, except for the One who has always been; the one that builds pyramids; raises temples; makes martyrs; composes sublime music; denies logic; praises the meek; receives souls into Paradise; dictates what to wear; smites the infidel; paints the Sistine Chapel; urges young men to die for the cause; blows up bandsmen by remote control; promises much; delivers little; fears no one and never dies, because the fear of Death is so much greater than honor, or goodness, or faith, or love. . . .

So, back to your question. What was it again?

Ah, yes, the black piñata.

You think I found the answer in there?

Sorry, sweetheart. Think again.

You want to know what I saw, Anouk?

Nothing. That's what. Big fat zip.

No answers, no certainties; no payback; no truth. Just air; a single belch of foul air rushing out of the black piñata like morning breath from a thousand-year sleep.

"The worst of all things is *nothing*, Anouk. No meaning; no message; no demons; no gods. We die—and there's nothing. Nothing at all."

She watches me with those dark eyes.

"You're wrong," she says. "There's something."

"What? You really think you've got something here? Think again. The chocolate shop? Thierry will have you out by Easter. Like all conceited men, he's vindictive. In four months time, you'll be back where you started, the three of you, penniless and on the road.

"Think you'll have Vianne? You won't, you know. She hasn't the courage to be herself, let alone be a mother to you. Think you'll have Roux? Don't count on it. He's the biggest liar of all. Ask to see his boat, Anouk. Ask to see his precious *boat*—"

But I'm losing her, and I know it now. She looks at me with no fear in her eyes. Instead there's something I can't quite make out—

Pity? No. She wouldn't dare.

"It must be very lonely, Zozie."

"Lonely?" I snarled.

"Being you."

I uttered a silent howl of rage. It's the hunting cry of One Jaguar, of Black Tezcatlipoca in his most terrible Aspect. But the child didn't flinch. Instead, she smiled and took my hand.

"All those hearts you've collected," she said. "And still you don't have one of your own. Is that why you wanted me? So you wouldn't be alone anymore?"

I stared at her, speechless now with indignation. Does the Pied Piper steal children for love? Does the Big Bad Wolf seduce Red Riding Hood out of a misguided need for company? I'm the Eater of Hearts, you stupid child; I'm the Fear of Death; I'm the Wicked Witch; I'm the grimmest of all fairy tales, and don't you *dare* feel sorry for me—

I pushed her away. She wouldn't leave. She reached out for my hand again, and suddenly, don't ask me why, I began to feel afraid—

Call it a warning, if you like. Call it an attack brought on by excitement, champagne, and too much pulque. But suddenly I was cold with sweat; my chest was tight; my breath came in gasps. Pulque is an unpredictable brew; it brings a heightened awareness to some; visions that may be intense but that can also drift into delirium, pushing the drinker to perform rash acts; to reveal perhaps more of themselves than is entirely safe for one such as myself.

And now I understood the truth: that in my eagerness to collect this child I'd somehow slipped; I'd shown my true face, and the sudden intimacy of it was unsettling, unspeakable, tearing at me like a hungry dog.

"Let go of me!"

Anouk just smiled.

And now true panic swept through me, and I pushed at her with all my strength. She slipped and fell backward into the snow, and even then I could feel her reaching for me with that look of pity in her eyes—

There are times when even the best of us has to decide to cut and run. There will be others, I tell myself—new cities, new challenges, new gifts. But no one will be collected today.

Least of all, myself.

I run, almost blindly through the snow, slipping on the cobblestones, reckless in my haste to escape, losing myself on the wind from the Butte that rises like a whisper of black smoke over Paris, on its way to who knows where—

Monday, 24 December
CHRISTMAS EVE 11:35 P.M.

I MADE A POT OF CHOCOLATE. IT'S WHAT I DO IN TIMES OF STRESS; AND the strange little scene outside the shop had shaken more than one of us. It must have been the light, said Nico; that weird light you get with snow; or too much wine, or something we ate—

I let him believe it. The others too as I led Anouk shivering into the warmth of the shop and poured hot chocolate into her mug.

"Be careful, Nanou," I said. "It's hot."

It has been four years since she drank my hot chocolate. But this time she drank it without complaint. Wrapped in a blanket, she was already half asleep; and she could not tell us what she had seen during those few minutes outside in the snow, nor could she explain Zozie's disappearance, nor the strange feeling I'd had at the end of hearing their voices from far away—

Outside, Nico had found something.

"Hey, folks. She lost a shoe." He shook the melting snow from his boots and put the shoe on the table between us. "Whoa. Chocolate. Excellent!" He poured himself a generous cup.

Meanwhile Anouk had picked up the shoe. A single shoe in luscious red velvet, stack-heeled and peep-toed and stitched all through with glamours and charms fit for an adventuress on the run—

Try me, it says.

Try me. Test me.

For a second, Anouk frowns. Then she drops the shoe to the floor. "Don't you know it's bad luck to put shoes on a table?"

I hide a smile behind my hand.

"Nearly midnight," I tell her. "Are you ready to open your presents?"

To my surprise, Roux shakes his head. "I nearly forgot. It's getting late. If we hurry, we'll just have time."

"Time for what?"

"Surprise," says Roux.

"Better than presents?" says Anouk.

Roux grins. "You'll have to see."

Monday, 24 December
CHRISTMAS EVE MIDNIGHT

THE PORT DE L'ARSENAL IS A TEN-MINUTE WALK FROM PLACE DE LA
Bastille. We took the last Métro from Pigalle, arriving just minutes before
twelve. The clouds had mostly cleared by then, and I could see slices of
starry sky, bracketed with orange and gold. A faint scent of smoke distressed the air, and in the eerie luminescence of the fallen snow, the pale
spires of Notre-Dame were just visible in the middle distance.

"What are we doing here?" I said.

Roux grinned and put a finger to his lips. He was carrying Rosette,
who looked quite alert, watching everything with the wide-eyed interest of
a child up long past her bedtime and enjoying every minute of it. Anouk
too looked wide awake, although there was a tension in her face that led me
to think that whatever had happened in Place des Faux-Monnayeurs was
not quite over. Most of our guests had stayed in Montmartre, but Michèle
was with us, looking almost afraid to follow the group, as if someone might
think she had no right. Every now and again she would touch my arm, as
if by accident, or stroke Rosette's hair, and look at her hands, as if she expected to see something there—a mark, a stain—to prove to herself that
it was all real.

"Would you like to hold Rosette?"

Silent, Michèle shook her head. I hadn't really heard her speak since I'd
told her who I was. Thirty years of grief and longing have given her face the
look of something too often folded and creased; a smile seems unfamiliar,

and she tries it on now as she might some garment that she's almost certain will not suit.

"They try to prepare you for loss," she said. "It never occurs to them to prepare you for the opposite."

I nodded. "I know. We'll manage," I said.

She smiled—a better smile than before, which brought a fugitive gleam to her eyes. "I think I will," she said, taking my arm. "I've a feeling it runs in the family."

It was then that the first of the city's fireworks went off, a chrysanthemum spray across the river. Another followed from farther away, then another, and another, arching gracefully across the Seine in arabesques of green and gold.

"Midnight. Merry Christmas," said Roux.

The fireworks were almost soundless, muted by distance as well as by snow. They went on for almost ten minutes more, spiderweb trails and rocket bouquets and shooting stars, and ringlets of fire in blue and silver and scarlet and rose, all calling and beckoning to one another all the way from Notre-Dame to Place de la Concorde.

Michèle watched them, her face calm and illuminated with something more than just fireworks. Rosette signed madly, crowing with joy, and Anouk watched with solemn delight.

"That was the best present ever," she said.

"There's more," said Roux. "Just follow me."

We walked down Boulevard de la Bastille toward the Port de l'Arsenal, where boats of all sizes are moored in safety away from the swell and turbulence of the Seine.

"*She* said you didn't have a boat." It was the first time Anouk had mentioned Zozie since the events at Le Rocher de Montmartre.

Roux grinned. "Look for yourself." And he pointed over the Pont Morland.

Anouk stood on tiptoe, eyes wide. "Which one's yours?" she said eagerly.

"Can't you guess?" said Roux.

There are more impressive riverboats moored along the Arsenal. The port takes crafts up to twenty-five meters, and this one is no more than half that size. It is old, I can see that from here, built more for comfort than speed, and its shape is old-fashioned, less sleek than its neighbors, with a hull made out of solid wood rather than modern fiberglass.

And yet Roux's boat stands out at once. Even from some distance away, there is something about the shape of it, the brightly painted hull, the plant pots clustered at the stern, the glass roof through which to see the stars—

"That's *yours?*" says Anouk.

"You like it? There's more. Wait here," says Roux, and we see him racing down the steps toward the boat moored down by the bridge.

For a moment he disappears. Then there's a flicker of flame from a match. A light comes on. A candle is lit. The flame moves, and the boat comes to life as candles burn on the deck, on the roof, on sills and ledges from stem to stern. Dozens—maybe hundreds—of them, glowing in jam jars, on saucers, shining out from tin cans and flowerpots until Roux's boat is lit up like a birthday cake, and we can see what we missed before: the awning, the window, the sign on the roof. . . .

He waves to us extravagantly, signaling for us to approach. Anouk does not run but holds my hand, and I can feel her trembling. I'm barely surprised to see Pantoufle in the shadows at our feet, and isn't there something else as well, some long-tailed and loping thing that matches him naughtily, step for step?

"Do you like it?" says Roux.

For a moment, the candles themselves are enough; a small miracle reflected in a thousand little points of light across the quiet waterway. Rosette's eyes are filled with them, and Anouk, watching with my hand in hers, lets out a long and languorous breath.

Michèle says: "It's beautiful."

And so it is. But more than that—

"It's a *chocolaterie*, isn't it?"

And, of course, I can see it is. From the sign (still blank) above the door to the little display window lined with night-lights, I can see what it's meant to be. I cannot begin to guess how long it took him to create this little miracle—how much time and work and love such a project must demand—

He's watching me with his hands in his pockets. There's a trace of anxiety in his eyes.

"I bought it as a wreck," he says. "Dried it out and fixed it up. Been working on it ever since. Paid for it over nearly four years. But I always thought that maybe one day—"

My mouth on his stops him midphrase. He smells of paint and gunpowder smoke. And all around us the candles are lit, and Paris is luminous under the snow, and the last unofficial fireworks are dying away beyond Place de la Bastille, and—

"Meh. You two. Get a *room*," says Anouk.

Neither of us has breath to reply.

It's quiet now under Pont Morland as we lie, watching the candles burn out. Michèle is asleep in one bunk, and Rosette and Anouk are sharing another, with Anouk's red cloak flung over them both, and Pantoufle and Bam standing guard in case of evil dreams.

Above us, in our own room, the glass roof shows us a sky sprawling and apocalyptic with stars. In the distance, the sound of traffic from Place de la Bastille might almost be the sound of surf on a lonely beach.

I know it's only cheap magic. Jeanne Rocher would not have approved. But it's *our* magic, mine and his, and he tastes of chocolate and champagne, and finally, we slip out of our clothes and lie entwined beneath a blanket of stars.

Across the water, music plays, a tune I almost recognize.

V'là l'bon vent, v'là l'joli vent

There isn't so much as a breath of wind.

EPILOGUE

Tuesday, 25 December
CHRISTMAS DAY

ANOTHER DAY, ANOTHER GIFT. ANOTHER CITY OPENS ITS ARMS. WELL,
Paris was getting stale, you know, and I love New York at this time of year.
A pity about Anouk, I guess. Chalk it down to experience.

As for her mother—well, she had her chance. There may be a little
short-term unpleasantness. Thierry, especially, will try to make his fraud
charge stick, though I wouldn't rate his chance of success. Identity theft is
so common these days—as I imagine he'll soon find out, when he looks at
his savings account. As for Françoise Lavery—there are too many people
who can swear Vianne Rocher was in Montmartre at the time.

Meanwhile, it's off to pastures new. There's plenty of mail in New York,
you know, and it goes without saying that a certain percentage of it may go
astray. Names, addresses, credit cards—not to mention bank details, final
demands, gym memberships, curricula vitae, all the trivia that make up
your life, just waiting to be harvested by someone with initiative. . . .

Who am I now? Who could I be? I could be the next person you meet walking down the street. I could be standing behind you at the supermarket checkout. I could be your new best friend. I could be anyone. I could be *you*—

I'm a free spirit, don't forget—

And I go wherever the wind takes me.